"LOOK AT ME, ELIZABETH," HE WHISPERED. "LIFT YOUR HEAD AND LOOK AT ME."

Slowly she did as she was bidden and found herself once again looking into those disturbing dark eyes. He traced the outline of her lips gently and then, noticing the seashells at her throat, chuckled.

"A sea nymph, are you?" he inquired. "How very fitting a choice . . . forever young and bewitching . . ."

His voice trailed away as he drew her lips down to his, and for a few fleeting moments Elizabeth forgot everything else, even the necessity of breathing . . .

ZEBRA'S HOLIDAY REGENCY ROMANCES CAPTURE THE MAGIC OF EVERY SEASON

THE VALENTINE'S DAY BALL   (3280, $3.95)
by Donna Bell

Tradition held that at the age of eighteen, all the Heartland ladies met the man they would marry at the Valentine's Day Ball. When she was that age, the crucial ball had been canceled when Miss Jane Lindsey's mother had died. Now Jane was on the shelf at twenty-four. Still, she was happy in her life and accepted the fact that romance had passed her by. So she was annoyed with herself when the scandalous — and dangerously handsome — Lord Devlin put a schoolgirl blush into her cheeks and made her believe that perhaps romance may *indeed* be a part of her life . . .

AN EASTER BOUQUET   (3330, $3.95)
by Therese Alderton

It was a preposterous and scandalous wager: In return for a prime piece of horse-flesh, the decadent Lord Vyse would pose as a virtuous Rector in a country village. His cohorts insisted he wouldn't last a week, yet he was actually looking forward to a quiet Easter in the country.

Miss Lily Sterling was puzzled by the new rector; he had a reluctance to discuss his past and looked at her the way no Rector should *ever* look at a female of his flock. She was determined to unmask this handsome "clergyman", and she would set herself up as his bait!

A CHRISTMAS AFFAIR   (3244, $3.95)
by Joan Overfield

Justin Stockman thought he was doing the Laurence family a favor by marrying the docile sister and helping the family reverse their financial straits. The first thing he would do after the marriage was to marry off his independent and infuriating sister-in-law Amanda.

Amanda was intent on setting the arrogant Justin straight on a few matters, and the cozy holiday backdrop — from the intimate dinners to the spectacular Frost Fair — would be the perfect opportunities to let him know what life would be like with her as a sister-in-law. She would give a Merry Christmas indeed!

A CHRISTMAS HOLIDAY   (3245, $3.95)

A charming collection of Christmas short stories by Zebra's best Regency Romance writers. *The Holly Brooch, The Christmas Bride, The Glastonbury Thorn, The Yule Log, A Mistletoe Christmas,* and *Sheer Sorcery* will give you the warmth of the Holiday Season all year long.

Available wherever paperbacks are sold, or order direct from the Publisher. Send cover price plus 50¢ per copy for mailing and handling to Zebra Books, Dept. 3709, 475 Park Avenue South, New York, N.Y. 10016. Residents of New York and Tennessee must include sales tax. DO NOT SEND CASH. For a free Zebra/Pinnacle catalog please write to the above address.

The Easter Charade
Mona Gedney

ZEBRA BOOKS
KENSINGTON PUBLISHING CORP.

Chapter One

"You know that we really have no choice, Edmund. We *must* pay a condolence call while we are this close to Braxton Hall. I wrote to Cecilia after Jasper's shocking accident last spring, but we do need to pay our respects in person since we are in the vicinity . . . and we need to see Nora, of course. It has been very nearly a year since our last visit. Come along now and see that the ostler has taken care of your grays properly."

Elizabeth Harrington spoke firmly as she guided her unwilling brother out of the comfortable coffee room of the posting house where they had stopped overnight and toward their chaise, where he paused to examine the handsome greys with practiced skill. Sir Edmund was a gentleman with an eye for horses and a rider of acknowledged excellence. His opinions were sought by the tulips of the turf at Newmarket and Epsom, and even the most knowing ones at Tattersall's coveted his judgmental nod before purchasing their cattle. He was at his best in such surroundings, happy with his clubs and his horses, but being in the company of a bevy of females like that at Braxton Hall always threw him into complete disorder, and he carefully avoided such situations whenever possible.

"Crammed his fences," Edmund announced as he reluctantly entered the carriage. "Always did. Too ham-handed by half. No feel for horses, none at all."

Elizabeth looked at him in amusement. "Edmund, Cecilia is our cousin. You cannot go to her talking in such an unfeeling way about how her husband very likely brought about his own death, no matter how poor a rider you considered him."

"Well, of course I shan't say anything so hen-witted as that,

Lizzy," he responded indignantly. "Not but what it isn't true." Then, lapsing into deep thought, he was silent for a few minutes as he watched the countryside roll past them. Suddenly, he sat bolt upright. "You don't suppose Caroline is at Braxton Hall, too, do you, Lizzy?"

Elizabeth did her best to hide her smile. Caroline Haverton had had her eye on Sir Edmund for twenty years and more and never lost an opportunity of singling him out for conversation. "It would be quite possible for Caroline to be with her still. I am sure that Cecilia would be grateful for her sister's help now that Jasper is gone." Glancing at his expression, she added bracingly, "We won't be staying overlong, so there is no need to look so blue-deviled, Edmund."

"That's all very well for you to say," he responded bitterly. "It won't be you she buttonholes and natters away at. You know that I don't like conversing with females I don't know."

"What a whisker, Edmund! You have known Caroline from the cradle."

"Just because she and Cecilia are our cousins don't mean I know 'em. Seeing them once every year or so for an afternoon call ain't what I call knowing them. You and Mama were the ones who always went visiting and had them up to town to stay."

"Yes, and you would carefully take yourself away whenever you knew they were coming," she teased.

"Only sensible thing to do. A parcel of females expecting me to do the pretty and go to all the rout-parties with them! What a cake I would have made of myself! I'm too old for that sort of thing."

Elizabeth dismissed his protest with a chuckle. "Don't talk as though you have one foot in the grave, Edmund. You're only forty. Anyone would think you were about to stick your spoon in the wall."

Sir Edmund looked at his sister fondly. He had been sixteen when she was born, and he had always taken an indulgent attitude toward her. Not that it had been difficult. She had always been a charming, amusing companion, and he had been secretly relieved when she had failed to accept any of the very flattering offers of marriage she had received. The offers had not been surprising, for not only was Elizabeth a lady of independent means, but she was also considered one of the beauties of the *ton*, her hair the color of shining copper, her eyes the deep blue of pansies.

What had been surprising, however, was her firm refusal of each offer she received. Like her beauty, her manner was not just in the common style. She was a young woman with crisp but lively manners and decided opinions. She thoroughly enjoyed the social whirl of London, nor was she above dallying in elegant flirtations, but never did she fall prey to the wiles of any of the gazetted fortune hunters that courted her attention. She was widely admired and never lacked escorts, but her fortune had made it possible for her to choose her own path in life, and she resolutely refused to share that path with any gentleman who did not meet her requirements for a husband.

All of the gentlemen who had offered for her thus far had been, in her eyes at least, lacking in some essential quality. Lord Lacey, handsome, eligible, and humorous, had been altogether devoid of depth of character. *Her* husband must be a man who was not only good-humored but also serious when the occasion demanded. Mr. Miles Mannering was too hasty-tempered; Lord Dabney, too dull; Sir Guy Hughes, too rackety. When her mother had pointed out that she should not expect her husband to be a pattern-card saint, Elizabeth had replied, "A pattern-card saint I do not expect and do not *want*, Mama, but I *must* have a refined and handsome gentleman, one who possesses intelligence, humor, kindness, and honor—and one who will not *bore* me. I do *refuse* to be bored for the remainder of my days."

"Going to be unmarried for the remainder of your days then, my girl," her brother had remarked succinctly.

"Better that than forever regretting my portion in life," Elizabeth had firmly replied.

And the rest of the *ton* had come to look upon her also as charming but eccentric, the latter characteristic allowed her unbegrudgingly because of her fortune and her pleasing manner, although in a lesser woman the decision to remain single would perhaps have been less acceptable. Even her rejected suitors bore her no grudge, both because she refused them so charmingly and because she accepted no one else.

Elizabeth's mother had accepted her decision not to marry, certain that eventually she would make a marriage choice, but, even after their mother's death, she and Sir Edmund had remained contented with their single lives. Aside from his mother, Elizabeth was

7

the only woman with whom Sir Edmund had ever felt entirely at ease. He would have been pleased to see her happily settled and would have gladly sacrificed his comfort for her own, but thus far he had not been called upon to do so.

"Best not go to Cecilia's using expressions like that one, Lizzy," he advised kindly. "She'd probably tell me I'm responsible for it and read me a lecture." He thought the matter over and added glumly, "Probably ring a peal over me anyway. Woman's a regular Tartar."

Elizabeth did not correct him. Cecilia did not look like a Tartar, but despite her fragile appearance – and she had in her youthful days looked very like a Dresden shepherdess – she had always been fully capable of having her own way in every situation. The soul of charm and graciousness as long as her wishes were honored, she could, as Edmund elegantly phrased it, "flay the flesh from your very bones" if she were crossed. And, Elizabeth reflected, she had undoubtedly been crossed by her husband's unexpected death, for his estate was entailed and all of Cecilia's children were daughters. Cecilia had most certainly counted on having another twenty or thirty years at Braxton Hall.

"Should count himself fortunate he's dead so she can't get at him," continued Sir Edmund, pursuing his thoughts diligently. "She'd have a thing or two to say to him about being so careless and getting himself killed with all those girls still to be spoken for. How many of 'em are there? Eight?"

"There are only four, Edmund. And I'm sure that they have been well-provided for in spite of the entailment. Jasper had a comfortable fortune of his own, quite apart from the entailment."

Sir Edmund was inclined to doubt this, having seen Jasper playing deep at Brooks's upon numerous occasions, but he forbore to mention this, his mind still on the number of daughters.

"Certain there's only four, Lizzy? Seems to me when we saw them last there was a whole roomful of them."

Elizabeth laughed. "Only because they are such lively children, Edmund, and because they wanted to play cards with you once they found you have a knack for it. They are very high-spirited girls, especially Nora." Her brow wrinkled a little as she thought about Nora. "We must take special note of Nora, you know, since she was Mama's godchild."

"Well, of course we will, Lizzy. You always send her Christmas packages and a little something for her birthday, don't you? Ain't that taking special note of her?"

"Yes, but perhaps we should be doing more, Edmund. I have been thinking . . ." Fortunately for Edmund's peace of mind, her words were cut off abruptly as the carriage came to a stop in front of Braxton Hall, a manor of mellow red brick built during the reign of James I. A very proper butler greeted them and ushered them into the morning room where Cecilia, looking deceptively fragile in a black silk gown, was reclining on an elegant Grecian chaise longue, upholstered in a roseleaf velvet nicely calculated to display her beauty to the greatest advantage.

"So good of you to come, Elizabeth . . . Edmund," she said in a failing voice, lifting her arms to receive Elizabeth's embrace and then dabbing at her eyes with a wisp of lace. "It has been so dreadful since last I saw you."

"I know it must have been," replied Elizabeth with quick sympathy. "You must miss Jasper dreadfully."

Cecilia looked slightly taken aback for a moment. "Oh, yes, that is so difficult, too," she agreed, "and the entailment of course is dreadful. We shall be homeless, my poor girls and I."

Elizabeth was shocked. "Surely not homeless, Cecilia? Although of course you can't stay at Braxton Hall because of the entailment, you can select another home in the vicinity—or perhaps you could even take a house in town. Edmund would be happy to assist you in such a matter," she added, recklessly committing her brother to a task that would have wilted his impeccable shirt points within minutes.

"I'm sure that it is very kind of you to offer, Edmund," Cecilia replied, nodding at the speechless Edmund and dabbing at her eyes again, "but I'm afraid that such a move would be quite beyond our means. Indeed, since the reading of the will, it has been a puzzle to determine how we can possibly manage on what is left to us after the entailment."

"Jasper surely could not have left you in such straitened circumstances," persisted Elizabeth, thinking that her cousin must be dramatizing her situation.

Cecilia's china blue eyes darkened in a manner that made Sir Edmund begin to fidget uncomfortably. "He most certainly did exactly that," she said in a sharper voice. "Jasper gambled away virtually all of his fortune and, knowing that he had done so, was so careless of his family as to race a horse that *everyone* knew was dangerous. The welfare of his family was a matter of so little consequence that he could shrug it off for the sake of a wager!"

Sir Edmund's eyes had brightened perceptibly during the last part of her tirade. "A wager? By Jove, I hadn't heard about that! What was the wager, Cecilia?"

Elizabeth's eyes caught his warningly as Cecilia's cheeks flamed. "Indeed, it is of no consequence what the wager was, Cecilia dear," she said soothingly. "That is so very like men, is it not? To forget everything for the sake of the moment? Had he paused to consider the matter, I am very sure that Jasper would not have risked your security so lightly."

Sir Edmund felt no such certainty, but he was relieved to see the bright color in Cecilia's cheeks fade as she leaned back against the sofa and pressed the back of her hand to her brow.

"You have no idea what torment I have suffered, Elizabeth," she murmured. "Not being a mother yourself, you could not be expected to understand what despair I have undergone when I thought of my portionless girls, soon to be cast out into the world. Why, when Norville was informed of Jasper's death and told that Braxton Hall was to come to him because of the entailment, he could have ordered us out then and there."

"Who is this Norville, Cecilia?" inquired Elizabeth.

"A very distant relation of Jasper's," she replied. "There was a cousin who was to inherit the estate, but he had died, and Norville was the next in line. They very nearly could not find him. He had been in Spain until our victory at Vitoria, at which time he was given a special assignment that took him across half of Europe. It was not until after the Battle of Leipzig in October that our solicitor finally made contact with him and informed him of his inheritance.

"We have been most fortunate," she added, "for he is every inch the gentleman. He understands my position completely. He even instructed the solicitor that, as he would not be residing in England for some time, he would like for us to remain at Braxton Hall if we wished to do so."

"Well, I am very glad to hear it," Elizabeth said. "A gentleman should realize what a dreadful shock this is to you and make every allowance for your distress."

"And he does indeed," she sighed. "Dear Norville . . . just the sort of son-in-law I would have selected. Nora is most fortunate."

Elizabeth stared at her. "What do you mean, Cecilia? In what way is Nora fortunate?"

"Why, Norville offered for her, of course. And he *is* a man with a comfortable fortune of his own, as well as his own estates, and now Braxton Hall . . ."

"Whyever did he offer for Nora?" Elizabeth broke in, then added as she saw Cecilia's lifted brows, "Not that Nora is not charming, of course—but I thought that he was in Spain. How has there been time for this to happen?"

"Norville returned this winter and came to visit us briefly during Christmas. He was most considerate and said that he had only come to tell me to take my time in making other living arrangements. After his visit he wrote to me and said that since he had come to understand my situation and had already planned to take a wife upon his return to England, he thought it only right that he offer for Nora and help me to take care of the other girls. So truly the gentleman," she sighed.

"He sounds very kind indeed, but what do you truly know of this man, Cecilia? And what does Nora think of his offer?" demanded Elizabeth. "This sounds altogether too quick and cold-blooded for my taste."

Cecilia shrugged one shoulder pettishly, annoyed at Elizabeth's failure to rejoice over her news. "In the three days he was with us at Christmas, he showed himself to be a sensible, well-behaved man, interested in our welfare."

Here Sir Edmund felt compelled to enter the fray. "What of his fortune and his other estates, Cecilia? Have you only his word on this? Could be a Banbury man, you know."

"He is no such thing, Edmund! Mr. Jarvis, Jasper's man of business, says that Mr. Norville is all that he says he is."

"Well, that's all right, then," said Sir Edmund, relieved.

Elizabeth looked incensed. "It certainly is not 'all right, then'! What of Nora's feelings in this matter? And, apart from his financial standing, what manner of man is this Mr. Norville? Would they suit?"

"Of course they would suit!" Cecilia snapped. "He is a gentleman, she is a lady. But Nora is being missish about the whole

11

matter."

The door burst open and Nora, a dark version of her mother's blond beauty, flew into the room from the hall where she had obviously been listening. "How can you say that I am being missish, Mother? How can you possibly wish for me to marry a doddering old man?"

Seeing Elizabeth, who had always made a pet of her, she threw herself into her arms and buried her face in Elizabeth's shoulder. "It is too dreadful, Elizabeth! Don't let her do this to me!"

Giving a dramatic sob, she added, "It is like being *sold,* Elizabeth! Every feeling revolts at the mere thought of it, but no one here cares for *my* feelings!"

Caroline Haverton, a plump, harried woman, hurried into the room and attempted to remove Nora from her resting place, but, limpetlike, Nora clung stubbornly to Elizabeth.

"It is quite all right, Caroline," Elizabeth said quietly. "I will take care of her."

Stroking Nora's tumbled curls soothingly, she led the girl to a sofa and drew her down beside her, talking softly all the while. Caroline followed her into the room, simpering at Sir Edmund and straightening the bows of her lace cap coquettishly.

"Now tell me what it is that you dislike so much about Mr. Norville, Nora," she instructed as soon as Nora had stopped sobbing.

"He is very old," she sniffed, applying Sir Edmund's reluctantly proffered handkerchief to her streaming eyes. "I daresay he may die before the year is out."

Elizabeth turned a startled gaze to Cecilia, who answered her unspoken question impatiently. "Andrew Norville is thirty-six, Elizabeth. Does that sound as though he is at death's door?"

Trying to ignore her brother's indignant snort as he thought of his own forty years of age, Elizabeth replied calmly, "Not at death's door, perhaps, but thirty-six does seem very old to sixteen."

"And he is prosy and talked of his duty to marry me, Elizabeth! His duty! Why, when I went to the assemblies at Taverton, no one there danced with me because they thought it their duty! They did so because they wished to! I won't marry an old man and be bored to death for the rest of my days!"

"Wouldn't be for the rest of your days," interjected Sir Edmund tartly, still smarting from the slur upon his age. "Said yourself that he was too old to last the year. Then you'd be a rich widow."

Elizabeth glanced at her brother reproachfully as she tried to stem a fresh tide of tears. She had felt a sharp stab of guilt when Nora made her plea for protection from a prosy old bore. Why should Nora have to submit to a fate that she herself had refused? Still stroking the girl's hair comfortingly, she determined that she *would* protect this sobbing child from such a fate. Finally, after assurances from Elizabeth that she soon would come up to Nora's room to talk to her in private, Nora allowed Caroline to lead her away.

When they had left the room, Elizabeth turned to her cousin in disbelief. "You would marry Nora to a man of thirty-six whom she doesn't even know? You surely cannot be serious, Cecilia. Why, the child is still in the schoolroom!"

Cecilia's chin set mulishly in a way Elizabeth remembered all too well. Cecilia was always most stubborn when least certain of the wisdom of her decisions.

"Nora was sixteen last May, Elizabeth. And you know very well that she has been attending assemblies at Taverton, for I wrote to you about it at the time, to tell you how well she seemed to take – or at least she did so until Jasper's death last autumn."

She dabbed at her eyes again with the morsel of lace as she recalled her role as the grieving widow, but then returned briskly to the businesslike manner that was more natural to her. "At any rate, there is really nothing else to be done. Norville's is by far the most eligible offer that she is likely to receive in her penniless situation, and he is in a position to help the rest of the girls and he said that he would do so. Why, we would not even have to leave Braxton Hall! We would stay in our home."

"That's all very well, Cecilia, and I understand truly how important that must seem to you, but I cannot agree that this is the thing to do. Give the matter a little more time."

"And what will time accomplish?" inquired Cecilia waspishly. "Except that perhaps Norville will have occasion to look round him and find someone else that he would like to marry. After all, he is just home from Spain, and we were fortunate that he met Nora so soon after his return."

"If he might be inclined to change his mind so readily, that is all the more reason to wait. How dreadful it would be for Nora if he

13

has made his offer too suddenly and then regrets it after marrying her! What would her life be then?"

"What fustian you are talking, Elizabeth! Not everyone has the same freedom to pick and choose as does Miss Elizabeth Harrington of Grosvenor Square!" Cecilia was so incensed that she forgot to languish on the sofa and sat bolt upright as she glared at her cousin. "Surely you are not going to talk rubbish to me about a love match! Norville is a gentleman! He will give Nora a secure place so that she will not lose the home she has always known, and they will go on most comfortably together!"

"And you will be able to go on most comfortably, too, I gather," commented Elizabeth dryly.

Cecilia's color rose again. Noting this, Sir Edmund, who had moved uneasily away from the two ladies as their voices grew sharper, hurried to the safety of the window and looked longingly toward the stables, where peace and sanity reigned. Above all things, he hated cap-pulling.

"And what of that, Elizabeth? Is it such a crime to wish to provide for myself and my daughters when we are facing a life of penury? What would you have me do? Set up household in a two-room cottage?"

Elizabeth, recognizing that she must change her strategy, seated herself beside Cecilia and patted her hand. "Of course not, Ceci," she said contritely. "I know how difficult this must be for you, and I don't mean that you need give up your idea of Norville completely." She paused a moment, thinking quickly. "Perhaps it would be helpful if we took Nora to London with us and had her stay a few weeks. It is too soon after Jasper's death to announce her betrothal just yet, and a change of scene would do her good. From what I just saw of her, having her removed for a few weeks would be refreshing for all of you."

Cecilia was studying her closely. "You do realize, Elizabeth, that I am not giving up the idea of having Nora marry?"

"Yes, of course, but a little time could give all of us a new perspective—and who knows what might happen in a few weeks?"

Seeing her cousin's raised eyebrows and anticipating Cecilia's next remark, she hurried to add, "And even though you are afraid that Norville may change his mind, if he is truly the gentleman you think him, he will understand the need to wait

14

and will not press you."

She paused a moment before delivering the *coup de grâce*. "And, practically speaking, Ceci, I don't believe it would be wise to allow him to see Nora just now. Her manner would scarcely be conciliating, and if she were to enact a Cheltenham tragedy, Norville might truly change his mind."

This point struck home and Cecilia nodded her head slowly. "That, of course, is very true. No man of sense, which Norville surely is, could listen to Nora rave about his having one foot in the grave without feeling some disgust."

Sir Edmund, who had been engrossed in watching the stableboy walk a particularly fine-looking bit of blood-and-bone and wondering how a cawker like Jasper had come to have such a prime one in his stable, was caught by the truth of her final remark.

"Well, of course, he could not! No person of sense would regard a man of six-and-thirty as one about to stick his spoon in the wall. I wonder that the child could be so bacon-brained as to say a thing like that."

"I do wish, Edmund, that you would try for a little more conduct!" snapped his cousin. "If you must use vulgar expressions, I should prefer that you do so elsewhere."

Elizabeth caught Edmund's eye and grinned. "You must forgive Edmund, Ceci. He has always suffered from a shocking want of conduct."

Ignoring Edmund's bleat of protest, she returned to the point in hand. "I think that your wisest course of action would be to allow Nora to come to us in London. She would be diverted from her present problems, and, although I realize that she is still in mourning, it has been a year and it would not be improper for her to attend some social functions with me. And I could see to it that she is properly outfitted, for she will soon no longer be in first mourning. Do let her come, Cecilia."

Sir Edmund sat down abruptly, seeing his carefully ordered world suddenly in shambles at his feet.

"You may be quite right," replied Cecilia slowly. "But there is a difficulty. Mr. Norville wrote that he would soon be in England again and would wait on us then. He will, I am certain, expect an answer at that time." She paused. "And that time, Elizabeth, is tomorrow. He wrote that he would arrive in time for dinner."

15

Elizabeth stood and straightened her skirts. "Then there is no time to be lost, Cecilia. Have Nora's trunk packed as quickly as possible, and Edmund and I will take her with us today. We begin our journey home tomorrow morning, and she will come with us." Carefully avoiding Sir Edmund's horrified gaze, Elizabeth walked purposefully to the door of the morning room. "I will go up and see Nora directly."

As she opened the door, a swirl of bright skirts and blond curls rushed into the room, and she turned and called roguishly to her brother. "Just see, Edmund! Here are the girls to bid you hello and to ask after your horses. And Caroline, too, come to talk to you while I am upstairs." As she closed the door gently, ignoring his desperate gaze, she saw Caroline drawing a chair close to him and the three girls clamoring for his attention.

Upstairs she found Nora seated in a window embrasure, her face pressed to the pane. Not even tears and tantrums had marred the picture-book prettiness of the small face she turned to Elizabeth, who could not wonder at Mr. Norville's readiness to offer for her hand. Nora's coloring had always reminded Elizabeth of a fairy-tale princess: skin as white as snow, lips as red as a rose, hair and eyes as dark as ebony. And her beauty, like that of Elizabeth herself, was not passive and quiet but vibrant and mercurial.

"Will you help me, Elizabeth? Can you keep my mama from marrying me to Mr. Norville?" She stretched out her hand pleadingly as she spoke, and Elizabeth took it in both of her own as she sat down beside her.

"I am certain that Mr. Norville would not wish for an unwilling bride, Nora," she replied mendaciously, "but we won't worry about that just yet. Your mama realizes that your betrothal could not be announced while you are still in mourning."

Nora's gaze brightened for a moment, but then she grew downcast again. "I am sure that was because of you, Elizabeth. She will still make me see him tomorrow, and we shall, as Mama puts it, come to an understanding. And then I shall be trapped, even if there is no formal announcement yet. I shall not ever be able to go to assemblies and balls again, except with Mr. Norville."

Her small face grew stormy as she considered the grim future. "Can you imagine it, Elizabeth?"

Elizabeth, fully prepared to offer her sympathy for the limitations this would impose on a young and sensitive girl, was cut short before she could begin to reply.

"Just think of it!" Nora continued bitterly. "Nora Norville! I shall be a laughingstock! Whoever heard of such a ridiculous name? Mama should surely see that I cannot marry anyone whose name goes so poorly with my own."

"I can see that such a thing must surely weigh heavily against the gentleman," said Elizabeth, her eyes laughing at this unexpected turn of the conversation. "Perhaps he is not wholly to blame for not realizing what a great burden this would be for you."

Nora drew herself up in a dignified manner. "I would not think that *you* would make a May-game of me, Elizabeth. I assure you that I most earnestly do not wish to marry Mr. Norville—not even if his name were . . . were . . ."

"William Shakespeare?" inquired Elizabeth, with an appropriately serious expression.

"That would be even stupider," responded Nora petulantly. "Not even if his name were FitzWalter!" she finished triumphantly, recalling a favorite name. Then, remembering her great trouble, she buried her face in her hands.

"There, there, child," said Elizabeth remorsefully, stroking her tumbled curls again. "I did not mean to laugh at you. Indeed, I want to help you."

Nora lifted her head and peered at her hopefully from between spread fingers. "What can you do, Elizabeth? Can you truly help?"

"Would you like to go to London with Edmund and me?"

Nora's eyes widened. "Oh, above all things, Elizabeth! That would be famous! I should love to go to London and go to the theatres and go shopping and see the sights!"

Her enthusiasm dwindled suddenly. "But Mama would not let me go, not with Mr. Norville coming to see us."

"Ah, but she has already agreed to it, Nora. You are to pack immediately and leave with us straight away. We start for London tomorrow morning, and you will stay with us at the Red Lion tonight."

Further speech was impossible for the moment because Nora had thrown her arms around her cousin's neck so tightly that her relative's breath was fairly cut off.

"But, Nora dear, I must tell you that this does not mean that your mama has dismissed all thought of Mr. Norville. You are simply taking a brief holiday with us."

"Yes, yes, Elizabeth, but that is still beyond anything great! I shall get to do some things at least as Miss Nora Lane before I become a married lady." Then, remembering her grievance, she grew less cheerful and added ominously, *"If* I consent to become one."

Ignoring her final words, Elizabeth said pleasantly, "Then let us go downstairs and tell your mama that it is all decided and that you shall come away with us directly."

"How jealous Cissy and Lisa and Jane shall be," Nora reflected complacently. "I shall write to them though," she added virtuously, "and tell them of all the things that we are doing. I daresay they will enjoy that."

Entertained by her childish chatter, Elizabeth could only marvel that Cecilia thought Nora old enough for marriage. It did not seem to her likely that Nora and Mr. Norville could have talked together at all, or certainly a man of six-and-thirty, no green boy to be sure, would have seen how completely unfitted she was to become a wife. Hopefully, given time to reflect, wisdom would prevail. Then, remembering Cecilia's predicament, she was less certain.

In the morning room they discovered Sir Edmund in what appeared to be desperate straits. He had Caroline on his left, seated as close to him as propriety would allow, her cap ribbons bobbing with animation as she described to Sir Edmund her trip to the linen draper's in Taverton. The girls, eager to begin a game of whist, were arguing among themselves as to who should have Sir Edmund as a partner. He was known to be an excellent player, and he and his partner would undoubtedly emerge victorious from the game. Playing cards with children usually held small appeal for Edmund, of course, but with Caroline in the room, a game of cards that would protect him from her constant attentions had become a matter of pressing interest.

"Now, now, girls," he was saying, attempting to disengage himself from Caroline, "there is no need to quarrel. I shall take turns being partner to each of you." And then, a sudden inspiration striking him, he added, "Or, better still, why not take me on a walk down to the stables and show me your horses?"

Their attention momentarily diverted from the game, Cissy, the youngest, exclaimed, "Tabitha, the stable cat, has had kittens, Edmund, five of them—the dearest things that you ever saw."

Edmund allowed himself to be pulled to his feet and hustled from the room. He felt little interest in a litter of kittens, but his route of escape was clear, and if Hastings was in the barn, he could ask him about that magnificent horse he had seen from the window.

"Cecilia, Nora has decided to come with us to London, and we have set Nanny to packing her things," announced Elizabeth, brushing by the nursery party as they made their exit.

"I shall tell Mr. Norville how sorry you are to have missed his visit," said Cecilia to her daughter, "and that you shall look forward to seeing him in a few weeks." She placed a marked emphasis on the fact that Nora would look forward to seeing him.

Nora made no reply, but her glance was mutinous as her mother turned her attention back to Elizabeth. "You understand, Elizabeth, that this visit is not to be an extremely long one. Nora may stay with you through Eastertide, but then she must return to Braxton Hall and take up her life here."

The remainder of the afternoon slipped by more easily than Elizabeth had imagined it could. Nora's trunk was packed; the children entertained themselves and Sir Edmund in the stables; Cecilia and Nora quarreled only twice. Sir Edmund had returned happily from his visit with Hastings, having inspected all of the horses, including the magnificent black Devon Boy, closely. He had made Cecilia a handsome offer for Devon Boy, had been accepted with alacrity, and had spent the remainder of the afternoon discussing with his coachman arrangements for the horse's removal to London with them.

So happily oblivious had Sir Edmund been to all else that it came as an unexpected jolt when, after tea and a fond parting from Cecilia and her family (especially fond because they were indeed parting), he and Elizabeth did not enter the carriage alone. Nora's trunk and boxes had been sent over to the Red Lion on a cart earlier, but Nora herself, attired in a traveling cloak and a plain little black poke bonnet, entered the carriage with them.

Seeing by her brother's expression that he had forgotten that Nora was to accompany them, Elizabeth said in a pleasant, matter-of-fact voice, "Won't it be a pleasure to have Nora with us in London, Edmund? We shall go to the plays and to Astley's and enjoy ourselves hugely."

19

There was a brief pause as Sir Edmund assimilated this new and most unwelcome information, seeing his peaceful days vanishing in a trice.

"Won't it be a pleasure, Edmund?" queried his fond sister in a tone a trifle stronger.

Reminded of his manners, he hurriedly and mendaciously agreed. "To be sure, a pleasure, Nora. A pleasure. To the plays. To Astley's." His voice faded.

"And you shall take us to ride in Hyde Park," said Elizabeth, attempting to bolster his spirits. "Just think of taking Devon Boy out for all of the pinks of the *ton* to admire."

Sir Edmund brightened perceptibly. "To be sure. Just the thing to take the wind out of Tom Mulberry's sails. He has been thinking that his new mount is not to be outshone." He settled more comfortably into the velvet squabs of the upholstery and contented himself with picturing his rival's discomfiture, while Nora, seated across from him, dreamed of unknown delights to come once they reached London. Elizabeth studied the two of them, wondering if she had made the wise choice in having Nora come with them. She had taken on a great responsibility, particularly when one considered that she was only four-and-twenty and an unmarried lady herself. However, as she thought of her mother and how fondly she had always regarded Nora, Elizabeth decided that she had done what had to be done by removing Nora from the imminent possibility of an ineligible marriage. It was clearly what Mama would have expected her to do for Nora, and Elizabeth was not one to shirk her responsibilities.

Chapter Two

The first day and a half of their journey to London was fairly un-eventful. Sir Edmund's valet and Elizabeth's maid, along with the bulk of their luggage, were sent ahead, and the rest of the party was able to leave the Red Lion at a reasonable hour. Sir Edmund had ridden Devon Boy alongside the chaise at a pleasant pace, for, al-though the bleakness of the countryside and the patches of snow on the meadows proclaimed that it was indeed the end of February, the road was dry and easy to travel. The weather had been unusually bitter during the weeks following Christmas, keeping them envel-oped in ice and snow, so Sir Edmund was grateful for this bit of dryness. He was comfortable enough, despite the cold, particularly since he did not have to be trapped in the chaise with Nora. The first evening in her company had convinced him that her tongue must surely be loose at both ends, for she had scarcely paused for breath in her talking from the time of their departure from Braxton Hall until the time Elizabeth led her up to her bedchamber at the Red Lion.

It was Elizabeth who had suggested he ride Devon Boy as they began their trip to London, and his expression had been much like that of a hare unexpectedly released from a trap. Although Nora's chatter was wearing, Elizabeth did not mind it as he did, and she reflected that there was no reason for Edmund to pay any greater price than necessary for her decision to rescue the child, although he had promised that he would help her with Nora. In fact, once she had pointed out to him that their mother would have expected them to exert themselves in behalf of her godchild, he had agreed and had even offered, in a burst of generosity that he would doubt-

21

less regret, to do the handsome thing and escort them about town.

"Edmund is an excellent horseman, is he not, Elizabeth?" inquired Nora admiringly, watching him from the carriage window. Sir Edmund was at his best in the saddle, his form both trim and commanding.

"He is indeed, Nora. He is quite noted for that and for his knowledge of horses in general."

"So is Mr. Norville," said Nora abruptly, her face clouding.

"Is he now? And did he tell you so?" inquired Elizabeth, wondering if Mr. Norville were inclined to think well of himself and announce it to the world.

"No, Hastings did," replied Nora. "He said Norville had excellent bottom, and after he saw him on Devon Boy, he called him a regular out-and-outer and said that he'd give a monkey to see him handle the ribbons."

Elizabeth kept herself from reminding Nora that this did not sound like a description of a man with one foot in the grave as she digested this latest bit of information about Mr. Norville. Undoubtedly Mr. Norville was quite aware of his prowess as a rider and consequently odiously puffed up with vanity. Many of the gentlemen of Elizabeth's acquaintance who could be described as "out-and-outers" were exceedingly arrogant, and she promptly placed Mr. Norville in their company.

Nora sat reflecting darkly on this evidence of Hastings's perfidy in admiring the enemy and added ominously, "But being a bruising rider does not mean that one has the right to marry whomever one chooses."

Elizabeth looked up as she heard her charge begin to chuckle.

"What *I'd* have given a monkey to see was Norville's face when he saw that Devon Boy was gone. I wager that he was more angry about that than about my leaving."

Elizabeth stared at her in dismay. "Nora! You don't mean to tell me that Devon Boy is part of the estate! Edmund and I thought that he belonged to your father as his private property!"

Nora shook her head. "He was to go with the estate, I believe. There was a paper of some sort about it, and at any rate Mother didn't want him. She doesn't like to ride and besides, it was Devon Boy that Papa was riding when he had his accident."

Elizabeth patted Nora's knee comfortingly, but it was difficult to bite back her thoughts about Cecilia's carelessness in placing Edmund in such an awkward position with Mr. Norville. It was the most monstrous thing that Cecilia should cause Edmund to look like a Jerry Sneak, making away with a horse that was obviously already known and valued. Telling Edmund would be a difficult matter.

"Did you never go riding with Mr. Norville, Nora?" she inquired, trying to speak in a natural voice. She would think about the problem with Devon Boy when she was alone. And it certainly was not the child's fault. Although she could have mentioned it at Braxton Hall, doing so would have placed her in an even more awkward position with her mother.

Nora hunched one shoulder pettishly. "He invited me to, and Hastings was to attend us, but I didn't wish to be with him, even with Hastings present."

"Did he make you so uncomfortable then?" Elizabeth inquired, immediately suspecting him of making unwelcome advances. It was a suspicion that Nora's next statement promptly dissipated.

"He was never amusing, Elizabeth! All of the things that he talked about were things that I care nothing about. What do I know of the war in the Peninsula?"

Seeing Elizabeth's disapproving expression, she added, "Well, he could have said just one or two things and then talked of something interesting. But he droned on and on about it, and every time he stopped, Mr. Jarvis, Papa's man of business, you know, would ask him something else and set him off again. I thought they would never have done with it."

She paused a moment and then continued enumerating her grievances. "And do you know what he intends to do, Elizabeth? It is the shabbiest thing! He intends to bury himself in the country and never go to London! I know, for he said so while he was visiting. Not in those words, of course, but that is what he meant, and so whoever marries him will be buried, too! He said that he will not have a house in London nor even visit there! He told Mama in his letter that we should live very happily on his estate in Devonshire. Happily! What a bouncer! I should be miserable there!"

Elizabeth reflected that Mr. Norville might be a bruising rider and an intrepid soldier, but he was certainly lacking in address. If he wished to fix his interests with a young lady, this was scarcely the way to have set about it.

Outside, a sudden gust of rising wind almost whipped Sir Edmund's hat from his head. Looking over his shoulder, he noticed with some anxiety that the overcast sky had turned almost black behind them. The distance from Braxton Hall to London was not a great one, but Sir Edmund was taking it in easy stages, for he had no intention of entrusting his beloved grays to a posting house to be brought along later. They had stopped earlier for a brief nuncheon, but the Black Swan, where they planned to break their journey for the night, was still several miles distant.

Sir Edmund's worries were well-founded. Within moments of the rising of the wind, sleet began to pelt down heavily. John Coachman slowed the chaise to a walk as the roadway grew icy beneath them.

"Beggin' your pardon, Sir Edmund, but we'll not make it to the Black Swan with the weather turnin' like this," he called.

"I was thinking that myself, John," Sir Edmund replied, choosing Devon Boy's path very carefully. "What is there along the road here? Do you recall if there is anything closer at hand?"

The postboy piped up, his teeth already chattering from the cold. "There's the Bull and Barleycorn a mile or so on down the road, sir. We'd best stop there before the storm breaks, or we'll find ourselves in a ditch for sure."

The other two being in complete agreement with him, they proceeded at a slow pace, the sleet gradually changing to snow. The postilion's view that they could make it before the storm broke turned out to be an unduly optimistic one, for Sir Edmund could scarcely see his hand in front of his face, so dark had the afternoon grown and so thickly was the snow whirling about them by the time they finally made their way to the door of a tiny inn at the outskirts of a small village. The innkeeper himself came out to guide the ladies inside, and Sir Edmund, determined to see that his cattle were cared for properly, escorted them around to the stables.

The Bull and Barleycorn was a small house, but Elizabeth was relieved to see that it looked well cared for. The entrance hall was hung with shining pewter pots, and the tiny parlor opening off of it had well-scrubbed whitewashed walls, an old clock whose ticking could be heard even in the entrance as they were shaking the snow from their cloaks, and a merrily leaping fire.

"Oh, how delightful that looks," exclaimed Nora, hurrying toward the fire to warm her hands.

"Allow me, child," said a pleasant voice, and a tall young man rose from the high-backed bench where he had been hidden and drew a stool closer to the fire for her.

"Thank you, sir," replied Nora stiffly, eyeing him with disfavor as she pushed back the hood of her cloak. "Although I am *not* a child, I appreciate your kindness." Mustering as much dignity as she could, she settled herself on the small oak stool, stretching her hands toward the fire, and turning her back to her benefactor as nearly as her circumstances would permit.

"I beg your pardon," said the stranger, who looked anything but penitent, his eyes bright with amusement. "Because of your height and the manner in which you ran to the fire, I mistook your age. I see now, of course, that you are indeed a young lady."

"How do you do, Lord Mallory?" inquired Elizabeth, recognizing the gentleman with misgiving. Of all the mischances, to run into a young man as dashing as this one when accompanied by an impressionable young girl! "I would not have expected to find you here."

"By all that's wonderful, it's Miss Harrington!" he exclaimed, turning to greet her with genuine warmth.

He was a tall, elegant young man with impeccable manners. His graceful person and charming manner had captured the heart of more than one young lady, although Elizabeth was not among their number.

He smiled down at her. "I might reply that I would not have expected to find you here, but that I am indeed delighted that I do."

Elizabeth felt the full weight of his charm, for his voice and expression indicated the absolute sincerity of his words. And of course few things in life are more delightful than the conviction that others find *us* delightful.

"That is very kind of you, Lord Mallory. We were on our way home to London when we were caught by this storm. My brother is outside now, seeing to our horses." Turning to Nora, she added, "I should like to present my late mother's godchild, Miss Nora Lane. She is coming to spend some time in London with us."

"God*daughter*," amended Nora, "I am no longer a child."

"Miss Lane and I met just now, rather informally, and I am afraid that she is displeased with me," he explained to Elizabeth.

Turning to Nora, Mallory bowed low over her small hand, the firelight deepening the color of his hair to a burnished gold. "I am delighted to make your acquaintance, Miss Lane. I had been dreading the evening, stranded as we are in the midst of nowhere, but now that I have such charming company, I look forward to it with pleasure."

Nora bestowed a forgiving smile upon him, and he proceeded to sit down and make himself agreeable. Elizabeth groaned inwardly and determined to make a push to remove her charge from such imminent danger. Mallory was noted among the members of the *ton* for his outrageous hoaxes and his sunny charm, while Nora's experience was limited to a few country beaux and a military gentleman of limited address: clearly the situation was fraught with peril. Cecilia would not thank her if Nora lost her heart to one of the most accomplished flirts in London.

"That is very kind of you, Lord Mallory, but we don't wish to intrude upon your privacy." She turned to the innkeeper, who was still hovering. "Could you show us to another private parlor since this one is already taken, innkeeper?" Elizabeth asked.

He shook his head at her unhappily. "This be our only parlor. Our trade at the Bull be mainly day trade."

Elizabeth looked alarmed. "You do have bedchambers available, do you not?"

His long face grew longer as he replied. "Only two, I'm afeared, miss, and the young lord has bespoken one of them. You and the young lady could share the other, but the gentleman with you must make his bed in here by the fire tonight."

Elizabeth had a fleeting vision of what Edmund's expression would be when he was welcomed in from the cold with this happy piece of news. "Your stable is adequate for our horses, is it not?" she asked anxiously. A bedchamber he might do without, but a good stable was an absolute requirement for Edmund.

The innkeeper was able to reassure her upon this head, telling her that they would be as snug as ever could be and no mistaking it.

"Well, that's a blessing. At least Edmund won't feel that he must spend the night out there," she murmured gratefully. To the innkeeper she added, "Perhaps you should show us to our bedchamber then."

He looked doubtful. "I will do that, miss, but I should be warning you that it's fearful cold in there. The missus is having a fire lighted now, but it won't do much against this wind and cold tonight. You'd be better off here with the gentlemen tonight. You wouldn't want to be sitting up there."

"I assure you, Miss Harrington, that he is speaking no more than the truth. I put my gear up there, counted the icicles that were forming, and hurried back down to this fire. And, if I'm not mistaken, the innkeeper told me that his wife is an excellent cook and will soon serve us dinner."

The innkeeper nodded. "She be that, my lord. We mayn't have enough rooms, but we do have plenty of food and drink for any that might come. This be Collop Monday, so there be plenty. Do you sit down, miss," he said coaxingly to Elizabeth. "I'll see to your things and the missus will bring you a cup of tea in jig time."

Seeing that she truly had no choice, Elizabeth allowed herself to be persuaded, and sat peacefully for a few minutes, appreciating the comfort of a crackling fire and steaming tea after the chill and discomfort of the last hour and ignoring the impropriety of their sharing a parlor with a gentleman they scarcely knew.

Nora excused herself and Elizabeth, thinking that she was going upstairs to their bedroom for a moment, thought nothing of it. When she reappeared, however, it was clear that her trip had been into the nether parts of the inn, for she carried with her a small orange kitten and a saucer of milk.

"Just look, Elizabeth. This is Sampson, one of Mrs. Netherspoon's kittens. Isn't he cunning?"

"I take it that Mrs. Netherspoon is the wife of the innkeeper?"

Nora nodded happily, her dark curls bobbing as she settled herself again on the small stool beside the hearth and encouraged Sampson to partake of his dinner. "Mrs. Netherspoon said that Tiger—that's Sampson's mother—had seven kittens. Now they only have Sampson and two others."

She studied Sampson as the kitten pawed at the edge of the dish. "He is very like one of our kittens at home. I thought about asking to bring it with me, but I knew Mama would not think that a good idea."

For once Elizabeth found herself in full agreement with Cecilia, feeling strongly that she did not want a small kitten as a traveling companion and picturing the reaction of Burton, their butler in Grosvenor Square, if they were to arrive with one—particularly an untrained one.

After soaking both front paws in the milk, Sampson had decided against drinking any and eagerly attacked the bows of Nora's small slippers, which were peeping out beneath the hem of her skirt. Nora squeaked in dismay and tucked her skirt firmly around them, but Sampson was not to be diverted—or at least not until Lord Mallory dangled a piece of string in front of his eyes and he turned to leap upon it.

"A very efficient rescue, Lord Mallory," said Elizabeth, smiling. "Much longer and Nora's bows would have been in shreds."

"I have had a great deal of practice in the way of rescues," he told her, dangling the string ever higher until Sampson was performing leaps worthy of an acrobat at a fair to reach it. "I have two younger sisters and a brother at home and they have a veritable menagerie. The one at the Tower of London is cast into the shade by theirs."

Looking down at Nora, he smiled kindly. "I am sure they would be delighted to meet you. Perhaps you could go on some outings with the girls and their governess."

Nora's eyes darkened when he mentioned the governess. Then she regarded him narrowly. "I'm sure that would be delightful. How old are your sisters, Lord Mallory?"

"Anne is twelve and Maria is fourteen. Between them and my brother George, who is ten, my mother and Miss Stevenson, the governess, have their hands full."

Nora had bristled visibly and had drawn herself up as much as a very short stool and her own diminutive stature would allow. "I should, of course, be very happy to make their acquaintance, Lord Mallory, although I am, of course, much older than they."

He lifted a quizzical eyebrow and she hurried to enlighten him. "I am practically seventeen, sir," she announced grandly.

"Are you indeed? Well, I would not have guessed it," he replied, compounding his offense. "I apologize for making you one of the schoolroom party." His eyes twinkled as she disengaged Sampson's small claws from her skirt and straightened it about her ankles with great dignity.

"That is quite all right, Lord Mallory. And I should not, of course, wish to appear rude. I would be very happy to meet your sisters – and George," she added grandly.

There was an abrupt knocking at the front door and then the sound of a curt voice calling for the landlord and the stamping of boots against the flagstones.

Again the impatient voice rang out. "Is there no one in this cursed place? Where is the porter? Are my horses to freeze to death while you take your comfort before the fire?"

They heard the reassuring rumble of Netherspoon's voice as he bustled in from the kitchen. "There will be someone right around to take care of them, sir. Will you be wishing to stay the night, too?"

"Well, of course I wish to stay the night, fool! Have you not looked out the window and noticed this devil of a storm? I must have a room and a private parlor."

Netherspoon could be heard explaining the situation and the stranger's abrupt dismissal of the claims of the others. "Let them fend for themselves," he told Netherspoon. "I am Lord Chawton of Mowbry Park. Just remove the baggage from one of the chambers and move my things in. As for those in the parlor, I believe that you can very well move them out to the kitchen and serve me in the parlor. Bring me a bottle of your best brandy right away, landlord."

The door opened and a tall, dark man in a many-caped greatcoat strode in, removing his gloves and flinging them down onto a table. Elizabeth's eyes had kindled as she listened to the exchange between Netherspoon and the new arrival, but Lord Mallory anticipated any protest she might be able to make as he stood to face the newcomer.

"I thought that I recognized your voice, Chawton," he said grimly, wearing a far different expression from that he had had while watching Nora with the kitten. "As you can see, it is just as Netherspoon told you. The parlor is already occupied by myself and these ladies, and the bedchambers are taken as well."

"Mallory! What an unpleasant surprise," said the newcomer, his glance as cold as the winter wind. "I am astounded to find you away from London and the gaming tables. What could have taken you from the charms of civilization to this wilderness, I wonder."

Mallory flushed. "My affairs are none of your concern, Chawton. I would suggest we step into the entry hall and discuss there what arrangements can be made."

Before he could continue, Sir Edmund entered, cheefully oblivious to the tension in the room. "I say, Elizabeth, I don't think we should remain in here. There is a much better fire out in the kitchen. I've asked Netherspoon to mix up some hot punch so that I can thaw away some of this cursed cold. In fact . . ."

By this time it had struck Sir Edmund that Elizabeth and Nora were not alone in the room, and he raised his quizzing glass to inspect the gentleman standing beside Nora. "Young Mallory, isn't it?" he inquired amiably. "Good to see you. I'll have Netherspoon brew up some extra punch."

Turning his scrutiny to the other gentleman, his warmth faded. "Oh . . . Chawton. Thought you had taken yourself off to Portugal or Spain or some such place."

The change in tone was not lost upon his subject. "I did, Harrington, but — as you can see — I have returned."

"So you have," replied Sir Edmund, with a marked lack of enthusiasm. "Well, in any event, Elizabeth," he said, picking up the thread of his conversation, "I believe that we'd best retire to the kitchen. There is a draft in here that will probably bring us all down with the influenza if we stay." He looked at his sister hopefully.

Elizabeth, doubtful that the unusual circumstances of the storm excused such a radical departure from acceptable behavior as sitting in an inn kitchen rather than a private parlor, allowed herself to be swayed as she considered how unpleasant it would be to share the parlor with a man of Lord Chawton's ilk. Far better to place Nora and herself in the company of the Netherspoons than such a man.

Nora added her entreaties to those of Sir Edmund, recounting the charms of the kitchen she had noted when she had gone exploring and discovered Sampson. Nothing, she assured Elizabeth, could be more charming than the kitchen of the Bull and Barleycorn, and no one more respectable than Mrs. Netherspoon, who presided over it.

To Sir Edmund's relief, she allowed herself to be swayed. Lord Mallory permitted himself to be drawn along with them, leaving Lord Chawton in possession of the parlor. Sir Edmund was eager for Mallory's company, knowing that he was not only a very pretty whip but at home to a peg with a deck of cards as well. Elizabeth, although she had misgivings about the wisdom of having Nora and Mallory in such close company, had felt the tension between the young man and Chawton. She had heard that there had been some unpleasantness when Mallory's older brother had last been home to London before his death in Spain. The rumormongers had noised it abroad that Chawton had won a veritable fortune from the young man in one night of gambling at Brooks's. Elizabeth, glancing at young Mallory's face, was unwilling to leave them alone together. Mallory might be a prankster and a flirt, but Chawton was what Sir Edmund called "a curst rum touch."

As they passed through the entry hall, they could hear a faint scratching between the gusts of wind.

"I believe there must be someone there," announced Sir Edmund, hurrying over to open it. As the door swung open, what appeared to be a small mound of snow staggered into the room and collapsed in a heap. Sir Edmund adjusted his eyeglass and peered down at it.

Nora took one look, pushed Sampson into Sir Edmund's unwilling arms, and knelt down beside it. "It's a dog! Why, it's no more than a puppy!" she cried, trying frantically to brush away some of the snow. "And he's very nearly frozen! Someone get a blanket—or, Edmund, let me have your scarf."

"What?" asked Sir Edmund, horrified. Being convinced that he had very nearly frozen and would undoubtedly contract an inflammation of the lungs that would carry him away if he did not protect himself, when he had removed all his outer garb, he had retained a cashmere scarf wrapped snugly about his throat, willing to sacrifice the elegant arrangement of his starched neckcloth for his health. "My scarf for a *dog?*"

"I shouldn't give it to her if I were you, Harrington," said Chawton, who had been watching in amusement from the door of the parlor. "That half-grown animal is not worth the price of the scarf nor the time it would take to dry him."

Nora turned on him like a small avenging fury. "Is he *your* dog?" she demanded.

He lifted one eyebrow nonchalantly. "Not anymore. He was a gift from a lady. Unfortunately, I did not want a dog, so . . ." he shrugged his shoulders indifferently.

"So you just turned him out into this storm to die?" asked Nora furiously, brushing away at the snow crusted on the pup's fur first with a small lace handkerchief and then, when that gave way, with the hem of her dark wool skirt, turning it into a sodden mass.

31

"I did leave him out. Whether he chose to die or not was his own affair," he replied carelessly, retiring into the parlor and closing the parlor door against them.

"That man should be left outside himself to see whether or not *he* will die in this weather!" she exclaimed, continuing to scrub her patient vigorously.

"Nora, dear, let us take the dog back to Netherspoon and see if he can help us," said Elizabeth gently, helping Nora to her feet and brushing her crumpled skirt, smoothing it as well as she could, and trying to wring from it some of the dampness.

"I'll take him," volunteered Lord Mallory, picking up the soggy bundle with no apparent regard for his well-cut coat of blue superfine, thus winning a look of approval from Nora.

Sir Edmund followed the procession, stroking Sampson absently and murmuring, "An ugly customer, Chawton." A terrible thought struck him. "I wonder if he took proper care of his cattle. Perhaps I'd better check on them." In Sir Edmund's book, a man could sink no lower than one who did not look after his horses properly. All too often the ostlers at public inns were guilty of giving the horses short rations and pocketing the difference. The ostler at the Bull seemed an honest fellow, but Sir Edmund had stayed to see to it that his horses received their fair portions and were properly rubbed down. Chawton obviously was not a man to trouble himself with such matters.

Chapter Three 🧺

Nora and her group were received in the kitchen with mixed feelings on the part of the Netherspoons. Their usual clientele was of a humbler variety, and the sight of Quality in their parlor was unusual enough, but their appearance in the kitchen, which also served as the common taproom, was unheard of. Their protests were overridden by the joint attack of Nora and Sir Edmund. Nora felt that her new charge would be much better off in the warmth of the kitchen with the prospect of good things to eat, and Sir Edmund felt precisely the same about his own situation.

Having been reassured by Netherspoon that Lord Chawton's horses had been taken care of, for he had seen to them himself, he could settle himself comfortably in a snug corner and enjoy a tumbler of hot punch with an easy mind, admonishing Mallory and Elizabeth to do the same. Discovering that he still held Sampson, he looked about helplessly, but the mother cat had removed herself and her other kittens to a less populated area, and Nora was occupied. Since Sampson seemed more inclined to nap than to attack, Sir Edmund reluctantly allowed his lap to become the kitten's resting place. Nora had prevailed upon Netherspoon to bring her some sacking and with that she toweled down the shivering pup and made a nest for him as close to the fire as Mrs. Netherspoon would allow. There Nora settled and devoted herself to feeding him bits of mutton and crooning to him in a comforting voice.

Elizabeth seated herself next to Nora, determined to keep an eye on that young lady and to make their unconventional visit to the kitchen as blameless as possible. She entertained herself for a blissful moment or two by envisioning herself dancing in a care-free manner at ball after ball in London, unencumbered and Nora-less. A moment or two was all that she allowed herself to indulge in, however, aware that neither she nor Nora should be in the common room of an inn, particularly in company with people that they did not know. Still, she comforted herself, they found themselves in exceptional circumstances, and they were simply trying to make the best of things.

The kitchen was a cheerful apartment: a deal dresser painted a dark brown proudly displayed polished pewter plates and dishes; one wall displayed bright copper pots and pans; Mrs. Nether-spoon's scrubbed pine worktable was dotted with interesting bas-kets and bowls that held the promise of dinner; a huge copper tea kettle steamed on the cast-iron range; a sea-coal fire blazed in the vast old-fashioned fireplace; bunches of dried herbs, sugar loaves, flitches of bacon, whole hams, and festoons of sausages hung from the blackened rafters. The smell of baking bread still lingered in the air and had been joined by the mixed fragrances of capons turning on the spit, roasting hare stuffed with herbs and bits of bread, and baking apple tart. In honor of Collop Monday, Mrs. Netherspoon was using up all of her meat left-overs before the beginning of Lent. A shepherd's pie, composed of layers of chopped mutton, minced onion, and mashed pota-toes, reposed in the fireplace oven, while Mrs. Netherspoon de-voted herself to preparing the humble toad-in-the-hole, slices of bacon coated in batter and deep-fried. She told Elizabeth with pride that all of these dishes, along with a pork pie she had on hand, a Cheshire cheese, and a dish of mushroom fritters, would constitute their dinner, nor need Elizabeth worry that she was us-ing up all of the pantry supplies, for tomorrow they could again be certain of very tasty meals, as well as Shrove Tuesday pan-cakes.

As she made her survey of the kitchen, Elizabeth was startled to discover that they were not its only inhabitants. She had as-sumed that because of the storm none of the locals would be out. At a small table in the far corner of the room sat one man alone, obviously not a gentleman, judging by his demeanor and the quality of his canary yellow coat and the arrangement of his plum-colored neckcloth. He seemed quite affable, smiling and bowing when he caught her eye with what seemed to Elizabeth a striking lack of propriety. Also, two other men and a woman occupied a settle against the back wall, a small deal table in front of them. These, too, seemed to be a humbler sort of customer, although, unlike the man in the canary-colored coat and plum neckcloth, they were quite self-effacing, seeming to wish to keep themselves to themselves.

Seeing her surprise, Mrs. Netherspoon said, "That's right, miss. I didn't think that you knew there would be more than just your party in here. It doesn't seem fitting for you to be in here, but I suppose it is much more comfortable on a night like this, and then there's your brother's health and the pup to think of. And the young lady has gotten the hem of her dress soaking wet, so she should be where she's warmest, too. All of these folks can be trusted to hold the line and be respectful—Jem Featherstone," and here she indicated the man in the yellow coat, who smiled and waved, "might put himself forward, but that is just the way he is. He don't mean anything by it. He's that way with everyone, but my John will settle him soon enough if he gets too frisky."

Dinner had the informality of a picnic for Elizabeth and her group. The food was plentiful and excellently cooked, and after the remains had been cleared away and they had complimented the glowing Netherspoons, they drew closer to the fire. Nora returned to her post next to the pup, who was showing signs of recovery. His rough black coat was dry, and his dark eyes were bright and watchful. Perceiving himself to be among friends, he ventured forth from his nest of sacking and began to sniff about inquisitively. Having been encouraged by Lord Mallory to inspect his shining Hessians, he repaid the favor by trying to chew their jaunty tassels. Discovering Sampson's saucer, he promptly dined upon all of the milk and bread, and, after wiping his milky whiskers tidily on the green figured print of Elizabeth's skirt, collapsed in a satisfied heap on Sir Edmund's foot.

He stared down at the pup with some displeasure. "Now, why do they come to me when they know I don't want 'em?"

Elizabeth laughed. "Because they know you will take care of them, Edmund. They probably know about you and your horses."

Her brother looked at her indignantly. "There's no comparison between a fine bit of blood-and-bone and one of these. Here, let's be gone now." He nudged the pup, who glanced up at him reproachfully but didn't budge.

"You underestimate him, Sir Edmund," remonstrated Mallory. "He is undoubtedly a Scots terrier and will make a wonderful ratter when he grows up."

"A ratter!" exclaimed Sir Edmund. "What would I want with a ratter?"

"He could keep the rats out of your stables, Edmund," replied Elizabeth, smiling.

"I have heard of one that could kill as many as fifty in five minutes," added Mallory. "And they go after bigger quarry, too. These little dogs aren't afraid to go after a cougar or a wildcat."

Sir Edmund regarded the small bundle on his foot with growing respect. "A small beast like that? Even full-grown he isn't going to be much over a stone in weight."

"But what he lacks in size he will make up for in heart." Startled by the sound of a new voice, they looked up to see Jem Featherstone, the man in the canary waistcoat. "Indeed, I have heard it said that all dogs are good, any terrier is better, and Scots terriers are the best. I believe that to be true."

"I do not agree with you about many things, Jem Featherstone, but I would agree with you about that," said a deep voice from the back of the kitchen.

"I thank you, Tom Macklin," said Featherstone, inclining his head gravely in that gentleman's direction. Macklin was a tall, raw-boned fellow with a kindly face. He and his sister and her husband sat comfortably at their table, regarding the newcomers with a profound but respectful interest.

Elizabeth was taken aback by this intrusion into their private group, but before she could say anything to put an end to it, Sir Edmund, who had been listening carefully, said, "Bosh! What is all of this fuss about a dog?"

Jem Featherstone stared at him reproachfully, his plump pink face growing even pinker. "We are not just talking about any dog, sir! We are speaking of a dog that is a gentleman!"

Sir Edmund looked at him in disbelief, searched for his quizzing glass, found it, and inspected Featherstone again, as though he could not believe either eyes or ears. "Calling a dog a gentleman? Speaking of rats, my good fellow, I believe you must either have rats in your upper works or be three parts disguised."

Affronted, Jem Featherstone drew himself up and said in a dignified voice, "What I say is perfectly true, sir. In fact, I will tell you a tale to prove my point."

"Wonderful!" exclaimed Nora. "A story! That is just what we need on such a gloomy evening."

Featherstone inclined his head gravely in her direction. "I venture to say that you will like it, miss." Without further invitation, Featherstone drew a stool closer to the fire and began his tale.

"Rufus is the name of our hero. Like the rest of his breed, he was dignified, honorable, courageous, and loyal to those he loved. He was a fighter, too, although not a vicious one. He only attacked to defend himself or his own.

"He belonged to a man by the name of Sammons who had a young son. When the child was only four, a dog from a neighboring farm, a large wolfhound, set upon him. Rufus leaped, caught the other dog by the throat, and hung on for dear life while the wolfhound tried to shake him loose and the little boy ran into the house.

"When Sammons came rushing out, both dogs lay bleeding on the grass. The throat of the wolfhound had been all but torn out, and Rufus had been badly hurt, but he could still wag his tail as his owner bent over him. The wolfhound died, but Rufus recovered, looking brisker and more confident than ever. Wherever Sammons went, we would see Rufus trotting right behind him.

"Two or three years after this, Sammons left his home on a fifty-mile journey. It was a very important one, for he was going to deliver the money that would make the final payment on his farm. It had taken him a year's hard work to accumulate the sum. Rufus was supposed to be locked in his master's bedchamber until later in the day to prevent his following Sammons, for the trip would be too long a one for such short legs. Unbeknownst to the rest of the family, however, Rufus had managed to squeeze himself through a partially opened window and had leaped into a pile of straw in a cart drawn up beside the house.

"The honest carter, our Tom Macklin," he continued, nodding toward the settle, "is a dog fancier himself, and when he saw the little dog making his escape, he unfastened his horse from the cart, got upon his back, and started after him.

"In the meantime, Sammons had been knocked from his horse by a highwayman on a deserted bit of the road. It was at this point that Tom Macklin got to the crest of the hill that overlooked the valley where all of this was taking place. He saw Sammons lying on the ground and the highwayman bending over him. Just then, Rufus, who had picked up speed after hearing the shot, raced around the bend in the road and launched himself upon the thief, who was so startled by the suddenness and force of the attack that he dropped his pistol and retreated.

"Rufus stood beside his master's still form, growling as the highwayman approached again, unimpressed by the size of his attacker. He tried to kick the dog away, but Rufus seized his knee above his boot tops. The man struck him again and again, but the dog refused to release him. Finally, doubled over with pain, the man managed to reach the pistol he had dropped in Rufus's first attack, aimed it, and fired. The little dog dropped at his feet, and the thief, determined to have Sammons's pocketbook after so much trouble, reached down to search his coat pockets.

"Before he could take the money, however, Rufus crawled to his master's side and fixed his teeth in the highwayman's arm. And, as you know," he nodded gravely to Tom Macklin, who nodded gravely back, "there is nothing more fearful than the bite of a Scots terrier. The power of his jaws is second to none."

Tom Macklin nodded in agreement and chewed the stem of his pipe reflectively.

"And so it was," he continued, "that when Tom Macklin arrived on the scene, Rufus still had the highwayman by the arm, although he was close to collapsing. The highwayman, after seeing the size of Tom, decided that he would submit quietly. When Sammons regained his senses, it was to see a masked man lying on the ground with his hands tied behind his back and Tom Macklin bending over Rufus, trying to tend his wound."

"And what of Rufus? Did he live?" inquired Nora eagerly, and even Sir Edmund looked interested in the response.

Featherstone shook his head sadly. "It was a mortal wound that he had sustained, and the life slipped right away from him after he had done his duty by his master. But he died with his head on his master's lap, having saved his home and farm for him. On the Sammons farm you'll find a headstone that reads: 'Rufus: Best of Friends.' "

The company sat silently for a moment, and even Nora was subdued. Then she picked up the pup and looked at him earnestly. "We'll name you Rufus."

Elizabeth and Sir Edmund exchanged an alarmed glance. "Don't grow too attached, Nora dear," cautioned Elizabeth. "Naming him will just make leaving him all the harder."

"No need at all," chimed Sir Edmund firmly. He plucked the sleeping Sampson from his lap and placed him on the floor, noting with disgust that his immaculate coat and riding breeches were now dotted with minute orange cat hairs.

Nora looked at them in dismay. "We can't leave Rufus here! That Man is not going to have another opportunity to mistreat him! And Mrs. Netherspoon promised me that I might have Sampson as my own."

Mrs. Netherspoon nodded her agreement, and Sir Edmund stared at his sister with a fixed gaze, silently demanding that she handle this situation.

"Upon my word of honor, dear child, that animal is quite safe from me," said Lord Chawton from the doorway where he had been standing for some minutes. "Its fate is a matter of complete indifference to me."

Before anyone could respond, he yawned gently and turned his attention briefly to Mr. Featherstone. "Such a charming story," he said sweetly, "although I must feel that my sympathies are with the highwayman."

Mr. Featherstone, sensing ridicule, bristled. "And who might you be, if I may be so bold as to ask?" he inquired.

Mr. Netherspoon hurried into the breach. "What may I be getting for you, my lord?" he asked Lord Chawton. "Don't you be kicking up a dust, Jem," he whispered to Mr. Featherstone as he passed him. Chastened, Mr. Featherstone subsided to his stool by the fire.

"I believe that I will have another bottle of brandy, landlord. And you may bring it to me here." Chawton sank gracefully into the chair at the corner table where Mr. Featherstone had been sitting. "It was getting rather dull in there alone, and if we are telling stories, I may find some amusement here."

The rest of the company looked uncomfortable and seemed to draw slightly closer together. Mr. Netherspoon took Chawton his brandy, and his good wife, eager to dispel the sudden chill in the room, said cheerfully, "It's a good thing that you came tonight, Tom Macklin, for I've fixed fat rascals just this very morning."

"Fat rascals!" exclaimed Nora. "What a curious name! What are they?"

"They are very like scones, miss, but they have currants and raisins in them. Tom Macklin is a North Riding man, and they remind them of his boyhood days. Don't they, Tom?" she inquired brightly.

Tom, obviously not much given to conversation, nodded and grinned, uncomfortable at being the sudden focus of attention.

While Mrs. Netherspoon was arranging the fat rascals on a plate, she added, "John is brewing up some hot punch for the gentlemen, and I am going to fix some hot spiced cider for the ladies. Then we may all be comfortable."

Sir Edmund's expression brightened perceptibly with the mention of the punch, so he was able to tolerate with some equanimity the sudden unannounced arrival of Sampson on his shoulder and Rufus on his boot.

Elizabeth excused herself to get her shawl and made her way quietly from the kitchen, carefully avoiding Lord Chawton, whom she heartily disliked. She was halfway up the stairs to her chamber when she heard the sound of stamping feet outside the door. Pausing a moment, she looked down to see who might enter.

The light from the lamp next to the door revealed that the newcomer was a man of slightly over medium height, his sturdy build emphasized by his greatcoat, which he promptly removed and placed on a bench. He took off his curly-brimmed beaver, shook the snowflakes from his dark hair, and tossed the hat on top of his coat. He did not appear to be greatly given to smiling, and his expression as he turned to face her was a grim and determined one.

He did not notice her at first in the shadows of the stairway, for she had not taken a candle to light her way, but as she turned to continue up the stairs, he heard the sound and looked up. "I beg your pardon, miss," he said. It was obvious from his tone that he was controlling his anger with some difficulty but that he was attempting to be polite.

"Could you tell me where I might find the landlord? Or perhaps," he added, almost grinding his teeth as he did so, "where I might find the owner of that very handsome black gelding in the stables? I believe he will be in company with two ladies."

Elizabeth looked down at him in some dismay, realizing that he must be referring to Devon Boy and that this must be Nora's Mr. Norville. She had a sudden wild impulse to laugh. Whatever else he might appear to be, Mr. Norville certainly did not look as though he had one foot in the grave. Indeed, he fairly pulsed with life — or, at the moment, with anger. Fortunately, she was able to restrain her laughter, for the thought of what Edmund's reaction to the loss of Devon Boy would be brought her back to reality with a jerk. What on earth was the man doing here? Had he followed them for the horse? Deciding that a direct approach was the best policy, she turned and walked down the stairs toward him.

"You must be Mr. Andrew Norville," she said cordially, extending her hand to him. "I am Elizabeth Harrington, Cecilia Lane's cousin."

He stared at her in amazement. "You are the lady who is chaperoning Miss Lane? I was left with the impression that you were a much older woman!"

Not a particle of address, thought Elizabeth, forcing herself to retain her smile. She did not wonder at Nora's unwillingness to be yoked with such a man.

"I shall wear a cap tomorrow so that you will think better of me," she replied lightly.

This pleasantry brought no smile. Instead, his brow became more deeply furrowed. "Caring for a young girl of sixteen is no laughing matter, Miss Harrington. I would think that you would

41

take the responsibility of a young girl's care more seriously."

Elizabeth ceased smiling. "You need have no fear, Mr. Norville. I will take excellent care of Nora. I should rather say that her mother need have no fear, for it is to Mrs. Lane that I am responsible, and not, sir, to you," she reminded him tartly.

"I believe, Miss Harrington, that Mrs. Lane told you of my intentions toward Nora." His aspect grew blacker by the moment, but Elizabeth held her ground.

"She did indeed, Mr. Norville. And I might point out that your intentions are precisely that—intentions—no more than that at this time. Nora is a young girl, and she deserves a young girl's pleasures, particularly after a year spent in deep mourning. She was my late mother's godchild, and she is coming to London with my brother and me for a visit."

"So I apprehend," he replied grimly. "I was not best pleased to learn that she was going to London when I thought that she was going in the company of someone of her own mother's age. I can scarcely be expected to be pleased to discover that her duenna is a young lady more nearly her own age."

"You must excuse my speaking frankly, Mr. Norville, since you have done so yourself," replied Elizabeth, determined not to be bullied. "I do not recognize any claim of yours on Miss Lane, and still less do I recognize any right of yours to criticize my ability to care for my guest. I am not a milk-and-water miss of sixteen, so do not be thinking that you can run roughshod over me."

"I trust that time spent with you, Miss Harrington, will not rob Miss Lane of the innocence of—as you so delicately phrased it—a milk-and-water miss."

Small white indentations had appeared on either side of Norville's nose, and Elizabeth could see that he was holding his temper by the merest thread. Exceedingly angry herself, she decided to test the strength of that thread.

"You were inquiring after a black gelding, Mr. Norville, which is how I knew who you were. Nora had mentioned that you had enjoyed riding him while at Braxton Hall. Perhaps my brother would allow you to borrow him for a turn in the Park sometime when you visit London . . . but I had forgotten! You do not visit London, do you? I believe you hold our city in contempt."

He smiled, but it was not a pleasant smile. "You have been misinformed. I do not hold London itself in contempt. It is rather that portion of its society that has nothing to do other than go to balls and gossip and game away money that could be spent in worthwhile ways that is the object of my contempt. I would not have had Miss Lane's freshness spoiled by contact with such a group of people for any price. And it is you that I must thank for bringing this about."

Elizabeth controlled herself with an effort and attempted to speak pleasantly, remembering that Cecilia had indeed almost promised Nora to him. "In truth, I think you *should* thank me. It is important, I think, for a young girl to have had some slight exposure to the world before she considers marriage."

"I do not consider that to be the case. In fact, I believe that it is much better if she has led a very circumscribed life, for she would be more amenable to having her opinions shaped by her husband."

Her eyes widened and she very nearly broke into laughter. "My dear sir, if you think that you will be shaping Nora's opinions because she is very young, I can only imagine that you have had no opportunity to talk with her. She may be only sixteen, but I assure you that she has very decided opinions about virtually everything."

"I believe that you exaggerate the case, Miss Harrington. Be that as it may, I understand that Miss Lane will be with you until Easter. Rest assured that I will be close by."

His tone strongly indicated that he would be on guard duty during Nora's London stay. Elizabeth, accustomed as she was to commanding the respect of those about her, controlled her temper with an effort. Assuming an air of archness that she calculated would most annoy him, she quizzed him with bright eyes and a brittle smile.

"How safe you will make us feel, Mr. Norville! But what can you mean, sir? Will you be staying in London despite your contempt for the place?"

He bowed stiffly, ignoring her raillery. "There are a few affairs

I need to see to there, but I will remain until Easter to see Miss Lane home to Braxton Hall. And now, if you will excuse me, Miss Harrington, I will find the landlord after I return to the stables and see to it that the ostler has cared for my horses. I shall most certainly see you again."

After his departure, Elizabeth sat down on the stairs to recover her composure. What a dreadfully arrogant, rag-mannered man! And she had allowed him to overset her to the point that she had lost her temper and behaved like a fishwife.

Chapter Four

By the time that Elizabeth had collected her shawl and returned to the kitchen, her cheeks and her temper had cooled
slightly and no one seemed to notice anything amiss. A glance
at Nora's cheerful expression revealed that Mr. Norville had
not yet joined them. It was obvious that the group had enjoyed
the story Lord Mallory had just told, for even solemn Tom
Macklin was still chuckling and shaking his head over "the
young lord's doin's." His story was one that Elizabeth already
knew, for the *ton* had chuckled about it for weeks after it happened. A wager had been made between Lord Mallory—who at
that time was still the Honorable Trevor Graham—and a friend
from his Oxford days, Sir Adrian Mayhew, and had been duly
entered in White's betting book. The winner was to be the one
who managed to provide the greater surprise for the other and
would be awarded fifty pounds by the loser. The judges were to
be three friends of theirs who would witness each surprise.

Sir Adrian, having planned carefully before making this wager, had sprung his surprise first, trusting that by acting so
quickly he would catch his quarry off guard. Within three days
after the wager had been made, Mallory had received a brief
note from an elderly uncle, who had lived retired in the country for years, announcing his imminent arrival at Mallory's
London home. Since his date of arrival coincided with a pre-
vious engagement that was to take Mallory away from town for
a week, Mallory assumed that this was the trick. Sir Adrian
knew of the engagement, indeed, he was to be a member of
the party, and Mallory determined that his friend expected him

to stay at home, preparing for the arrival of his uncle. Declining to be taken for such a Johnny Raw, Mallory had smilingly joined his friends for the week at Newmarket.

Great was his surprise when he returned to London and found his Uncle Henry firmly installed in Mallory's own study and the best guest bedchamber, accompanied by his valet, his coachman and groom, two footmen, three trunks, assorted portmanteaux, and two elderly spaniels. He had called his bemused nephew to order for having been so rattlebrained as to be absent on the day of his arrival, but had remarked cheerfully that he had managed to make himself at home (a statement that was all too obviously true) and that he was now ready to begin dispensing the advice that his nephew had requested in his very urgent letter. When Mallory had thanked him profusely for his concern and delicately inquired the length of his intended visit, the old man had reminded him that his invitation had been for a period of ten weeks. Mallory had tottered from his study to find his friends in a state of collapse in the corridor.

Sir Adrian had braced himself for Mallory's return attack, but the weeks had passed and nothing had happened. Almost had he persuaded himself that Mallory recognized that he, Sir Adrian Mayhew, held the whip hand and that there was no point in attempting to retaliate when the blow fell. Sir Adrian, in company with his old friends, had gotten jolly over port wine and roasted oranges and lemons, as they had in their Oxford days. He was always an exceedingly sound sleeper, but particularly so after such an evening.

The next morning he had awakened a little later than usual and felt, as he looked about his chamber, that something was not quite as it should be. As he grew more alert and his valet assisted him with shaving and putting on his town toggery, he became certain that this was so. Sir Adrian had a very snug set of rooms—and they were still very snug—but everything appeared to have been reversed. When he turned from his mirror to leave his bedchamber, it came to him that he had turned away from the actual door instead of walking toward it! When he opened the door of what should have been the dining room, he discovered instead his small drawing room. Now thoroughly confused, he tried the door which should have entered the drawing room and discovered his misplaced dining room. When he sat down at the dining room table for his breakfast of beefsteak and beer, his place had been set on the wrong side of the table. Staring at his valet, he demanded to know who had moved the rooms out of place. Winters stared back at him a moment, then asked with some concern if he were feeling quite the thing.

Sir Adrian had grown more and more convinced that he must still be a little bit on the go, and he finally decided that he must get out and clear his head with a walk. When he started to put on his hat, a letter had floated to the floor. Opening it, he had discovered gibberish instead of writing. He was mystified until it occurred to him that he had seen this trick done in his schoolboy days. Holding up the letter to the mirror, he had read the following:

> Right is left
> And left is right.
> Such a situation
> Deep confusion does invite.
>
> Forward is backward
> And down is up.
> Perhaps it comes
> From too much port in your cup.
>
> Or, my dear Mayhew,
> Perhaps it could be
> That things really are
> Exactly as you see,
>
> For your rooms
> In Duke Street are found,

Mallory's elaborate hoax had taken weeks to prepare, for he had hired a set of rooms that was the mirror image of Sir Adrian's and had furnished it in the same manner. He had also managed to enlist Winters's help, a desertion that took Sir Adrian some time to forgive. They had moved him during the night and waited to see his reaction when he awakened.

"I see that you spend your time in very rewarding ways, Mallory," drawled Lord Chawton from his corner of the kitchen. "Such energy and money as you must expend on your hoaxes. You quite exhaust me."

Mallory flushed, annoyed by the contempt in his voice. "It might have been a halfling's trick, Chawton, but at least I do not need to be ashamed of the things that I have done. *My* activities can bear the light of day."

"Indeed?" Chawton swung his quizzing glass thoughtfully. "Almost all of us have something — some little thing — that we would like to hide." He stared at Mallory meditatively and added slowly, "Or sometimes it is some secret in our family that we wish to conceal."

Mallory stared back at him, his eyes hard and bright.

"Perhaps, since everyone is telling stories, I might tell one, too," said Chawton.

There was an awkward silence. No one, not even the obliging Netherspoons, felt the smallest desire to hear him speak about anything, but Chawton interpreted their silence as consent and began his tale.

"There was once — in a faraway land, of course — a man who was asked to go on a very long and very important journey. He was a loyal servant of his own king — they always are in the stories, you know — and so he agreed. He was to deliver a gift of great value and a message to a king in a country far away from his own — beyond the sea and beyond great mountains. And so he bid goodbye to his loving family and set off on his journey.

"He traveled many hard miles and had many adventures, even

48

being set upon by thieves in a dark forest, but he finally reached his destination. He rested and then attired himself to complete his mission. The king was expecting him and sent a carriage to bring him to the court. The night was dark and cold and windy, and the torches that the link boys held were guttering in the wind. A footman held open the door of the carriage, but our gentleman paused as he was about to enter, as though he were thinking deeply, then turned back, saying he must go back to his room for something he had forgotten. He walked around the front of the carriage, past the horses' heads, and into the darkness.

"The carriage waited for several minutes; then the footman entered the inn to remind the gentleman that the king was waiting. The landlord sent a servant up to his room, but they found it empty. His trunk and portmanteaux were there, but there was no sign of the gentleman. No one had seen him reenter the inn. In short, he disappeared that evening and was never seen again."

Chawton glanced at his audience. Mallory was staring at him intently. All of them, in fact, seemed to be caught by his tale.

"Is this a true story?" asked Nora breathlessly.

"Of course not," replied Chawton nonchalantly. "Nothing but a fireside tale."

"Was there no hint, no clue at all as to his whereabouts?" she persisted.

Chawton looked amused. "I was saving that for the very close of my story. As a matter of fact, a scrap of paper was found on the table in his room. On it someone had hurriedly written a nonsense riddle."

"A riddle! I *do* love them! What was it?" demanded Nora.

"As I said, it was a riddle. It went like this:

> *I am the beginning*
> *I hold the key*
> *I am winter's end*
> *From summer I flee*

It makes no sense at all," Chawton repeated, studying the faces before him, particularly that of Lord Mallory. As for Mallory, his eyes never left Chawton's face.

"And what of the 'gift of great value,' Lord Chawton? Was that found in his room?"

Everyone, Chawton in particular, looked startled to hear a new voice, and when he turned to face the speaker, he paled visibly.

"Norville! I did not know that you were back in the country!"

"I did not imagine that you did," replied Norville smoothly. "But I am delighted to have been here in time to hear your very interesting story. Do tell us, Chawton. Did the gift disappear as well?"

Chawton looked more uncomfortable than ever. "Yes, the gift vanished with him."

"Nabbled it," said Jem Featherstone knowingly, rubbing the side of his nose. "Though I don't see why he waited until the last possible moment to disappear. Seems like a dashed queer start! Why not nip off somewhere along the way?"

Norville looked at him approvingly. "A very apt observation. Why indeed should an intelligent man do such an exceedingly foolish thing?"

Nora had pulled convulsively on the skirt of Elizabeth's dress at Norville's unexpected entry into the conversation. "That is Norville," she had whispered in a panic. "He must have come for me, Elizabeth. Don't let him take me home!"

"Don't be foolish, Nora. Of course he will not take you home. That would be most improper and Sir Edmund would not allow it. Nor would I," she added in a martial tone.

A little comforted, but still keeping a wary eye on Norville's stern face, Nora turned her attention back to the story. "What of his family, sir? Did they never hear of him again?"

Chawton shook his head, apparently eager to have done with the conversation.

"Could he not have been kidnapped?" she persisted. "For if he disappeared of his own will, even if he stole the gift, surely he would have let his family know that he was alive."

Norville smiled at her. "One would certainly think so, Miss Lane," he agreed.

At this direct acknowledgement of her presence, Nora shrank even lower on her stool. Mallory looked up sharply, distracted from his study of Chawton by Nora's reaction to Norville.

"I see that you are acquainted with at least one member of our group, sir. Are you by any chance the Lt. Colonel Andrew Norville who was in Spain with the 14th Light Dragoons a year ago?"

As Norville nodded his head, Mallory smiled and extended his hand. "I am Trevor Graham, now Lord Mallory. It is you I have to thank for writing to my family after my brother's death. It was a great help to us, particularly my mother, to hear about it from someone that he regarded so highly."

Norville took his hand. "Michael was a fine man. We miss him sorely."

"And so you served in the Peninsula as a member of the Duchess of York's own Light Dragoons?" inquired Jem Featherstone knowledgeably, rubbing the side of his nose more vigorously. "It is an honor to be sharing a fire with you, sir, an honor!"

Seeing Mallory and Norville deep in conversation and his effusions acknowledged only by a brief nod, Featherstone turned to Tom Macklin and the Netherspoons, who were regarding Norville with obvious admiration, and continued to expound upon the victories in the Peninsula. His recital was interrupted, however, by the mixed sounds of cursing and yelping.

Chawton had taken advantage of this interruption to make his departure. Rufus, who had also taken advantage of the confusion to investigate the farther reaches of the kitchen, had had the misfortunc to blcnd with thc shadows, and Chawton had tripped over him. With a loud imprecation that brought conversation to a halt, Chawton lifted the hapless pup on the toe of his boot and flung him against the wall. Rufus tumbled to the floor in a small, motionless heap as Chawton slammed the door behind him.

51

Nora and Elizabeth rushed to gather up the dog, and together they replaced him gently in his nest by the fire. Tom Macklin silently joined them, checking the small form carefully. With their attention focused entirely on Rufus, they did not notice Mallory and Norville quietly follow Chawton from the room.

"Will he be all right?" Nora asked Macklin tearfully as Macklin probed the pup gently with hands almost as large as the pup itself.

Macklin nodded. "I think so, miss. He's a rare lump coming on the side of his head, but I think that's the lot of it."

"What a cowhearted thing to do!" expostulated Sir Edmund, who had been watching the whole scene with deep disapprobation. "The man shouldn't be allowed out without a keeper!"

Relief was great when Rufus began to whine and move his head slowly. Even Sir Edmund was moved enough to suggest that a warm bran mash might be just the thing to aid in his recovery. Rufus was made much of and tucked into his warm nest, Sampson expressing his opinion of this blatant favoritism with protesting, plaintive meows until, finally accepting the situation with a philosophical air, he curled up into an orange ball beside the pup.

So oblivious to all else had the group in the kitchen been that it came as a surprise to see Mallory and Norville enter the room from outside, goodnaturedly shaking the snow from their boots and coats. So pleased with themselves did they look that Elizabeth could not restrain herself.

"Where have you been?" she inquired.

"Seeing to it that Lord Chawton was properly outfitted for his journey," responded Mallory cheerfully.

"Surely he did not leave in this weather!" she exclaimed.

"He was not at first certain that he wished to," admitted Mallory, "but after a brief discussion he could see the wisdom of making his departure now."

"Drew his cork for him, did you?" asked Sir Edmund approvingly. "I've heard you're very handy with your fives, Mallory." He arose and approached Norville. "I daresay you may not remember, Norville, for it's been a long time since last you were in London, but we met there at White's one evening."

"I do indeed remember, Sir Edmund," he replied, extending his hand. "I had seen you earlier that day in the park, riding a very handsome bay, and I tried to convince you to sell her to me."

"That would have been Highstepper," said Sir Edmund reminiscently. "None like her to be found today," he said sadly. Then his expression brightened, and Elizabeth was filled with misgiving, for she was sure he was going to talk about Devon Boy. "Although, Norville, you would not believe the sweet-goer I just found at my cousin's."

Elizabeth could not bring herself to look at Norville's face. Why, she asked herself, could Edmund not attend to anything other than conversation about horses? He obviously had not listened to Cecilia, and he had no notion at all that Norville had anything to do with Cecilia or Nora or Devon Boy. Nothing at all to do with Braxton Hall, in fact, though Norville was now its owner.

Here she had underrated her brother, however. After recounting some of Devon Boy's finer points, sure that Norville could appreciate them, his brow wrinkled as he regarded him thoughtfully. "You couldn't, by any chance, be the Norville that my cousin Cecilia was speaking of, a distant relation of her husband, Jasper Lane?"

Elizabeth groaned inwardly, but Norville seemed to take it in good part. His face grew slightly less severe as he acknowledged the connection. Elizabeth, seeing that Nora and Lord Mallory, ably assisted by Tom Macklin, were devoting their attention to the livestock, could only hope that Edmund's evil genius would not cause him to pursue this line of thought to its logical end.

"A sad business, that," continued Sir Edmund. "It all came of a wager, according to Cecilia. I don't suppose you'd know just how it happened?"

"As a matter of fact, I know very little about it. Mrs. Lane did not, of course, wish to discuss it."

"Too heavy-handed," asserted Sir Edmund, voicing again his

53

chief grievance against the dead man. "Always thought himself bang up to the mark, a regular top-sawyer." He shook his head. "Couldn't usually pick his cattle either. Forever buying beasts that were touched in the wind. Can't imagine how he came to have a prime 'un like Devon Boy."

"I can tell you that, Edmund," said Nora, who had suddenly become aware of the conversation. "He won Devon Boy from Squire Thomas in a game of whist. Mama said that the squire lost on purpose because Devon Boy was the devil's own horse and he wished to be rid of him."

Elizabeth, uncomfortably reminded of the impropriety of their circumstances now that Norville was observing them, murmured in a low voice, "Nora, dear, remember your language, please."

"Why, the squire must be all about in his head!" remarked Sir Edmund in astonishment. "Devon Boy is as sweet a goer as I've ridden—almost the equal of Highstepper."

"I would agree with you, Sir Edmund," said Norville. "He is a fine animal. No temper—just spirited."

"Exactly so! I can see that you must have taken him out while you were at Braxton Hall," replied Sir Edmund.

Anxious to change the course of the conversation, Elizabeth turned to Nora. "Have you thought any more about the riddle, Nora?"

Nora's eyes brightened. "Do talk about it. I'm sure we could work it out. Now, how did it go again?"

Jem Featherstone, feeling that he had been too long left out of the conversation, repeated it for her, adding, "I have been devoting some thought to this matter, miss, being very fond of a riddle myself and quite handy with them if I do say so, and I think that the beginning alluded to might be the letter *A*—as being the beginning of the alphabet, you see."

Nora looked at him admiringly. "That is very clever of you. I hadn't thought of that."

Praise obviously agreed with Featherstone, for he seemed to grow plumper before their very eyes. Eager to encourage the conversation, Elizabeth threw in her bit. "It could be the number one. That is also a beginning."

"Yes," Mallory interjected. "But the beginning of *what?* This could be the beginning of anything—the alphabet, a song. It could be alpha rather than *A* for the beginning of the alphabet. Or perhaps it refers to the beginning of time—perhaps Adam as the first man."

"That's very true." Nora looked discouraged for a moment, then plucked up a bit. "What about the second part—the 'I hold the key'? The answer to that must surely be a lock."

Tom Macklin nodded slowly, puffing his pipe as an aid to reflection. "Aye, miss. I think you would be in the right of it there."

Jem Featherstone had a constitutional dislike for ideas that were not his own, so he prepared to take issue. "That might well be, of course," he said condescendingly, "but it depends on what kind of key is meant. A pianoforte also has a key."

"So it does. I hadn't thought of that either," admitted Nora.

The Netherspoons had been listening indulgently, but deciding that it was time for their guests to have the inn to themselves so they could prepare for bed, firmly discouraged anymore riddling on the part of Mr. Featherstone. Good-nights were said all round, and the townsfolk put on their coats and left by the kitchen door.

Sir Edmund shivered as the cold wind blew a scuttering of snow past his boots. "At least we'll have a snug bed tonight, my dear," he said to Elizabeth, blissfully unaware of what lay ahead of him. Elizabeth and the Netherspoons exchanged glances.

"Edmund, the inn has only two bedrooms, I'm afraid."

Edmund did a quick mathematical calculation, and his expression made it clear that the result was not pleasing. "And what am I to do?" he asked in a resigned tone. "Make my bed by the fire here?"

"That's the ticket!" said Netherspoon in an encouraging tone. "The missus and I will make you and Mr. Norville as snug as though you were wrapped up in cotton wool!"

"Coming it a bit too strong, Netherspoon," responded his victim. "But I suppose there's no other choice." He glanced about the floor, as though looking for the softest spot.

"Take heart, Sir Edmund," said Norville briskly. "This is much better than many of the places I've had to sleep in Spain. We can count ourselves fortunate. We could be out in the snow like Chawton."

Considerably heartened by the thought that Chawton was in far worse loaf than he, Sir Edmund allowed himself to be reconciled to the prospect of sharing the hearth with Norville, Sampson, and Rufus, reassured by the Netherspoons that the fire would be kept blazing and that hot punch would be readily available in case the chill became too great to be endured. As Elizabeth and Nora were abandoning the kitchen for their bedchamber, they could hear Sir Edmund saying, "And now, Norville, about Devon Boy . . ." They closed the door behind them, leaving Norville to his tender mercies.

Chapter Five

The snow stopped with the dawn, and by the time Norville stirred, the sun had spread a rosy glow over the frosted fields and rooftops. The Netherspoons had been as good as their word, for the fire still crackled cheerfully. They were bustling about the kitchen, and the smell of breakfast filled the air.

"I've took the liberty of laying some things out in the parlor and heating some water for shaving, sir," said Netherspoon when he saw that Norville was awake. "It still be cold there, even with a fire, but private. You'll find your gear in there."

"Thank you, Netherspoon. I will feel much better after shaving and changing." He turned to look with amusement at Sir Edmund, who was still sleeping soundly, Rufus and Sampson curled next to him in the folds of his blanket.

When he returned to the kitchen thirty minutes later, he found Sir Edmund seated close to the fire, a mug of hot coffee in his hand.

"There you are, Norville. I shall take my turn now." He looked down at the wreck of his cravat. "It's just as well that my valet can't see me now. He won't be best pleased when he tries to remove all of the hairs of the livestock either." He brushed ineffectually at his coat and breeches.

When he rose to leave the fireside, Rufus and Sampson rose, too, fully prepared to accompany him. It required great firmness on Sir Edmund's part and considerable coaxing on Norville's to convince them to stay. The winning card was played by Mrs. Netherspoon, who placed two small dishes of table scraps and milk in front of the hearth, and Sir Edmund made his escape thankfully.

While Norville thoughtfully watched the pair of them at their breakfast, Elizabeth made her appearance. Seeing that Norville was the only one by the fire, she almost turned back to her room again, but he looked up and saw her, a pleasing picture in a woolen gown of hunter's green, her copper curls caught back from her face by a ribbon of the same color.

"Ah, Miss Harrington—just the person I have been wishing to speak with. Please come and have a seat by the fire."

She did so reluctantly, hoping that Edmund would soon appear. "Did you sleep well?" she inquired politely.

"Like the dead," he assured her. "I believe that your brother and his companions also slept soundly."

"His companions?" she inquired, startled. Then, her eyes dancing, she looked down at the pair dining by the fire. "Did they sleep with Edmund? How annoyed he must have been, poor man."

"He left plucking animal hairs from his clothing and bemoaning the absence of his valet."

"Poor Edmund. He does enjoy his creature comforts very much, so this is especially dreadful for him."

Norville changed the subject abruptly. "I should like to apologize for my lack of manners yesterday, Miss Harrington."

Before she could manage a syllable in reply, he continued. "I can only tell you that, although my manner of speaking to you was unforgivable, I very much meant the things I was saying. I wish that you were not taking Miss Lane to London. It may do her some good, as you say, but I cannot help but feel that it will do her much more harm than good."

He saw that Elizabeth was about to speak, and said, "Please do hear me out, Miss Harrington. A time in London may very well entertain her and give her a little town polish, a very thin veneer, shall we say, but it is much more likely to teach her to flirt, to fritter away her time in mindless occupations, and to be discontented with her normal life at home."

Elizabeth saw that, although his tactics had changed, his goal remained the same: to keep Nora safely in cotton wool at home,

58

awaiting his convenience. She was determined that his new conciliatory manner would not throw her off her guard, so her reply was brisk.

"But she has not had a normal life at home, Mr. Norville. There has been virtually no social life for her for almost a year. That cannot be termed normal."

"But it makes her all the more susceptible to any of the temptations in town. She will learn to think only of her gowns and the parties she will attend the next day. I like her simple manners and appearance; she is a refreshing change from damped muslins and cropped curls."

He paused a moment, and before Elizabeth could inform him that *she* lived in London and managed to think of other things than gowns and parties, he continued. "And there will be lures thrown out by the town bucks who will be attracted by her youth and beauty even though she has no fortune. To be frank, *because* she is lovely but has no fortune, she may very well receive unwelcome attentions—not from any real gentleman, of course, but from some who have the name but not the manner of a gentleman." He paused again, and his chin set more firmly as he looked at Elizabeth. "She may be particularly vulnerable because she has no real protector, for you, Miss Harrington, are far too young to see to it that those about her hold the line."

"It may come as a great surprise to you, Mr. Norville," she replied stiffly, "but I had my first season seven years ago, and I manage to go on very well, without the unwelcome attentions of rakes. And," she added firmly, "I *do* manage to think of more than gowns and parties."

He smiled. "Yes, I am sure that is true. But then, you are Miss Elizabeth Harrington of Grosvenor Square, are you not? A young lady of independent fortune, accustomed to the ways of the *ton*, certain of commanding respect wherever you may go? In short, Miss Harrington, you are a person of consequence with all of the protection that name, position, and fortune bring. You are not vulnerable as Miss Lane is."

"I must remind you that my brother, Sir Edmund, could be counted as Miss Lane's protector."

He smiled once again, the briefest and most mirthless of

smiles. "I can see that you think you have landed me a facer, but I remember Sir Edmund from my younger days, Miss Harrington, and I would confess myself much surprised if he has changed. He will occupy his days with his horses and his clubs, not with breakfasts and balls."

Elizabeth bit her lip, unable to deny the truth of this. "Nonetheless, Mr. Norville, Miss Lane was my mother's godchild, and I feel a particular obligation to her. I have promised her this holiday in London, and I shall take very good care of her. And I must remind you, sir, that her mother gave her readily enough into my care."

"So she did," agreed Mr. Norville, "and I very much doubt that she would approve of having her daughter in the taproom of an inn, keeping company not only with people beneath her station but also with one man who is a notorious rake and another who is one of the most accomplished flirts of the *ton*."

He paused. "In view of this situation, and since I have a particular interest in Miss Lane's well-being, I shall, as I mentioned earlier, be at your disposal in London."

"If you plan to call upon us there, then I would suggest to you, Mr. Norville, that you begin by trying to make yourself agreeable to Miss Lane. That appears to be something you have overlooked."

She had the satisfaction of seeing that she had disconcerted him, but further conversation was prevented by the arrival of Nora, Sir Edmund, Lord Mallory, and breakfast. Although the owners of a very small inn, the Netherspoons were generous hosts, and breakfast required the full attention of their guests. There was a large steak and kidney pie, bacon and poached eggs, toast and muffins, doughnuts and cold ham, loaves of brown bread, and another Cheshire cheese. While they were eating, Jem Featherstone and Tom Macklin, along with several of their cronies, appeared, also apparently intent upon breakfast. Featherstone, in fact, entered the inn chanting:

> *A-shrovin', a-shrovin',*
> *I be come a-shrovin',*

A piece of bread, a piece of cheese,
A bit of your fat bacon,
Or a dish of dough-nuts,
All of your own makin'.

A-shrovin', a-shrovin',
Nice meat in a pie,
My mouth is very dry.

"And when is your mouth *not* very dry, Jem Featherstone?" inquired Mrs. Netherspoon tartly.

"Now, now, Nell, you know that it's just a rhyme, a Shrove Tuesday rhyme for the young ones . . . although my mouth *is* a trifle dry, and I could do with some 'nice meat in a pie.' "

"And I'm sure you're very welcome to it," said Mr. Netherspoon affably. "Take a seat and help yourselves," he encouraged them.

"I'd forgotten that this is Shrove Tuesday," commented Lord Mallory. "This is an important day in my little brother's life."

"Why is it of particular importance to your brother?" inquired Elizabeth politely. "If I remember properly, you said that he was ten years old."

Mallory nodded. "George will go up to Eton next fall, but my mother has wanted him near her for the time being, and he has been attending Westminster School. At eleven o'clock this morning there is a procession: the beadle, carrying his silver-topped mace, enters the Great Schoolroom, followed by the dean's verger, the dean of Westminster, the headmaster, and the cook with his frying pan. The cook is the focus of all eyes, for he must toss the pancake in his pan up and over the iron curtain bar that separates the Upper and Lower Schools. When it comes down, all of the boys in the school make a dive for it. The boy who emerges from the fray with the pancake—or the greatest part of the pancake, and they do use scales to weigh the pieces—receives a golden guinea from the dean. Then the dean 'begs a play'; that is, he asks the headmaster to give the boys a holiday. The boys call it the Pancake Greaze, and George is quite convinced that this year he will manage to win the guinea."

Mrs. Netherspoon had listened open-mouthed to Mallory's description of the occasion. "Well, I never heard of the like," she said as he finished. "Just imagine—all of those boys diving for one single pancake. I wouldn't want to be next or nigh that room at all."

The rest of the group seemed disposed to agree with her strongly, the fearful vision of a mob of boys descending with gusto upon a single pancake striking them most forcibly.

"At least the snow spared us last night from our village boys having their bit of fun," remarked Netherspoon.

"What kind of fun?" inquired Nora, who always wished to be well-informed about whatever was taking place.

"Lensharding," answered his wife for him. "They take themselves about throwing bits of broken crockery at the door of any house where they don't receive a bit of money." She sniffed. "Call it fun if you like, John Netherspoon. It's more like highway robbery. I was right glad to see the snow call a halt to it."

"Now, now," he said soothingly. "There's no real harm done. They just like their bit of fun."

"There'll be no football through the street today either," commented Jem Featherstone. "The snow has stopped, but it is still difficult to pass along the street, and the sun'll not be melting it down enough for them to get out with their ball and kick it all along the way from Denton's stables to the rectory."

"Just as well," returned Mrs. Netherspoon, sniffing again. "Likely be breaking windows like they did last year. Took out the greengrocer's window," she told her guests, "and the chemist's. We have latticework over ours, so we've a bit of protection."

"Do they always play on Shrove Tuesday?" asked Nora, delving again.

Netherspoon nodded. "Just a bit of sport before Lent begins tomorrow," he said, looking at his wife. "No real harm in it at all."

His wife appeared inclined to argue the point, but Mr. Norville intervened unexpectedly.

"In northern Spain," said Norville, tactfully diverting Mrs. Netherspoon, "Shrovetide marks the end of Carnival, and Gregoire, a huge stuffed figure, is pulled about in an oxcart decorated with greenery, and everyone celebrates, but tomorrow, Ash

Wednesday, everything changes. Gregoire is tried and condemned and burnt upon a pyre, with the people leaping about and throwing brands of fire. Then all of the joy turns to sorrow and they sing songs of mourning because it is the beginning of Lent, a time of fasting and privation."

Everyone at the table looked fascinated but vaguely disapproving of such foreign carryings-on. "Why ever would they do a thing like that?" asked Mrs. Netherspoon. "It doesn't even sound Christian."

Norville smiled at her. "I doubt seriously that it is," he agreed. "The same idea appears in a good many countries, and it seems to be tied to very ancient ideas, perhaps to the long-ago times when a human sacrifice was considered necessary to drive away the winter and release the spring. Gregoire is the victim now."

"Heathen notions," announced Mrs. Netherspoon disapprovingly, disposing of them with a shake of her head and turning back to her cooking. The others looked as though they agreed with her strongly, much preferring their own familiar ways.

Elizabeth was interested in spite of herself. "You must have seen a great deal of the way the people live there," she said to him as the conversation became general. "Did you like that— quite apart from the war, I mean?" she hastened to add.

He looked amused. "The war itself, of course, was not likeable, but the people and the country were a different matter entirely. It was my privilege to get to know more about them."

Nora was looking bored. The conversation had turned, as it always seemed to with Norville, to the war. She turned to Lord Mallory.

"Have you any more stories to tell about your hoaxes?" she asked hopefully, certain of amusement in this quarter.

"Not just now, perhaps later," he returned, not even glancing at her. Nora swelled with indignation, but it was lost upon him. Mallory's attention was focused entirely on Norville.

"You do truly know a great deal about the people, Norville, for I remember some of my brother's stories about you. He wrote that you were the most remarkable spy imaginable, that because of your knowledge of the people and your command of the language, you could mix with any level of Spanish society, from muleteer to hidalgo, and make them believe that you were one of them. And that your powers of observation were so keen that your reports were invaluable when you returned."

Norville drank his coffee reflectively. "It seems that Michael must have done an unconscionable amount of letter-writing. He was quite busy himself, so I can't imagine how he managed it."

Mallory grinned. "Michael said that you allowed him to come with you upon occasion. He also said that you could pass yourself off as a Frenchman or a German as well."

"With a little practice, I am hoping to become a passable Englishman and settle down," remarked Norville dryly, glancing across the table at Nora, who promptly flushed a rosy red and retired behind her napkin.

Mallory watched this interchange with a puzzled expression, but before he could think about it further, Sir Edmund, who had been listening to their conversation with the air of one who has just made an important discovery, plunged into the conversation.

"I say, Norville, you must be the very man in Alvanley's story!" he exclaimed.

Norville looked at him, eyebrows raised, waiting for an explanation. Sir Edmund nodded decisively, like a man certain of his ground. "Yes, it is about when you were taken prisoner while on a mission for Wellington. Your captors were planning to take your possessions and then kill you, but they didn't realize that you could understand what they were saying. You managed to set up a decoy after they had taken your watch and money, and you wriggled into a flour sack at the mill where they had made their camp and threw yourself across a pack horse belonging to another traveler and made your escape. When you got rid of the flour sack and the fellow turned around and saw you, he thought he had hold of a ghost because you were covered with flour. Wellington congratulated you when you returned to camp with your report. Alvanley was telling this at White's, and someone wanted to know what you said to Wellington. Alvanley said that you made a very *flowery* speech." Sir Edmund sat and chuckled for several moments at this morsel of wit. "A *flowery* speech!"

"Great Scott!" said Norville blankly. "I'd no idea I was supplying fodder for the gossips at White's."

"Indeed you did," Sir Edmund assured him. "That one was told and retold until Alvanley announced that he would have to call out the next man who asked him to repeat it."

"Well, we can be grateful for that at any rate. I hope he did so. We need not have that story again or any others like it," said Norville.

He was, however, quite wrong. To Nora's disgust, the others clamored for more tales of Spain, and Norville was fairly cornered. The snow still held them back from their travels, for it had not melted enough to make the roads passable, and there was nothing to do other than sit by the fire, eat, and talk. Elizabeth was quite prepared to be disgusted with him, sure that he would set himself up as the hero of each piece, but he did not. Instead, he created for his listeners a very vivid sketch of life for the troops in Spain, of the lives of the villagers in their area and their customs, of the courage shown and hardships sustained by both of these groups. According to Norville, in the final days before the complete withdrawal of Joseph Bonaparte and the French troops from Spain, the Spanish peasants would reveal no information to them about the movement of the English army. To Wellington and his people, however, they gave detailed reports about the condition and placement of the French.

Although he did not say so directly, Elizabeth gathered that Norville had been attached to the duke's staff and had moved about from assignment to assignment. He described for them the flight of the French army from Spain after the Battle of Vitoria. With them had gone King Joseph, Napoleon's brother, abandoning his personal baggage, which included wagon after wagon filled with the plunder taken from Andalusia: jewels, artwork, gold—even a military chest filled with gold for payment of the French troops. Of more immediate value to the British were the guns and ammunition stores abandoned in their hasty retreat. She longed to ask him if he too had taken a share of the spoils, but she did not.

Despite herself, she found that she was interested in what he had to say and pleasantly impressed with his lack of self-importance as he said it. She found herself wondering too why he had not brought back some young Spanish lady as his wife, for she was certain that there must have been many who would have been willing. Instead, he had chosen Nora, who could scarcely have been less willing and who certainly did not value the qualities that he had to offer. It seemed a very perverse approach to marriage.

The day passed quietly and pleasantly enough for everyone, even, at last, for Nora. She had Rufus and Sampson, of course, and then Mrs. Netherspoon obligingly supplied her with jackstraws and a deck of cards and she managed to inveigle Elizabeth, Tom Macklin, and Mallory into playing with her. Norville stood briefly by Elizabeth just before dinner, watching Nora at play with Macklin and Mallory, and said quietly, "Although the circumstances here are most unusual, Miss Harrington, you must admit that this is not at all the kind of situation that Miss Lane should find herself in, nor would her mother be pleased by it."

Elizabeth was forced to concede the truth of the statement, but she did it silently, unwilling to agree with him aloud. It was, after all, scarcely her fault that the weather had been so outrageous this winter. They had not seen a winter like this within living memory. And Norville was holding her responsible for this ridiculous situation!

Rather than reply to his comment directly, she reverted instead to her earlier criticism of him. "It would seem to me, Mr. Norville, that you could attempt to make yourself more agreeable to the child. I have not seen you taking pains to entertain her today."

"That is quite true," he said coolly. "I do not propose to alter the way I do things in order to please. I am who I am." And he turned to walk away.

"That's all very well, Mr. Norville. But . . . she is who *she* is as well."

He turned and looked at her and, to her surprise, smiled. "A home shot, Miss Harrington," he replied, and strolled from the kitchen, leaving her wondering about the workings of his mind.

Dinner was again a substantial affair over which the Netherspoons had labored long. True to her promise, Mrs. Netherspoon produced a platter of golden Shrovetide pancakes which disappeared so quickly that she had to make a hasty return to the stove.

66

Over the last of the pancakes, Lord Mallory looked across at Norville, his words coming slowly, "I was wondering, Norville, if you noticed anything particularly odd about Chawton's story last night."

Norville looked at him inquiringly and he added, more slowly still, "What I mean is that it reminded me of Sir Howard Gregory's disappearance."

Sir Edmund came to life at the mention of Gregory. "A very good man, Gregory. An excellent judge of horseflesh. None better. Losing him was a serious business."

Norville regarded him with a twinkle in his eye, but agreed. "Losing Gregory *was* a serious affair. He was apparently sent to convince both Tsar Alexander and the Prussians that their countries should not listen to Austria's wily Metternich, who wished to negotiate a Continental peace with Napoleon that would leave England in the cold. Gregory was to show them that they needed us. It was no accident that he disappeared before he could speak with them. Someone was trying to prevent an agreement between our governments."

Elizabeth looked puzzled. "But why would a man like Chawton be telling that story? What could he possibly have to do with Sir Howard?"

"That is precisely what I had wondered," said Norville. "I would like very much to know what the connection is. He seemed disinclined to discuss the matter with me before he left so hurriedly last night."

"Even if he were connected with his disappearance—and I certainly don't see why Chawton *would* be connected with it, even though he is something of a loose fish—why would he give us a riddle?" asked Elizabeth thoughtfully. "What has the riddle to say to anything?"

Neither Mallory nor Norville responded to her question.

Nora had been listening wide-eyed. "Do you mean that *was* a true story and there really was a disappearance?" She gave a single bounce on her chair. "Then we *must* concentrate on the riddle. Now let me see . . . 'I am the beginning . . .' "

Chapter Six

The next morning found the roads in a passable condition, and the travelers gratefully gathered their belongings, thanked the Netherspoons, and made their way toward London. Sir Edmund rode inside with Elizabeth and Nora, the groom bringing Devon Boy carefully along behind them. On the seat beside Sir Edmund rode two wicker baskets, one containing Rufus and the other Sampson. He had succumbed to Nora's pleas, trying not to imagine what his household staff in Grosvenor Square would think of the new additions to the family. But he had added, "But they won't sleep with me and that's final. You'll have to find another place for 'em."

"Why is Norville coming to London?" Nora inquired in a pettish tone. "I thought he was never going to spend time there again, and now, just as I am about to enjoy myself, he decides to change his mind and come along."

Elizabeth looked at her in amusement. "I believe that he is paying you the compliment of wishing to be where you are," she said diplomatically, unwilling to tell her charge that he was coming to keep an eye on her.

"What a bouncer!" exclaimed Nora inelegantly, burrowing farther into her cloak. "At any rate, I don't want to be where he is, Elizabeth. I do hope we shan't be tripping over him at every turn."

Elizabeth was hoping the same thing. She preferred not to have him studying her every move with Nora, sharply critical as she knew he would be of whom they would see and where they would go. She disliked the idea of being under surveillance.

68

"Norville seems a very good sort of fellow. We should have him to dinner when we get back, Elizabeth," announced Sir Edmund with a blissful disregard for everything the ladies had been saying. "He's a good eye for cattle—and he tells a good story."

Elizabeth and Nora received his suggestion with a lack of enthusiasm which he did not notice as he recounted for their benefit some of the stories they had heard Norville tell the day before, as well as a few stories involving horses which they had not yet heard. It seemed a very long trip to all of them, Sir Edmund worrying alternately about Devon Boy and his grays, Nora bored past belief except when she was playing with Rufus and Sampson or trying to work out Chawton's riddle, Elizabeth trying to think of a way to reconcile her household staff to the livestock's arrival and of a way to put Mr. Norville properly in his place and keep him there.

Their chaise rolled down Oxford Street, and Nora pressed her face to the window to admire the brightly lighted shop windows, some filled with lengths of rich fabrics, some with pyramids of fruit, some with crystal and silver, some with articles made of Brussels lace. They rolled past busy shoppers, past the gingerbread man, standing with his basket on the corner, past a man with a pack of hearth brooms and rush baskets on his back, past an old man selling morocco slippers in all colors and sizes.

When they arrived in Grosvenor Square late that afternoon and were greeted by Burton, it was obvious to Elizabeth from his affronted expression that she would have to be extremely diplomatic if she hoped to reconcile the butler to the presence of Rufus and Sampson. Having shown Nora to her room and assigned a young maid to look after her and having placed Rufus and Sampson in the temporary—and reluctant—custody of Burton, who promptly handed them to one of the footmen, it was with deep gratitude that Elizabeth finally reached her room and the ministrations of Silvers, her maid.

Life seemed more bearable after a nap and a hot bath, and she went down to dinner in a much more cheerful frame of mind, wearing a very fetching gown of blue silk trimmed with white knots, her red curls confined to a knot at the nape of her neck by two pearl-trimmed combs. Nora looked at her enviously, feeling drabber than ever in a plain gown of black crepe.

Intercepting her glance, Elizabeth reassured her, "Do not give it

69

another thought, Nora. Tomorrow we will order some new gowns for you."

Infinitely cheered, Nora was able to sit down to dinner with a hearty appetite. Inquiring after the health of Sampson and Rufus, she found that they were temporarily residing in the storage closet adjoining the pantry, whereupon she protested that they must, of course, be brought out immediately. Burton reluctantly brought them from their quarters, obviously in full agreement with Sir Edmund, who protested admission of the livestock to the dining room.

"But, Edmund, they dined with us at the Bull and Barleycorn," Nora reminded him.

"So they did, my dear, but that was quite a different matter. There was little choice."

"And they even slept with you," continued Nora relentlessly.

Studiously avoiding Burton's shocked expression, Sir Edmund admitted that this too was true, repeating that circumstances were now quite different.

"But they are so happy to see you, Edmund," she pointed out with obvious truth, for both of them had found his boots beneath the table and arranged themselves comfortably over them.

"Perhaps you would like to keep them in your room, Nora," he said hopefully.

She clapped her hands. "Indeed I would, Edmund. That would be delightful!"

Edmund was far from sure that this would be the case, but he thought that it would be an improvement over having them under the servants' feet in the kitchen or *on* his in the dining room or, worse still, in his bedchamber.

Since they were dining alone, Edmund did not remain at the table when the ladies rose; instead, they all, Sampson and Rufus included, retired to the drawing room, and Burton brought in the tea tray. Having made the heroic gesture of staying at home for dinner on his first night back in town instead of retiring immediately to the elegance of White's or the camaraderie of Limmer's, Sir Edmund rewarded himself by looking over the stack of neatly pressed newspapers that Burton brought in to him. Nora was seated on the lovely Aubusson carpet that Sir Edmund and Elizabeth's father had purchased on his Grand Tour, entertaining herself by dragging a ribbon across the floor in front of the kitten and the pup. Elizabeth, having watched them only long enough to assure herself that Rufus was not about to mistake the leg of the Pembroke table for a bone nor was Sampson displaying any interest in the green velvet curtains, turned to peruse the mail that had been awaiting her return.

"This is a bad business," murmured Sir Edmund, looking over the accounts of the French victories at Montmirail and Montereau. "Boney is pushing us back again," he informed Elizabeth, looking up from his papers. "He's a damned clever fellow for a Frog, and he's making fools of us all again. Thought we'd put him into the basket and popped the lid on him when we chased him into France, but now he's giving all of us—the English, the Russians, the Austrians, the Prussians—a run for our money. It's Carlton House to a Charley's shelter that if Castlereagh can't get the rest of that lot to go along with us that Boney'll slip through our fingers again."

He thought deeply for a moment, then added, "Our men have good mounts, too, they say. Can't be the fault of the horses."

"Of course not, Edmund, but as you pointed out, there are so many Allies trying to work together. We know they are having trouble agreeing on what needs to be done."

Sir Edmund frowned. "Shouldn't wonder if Castlereagh made a mull of it last autumn. Shouldn't have sent young Aberdeen to Frankfurt. Should have gone himself and avoided all that brouhaha."

"Well, he has gone now, so perhaps they can still bring themselves about," his sister consoled him. Then, noting Nora's expression of disgust at the topic and remembering that this was her first night in London, Elizabeth determined to make it pleasant for her at least in a small way.

"I have a surprise for you, Nora, or rather, it is a surprise that was planned for you by my mother."

Nora sat straighter, her eyes sparkling. "What is it, Elizabeth? May I see it now?"

"Indeed you may," she assured her, ringing the bell for Burton. "It is in Silvers's care. I'll just have Burton send up for it."

Burton returned a few minutes later bearing a small box of blue velvet. Before giving it to Nora, Elizabeth said, "This was selected by Mama several years ago, and she planned to give it to you when you came out. It seems to me that now is a very good time for you to receive it."

Nora opened the box carefully. Inside was a dainty ring with stones of nephrite, opal, ruby, and amethyst. "It's lovely, Elizabeth," she exclaimed, slipping it out of the box and onto her finger. "Is it a Harlequin ring like yours?" she asked, referring to the ring Elizabeth always wore, set with varied stones to look like the motley of that famed pantomime figure.

"No, this is a regard ring, Nora," she explained. "Notice that the stones have been arranged so that the first letter of the name of each stone is a letter of your name: nephrite, opal, ruby amethyst; N-O-R-A. Mama thought you would enjoy that."

"Oh, I love it!" she exclaimed. "I have never heard of a ring that spells your name. Have you one, too, Elizabeth?"

Elizabeth smiled. "No. Mine is such a long name, you see. I have my Harlequin instead."

"I shall wear it every day," she announced proudly. "It is the first real piece of jewelry that anyone has ever given me." She walked over and held out her hand to Edmund so that he could admire it.

"Very nice," he said indulgently, gently disengaging Sampson's claws from his knee and handing him to her. "Always thought those rings were clever. Rather wished for one myself. Of course," he added thoughtfully, "could be walking around with a ring that said just about anything if you didn't know how to tell."

"You would think of that, Edmund," laughed his sister. "Perhaps we shall have to get you one."

Nora looked at him pertly as she gathered up Sampson and Rufus for bed. "But instead of *Edmund*, your ring would have to spell *horse*."

Sir Edmund chuckled as she departed; then he took leave of Elizabeth for White's, eager to catch up on everything that had transpired during his fortnight's absence. Fish, his valet, could have called to Nora's attention the possibility that Sir Edmund's ring might have to spell more than *horse*, for when he pulled the curtains the following morning, he was dismayed to find Sampson curled up at the foot of the bed.

Chapter Seven

Much to Nora's delight, she and Elizabeth set forth to survey the smart London shops after breakfast the next morning. Feeling that she had stepped into Ali Baba's cave, she examined Italian silks and Manchester velvets, Indian muslins and Chinese crepes, chickenskin gloves guaranteed to soften and whiten hands and arms, tippets of feather and fur, ribbons and laces and plumes, dainty slippers in a rainbow of hues.

"It is time to remove you from those blacks, my dear," said Elizabeth firmly.

"I *am* tired to death of black," Nora admitted, fingering her skirt, "and I know that Papa hated to see women forever in black. But Mama said that it was proper to wear it so long. I began to think I should never be able to wear colors again." She sighed. "And I look like a ghost in black."

"Well, you certainly would not want to fail to show respect for your father, but you can wear something other than black now. And you must remember," she added, thinking of Cecilia, "your mother looks lovely in black, so she does not mind wearing it so much."

It was a small-minded remark, she knew, but since Cecilia was always very conscious of her own appearance it did seem as though she could spare a bit of thought for her oldest daughter. Lovely though she was, black was definitely not the color for Nora—or at least not unrelieved black. It seemed to drain the life from her complexion, whereas it simply emphasized the transparency of Cecilia's. There was no need to keep the child in it overlong simply because it was becoming to her mother.

"Now that we are into March, the weather will be growing warmer soon, although that is difficult to believe when it is still so cold and we've had such a terrible winter," said Elizabeth thoughtfully as they examined materials. "We must bear that in mind as we choose."

In the end, Nora had ordered two round gowns, one of cotton in a delicate print, one of amber merino, trimmed in knots of black and deeper gold; an embroidered muslin with a spencer of figured silk; a walking dress of green-gold satin piped in black; two tunics, one of gold satin, one of bottle-green Chinese silk, to dress up her old black round gowns; a Spanish pelisse of moss green sarcenet trimmed with Egyptian crepe; and the crowning glory, an evening gown of primrose silk, trimmed with black satin roses. Elizabeth was well aware that Cecilia might not approve, but she felt she had made the concessions to propriety with black trim. Assuring Madame Devereaux that she would be ordering more dresses for Nora as well as for herself very soon, Elizabeth gathered up her charge and departed. Two of the dresses and the tunics were promised for the very next afternoon, and Nora spent the afternoon blissfully shopping for gloves, a pair of green kid slippers, a new reticule, an Indian shawl, and colored ribbons and plumes to brighten her hats.

Exhausted but triumphant, they returned home to find that both Mr. Norville and Lord Mallory had left their calling cards. Nora was displeased with the information; she did not want to meet Mr. Norville simply because she had no desire to see him, and she did not want to meet Lord Mallory until she had her new outfits.

"For I will not have him think that I am a child," she told Elizabeth with a raised chin. "He will try to send me off with his younger sisters and the governess as though I were still in the schoolroom."

"Well, never mind, Nora," Elizabeth said soothingly. "They will not come again today, and we will worry about tomorrow when tomorrow comes. And besides," she added, her eyes twinkling, "I have another surprise for you."

"What is it?" exclaimed Nora. "You have already done so

much, Elizabeth—the ring and the gowns. What else could there be?"

"My hairdresser will be here shortly. I made the appointment before we left London, but I am quite certain that he will be happy to take the time to crop your hair for you."

"How famous!" crowed her young charge. "I shall have curls cut around my face as I have been wishing to for months! Oh, I do thank you, Elizabeth," she cried, throwing her arms about her cousin's neck. And Elizabeth closed her mind firmly to Norville's comments about cropped hair. As yet, he had no control over Nora and her appearance, and she had no intention of letting him think that he did.

And two hours later, examining the work of Mr. Fotheringay's skilled scissors, Elizabeth had to admit that her idea had been an excellent one. Short dark curls framed Nora's face although the rest of her hair remained long and was pulled into a cluster of ringlets.

Instead of admiring her own reflection, however, Nora was looking at Elizabeth, who had cut her long hair *à la Titus,* a short style featuring a center part and disheveled curls. "You look absolutely beautiful," said Nora reverently. "Mama is said to be a beauty, but you look like someone who should be in a portrait hanging in a great hall."

Elizabeth looked at her and said dubiously, "That sounds as though I look quite out of date."

"Oh, no!" Nora exclaimed. "It's just that you look like a great lady—one who should be in such a picture."

Laughing, Elizabeth invited her charge to accompany her to the library to display their new coiffures to Sir Edmund. They found him there with his two companions and his newspaper, and he made a very satisfactory audience as they preened and posed for him.

"Very dashing," he commented, removing Sampson, who was using his immaculate biscuit-colored trousers as a scratching post, from his leg. Holding the kitten by the nape of the neck, he handed it to Nora, saying, "Take this up to your room, please, Nora, and leave him there with the other one. And be certain to close the door." "The other one" looked up from his recumbent position, then rolled back over to sleep.

"We don't need them down here to bother people," he commented firmly. "I almost forgot to tell you, Elizabeth. I knew that you said that you and Nora were dining at home until Nora's things came from the mantua-maker, so when Mallory and Norville called before I left for the club this morning, I invited them to dinner tonight. Told them it would just be an at-home."

"You did what?" asked the ladies, almost simultaneously.

Sir Edmund looked at his sister in surprise. She had always been a pleasant, easy-going hostess, ready to welcome any unannounced guests that he might decide to bring home with him. "Something wrong, Lizzy?" he asked in concern.

Elizabeth regained command of herself. It was, after all, not Edmund's fault that Norville was such a thorn. She knew, moreover, that Nora wanted to meet neither of them, and she herself was uncertain about the wisdom of throwing Nora and Mallory together, innocent though it seemed. However, it was done, and she must handle the matter as graciously as possible.

"No, of course there's nothing wrong, Edmund." She managed a smile and directed a quelling look at Nora to restrain any outburst from that quarter. "I must talk to Cook about dinner."

"No need," announced Sir Edmund proudly. "Had Burton do it after I invited them this morning."

Congratulating Sir Edmund on his thoughtfulness, she swept Nora upstairs to see what could be done to refurbish her wardrobe before dinner. Between them, she and Silvers managed astonishingly well, and it was a very contented Nora who tripped down to dinner that evening. Silvers had found a scarf of filmy green that they draped becomingly about the neck of Nora's plain black gown. That, added to a new comb for her hair, a pair of earrings from Elizabeth, her new green slippers, her ring, and her consciousness of having a dashing new hairstyle, made her as contented as she could be short of a new gown. Elizabeth, unwilling to present too striking a contrast to her guest, wore a high-necked gown of russet silk and a matching bandeau about her hair.

Their guests were already with Sir Edmund in the drawing room when they arrived, and it took but a single glance at Norville's face to be aware of his displeasure with Nora's new hair style. It was the first thing that Mallory commented upon when they entered.

"Miss Lane, a new look, I see." He held up his quizzing glass in a critical manner. "Yes, quite the thing now, aren't you? One day in London and you have already begun to change."

Elizabeth studiously avoided Norville's eye as Mallory turned his attention to her. "And, Miss Harrington, I see that you look as radiant as always."

Norville bowed stiffly to both of the ladies and turned his attention back to his conversation with Sir Edmund.

"You should see, Lord Mallory, the lovely gowns that we purchased today! Of course, you *will* see them, I'm sure," she added ingenuously as she rattled on, describing for him each detail of their shopping. It was obvious to Elizabeth that Mr. Norville was attending to what she was saying, even though he was keeping pace with Edmund in their conversation. His brow grew more creased and his eyebrows drew closer together as Nora described the pleasures of the day. It was, in fact, with gratitude that Elizabeth heard Burton announce that dinner was served.

Dinner was generous but simple; it was plain that Sir Edmund had ordered it. They sat down to soup, fish, a round of beef, partridges, and apricot tart. Mallory's easy manners made it possible for all of them to be comfortable, and, sensing the constraint on the part of everyone but Sir Edmund, he devoted himself to setting them all at ease. Upon inquiring into the news they had heard since their return, he unwittingly spurred Sir Edmund into speech.

"The most amazing thing, you won't believe what I heard at White's today! I believed it myself, though—quite time, I thought, so perhaps you will, too," he remarked, leaving all of his listeners, save Norville, who had been there too, in a fog.

"What is it that's so amazing, Edmund?" inquired his sister.

"We are advancing! We're turning the tide against Boney again!" he exclaimed, applying his napkin to his chin with vigor. "And about time! I thought the Frogs had us again, but we're on the march!"

"If we can't stand together," commented Norville dryly, "they

77

will have us again. I trust that the Allies will manage a bit better this time. We may not have unlimited opportunities."

Elizabeth, seeing Nora's expression at the introduction of the war into the table conversation, decided that it was time for them to retire to the drawing room and leave the gentlemen to their port. Gratefully, Nora joined her.

Fortunately, by the time the gentlemen joined them, they seemed to have disposed of the war to their satisfaction and had advanced to other important topics, like horses, and were discussing with enthusiasm a pair of handsome bays that Mallory was considering selling.

"Don't do it, my boy!" exclaimed Sir Edmund. "You'll look many a day before you find their like again."

"I know it," agreed Mallory ruefully, "but the thing is that I don't need 'em. They were Michael's—I already kept my own stable and then I added all of his cattle."

"Well, think it over before you do it," advised Sir Edmund.

"I'll do it, sir," he agreed readily and turned to smile at Nora. "My mother and sisters—and George, of course—send their regards to you and Miss Harrington. My sisters particularly wanted me to tell you that they wished to call on you as soon as you are ready to receive them—and they especially would like to meet Rufus and Sampson, if you wouldn't mind."

The mention of his sisters had put Mallory on shaky ground, for Nora suspected him immediately of placing her back in the schoolroom set with them, but the mention of her pets quite disarmed her.

"Of course they may call. Tomorrow if they would like." She turned to Elizabeth. "That would be all right, wouldn't it?"

"Of course it would. I have met them, but it's been quite some time ago, and I'm sure they must have changed tremendously."

"Oh, they have, indeed," Mallory assured her. "Maria is about to turn fifteen and considers herself quite the lady. She practically eats me alive if I forget and treat her like a schoolroom miss." His eyes danced wickedly as he glanced at Nora.

"I should think she would," said Nora with dignity. "Nothing is more lowering to one's feelings than to be treated like a child when one is *not* one."

Feeling uncomfortably sure that she had become too entangled in her *one's* and deciding to punish her tormentor, Nora turned her back on Mallory and smiled gently at Norville. Taken by surprise, for he had been studying the two of them and drinking his tea quietly, not expecting her to speak to him, Norville smiled back at her. Not having seen his real smile at all, Elizabeth was amazed at the difference it made in his appearance. Gone was the grimness, the disapproval.

"I know that you are not fond of London, Mr. Norville," Nora said graciously, "but I hope that you have found your day pleasant."

Amused by her air of dignity, he responded in the same manner. "It's very kind of you to inquire, Miss Lane. I did indeed find myself somewhat at loose ends, but that did not last long, for I encountered an old friend—and then, of course, Sir Edmund was good enough to extend this dinner invitation when I called to be sure that everything was well with your party after the journey."

He looked at her with a direct gaze, glancing at her hair, and Elizabeth held her breath, waiting for some cutting remark. "And I can see that everything is well with you, Miss Lane, for you look charming. *Your* first day in London has obviously agreed with you."

Elizabeth, having been prepared for the worst, found herself unaccountably annoyed by his chivalrous remark. So out of character, she told herself with irritation.

Nora turned a delightful pink at his unexpected compliment and felt called upon to chat with him a little more. Glancing down at her hand, she exclaimed, "Elizabeth—I mean, Miss Harrington—presented me with a ring that my godmother left for me."

She held out her hand to Norville so that he might see it clearly. "You see," she explained, as he took her small hand in his, "the nephrite is an *N* for the *N* in Nora, the opal is an *O,* the ruby an *R,* and the amethyst an *A.* Nora!"

"Delightful," he murmured, still holding her hand, and looked at her face rather than the ring.

Nora pulled her hand back hastily, saying, "Yes, isn't it? I had

79

never heard of a regard ring before, but I think it a very pleasing idea."

Lord Mallory looked as though he found the whole subject less than pleasing, but commented graciously that it had been most kind of Mrs. Harrington.

"My mother was always fond of jewelry and such trumpery," said Sir Edmund fondly, again impervious to the undercurrents in the room. "My father used to swear that she kept Rundell & Bridge in business."

"Which was a great untruth," said Elizabeth firmly. "It was our father who kept the jewelers in business; it was our mother who knew a great deal about gems and about the history of jewelry. She even had a few rare pieces that she had collected over the years."

Nora looked up quickly. "Did she really, Elizabeth? Could we see them? Would you mind showing them?"

"Of course not," she replied, somewhat startled by Nora's reaction. On the other hand, she told herself as she went upstairs to collect the box that was always in Silvers's keeping, it was not really surprising, for Nora seemed enchanted by jewelry.

She returned to the drawing room bearing a large flat velvet case, which she placed on a low table, and the others gathered around her. Opening the case, she revealed about twenty rings. Selecting one, she held it up for them to see.

"This is a talisman ring," she explained, holding out a gold ring, its face delicately engraved with St. Christopher holding the infant Christ. "To wear it was to protect yourself against sudden death, especially death by drowning."

Nora handled it curiously, but with respect, and passed it on to Sir Edmund.

Elizabeth pointed to another ring nestled in a corner of the case. "This one, on the other hand, was not to protect the wearer from sudden death. This ring carried death. In fact, it was called the *anello della morte*, the ring of death."

"What do you mean?" asked Nora, round-eyed.

"This one is supposedly like a ring worn by Cesare Borgia. The bezel, as you see, is wrought in the shape of a lion. The lion's claws are sharp and hollow and were filled with poison.

One hearty handshake with your enemy and you had disposed of him. We were never allowed to touch that ring for fear some of the poison might linger."

Nora drew back. "I would not want to keep such a thing," she said. "Why do you still have it, Elizabeth?"

"I have kept it, of course, because of my mother. But I have wondered about the Royal Society of Antiquities. They are beginning to collect some things for a museum. Edmund and I may consider presenting the rings to them."

"It seems that would be a wise idea, Miss Harrington," said Norville. "Your mother appears to have gathered quite an exceptional collection."

Nora shivered. "It is not one that I would want."

"But most of the rings are quite charming, Nora." She picked up a dainty gold ring. "This is a posy ring—the inscription, the posy, in this one reads "Within thy brest my harte doth rest."

She selected another. "And this, 'Love me and be happy.' The gentleman who presented this to his lady was very sure of himself," she commented, glad to see that Nora's expression had brightened.

"Perhaps the answer to the first part of the riddle is a ring. 'I am the beginning'—perhaps it is a betrothal ring or a wedding ring—the beginning of something," said Nora, who had still been puzzling over Chawton's riddle.

"I had not thought of that, Nora, but it is possible," said Elizabeth. She turned to Mr. Norville. "But you are quite in the right about these rings, I believe. These should be in a place where others may enjoy them too. I know a little about the rings, but fortunately my mother kept a journal with records about each ring. She was very knowledgeable—she told some wonderful stories about famous jewels in history. She wrote those down as well."

Elizabeth closed the case and the conversation turned to other matters, including Lord Mallory's request to view Sampson and Rufus so that he could report to his sisters that all was well with them. Nora retired to collect them from her room, leaving Sir Edmund to consider ways in which he could best protect himself from the onslaught of both animals.

"You did not tell us about your little brother and how he fared on Shrove Tuesday," said Elizabeth to Mallory. "Did he manage to retrieve the pancake?"

Mallory chuckled and shook his head. "From the sound of it, there wasn't more than a tiny bit of it left after they had all set upon it. The guinea went to a boy from the Upper School, so poor George lost his last chance to win. He was quite cast down about it, but he bucked up amazingly when I gave him a guinea of his own. He decided that under the circumstances he could dispense with the honor of winning and simply accept the money."

When Nora returned and attention became focused on the animals, Elizabeth could not resist turning to Mr. Norville and saying teasingly, "I thought that you did not approve of cropped hair, Mr. Norville."

He glanced at Nora and then at her own crop of coppery curls and smiled. "It is possible that I was mistaken, Miss Harrington. I find that it depends upon the lady. Tonight I can say nothing against the style."

She looked at him curiously. "I would not have thought you a flirt, Mr. Norville. And yet tonight I almost felt, as Nora's chaperone, that I should interfere when you held her hand overlong."

"But you did not," he reminded her.

"It took me by surprise, sir, for I did not expect it of you."

He looked at her gravely. "Perhaps you should be on your guard, Miss Harrington. That happened tonight in a small party at home. How will you be able to watch over Miss Lane in a more public gathering?"

She gasped. "Were you *testing* me, sir? Deliberately flirting with that child to see if I would spring to her defense?"

He bowed slightly. "Let us say, Miss Harrington, that I was following your very acute suggestion and attempting to make myself agreeable to the young lady."

It was fortunate that Sir Edmund called just then for Elizabeth to rescue him from the depredations of the livestock, Nora and Mallory being of no help whatsoever. When she had done so, she had regained a tolerable amount of control and was able to bid good night to their guests with at least the appearance of composure, having assured Lord Mallory that his mother and sisters would be very welcome to call the following day.

When Mr. Norville indicated that he wished the privilege of calling as well, she was even able to force herself to smile, saying, "It is always pleasant to have a caller as *agreeable* as yourself."

His eyebrows raised slightly, acknowledging her thrust. Glancing at the velvet jewel case containing its *anello della morte,* he commented lightly, "I shall be most careful, Miss Harrington, if you wish to shake hands with me at any point."

As Elizabeth brushed her hair and prepared for bed later that evening, she mulled over the puzzling contrasts in Mr. Norville's character: abrupt, aloof, critical—then disarmingly charming (*disarming,* being the key word)—and then, once more, unexpectedly and unforgivably critical. Elizabeth brushed her hair with a vigor that would have brought tears to the eyes of a lesser woman as she thought about the evening. Silvers, convinced that her mistress would soon do herself damage, gently removed the brush from her hand. As Elizabeth placed her head on the violet-scented pillow, her last waking thought was "I wonder if the poison in that ring still retains its power." And upon that pleasant thought she drifted away.

Lord Mallory called promptly the next day, escorting his sisters and proffering the apology of his mother, who was indisposed. Anne and Marie were both lively, pretty girls, with the same ease of manner that their brother possessed. Sampson and Rufus were brought in and duly admired and made much of, and before their call was over, the three young ladies were on very amicable terms. Indeed, by the time they left, Nora and Elizabeth had promised to attend a family theatre party the next day, for Anne and Marie were going with their mother for their first time to see Kean act and Nora was equally eager to see the latest London rage; and Nora had also been invited to walk in the park that very afternoon with the young ladies and their governess if the weather remained fine. Despite the mention of the governess, Nora was eager to see everything possible and had begged to be allowed to go, so Elizabeth had granted her permission.

Mr. Norville, who had arrived in time to hear the invitations accepted, drew Elizabeth apart to speak to her privately. "Do you not think, Miss Harrington," he inquired gravely, "that these attentions are too particular? It would perhaps be better if Miss Lane were introduced to a variety of people."

Elizabeth, who had just been thinking that Mallory must not be allowed to live in their pocket, was irritated by his remark.

"I had not planned for Miss Lane to become truly active until her new wardrobe arrived so that she would be properly outfitted. The fact that she has been thrown prematurely into company—beginning, I might add, with your own call yesterday—has not been of my planning."

"But the problem exists just as much as though you *had* planned it, does it not?" he inquired gently. "I am sure, however, that you will take steps to correct the situation."

"You may be quite certain of that, Mr. Norville," she assured him stiffly. "Nora will not receive the particular attentions of *any* one gentleman while she is staying under my protection."

"I see that I am *persona non grata*," he answered, bowing, "so I will take my leave with the others."

"Indeed, I did not mean to be rude, Mr. Norville," she replied, extending her hand frankly. "You are quite right, of course, about giving the wrong impression by being too much with the Grahams, but surely there can be no harm in being with the young ladies."

He looked at her extended hand and smiled. "Is it quite safe, Miss Harrington, or are you wearing the *anello della morte?*"

She returned his smile in spite of herself, noting again what a different person he looked to be when he smiled. A pity he didn't do so more often. Perhaps Nora would find him less boring. Elizabeth herself, however, having experienced his charm once, felt certain that she would not be taken in by him again.

"It is quite safe, I assure you. I am not armed. But do tell me, sir, what harm there could possibly be in spending time with Mallory's sisters?"

"I should be very much surprised," he replied, his smile disappearing and the familiar crease appearing between his eyebrows, "if young Mallory does not put in an appearance on both of these occasions. He seems quite drawn to Miss Lane and his attentiveness in calling has been most particular."

Elizabeth admitted to herself that Norville was quite right, but aloud she simply said, "Mallory has been quite taken with Nora's menagerie and says that he wishes to see how they are going on."

"Yes. I am aware of what Lord Mallory *says* his interests are. Even though I do not spend my life in London, however, I am also aware that Lord Mallory is considered a very dashing young gentleman and that to be distinguished by his attentions is enough to make a young lady sought after by others."

Quite so, thought Elizabeth to herself. Others would undoubtedly wish to know who Mallory's latest flirt was. And as long as Nora's affections were not engaged, it would do her no harm. Aloud, she simply replied, "Lord Mallory is a gentleman. I shall hope that all of those that are interested in Miss Lane are of the same quality."

As though offended by her implication, Mr. Norville departed in the wake of the others, leaving Nora happily anticipating her two outings and Elizabeth busily planning others that would widen her circle of acquaintances. When the first of Nora's new gowns arrived that afternoon, she rushed to don the amber merino before the Grahams called for her, borrowing a blue wool cape trimmed with fur from Elizabeth to protect her from the chill. Looking at her animated little face framed by the fur-trimmed hood, Elizabeth found herself feeling that it would be just as well if Mallory did not join them on their walk. Nora looked far too taking; even a young lord accustomed to having lovely young women seek his attention might not be proof against beauty combined with such innocent, enthusiastic enjoyment.

Nora returned from her walk overflowing with things to tell Elizabeth. They had convinced Miss Stevenson to have the coachman set them down before they came to the park so that they could look in the shop windows along the way, and there had been such quantities of things to see. There had been silversmiths and linen shops, confectioners and fruiterers, and a man selling muffins, ringing his bell and crying, "My bell I keep ringing and walk about merrily singing my muffins!" The apple man had a pan of lighted charcoal upon which he was roasting apples on a tin plate. The girls had stopped to purchase some and they had, of course, been delicious. Miss Stevenson had exclaimed a little over the propriety of young ladies eating on the street corner, but they had overridden her. There had been an organ grinder with his monkey, which was dressed in the most cunning little red jacket and hat. And she had seen several dashing young dandies in their curricles, too, and one of them—*the* most dashing one—had stopped to speak to Anne and Maria, for he was a friend of their brother's, and he had asked to be introduced to Nora!

Dizzied slightly by this enthusiastic onslaught and devoutly grateful that Mr. Norville had not been present to hear it, Elizabeth asked, "And who was this dashing young man, dear?"

"His name is Sir Adrian Mayhew. Do you remember Lord Mallory's story about switching the rooms? He is *that* Sir Adrian. He was extremely pleasant, Elizabeth, and so pleased to find that we were going to see Kean in *Richard III* tomorrow night, for he is, too. He said that he wishes to compare Kean's performance to that of Mr. Kemble."

Elizabeth, who was quite sure that such a thing had never entered Sir Adrian's mind until meeting Nora, recognized that her duties as a duenna were likely to be onerous indeed. Sir Adrian was a noted Corinthian, a boon companion of Mallory's, and quite as desperate a flirt as his friend. Lord Mallory's attitude toward Nora thus far had been quite brotherly, but he had been much more constantly in attendance than any brother would have been.

"Did you meet Lord Mallory while you were out?" she inquired.

"Oh, yes," said Nora blithely. "He came along in his curricle while we were talking to Sir Adrian and told us that we should return to the carriage because it was becoming too cold for us to be out. He seemed quite annoyed to find Sir Adrian there. It didn't trouble Sir Adrian though. He just laughed and said, 'Trevor, you devil!' then bid us good-day and rode away."

It was quite clear to Elizabeth that she was going to have to expand Nora's social circle quickly, and she paused for a moment, thinking how lovely it would be if she could simply devote herself to her own affairs without having to feel like a mother hen. She put aside the thought as unworthy, however, knowing that she had invited all of this upon herself and that she must now face the consequences.

Facing those consequences the next night at the Drury Lane was almost more than she could bear, however. She was pleased that Lady Mallory was feeling more the thing and could join the girls and Elizabeth, but they were very soon joined by Lord Mallory and immediately afterwards by Sir Adrian, both of whom obviously planned to stay for the evening. Nora looked absolutely breathtaking in her new primrose gown, and her excitement about both the evening and the gown had brought a most becoming flush to her cheeks. Her circle of admirers grew during the first interval, all friends of Mallory's or Sir Adrian's who had discovered pressing matters which required the attention of those two gentlemen.

Mallory did not appear particularly gratified to see these gentlemen, and he turned to the ladies of his party and invited them to come down to the Green Room where they might be able to meet Mr. Kean. They responded with alacrity, Elizabeth in particular feeling eager to dispense with the company of so large and energetic a group.

They were not able to meet the electrifying Mr. Kean, for he had not yet put in an appearance, but to the delight of all the ladies, they were able to meet Miss Fanny Kelly, who was to appear later that night in the farce. While they were talking, Mallory excused himself, telling the ladies that he would be back in a few minutes to escort them back to their seats.

"She is not particularly pretty," commented Nora later as they were standing alone and looking about the group in the Green Room, "but her face is very pleasant. I would never forget what she looks like."

Sir Adrian agreed with her. "She is a very charming lady."

She suddenly clutched Elizabeth's arm. "Look, Elizabeth! Who is that man, the tall, dark-haired man that walks with a limp?" All of the ladies turned to look, trying to stare without giving the appearance of doing so.

"Why, that is Lord Byron!" Elizabeth whispered, quite excited herself. "I have never met him, but I have certainly heard all about him."

"What a handsome face," mused Nora. "I wonder if he is in love with Miss Kelly," she wondered, watching him smile down at that lady.

Elizabeth watched them carefully, still trying not to stare. "I don't think so. He certainly likes her, I believe, but his look is not very loverlike." She paused. "Whatever is he doing? Oh, look, Nora, Byron is getting a sword. He's showing Miss Kelly how to use it."

"She must have a breeches role coming soon," commented Sir Adrian. "In which case she will have to know how to wield a sword properly."

"Oh, I should like above all things to play a breeches role myself," declared Nora. "Well, I would!" she said defensively as the others stared at her. "I should love to dress up in breeches and have all of that freedom, even if it meant learning to use a sword."

Sir Adrian clicked his heels together and bowed low. "I am at your service, Miss Lane," he announced. "I would be happy to teach you swordsmanship at your convenience."

Seeing new pitfalls ahead, Elizabeth hurriedly told him that she did not think that needed to be one of Miss Lane's first activities in London. Perhaps later, if time came to hang heavily on her hands. Having averted that difficulty for the moment, and again deeply grateful that Mr. Norville had not been present to hear Nora's earnest desire, she turned to find herself facing that gentleman.

"Good evening, Mr. Norville," she said graciously, deciding to act as though the breeches interlude had gone unnoticed.

Before he could respond, however, a voice from behind her exclaimed, "Andrew Norville! How very glad I am to see you again!" and Lady Mallory came toward them, offering Norville her hand. "I know that Trevor told you how very grateful we are to you. Michael wrote us a great deal about you and your kindness to him."

Norville bowed to her. "It was my pleasure to know your son,

Lady Mallory. I was happy to be of service to him . . . and to you."

"I have told Trevor that you must come to call. Please do, Mr. Norville. We would count it a kindness on your part."

Norville smiled and thanked her, assuring her that he would come to see her and that they could talk of Michael. Then, as she was gathering her daughters and Nora, he turned to Elizabeth, who had been hoping to avoid the pleasure of a tête-à-tête.

"A *breeches* role?" he inquired, brows raised. "She does not merely want to be an actress, but one that plays men's roles to boot?"

Elizabeth shrugged her shoulders lightly. "She is just . . . spirited, Mr. Norville. But very tractable, I am sure," she added dryly. "I am certain that you can mold her opinions about acting—perhaps you could even assist her with the fencing."

Realizing that discretion was the better part of valor, she turned away from him and hurried after her party before he could reply. Glancing back into the crowded Green Room before she left it, Elizabeth caught a glimpse of Mr. Norville, who appeared to be still watching her, and, in the far corner, Lord Mallory, speaking hotly with someone whose face was at first hidden. As he turned, however, she could see who it was—Lord Chawton. Now what, she asked herself as they returned to their box under Lady Mallory's supervision, would Mallory be discussing with Chawton and why would he be so distressed?

She had little time to devote to the question when she returned to their box. The play resumed, and from the time the small, dark man who had taken London by storm came on the stage until he left it, she, like the rest of the audience, sat mesmerized. His approach might be radically different for conservative, tradition-bound Drury Lane, but there could be no denial of his power over an audience. At the end of the act, people were standing and applauding wildly, some even standing on their seats.

Mr. Norville did not come to their box during the next intermission, but Elizabeth saw him enter a box across the way and bend over the hand of a lovely woman with long, fair hair. Lady Mallory followed her gaze and Elizabeth heard her gasp.

"Why, I have been so caught up in the play that I had not even noticed her! I did not realize that she was back in England!"

"Who is she?" asked Elizabeth curiously. "I don't remember seeing her before."

"You wouldn't have, my dear. You are too young. That is Lady Caroline Sale—or she used to be. She has been Lady Brill these twelve years and more. Poor Norville!"

"Why poor Norville?" asked Elizabeth, frowning.

"He was engaged to her then and as deeply in love as I have ever seen a man be. He went to Stoneybrook, his home in Devon, to see to it that everything was in order before he married her and took her there, and when he came back to London, he found that she had eloped with Lord Brill, quite the most notorious rake in town."

She paused, remembering.

"What did he do?" Elizabeth asked.

"Why, he went after them. He thought that she was too young to know what she was doing. It was during the Peace of Amiens and he followed them as far as Paris, but when he found them, they had already married, and Caroline refused to come home with him. He didn't return to London. He went to Stoneybrook and when the war broke out again, he joined. His mother was a girlhood friend of mine, and she told me just before her death that Andrew did not plan ever to marry. Poor woman," she sighed. "Andrew was her only child and she worried over his unhappiness to her dying day."

"Is that Brill?" Elizabeth asked as a tall blond man entered the box.

Lady Mallory shook her head. "I don't know who that is—nor do I even know if Brill is still alive. As far as I know, this is Caroline's first time to return to England in all those years."

Elizabeth watched Norville leaving the box, Lady Brill turning to call after him, and wondered. Perhaps he would no longer be so interested in Nora. And, if he were, she thought, this explained a great deal about his fear of the effects of London society on young girls.

Chapter Eight

Elizabeth had ample time to reflect upon the question of Lady Brill and Mr. Norville if she desired to do so, for the gentleman in question did not appear in Grosvenor Square for several days. Their time, however, was so filled with activities that his defection was scarcely noted, by Nora at least. Elizabeth conscientiously took her young charge calling on several ladies whose patronage would assist her, and as soon as it became known that Miss Harrington had a delightful young guest, cards of invitation for Nora came in quite as steadily as those for Elizabeth. Nora walked out once with Anne and Maria during this time, accompanied again by Miss Stevenson, but there was little time during the day that was not scheduled with some activity. It had even been necessary to order additional gowns to keep pace with her social activities. All of the affairs she had attended thus far had been relatively small ones, and Nora had yet to have her first real ball. That would be at Mrs. Pritchard's home the next evening, and Nora was already weak with excitement.

At least Mr. Norville would not be able to accuse her of allowing Nora to become too particular in her attention to young Mallory, thought Elizabeth virtuously—if he were even interested in Nora any longer, now that the fascinating Lady Brill was in town. It was true that Mallory still called with regularity and that they had seen him at several small affairs they had attended, but Nora had begun to attract her own circle of admirers, so when Mallory came to call now, it was virtually impossible for them to engage in a tête-à-tête. So occupied had Elizabeth been with chaperoning Nora that Lord Lacey, one of her faithful admirers, had felt compelled to remonstrate.

"Who *are* these dratted puppies I keep tripping over when I come to see you, Elizabeth? And why must they collect in *your* drawing room?" he demanded.

"I suppose that you are not referring to Rufus, are you, Hamilton?" she inquired, her eyes alight with amusement at his discomfiture as he looked around the room. Rufus reclined in solitary state at Nora's feet, Sampson having retired to the kitchen to look into the possibility of a light nuncheon.

"Well, of course I am not, dear lady. I am referring to *them*." He radiated disapproval as the sweep of his hand indicated four or five young fribbles gathered about Nora.

"As you see, Hamilton, Nora is holding court. I am amazed that you are not a member."

"I? I am not a cradle-snatcher—"

"That is not very chivalrous of you," Elizabeth interrupted, "and do you mean to indicate that I am at my last prayers?"

"You know full well that I think that you are the loveliest, wittiest, most accomplished woman of my acquaintance, Elizabeth," he replied with feeling, "and that I would marry you at any moment. You have only to name the time and I would lay my fortune at your feet."

"Yes, and we know that you are perfectly safe, Hamilton, so you may offer with impunity. And, for the moment, I must play propriety for Nora, and you must help me."

"Anything to be of service to you, dear heart." He paused and considered, and then, his sense of self-preservation overcoming his ardor, he asked with some misgiving, "What, precisely, do you mean by helping you, Elizabeth?"

"I should like it very much, Hamilton, if you would escort us to Sadler's Wells today. Edmund is away, and I don't wish to have any of Nora's court accompany us, but I had promised her that we might go. So of course I thought of you."

"Of course," he replied, somewhat weakly. "What is it that we are going to see?"

"You will be delighted with it. I know only that there is an act by performing dogs, as well as a tightrope walker and tumblers.

I am not certain what else we may be fortunate enough to see, although I believe there is an egg-dancer as well."

He stared at her. "Are you telling me, Elizabeth, that you wish to go to Sadler's Wells to see these things?"

"Not precisely that I wish to, Hamilton, but that I am really obligated to do so. Nora wishes to see them—particularly, I think, the performing dogs. I believe that she is thinking of trying to train Rufus." She paused a moment, thinking. "I do hope that she won't because I don't believe Edmund would be pleased to have a dog performing in the drawing room."

"What will you do tomorrow to equal this thrilling outing, Elizabeth? And I hasten to add that I am engaged for the whole of tomorrow and am leaving for Bath on the following day."

"What a shocking lack of gallantry, Hamilton! I need not attempt to equal it tomorrow, for tomorrow night is the Pritchard ball and Nora is quite beside herself about it. *Will* you accompany us to the theatre today?" she inquired, returning to the matter at hand.

"How can you doubt it? I would be delighted to escort you."

"I do thank you, Hamilton, for I know that it is not at all what you would wish to do, but I did promise Nora. She has been dreadfully disappointed that she will not be able to attend Astley's while she is in London. I had quite forgotten that they do not open until Easter Monday, and I am not certain that she will still be with us then. This will at least atone in part for that."

Sadler's Wells had come by its name honestly. A highway surveyor named Thomas Sadler decided in 1683 to create a pleasure garden there, discovering on the property an old music room and a medicinal well, one that had been noted for its healing power during the Middle Ages. Mr. Sadler had rebuilt the music room and established a pleasure garden where people could be entertained as they took the waters. In 1765 a stone theatre had been built in its place, and in 1801 Edmund Kean had performed there as a child. It provided a variety of entertainments, from ballad operas to ladder dancing. Plans were in store for a more unusual type of program called "nautical drama," with rousing titles like *The Tars of Old England,* which would simulate naval battles with the aid of a 90-foot long, 3-foot deep tank of water on the stage.

Lord Lacey enjoyed himself more than he had expected to. Their box had an excellent view, and he made himself comfortable with the homely pint of port that came with the ticket. He was pleasantly surprised by the Great Merrivale's Astounding Canine Carnival and listened indulgently as Nora reviewed her plans for beginning an immediate program of study for Rufus so that he too could reach the exalted heights of the Great Merrivale's performers. The rest of the program was equally as lively and diverting, and they were quite pleased with their outing.

For Nora, however, the *pièce de résistance* was the egg-dance. She had never heard of such a thing, so she watched carefully as the gaily dressed dancer came out onto the stage, a roll of carpeting under her arm.

"Is she a gypsy?" whispered Nora, inspecting her gold hoop earrings, dark hair, and vivid clothing with wide-eyed interest.

"It's quite likely," responded Elizabeth. "She looks very like one."

The dancer carefully rolled out the carpeting, setting a lighted candle at each corner of it. Then, taking a basket of eggs, she painstakingly laid them out in a pattern on the carpeting, measuring her steps as she did so. Finally, she tied a kerchief of turkey red about her eyes, slipped a pair of castanets upon her fingers, and signaled to her violinist. Precisely as his plaintive melody began, she started her dance, stepping nimbly over the dozen or so eggs, never causing one to move by as much as a fraction of an inch. Little by little the tempo of the music accelerated and with it her movements as she wound in her mazelike patterns among the eggs, stepping more and more briskly, sometimes even leaping and alighting in a half-kneeling position. When the music ended, she rolled all of the eggs gently into a small heap with her foot, then slipped the kerchief from her eyes, and bowed to the appreciative audience.

"She was really very amazing," said Lord Lacey. "Imagine dancing about among all of those eggs! I would have mashed them into that bit of carpeting within the first five steps."

"Surely not, Hamilton," laughed Elizabeth. "I have seen you

dance most gracefully in the ballroom. I cannot believe that of you."

"I do hope that I shall have partners for the dances tomorrow night," said Nora anxiously, reminded of the Pritchard ball. "I should hate to be left while everyone else has someone to stand up with."

"I don't think you need worry, Nora. You won't lack for partners. Your difficulty may be having enough dances for all of the partners who will wish one."

"I am sure that will be the case," agreed Lord Lacey gallantly. "I trust that you will do me the honor, Miss Lane, of saving me one . . . preferably a quadrille."

Nora dimpled. "I will be delighted, Lord Lacey. Now I am assured of at least one dance."

The evening ended pleasantly. Lord Lacey was conscious of having fulfilled his obligations admirably; Elizabeth had provided Nora with at least one of the outings she had promised—and without any questionable gentlemen accompanying them; and Nora had seen not only the egg-dance, which she burned to try for herself, but also the Great Merrivale's performing dogs, and she was convinced that Rufus was the equal in intelligence and physical coordination of any one of them. Proper training would reveal his talents.

Morning found Nora again holding court for her admirers, and it was with difficulty that Elizabeth restrained her from sending for candles and a basket of eggs so that she could demonstrate the egg-dance on the Aubusson carpet. She was forced to make do with a lively description and an imitation of one of the graceful leaps. Mallory and Norville entered the drawing room together, just in time to see her alight in the dramatic, half-kneeling position of the egg-dancer. Mallory applauded while Norville raised his eyebrows almost to his hairline and locked his gaze with that of Elizabeth's.

Seating himself quietly next to that lady, he murmured, "I had thought that she would content herself with practicing swordplay for a breeches role, but I see that she has moved on. Miss Harrington, have you *no* control over her?"

"Oh, yes," she replied cheerfully, determined not to let him rattle her. "She had wished to use real eggs in the dance, but I convinced her to make do with bits of ribbon to mark their places." Here she indicated the ribbon markers on the carpeting. "Burton was grateful for my intervention."

Mr. Stanton Scott, one of the youngest members of Nora's court, was distressed to learn that she had been to Sadler's Wells the day before.

"I w-wish that I had known you were going," he stammered, overcome by his own audacity, "for I w-would have gone to protect you."

"To protect me?" Nora exclaimed. "What would you have protected me from?"

"Highwaymen!" he answered promptly.

"What a bag of moonshine!" returned one of his disrespectful companions. "Scott is merely wishful of cutting a dash for you, Miss Lane."

Mr. Scott glared at the offender. "It isn't a bag of moonshine! Lady Campion was robbed last evening as she was returning home by way of Knightsbridge."

"Was Lady Campion harmed?" asked Elizabeth with concern.

Mr. Scott shook his head. "She said it was a real adventure. The highwayman wore a black domino and a black half-mask over the upper portion of his face even though he was quite hidden in the shadows."

He looked a little puzzled as he continued his tale. "She said that his manners were very courtly—that he was quite the gentleman."

"But he *did* rob her?" asked Nora.

Mr. Scott shook his head. "Oh, yes. He took the ruby ring she was wearing and her pearls and a diamond pin—but he was very apologetic."

"There's Dutch comfort for you!" exploded one of his listeners.

"Well, she said it *was* a comfort to be robbed by a gentleman. When her coachman tried to pull a pistol on him, the highwayman simply told him not to think of doing such a foolish thing unless he wished to shoot his bolt."

"Now that *is* gentlemanly," said Mr. Keeley, with all of the annoying persistence of a gadfly.

"Well, it *was* if you only think about it, Keeley! He could have shot the man. Lady Campion said he had a long-nosed pistol in his hand the whole time."

Mr. Scott turned back to the object of his devotion, and nervousness overcame him again. "So, Miss Lane, if you drive out again, p-pray let me know so that I might escort you."

Mr. Keeley snorted. "And what good would that do her, Scott?"

"I would protect her!" said Mr. Scott ferociously, or as ferociously as his mild manners would allow.

"You and how many others?" inquired Keeley, and he bowed to Nora. "I, on the other hand, Miss Lane, would be fully capable of protecting you from such disreputable riffraff. Please do allow me to see you to the ball this evening."

Before the quarrel could escalate, Elizabeth decided it was time to intercede.

"That is very thoughtful of you, Mr. Keeley; but Miss Lane already has an escort. She will be delighted to see you at the ball, however."

Thus reminded of their manners, the young gentlemen arose to take their leave, all of them attempting to engage Nora for as many dances as possible.

After they had departed, leaving Mallory and Norville in possession of the drawing room, Elizabeth asked, "You are remembering, Nora, not to allow any young man to engage you for more than two dances?"

"Oh, yes, Elizabeth! And just think—nearly all of the dances are already spoken for!"

Mallory bowed gallantly. "I hope that you will save one for me, Miss Lane."

She curtsied. "I should be happy to, Lord Mallory, if you think I am quite old enough to dance."

He considered the matter carefully for a moment, then nodded. "Just old enough, I believe. Now—do show me the egg-dance. I saw only the close of it."

Nora needed no encouragement and proceeded to give her demonstration again. Elizabeth watched Norville from the corner of her eye, but he made no move to interfere—nor, she thought, did he seem to be even noticing what was going forward. He was deep in thought and had not even attempted to engage Nora for a dance. She wondered if his thoughts were with Lady Brill.

At the end of Nora's egg-dance, Mallory had applauded and Sampson, somewhat lethargic from his profitable journey to the kitchen, had reentered the drawing room and was occupying himself by absently swatting the ribbon egg markers about the floor.

"We were always very fond of decorating eggs when I was a child. Were you?" inquired Mallory, diplomatically ranging Nora on the side of the adults.

"Oh, yes," she replied. "Nanny used to take my sisters and me out to pick the things that we would need to color the eggs—spinach leaves or anemone petals for greens, logwood chips for purple, gorse or onion skin for yellow, cochineal for scarlet. Or sometimes we would take ribbons of different colors and bind them about the eggs before boiling them."

Mallory nodded, remembering. "My sisters and George will be coloring eggs this spring, I am sure. Perhaps you and I could help them."

Before Nora could assent to this, he remembered something else and continued. "Did you ever write your name, or a message, on the egg after it is dyed?"

Nora nodded. "We always wrote our names with white wax pencils on the eggs we had dyed, but we never wrote messages. That would have been more clever."

Mallory chuckled. "George always expects to find one egg that has a message on it, and the message is supposed to lead him— or whoever finds it—to a hidden prize. There is always one like that in our hunt, and George always expects to find it. If he doesn't, the rest of us regret it, so we always try to arrange for him to be the one to discover it."

Nora laughed, but she stopped abruptly and sat up so stiffly that Mallory thought she might be ill.

"Are you all right, Miss Lane?" he asked anxiously.

Her wide-eyed gaze suddenly fixed upon his face. "That is it!" she exclaimed. "That is the answer to the first riddle!"

"What is?" he asked, puzzled.

"Egg! That is the answer to 'I am the beginning.' " She turned to Elizabeth and repeated it. "Don't you think that might be the proper answer?" she demanded.

"Well, an egg is most certainly a beginning," replied Elizabeth, smiling at her enthusiasm and glancing at Norville to see if he had emerged from his brown study enough to note what was taking place.

Mallory's brow cleared. "You could be right," he admitted. "What about the second part?"

"I still think that the answer to that is a lock," she insisted. "And Mr. Macklin at the inn thought that I had it right, too."

"Well, most certainly the answer to each riddle is not the same word," said Mallory thoughtfully, " for the answer to 'I hold the key' would not be 'egg.' "

Elizabeth sat quietly, not particularly mindful of the riddles, watching Mr. Norville's absent expression. With Mallory's last words, he seemed to refocus himself with an effort and made an attempt to join the conversation.

"It hardly seems likely that the same word would be the answer to all of the questions," he agreed. "How did it all go again?"

Nora, who had memorized it on the spot at the Bull and Barleycorn, replied promptly:

> *I am the beginning*
> *I hold the key*
> *I am winter's end*
> *From summer I flee*

"I am impressed, Nora," said Elizabeth, smiling. "I had forgotten the last portion of it."

"I've thought about it a good deal," she replied, "and it does seem as though we ought to be able to solve it. Although I still can't imagine why that dreadful Lord Chawton told us about it, I can't forget about it. Riddles prey upon my mind until I can puzzle them out."

Mr. Norville was watching her with amusement. "What would you do as your next step in solving it?" he asked.

Nora looked at him seriously. "I am quite sure that I know the answers to all four questions, for it is spring that is winter's end and autumn that flees from summer. But I don't understand what they mean."

She paused and the others waited, for she was obviously thinking deeply. "Lord Mallory said that there was a real man who disappeared like the man in the story—a Sir Howard Gregory. I think that we should visit his family and see if they can help us."

If she had said that she was considering moving to China for the summer, her listeners could not have been surprised. Even Mr. Norville, who had asked the question, was startled.

"Well, he does have a family, doesn't he?" she inquired, when no one commented upon her idea.

Recovering himself first, Lord Mallory demanded, "And what will we ask Lady Gregory when we call on her? She will think we have windmills in our heads if we arrive on her doorstep to question her."

"It will be that or she will have us shown the door for our brass-faced curiosity," added Elizabeth, shuddering at the thought of intruding on the widow.

"Well, you asked me what I would do and I told you," said Nora huffily.

"I think you are quite right," said Norville suddenly, and they all, Nora included, turned to stare at him.

"It is a very reasonable approach," he defended himself. "If you want to know the answer to a question, you go to those most nearly involved, and in this case that would be Lady Gregory."

Feeling vindicated, Nora straightened her shoulders and glared at Mallory, who grinned. "And when do we all call on Lady Gregory?" he inquired.

"*All?*" echoed Elizabeth feebly.

"*All* of us," repeated Lord Mallory. "You would be particularly essential, Miss Harrington, for Lady Gregory would know you best."

"Very well, then," said Mr. Norville, rising. "I will see all of you tomorrow morning, and we will pay our call. If that would be convenient," he added, bowing to the ladies.

"Yes, we would be able to go, would we not, Elizabeth?"

replied Nora, taking the lead, for Elizabeth was still trying to picture what she would say to Lady Gregory.

"Yes," she responded without enthusiasm. "Tomorrow morning would be as appropriate a time as any," she added caustically, but her sarcasm was overlooked. Nora had turned back to Mr. Norville.

"Are you not going to the Pritchards' ball tonight, Mr. Norville?" she asked.

He smiled down at her, his rare smile again transforming him. "Yes, I had forgotten. I will look forward to seeing you there."

After the door had closed behind the two gentlemen, Nora commented wonderingly, "He did not even ask me for a dance, Elizabeth."

Elizabeth had not expected that Mr. Norville would ask herself to stand up for a dance, but she had indeed expected him to engage Nora for at least one. He is thinking of Lady Brill, she told herself. Nora may well be free of him soon.

It was amazing that she could derive so little comfort from that thought.

Chapter Nine

Although the Pritchards' ball left Elizabeth with much to think about, it did not improve her spirits. For Nora, arrayed in a ball gown of white crepe trimmed with black velvet ribbons spangled with gold, it was otherwise. From the moment she and Elizabeth and Sir Edmund were announced, it mattered not a particle that the rooms were overcrowded and overheated. She danced every dance and had to turn away partners. Heads turned as she danced by, and she could not but be aware of it. Even the fact that Lord Mallory told her that she looked "as fine as fivepence" in an odiously patronizing manner, quite as though she were one of his sisters instead of a young lady bidding fair to become the belle of the ball, and did not ask for a second dance did not spoil her evening. The fact that he danced two dances with Elizabeth and then disappeared into the cardroom was nothing to her, although it did not escape her attention.

More than one person turned to watch Elizabeth and Mallory as they danced, for he was a striking figure in his own right, golden-haired and graceful, but paired with her slender elegance and flaming hair, they presented a compelling picture. This was apparently lost upon Mr. Norville, however, for his eyes never lifted from his partner's face, and she appeared equally absorbed in him. The breathtaking and faithless Lady Brill! Not everyone learns the first time, thought Elizabeth as she watched him from beneath lowered lashes, although one would expect more of an intelligent man. Particularly of an intelligent man who had recently offered for an innocent young girl.

"Blue-deviled, Miss Harrington?" asked Lord Mallory, looking down at her in concern at the end of their first dance.

"Just a trifle moped. Do I look so frightful, Lord Mallory?" she parried, attempting a lightness she did not feel.

"Fishing for compliments, Miss Harrington?" he inquired, his eyes twinkling. "How unworthy of you! You have no need to do so, I assure you. I will gladly give them freely."

Before she could stop him, Mallory had begun a poetic enumeration of her many attributes, from the flame of her hair to the neatness of her ankle, exercising such hyperbole in his comparisons that she laughed in spite of herself.

"Stop roasting me, you absurd creature," she chuckled.

"If you do not stop now, Mallory," said a quiet voice, breaking into his free flow of outrageous compliments, "there will be nothing left for anyone else to say to Miss Harrington."

"I had no notion, Norville, that you were going to do the pretty as well. Would you like to begin where I have left off?"

Mr. Norville shook his head. "I'm afraid I do not deal in Spanish coin, Mallory. I must leave that to others. I merely wished to have a few words with Miss Harrington if she can spare me a moment."

Elizabeth nodded her agreement and Mallory looked indignant. "Well, of all the slowtops, Norville!"

He turned and bowed gallantly over Elizabeth's hand, saying in a low voice, "Well, you do look in a little better loaf now, my dear. Call upon me if you fall into the dismals again." Straightening, he gave her a speaking look and added in a louder voice, "I shall be back to claim the next dance, Miss Harrington."

Norville watched him thoughtfully as he threaded his way through to the cardroom. "I see that you and young Mallory are getting on well."

"That was just a farrago of nonsense that you heard. Lord Mallory was trying to put me to the blush and he succeeded admirably."

He studied her face. "I can see that he did. I was too hasty when I upbraided you for allowing Mallory to run tame in your home, Miss Harrington. I had not realized that you were the object of his gallantries. I must apologize."

Elizabeth flushed again. "I wish you will not be funning me, Mr. Norville. There is nothing between Lord Mallory and myself except friendship. If we choose to amuse ourselves in such a manner, we do no one any harm."

She took a deep breath, fighting down a desire to inquire into his relationship with Lady Brill, who was now watching them from across the room, and forced herself to smile and say lightly, "And now, Mr. Norville, what was it you wished to speak with me about?"

"About Miss Lane. I have been thinking about your comments to me—that Miss Lane is too young to be married, that she needs more time, that she needs to look about her a bit. Also," and he hesitated here a moment, "that you believed we would not suit."

He paused and looked across at Lady Brill, who smiled and beckoned to him. "I still do not think that you are correct about those matters, but we shall see. I wanted you to know that I am thinking about them."

He saw Mallory coming back toward them and excused himself, walking to join Lady Brill. I should imagine you certainly are thinking about them, Mr. Norville, Elizabeth said to herself. Only it is not Nora that you are concerned about; it is Lady Brill and yourself.

Mallory indicated Nora in a corner of the ballroom, surrounded by a throng of admirers. "In high croak tonight, ain't she?" he asked, grinning.

"I'm afraid so," agreed Elizabeth ruefully. "She told me this afternoon that she wanted to become all the crack, and I believe she's going to do it."

"I shouldn't be surprised. She'd like nothing better."

"Not unless it meant having a breeches role in a play or becoming an egg-dancer or training Rufus to perform on the stage," Elizabeth replied.

It was when they went into supper that evening that they heard again about Lady Campion's highwayman. The room was buzzing with the news. When Lady Campion's maid had awakened her that morning, following the evening of the robbery, she had discovered on her mistress's pillow a pink enamel Easter egg containing a tiny scroll tied with a scarlet ribbon. Opening it, they had read the following:

> *Do not pause when this you see—*
> *Turn around and take steps three.*

104

Lift the cushion, lift the lid;
Inside are all the jewels hid.

"And *were* they there?" asked someone, astounded.

"Yes, indeed," said Lady Campion's grandson. "They took three steps to the windowseat, did exactly as the note said to do, and there they were: her ruby ring, her pearls, and her diamond pin!"

"But why would anyone rob her and then return the jewels to her?"

"And *how* did he manage to return them without being seen?" asked a second voice.

Lady Campion's grandson smiled. "My grandmother says she doesn't know and she doesn't care. What she *does* know, she says, is that he was a gentleman, first and last, with manners as fine as any duke."

Sir Edmund, who had been listening to all of the conversation with raised eyebrows, countered, "Fellow sounds a little confused to me. What kind of duke robs a lady of her jewels and then sneaks into her bedchamber to give them back again?"

"The Duke of Diamonds," someone suggested. "After all, he steals only the best."

"He would have been properly in the suds if Lady Campion had awakened while he was in the room," commented another.

"I should love to be held up by a highwayman," said Nora, her eyes sparkling.

"Well, of course you would," agreed Elizabeth. "So would we all. What could be more diverting than giving up your jewels at gun-point?"

"But, Elizabeth, he was so gallant—and besides, he *did* give them back."

Sir Edmund looked at her in astonishment. "You must be all about in your head," he gasped. "Next I suppose you'll think it's all fun and gig that the fellow comes into your house at night and sneaks about to return them!"

Nora tilted her chin up. "I think he was very courageous and very chivalrous to do so."

"Well *I* think it's all a hum," said Sir Edmund firmly, rising to go retire to the cardroom. "It sounds like a Banbury story first to last."

As it happened, Sir Edmund was in the wrong of it, for before the evening was over, there was another ripple of scandal that reached even into the cardroom where he and Mallory, along with a good many other gentlemen who were disinclined to dance, were ensconced. There had been another robbery.

"*Another* robbery?" exclaimed Sir Edmund, outraged. "Is Lady Campion here?"

This time, however, the victim had not been Lady Campion but Mrs. Evelyn Pritchard, in whose home the ball was being held. When she had gone up to her chamber for a few moments, she had been greeted by a stranger in a black cloak and mask, who had bowed and regretfully asked her to relinquish the diamond necklace, earrings, and bracelet she was wearing, as well as her emerald ring. Before leaving her, he had suggested that she wear her set of sapphires when she went back downstairs, for they would look most becoming with the gown she was wearing.

"Well, of all the cheek!" exclaimed Sir Edmund. "Does Mrs. Pritchard have a set of sapphires?"

Mr. Scott, Nora's admirer, nodded. "Mrs. Pritchard is my aunt," he commented. "She doesn't wear the sapphires often, but she does have a set—has had them for years."

"But how did this fellow know about them?" asked someone.

There was a brief silence, then Lady Campion's grandson said grimly, "It appears that our Duke must be one of ourselves—someone who would know what jewels a lady has and is free to enter our homes at will—as a guest."

Sir Edmund and Nora could scarcely talk of anything else on their way home in the carriage that night, the highwayman having eclipsed even Nora's first London ball. Elizabeth was quiet and withdrawn, concerned not with the Duke but with Norville and Lady Brill. Now that it appeared he might no longer feel an interest in Nora, Elizabeth's conscience was beginning to nag her. What would Cecilia say if Nora lost Norville and could not replace him with another suitor? What would happen to Nora's family? If it occurred to her that she might be distressed for any other reason, she firmly refused to think about it.

The following morning the news swept like wildfire through Mayfair that Mrs. Pritchard too had discovered an Easter egg containing a tiny scroll bearing a riddle—this one on top of her dressing table. When the simple riddle was solved, she found her diamonds and her ring.

There is nothing that polite society loves like a scandal, and this one offered delightful possibilities for speculation. The Duke became a favorite topic of discussion and his identity a favorite subject for wagers. Everyone had a theory, and all of the ladies hoped that they might soon be the object of the Duke's attentions.

Sir Edmund, seated with his paper in the drawing room the next morning after the ball, snorted. "What sort of highwayman is this Duke?" he demanded. "He wasn't even on his horse last night! No self-respecting highwayman would resort to being a common house thief."

"Yes, but I don't think he *is* common, Edmund," said Elizabeth. "That's why he is attracting such attention."

Nora looked thoughtful. "I did not think of it last night because I was so excited, but it seems very strange to me that we keep finding riddles . . . and eggs."

Sir Edmund and Elizabeth stared at her.

"It is true," she defended herself. "Think of Lord Chawton's story and now this. Was Chawton there last night?" she asked.

Sir Edmund nodded slowly. "Saw him in the cardroom for a bit after I went down to supper. Didn't stay the whole evening though."

"You see!" said Nora triumphantly. "He probably left to rob Mrs. Pritchard."

"But they say that the Duke has very courtly manners," objected Elizabeth. "Surely we could not say that of Chawton."

"True," sighed Nora, "but it does seem strange to stumble across so many riddles."

When Lord Mallory arrived a few minutes later, ready to sally forth to call on Lady Gregory, she presented her observation to him.

"I agree with Miss Harrington," he said firmly. "Anyone who could think Chawton charming would have to be as queer as Dick's hatband. Hiding him behind a mask and domino wouldn't improve his address."

Turning to Elizabeth, he smiled and took her hand. "All over your blue megrims?" he inquired.

"Quite over them," she responded gratefully. "It was very kind of you to be so concerned about me last night—and the daffodils that you sent this morning are beautiful. There are no flowers more cheerful than they are; it lifts my spirits just looking at them."

"Well, that's what I thought about them," he admitted.

"I didn't realize those were from you," said Nora somewhat blankly, looking first at the huge bouquet of golden blossoms and then at Mallory and Elizabeth.

Mallory continued talking to Elizabeth as though he had not heard her. "I should have enjoyed a third dance with you last night if it hadn't been for the confusion the Duke caused."

Nora frowned. "Elizabeth told me it wasn't good *ton* to stand up with a gentleman more than twice unless you were engaged to him."

Mallory disregarded her criticism cheerfully and said, "Very dashing you looked last night, Miss Lane. If we are going to escape before your callers begin to besiege you with flowers, we had better toddle along."

They had just begun the process of toddling, Lord Mallory having been foresighted enough to bring his chaise, when Mr. Norville joined them.

"I didn't think that you would be going with us this morning," said Elizabeth somewhat frostily.

A very slight smile curved the corners of his mouth. "And why did you think that, Miss Harrington?" he inquired. "I thought that I had made it quite plain that I thought Miss Lane's idea an excellent one."

Nora held her head a little higher at this.

"I merely meant that I thought you might be otherwise occupied this morning," replied Elizabeth vaguely, thinking of Lady Brill.

"I see," he replied. And she had the very uncomfortable feeling that he probably did.

Nora, who had been feeling unaccountably put out by Mallory's defection to Elizabeth, decided that in Mr. Norville she had perhaps found someone who would respect her suspicion of the riddles, and she proceeded to point out to him the coincidence that they had encountered more than one riddle in a very brief span of time.

He listened attentively and then pointed out that there had been more riddles than those of Chawton and the Duke. When the others looked at him blankly, he reminded them that Mallory's own story at the Black Swan had been something of a riddle in itself. There was a brief silence while they digested this. Then Mallory chuckled.

"Are you suggesting that I am the Duke, Norville?" he asked.

"Not at all, Mallory. Just pointing out that there are more riddles about us than we are sometimes aware of."

Mallory was satisfied with his reply, but Nora studied Mallory furtively as the carriage bowled along, taking them to Curzon Street and Lady Gregory. If she was somewhat puzzled by the arrival of four virtual strangers on her doorstep, Lady Gregory was far too well-bred to betray it. Having seated them courteously in her drawing room and rung for the tea tray, she looked hopefully at Elizabeth, the visitor best known to her.

Before she could speak, however, Norville smiled at Lady Gregory. "Please forgive us for intruding, Lady Gregory. As Miss Harrington told you, my name is Andrew Norville. We met once a very long time ago—almost fifteen years ago now—at a dinner party given by Lord and Lady Randall."

Lady Gregory studied his features for a moment, then smiled as recognition dawned. "Yes, of course, the young man from Devon who liked to ride and who wanted to do something exciting with his life!" She smiled at him. "And have you?"

He bowed his head. "I eventually purchased a pair of colors and Sir Howard was kind enough to take an interest in me when we met in Paris during the Peace of Amiens. Because of that, I was employed upon a number of special missions during my time in the army. I was very grateful to him for his help."

Her face softened at this mention of her husband. "Sir Howard was always very interested in helping the careers of young men whom he considered particularly able. I am glad that he was able to be of assistance to you."

She looked at him directly. "Are you here because of my husband's disappearance?" she asked.

Norville nodded. "We have encountered some very curious circumstances and we would like to ask you one or two questions if you would not find them either impertinent or painful."

"They may well be painful. It seems as though I have done nothing other than answer questions for over a year now, and somehow they don't become easier to answer."

She sat up a little straighter as though bracing herself for them.

"I will do my best to help you. What would you like to know first?"

"I know that you have been asked this before, but did you by chance find anything unusual among your husband's possessions when they were sent home to you?"

She shook her head. "In fact," she added, "there was something missing that *should* have been there."

They all looked at her eagerly. "What was missing?" asked Norville.

"His Easter egg," she responded promptly. Nora, perched precariously on a dainty, spindle-legged chair, almost lost her balance at this additional Easter egg reference, and it was with difficulty that she held her tongue.

Lord Mallory stared at her. "Your husband was bringing home an Easter egg?" he asked incredulously.

Lady Gregory nodded her head. "Sir Howard has—had—a collection of them. I will have to show it to you before you leave today. He wrote to say that he had found a very unusual one that he was anxious to add to it."

"Did he say in what way it was unusual?" asked Norville.

"He didn't actually describe it to me. He did say, though, something about a paradox."

"A paradoxical *egg?*" Nora, scenting another riddle, entered the conversation.

"I wonder what he could have meant by that," said Elizabeth slowly.

"I have absolutely no idea," replied Lady Gregory. "I admit that it sounds most peculiar. He did not explain it and I did not hear from him again," she added slowly. "That was my last letter from him . . . and when they brought me his trunk and his other possessions, there was no sign of the egg he had mentioned. I looked specifically, and I asked about it because he had mentioned it, and I wanted it to remind me of him."

There was a sympathetic pause, and then Elizabeth asked slowly, "Was there anything else missing that you know of, Lady Gregory?"

She shook her head slowly.

"Did you know what his mission to St. Petersburg was?" inquired Norville.

"As you know," she explained slowly, "after Napoleon's defeat in

110

Russia, Metternich sent Baron Wessenberg of Austria here to convince us to allow Austria to mediate a peace with Bonaparte, but our government rejected any peace which ignored our objectives in regard to Maritime Rights and the Low Countries and did not fulfill our pledges to Spain and Portugal. The baron was not received in London society and after his departure, there were those in our government who were afraid that Metternich might try to establish a Continental peace which would exclude Great Britain."

She stared down at her hands a moment, twisting her wedding band absently. "They decided to send my husband on an unofficial mission to Tsar Alexander, hoping to convince him and the Prussian, Baron Stein, who had fled Bonaparte and joined him, that they should not comply with the Austrians and cut out our country from the negotiations."

"Did he take any gift of value with him?"

She flushed painfully. "I know now that he must have, of course. But I did not know at the time. I have no idea what it was, except that it was valuable enough to provoke an attack."

"Did anyone mention to you a slip of paper with a riddle that was found in Sir Howard's rooms?" asked Norville gently.

She shook her head again. "A riddle? He was very fond of them, of course. But I was not told that one was found. Do you remember what it said?"

Nora spoke up promptly:

> *I am the beginning*
> *I hold the key*
> *I am winter's end*
> *From summer I flee*

Lady Gregory listened carefully and then, taking a slip of paper, asked Nora to repeat it again, and she carefully copied it down and reread it.

"I don't know what it could mean, but I assure you that I shall think about it." Her voice grew firmer. "I have not been satisfied with the lack of explanation about my husband's disappearance. I have had to listen to rumors begun by scandalmongers, hinting that Sir Howard deliberately disappeared, taking with him something that was not his. I *know* my husband. He could not have done such a dishonorable thing. Sir Howard did not leave of his own choice. He was taken—which means that either he is still held somewhere—" and here her voice shook slightly, "or that he is dead."

Elizabeth placed her hand upon the older woman's shoulder comfortingly, and Lady Gregory glanced at her gratefully. "I do not believe that he would have been held so long with no word, no ransom note. So my children and I have come to believe—and reluctantly to accept—that he is dead. But we cannot accept the thought that he would betray both his country and his family."

"You have two children, do you not?" asked Norville, and she nodded.

Mallory interjected, "I know your son Paul. He attended Oxford when I was there."

"Yes, Paul had hoped to pursue a career in diplomacy like his father, but . . ." She held up her hands in a gesture of defeat. "There is very little opportunity for a young man whose father has been accused—no matter how unofficially—of treason. My daughter at least lives very far from London with her husband. Scandal cannot touch them so readily and for that I am grateful."

Elizabeth watched her with admiration. Even though she had obviously suffered from the loss of her husband, she had not allowed herself to become embittered or self-pitying, and her faith in her husband's honor remained unshaken. Though she was fragile-looking, with silver hair, she was a woman of whipcord strength.

"Perhaps you would like to see Sir Howard's collection that I spoke of?" The others murmured politely that they would, but as they rose from their places to accompany her, Lord Mallory, his face unnaturally flushed, turned to speak to her.

"There is something that I must tell you, Lady Gregory, that will undoubtedly cause you pain—which is something I very much regret—but I assure you that it causes me pain as well."

They all regarded him with astonishment, not only because of what he was saying but also because of his manner. Mallory was always genial, his manner polished, his attitude frivolous. The man before them, however, was deathly serious.

Lady Gregory paled a little, but she spoke quietly. "I am listening, Lord Mallory."

"I had not intended to tell anyone, but I believe that you have a right to know this." His voice was a trifle unsteady, and he had to take a moment to regain his composure. "My older brother Michael entered the army, despite the fact that he was the oldest and my father's heir, because he had a great need for adventure, and my father felt that the army gave him a legitimate way to satisfy that need, whereas if he remained in London, he might simply devote himself to gambling and a roistering life as substitutes for real adventure."

"Your father was a wise man," said Lady Gregory as he paused.

"He was most certainly that," Mallory agreed. "Michael distinguished himself in combat—Mr. Norville can attest to that," he said, nodding at that gentleman. "And because of the reputation he achieved as a man of courage and honor, he was asked to act as a courier. He was home on leave at the time. It was last winter."

He looked Lady Gregory directly in the eye. "He was asked, Lady Gregory, to carry a package from here to St. Petersburg, where he was to meet your husband and give it into his care."

"And did he do so?" she asked.

Lord Mallory bowed his head. "I believe that he did so, my lady, and that he left St. Petersburg immediately, before the disappearance of your husband. But I have no proof. The mission itself was a secret, so although when he left I did know that he was not going directly back to Spain because he had a mission to complete, I did not know where he was going nor what he was to do. He was killed in action shortly after his return to Spain, so I know nothing of whether or not he actually delivered the package. I only know what I believe to be true."

"And you think this knowledge must be painful for me because it would mean that my husband had the package, the gift, whatever we wish to call it, when he disappeared?"

Mallory nodded, and she smiled.

"I can appreciate your belief in your brother's innocence because I also believe in my husband's innocence. It is not necessary that one of them be the guilty party. There are other possibilities."

"Indeed there are, Lady Gregory," agreed Norville, "but identifying other possible candidates and proving their guilt would be a difficult matter."

Elizabeth took Mallory's arm gently. "Forgive me for asking, Lord Mallory, when you were really addressing your story to Lady

Gregory and my presence here is just a happenstance, but—" Here she broke off.

"Please ask, Miss Harrington. I promise that I will not be offended," he replied.

"How did you know of the package when your brother had not told you any particulars? And that he was to deliver it to Sir Howard in St. Petersburg?"

Nora's eyes widened, for she had not considered this, so engrossed had she been in the story itself. Mr. Norville and Lady Gregory watched closely, waiting for his reply.

Mallory colored again. "You will recall the—gentleman—whom we encountered at the Bull and Barleycorn?"

All save Lady Gregory nodded.

"Although his estate is not far from Chanderley, I had not been personally acquainted with him until several days prior to that encounter, when he presented himself to me and requested a private interview. He said that it had to do with Michael."

Here Mallory took a deep breath. "I thought perhaps it was a gaming debt that Michael had not taken care of because he was called away from London so suddenly. I had known, of course, that Michael lost very heavily to this man one night at Brooks's, and I thought that more might be owed. But that was not it. Lord Chawton told me that he had information about Michael's mission that would dishonor him and our family were it known."

"Blackmail!" exclaimed Norville grimly.

Mallory nodded heavily. "But he did not want money. He wanted the package. He told me what Michael's mission had been and that Sir Howard had disappeared before receiving the package. Chawton said that Michael must have known of his disappearance, either because he was involved in it or because he saw it. In either case, according to Lord Chawton, he simply decided to keep the package for himself."

"How would Lord Chawton have known anything about this mission?" asked Lady Gregory sharply. "He is a gamester, not a man connected with political affairs!"

"I was thinking much the same thing, Lady Gregory," agreed Norville. "It would be most interesting to know where he got his information. And I would be interested to know, too, Mallory, how Chawton persuaded you to believe this."

"He showed me Michael's signet ring. He never allowed that ring to leave his hand. I knew that it was not returned home with his other belongings after his death, but I thought perhaps it had been taken from his hand by a looter after he was wounded."

"And did Chawton tell you how he came to have the ring?"

Mallory nodded. "He said that Michael could not cover everything he lost in play that last night at Brooks's, but he promised that he would soon be able to. He told Chawton about his mission and that he would be carrying something of great value. He promised that when he had completed his mission and returned to Spain, he would send Chawton the money that he still owed him. He gave his signet ring as a pledge."

Mallory turned to Lady Gregory. "I cannot believe that my brother would have been so dishonorable as to betray the information about his mission to anyone, and certainly not to a man like Chawton. But the fact remains that Chawton holds his ring. He has told me that if I do not turn over the contents of that package to him within the next month, he will make this information widely known in London, beginning with my mother."

"Where had you been when we met you at the inn?" asked Norville.

"To our home at Chanderley. If there were any truth at all in Chawton's story, I thought perhaps Michael might have sent something there." He sat down with his head in his hands. "But there was nothing. And Chawton must have followed me. Then he told his miserable story to remind me of the power he holds over me."

"But what about the riddle?" asked Nora. "What has the riddle to say to anything? Does Chawton know the answer to it?"

"I think not," replied Elizabeth, who had been rethinking the evening at the Bull. "The story was a reminder to you, Lord Mallory, but the riddle . . . perhaps he wanted to see if you recognized it. It does not seem to me that he would use it unless he either wanted to plague you with it or wanted to see if you could solve it. So it must truly be a key, but one that Chawton does not know how to use."

Norville looked at her almost approvingly. "You are most discerning, Miss Harrington."

"I must suppose, Mr. Norville, that you mean that I am very discerning for a frivolous member of the *ton*," she replied briskly, turning her attention back to Lord Mallory. "I think, dear sir, that we must try what we can to unravel this problem."

"I appreciate your concern, Miss Harrington, but please do not feel that you are obligated to become a party to this."

"Nonsense! Miss Lane and I would feel terribly put upon if we were not allowed a part in this. Would we not, Nora?"

Nora had not been best pleased to be left on the fringes of the conversation, particularly since she felt that she had answered the riddle, so her tone was more restrained than it might otherwise have been.

"Certainly," she responded in a careless manner. "If, of course, Lord Mallory feels that we might be of any assistance."

"I trust that I am included in this," interjected Lady Gregory.

"Indeed you are," Lord Mallory assured her. "I felt that I must tell you, little though I wanted to confess it."

Mallory looked at Norville, who had become silent during the interchange. "And what of you, Norville? Do you wish to disassociate yourself from me and from this problem?"

There was a tiny pause as Norville glanced at Elizabeth and Nora. "Not at all, Mallory, not at all. I begin to feel that I, too, have a personal interest in this matter."

Chapter Ten

Lady Gregory straightened her shoulders and announced briskly, "Well, now that we have established that we are all in this together, I believe that we should begin."

Nora decided that she had stayed in the background long enough. "We should begin with the riddle. They did not tell you, Lady Gregory, but I believe that I have the answers to all of the questions in the riddle."

Lady Gregory looked at her admiringly. "How very clever of you, dear. Do tell me what you decided."

"Well, the 'I am the beginning' is an egg, and . . ." Nora trailed off suddenly, her eyes sparkling, as an idea began to take shape. She gasped. "Why, I hadn't thought about that for a second! I just sat here and listened to the stories without thinking about it!"

"About what?" asked Elizabeth, puzzled.

"The egg! If the answer to the first riddle is 'egg,' perhaps there is a connection to Sir Howard's egg that he was going to add to his collection! Or at the very least it is an odd coincidence."

This time Lady Gregory's admiration was genuine. "Now that is truly clever, Miss Lane. Let me take you to the Red Saloon as I was about to earlier and show you Sir Howard's collection. Perhaps we will think of something else as we examine them."

The Red Saloon was, they discovered, entirely given to Sir Howard's eggs. The walls were lined with glass cases like library shelves, all of them velvet-lined and some of them locked.

"Not all of the locked cases contain eggs that are costly, of course," Lady Gregory explained, "but some are very delicate

117

and Sir Howard did not want the servants who were dusting to open the cases and perhaps break some. And then some *are* truly valuable."

"Well, I must say!" exclaimed Mallory as he stared about him. "We always thought we had quite a few eggs at Eastertide, but we were not a patch on Sir Howard! How many are there, Lady Gregory?"

"I believe there are approximately four hundred," she replied matter-of-factly.

"Look at these!" Nora stood in front of a case containing glass eggs in lovely shades of blue, red, yellow, and purple, each of them inscribed with a saying. She bent closer to the glass so she could read aloud the inscription on one, *"With all my love and all my faith this Easter egg I give to you."*

"Those are Alsatian," explained Lady Gregory. "The glassblowers made them to give to their sweethearts."

"Here are some others that are inscribed," called Elizabeth, who had wandered to the other side of the room.

"I believe that you can read them reasonably well," said Lady Gregory, coming over to her. "Sir Howard arranged them so that the inscriptions would show to best advantage. There are several different types of messages. This one," and here she pointed to a large red one, "is religious:

Through Christ we, too, have a new beginning.

And these are eggs that boys and girls in the Tyrol exchange. This one reads:

> *Grant your love*
> *This I beg*
> *To the one who gives*
> *This Easter egg.*

I wonder if the wish was granted."

She chuckled. "The giver might have gotten back either of these replies:

118

If in all the wide world
There were no one but you,
I still could not promise
That I would be true.

or, if the lover were fortunate:

This Easter egg
Is my promise true.
By Eastertide next
I will marry you."

"I thought the messages we wrote on our eggs were long," commented Mallory. "We never could have managed to get all of this onto one."

"It is said that Mozart wrote one of his first songs to go on an Easter egg," commented Lady Gregory. "But I am like you, Lord Mallory. I did very well to place my name on one that I was designing. The Swedes were more practical—and more private. They painted flowers on their Easter eggs and slipped their love notes into the hollow shell."

"Why does this one have a little tree on top of it?" asked Nora, pointing to a wooden egg topped with a tiny decorated fir tree.

"That is from Strasbourg and it's called a Nazareth egg. They give it at Christmas, so it is topped with one of their Christmas trees—like the one the Duchess of York puts up at Oatlands. The little tree comes off, and as you'll see if you look at the one next to it, it can be topped with a little wooden Easter hare."

"How clever," commented Elizabeth. "A very practical approach so that you purchase fewer eggs."

"These are Sir Howard's own pace-eggs that he decorated or that were given to him by family members."

The others paused respectfully. Inside the case were delicately tinted eggs, one with a squirrel on it, one with the imprint of a rose, another with that of vetch and fern.

Picking up a brightly flowered enamel egg, Lady Howard

opened it to reveal a tiny heap of inexpensive golden rings. "Sometimes the eggs are used to hold an expensive gift and sometimes to hold playthings like these."

"And these!" exclaimed Elizabeth, pausing at another large glass case. "These aren't Easter eggs."

"No," replied Lady Gregory, opening the case. "The shape of the egg is so popular that it has been used for a variety of items." She picked up a carved boxwood egg and unscrewed it into two halves. "This is a pomander, to be filled with potpourri—or some fill it with coriander seeds to repel moths. This one is a vinaigrette," she said, pointing to a yellow Battersea enamel egg. "And the one next to it is a snuffbox."

Elizabeth was enchanted to discover an ivory egg sewing box, a blue glass scent bottle, a sponge box—all in the shape of an egg. In the case also rested a green glossy egg of malachite which Lady Gregory said the Russians used as hand coolers.

Other cases contained eggs etched with vivid patterns, some like embroidery patterns, some with bright geometric designs, others with scenes painted upon them. There was every conceivable color and material.

Lady Gregory paused a moment and looked about the room, her eyes bright with unshed tears. "Sir Howard loved these," she said softly. "Apart from their beauty or oddity, he loved the symbolism, the idea of renewal that has always been associated with the egg."

"They are fascinating," agreed Elizabeth, bending closer to examine a blue egg that had caught her eye. On one side was a picture of the Resurrection and on the other a lovely pattern of scarlet flowers. "This isn't an actual egg, is it, Lady Gregory?"

"No, that is a Russian wax egg. The colors that you see are tiny colored beads that have been embedded in the wax. The people use ribbons to attach them to their family icons."

It was the final case, a round one with several shelves that stood in the middle of the room, that amazed them most. There they found several handsome porcelain eggs that had been painted in Russia. Aside from the Resurrection scene, the eggs portrayed a delightful small cherub, the majestic Cathedral of the Archangel and Belfry of Peter the

Great in Moscow, a pair of glowing peacocks.

On the shelf above that were three eggs, two of which lay open. The first was a white enamel egg lined with blue velvet. In it sat a small golden chicken and next to it a tiny golden egg.

"I had always understood that it was the goose that laid the golden egg," remarked Mallory, bending closer to examine it. "But despite the temptation of riches, I think that I prefer the basket of flowers."

"I can see that you have a real affection for daffodils," said Elizabeth, for the woven gold wicker basket inside the second egg contained a bouquet of those flowers in bright yellow enamel. The exterior of that egg was the same yellow enamel crusted in pearls. "And I agree. It is lovely."

"And this one you must see in motion," said Lady Gregory, unlocking the case and reaching for the third egg. It was a golden egg, and she looked at Lord Mallory laughingly, "This must be the egg you were waiting for."

Raising its golden clasp, she opened it and lifted out a small golden knight on his charger. "This is St. George," she told them, "and here is his dragon."

Under the velvet liner of the egg were two tiny keys. Taking them, she carefully wound each small figure and set them on a table. St. George lifted his lance and his charger reared and then somewhat stiffly approached the dragon, which bent its head and moved forward, too, in an awkward sort of dance.

"They are wonderful!" cried Nora, clapping her hands. "I would love to have a knight and a dragon like these!"

"They were his pride and joy," said Lady Gregory. "As you can see, I left the top shelf of the case empty for his new treasure that he was bringing home? I thought perhaps it would replace St. George . . . but I suppose that it will remain empty."

Norville, who had been watching and listening attentively as she conducted them on their tour, smiled at her gently. "Perhaps not, Lady Gregory."

When the others had demanded to know what he meant by that comment, Norville had simply smiled, declining to explain. Lady Gregory had studied him closely and, as they took leave of her, had offered him her hand, saying simply that she looked forward to hearing from him soon. Nora and Lord Mallory continued to interrogate him during the carriage ride back to Grosvenor Square, but he had parried all of their questions.

As he helped the ladies to alight, he looked questioningly at Elizabeth. "Have you no questions for me, Miss Harrington?" he asked.

"I am certain that you would not choose to answer them, Mr. Norville, so—no—I have no questions." Elizabeth was determined not to give him the satisfaction of refusing to answer her questions.

He looked at her searchingly for a moment as though he were trying to determine whether or not this was anything more than a fit of pique. Then, bowing, he said his farewells to the ladies and Mallory there on the sidewalk and departed.

Mallory watched him walk away. "I wonder what he suspects," he mused aloud.

Nora was vexed. "What could he have meant?" she exclaimed. "Why does he think Lady Gregory will ever receive the egg that her husband was bringing home. Why will he not tell us? He is the most high-handed, *annoying* man!"

Elizabeth was strongly inclined to agree with her, but seeing that Nora was about to work herself into a passion that would do none of them any good, she replied in a calm voice.

"No doubt he will tell us in his own good time. After all, Nora, you answered the questions of the riddle—and they must be connected with this."

Nora brightened at this. Burton, who had been waiting patiently at the door, was finally able to usher them into the house. As they walked into the drawing room, she pulled off her York tan gloves and dropped them on a chair.

"But what could the connection be, Elizabeth?" She sat down and absently began twisting her ring, Elizabeth and Mallory watching her in an equally absent manner. Suddenly, Elizabeth sat bolt upright in her chair.

"Of course! That's it—Nora!" she exclaimed, somewhat incoherently.

Her companions regarded her blankly. "*What* is it?" demanded Nora.

"Nora—the ring, I mean—perhaps that is how the riddle works! Perhaps it is an acrostic!"

"Do you mean that it works like Nora's ring? The first letter of the name of each stone spelling her name?" asked Mallory, becoming more animated by the moment, and, in the excitement, forgetting to refer to Nora in a more formal manner.

Understanding dawned in Nora's eyes as Elizabeth hurried into the library for paper and pen. Carefully, they wrote out the answers to the questions: Nora dictating, Elizabeth recording, Mallory reading over Elizabeth's shoulder.

"'I am the beginning'—the answer to that was 'egg,' so you must record an *E*," ordered Nora, and Elizabeth obediently wrote it down. " 'I hold the key.' That is 'lock,' so we have an *L*," she continued.

"Then spring is winter's end, so we have an *S* and autumn flees from summer, so the last letter is *A*. Elsa!" she exclaimed triumphantly.

"Elsa?" Elizabeth and Mallory stared doubtfully at one another. "Who could that be? Is that the name of Sir Howard's daughter?"

"No, his daughter's name is Emma," replied Lord Mallory slowly. "But the thing is," he continued, "this isn't really an acrostic because Elsa isn't being described by all the clues."

"It is all that we have at the moment, Lord Mallory, so I believe that we should pursue it," said Nora firmly.

"Emma begins with an *E*, too," noted Elizabeth, paying no attention to their digression. "Is it possible that the other three answers are incorrect and we should have 'Emma' rather than 'Elsa'?"

Diligently, they reexamined their answers, determined that Norville would not solve the mystery alone. They reconsidered each answer. Could a money-box be said to hold the key? Or a chest? Or a door? Still, those all truly used locks to hold the key in question, and only the money box began with an *M*. There was a brief but lively argument as to whether or not May could be counted as the end of the winter, Mallory believing that it could be, Nora and Elizabeth putting up a spirited defense for spring as the answer. Finally, they all agreed that "Elsa" must be the right answer, particularly since Lady Gregory had indictated that her daughter Emma knew nothing more than she did about Sir Howard's disappearance.

"Very well," said Elizabeth, tapping her fingernail lightly against the writing table at which she was seated. "It must be Elsa. Now the question is—who is Elsa? Do either of you know anyone by that name?"

Mallory and Nora both shook their heads regretfully. "Nor do I," she responded slowly. "I cannot help but feel that there is an easy way to determine her identity. I suggest that we return to Lady Gregory and ask if she knows of anyone named Elsa. After all, if Sir Howard left this riddle as a clue, he must have expected *someone* to be able to work it out. Who is more likely to know than his wife?"

Nora, who always preferred action, agreed promptly. "We will show her the acrostic and see what her suggestions might be," she agreed, reaching for her gloves.

"We will certainly show this to her but not, I think, today. We cannot intrude a second time and, quite apart from that, we have promised Lord Dabney that we will drive in the Park with him today," replied Elizabeth. Lord Dabney, pompous and prosy, had continued to call upon Elizabeth with regularity even though she had refused his offer of marriage six years ago. Although he was not a favorite, he was dependable and devoted, and she felt that he deserved a special mark of attention from time to time.

"It's too cold," began Nora in a plaintive tone, but Elizabeth interrupted her briskly.

"Nonsense! It was not too cold to drive to Lady Gregory's, nor did you think it was too cold to drive there once again."

Nora, who was bored by the gentleman, showed signs of obstinacy, and while she gathered the shreds of her patience, Elizabeth had a moment to reflect upon how alike a mother and daughter could be. She glanced up to find Lord Mallory smiling at her in an understanding manner, his eyebrows arching as he glanced significantly at Nora.

"Is there anything I can do for you, Miss Harrington?"

"You have been extremely kind already, Lord Mallory. We do thank you for escorting us to Lady Gregory's." She paused a moment, then offered him her hand and added, "I am most sorry for your trouble, and I trust that it will all be set right."

He took her hand and pressed it lightly to his lips. "Thank you, Elizabeth. And, if there is nothing I may do for you, I must be on my way. I will do myself the honor of calling upon you tomorrow."

Turning to Nora, he added, "I am certain that my sisters will wish to call upon you as well." And nodding a brief farewell to her, he departed.

"Well, I never!" she exclaimed. "What an absence of manners—he scarcely took note of me at all! And I had no idea, Elizabeth, that you would encourage such a lack of propriety as allowing Lord Mallory to call you by your given name and to kiss your hand! I am *greatly* surprised!"

"I am rather surprised myself," Elizabeth replied thoughtfully, wondering what had initiated such gallantry on Lord Mallory's part. Then, in a more lively voice, she added, "Do go to your chamber and prepare for our ride, Nora. Lord Dabney will call for us promptly at five."

Grimacing, Nora took herself to her room to do so. Driving out with Lord Dabney and Elizabeth hardly suited her idea of an activity appropriate for a young lady who wished to be cutting a dash in London society. Lord Dabney was wealthy, he was important, he was fashionable, he was dependable—and he was definitely dull. Playing gooseberry with them would do nothing to add to her credit. He paid Elizabeth the same florid compliments time after time, and she wondered that Elizabeth chose to spend any time at all with him. Such thoughts led her inevitably to Norville.

"You have told me yourself, Elizabeth, that *you* refused several eligible offers because you decided that *you* would never marry a man who would bore you."

Remembering that Nora might indeed have to marry Norville, Elizabeth reflected ruefully that her mama had been right when she had said that all of her chickens would eventually come home to roost when she refused all of her offers in such a high-handed manner. She tried to mend the damage done by her careless tongue.

"I was very young when I said that, Nora. I thought that a man had to be handsome and dashing and fascinating, in addition to having all of the virtues I demanded. I have since learned that there are some qualities that are more important for a man to possess than others."

"Like what?" queried Nora skeptically.

"Like dependability and kindness, to mention two." Norville hopefully has at least one of the two, Elizabeth reflected silently.

"Gammon!" replied her charge, obviously unimpressed. "Does Lord Danby possess those qualities?"

"Certainly."

"And do you plan to marry him?"

Elizabeth, caught off guard, replied honestly, "Of course not."

"And why not, Elizabeth? Is it because Lord Dabney is not handsome and dashing?"

"No."

"Then why?"

"There isn't time to discuss it before Lord Dabney arrives, Nora," replied her cowardly duenna, promptly taking the easy way out of a difficult situation.

The ride was not a successful excursion. Nora insisted upon taking Sampson and Rufus on the pretext that they had had too little fresh air since their arrival. Despite being allowed to bring them, she still indicated at every point possible during the ride that she had been forced to come along. Elizabeth kept up a steady stream of light chatter to try to keep Lord Dabney from noticing Nora's lack of manners. Lord Dabney, between wondering why Miss Harrington had so suddenly become a chatterbox and why it had been thought that two small but lively animals were suitable passengers for his elegant chaise, was suitably morose.

Despite the chill in the air, a thin, watery sun had appeared in the late afternoon sky. Nora, seeing familiar figures in the distance, begged prettily to be set down for a few minutes so that Sampson and Rufus could take their exercise. Elizabeth was made immediately suspicious by the winning manner that she had assumed and informed Nora that she too felt the need of a little exercise. Lord Dabney, reading a more sinister meaning

126

into Nora's statement and fearing for his new upholstery, said hastily that they would all be walking for the next few minutes.

Nora was joined almost immediately by Anne and Maria Graham, and the three of them were followed closely by the vigilant Miss Stevenson, then by Elizabeth and Lord Dabney. To the annoyance of the latter, a rider trotted briskly up beside them and Lord Mallory bowed and spoke.

"Miss Harrington, it is a pleasure to see you again today. May I say that you look charming?" He glanced appreciatively at her handsome blue velvet pelisse and the matching bonnet with its dashing ostrich plume.

Lord Dabney, taking note of Mallory's reference to seeing her again, said in an aggrieved tone, "I called to see you this morning, Elizabeth, but Burton informed me that you were out."

"And so she was," responded Mallory wickedly, doffing his high beaver to Elizabeth and spurring his mount into a canter to join the young ladies ahead, leaving Elizabeth to soothe Dabney's ruffled dignity.

"Good afternoon, ladies. A fine afternoon for a walk," he said affably.

Nora nodded as stiffly and formally as Rufus, who was tugging at his leather lead, would allow. Mallory's defection from her court of admirers still rankled, although she had decided that he must have a curious predilection for older women, an observation which would have delighted Mallory and done nothing to endear her to Elizabeth.

Mallory's small sister Anne was clutching Sampson tightly to her green woolen cape to prevent his making an escape into the bushes nearby.

"I see that Sampson is in need of a leash of his own," her brother observed, dismounting to ruffle the kitten's fur and his sister's flaxen curls. When he stooped to pat Rufus, the pup went berserk, indicating by his frantic attempts to reach Mallory's boots that Mallory was his dearest and oldest friend from whom a cruel fate had separated him for months.

"What a very touching scene," observed a caustic voice from behind them. Lord Chawton, seated on an elegantly groomed black gelding, stared down at them disdainfully. "I see that you did not rid yourself of that small beast, Miss Lane. I thought that certainly wiser heads than yours would prevail."

Mallory was silent a moment before replying. "Not everyone agrees that leaving animals out to freeze is the way to solve a problem."

Chawton shrugged. "Not everyone can deal realistically with a problem," he countered. "And of course there is more than one way to trim any population or to face any problem." Without waiting for any response, he turned and joined the other riders that were passing.

Nora shivered slightly as he departed. "He frightens me," she murmured. "Even his voice and his eyes seem threatening."

Mallory watched him until he was out of sight, his brow creased in thought. "You need not worry, Miss Lane. It is not you he wishes to frighten."

"What do you mean, Trevor?" clamored his sisters as Miss Stevenson fluttered anxiously in the background. "Who is he trying to frighten? Is it you?"

"No, of course not," he replied hastily. "Why would he be interested in me? He is just an ill-mannered boor who tries to impress people."

Lord Dabney looked at Elizabeth intently after listening to this exchange. "What does Chawton have to do with anyone in this group, Elizabeth?" he asked in a disapproving voice.

Without waiting for a reply, he lowered his voice and added, "You know, do you not, the unfortunate story about Chawton and Lord Mallory's late brother?"

Elizabeth nodded. "He is just making himself unpleasant, Gervase, something for which he seems to have an uncommon talent. I believe he is trying to antagonize Lord Mallory."

"Mallory would do best to ignore Chawton completely," said Dabney grimly. "He is a man of few principles and a fine shot on top of that."

Elizabeth laid her hand on his arm in alarm. "Do you think he means to force Lord Mallory into a duel?"

"It is possible. He has been known to chivy young men into challenging him."

"But why? What possible motive could he have for calling out young men who are not prepared to face him?"

"Possibly because of his short temper," Dabney responded, "or possibly because they have lost a great deal of money to him in very questionable card games. Or possibly, Elizabeth, there are other, darker motives for a man like Chawton."

He paused a moment, his thoughts obviously disagreeable ones. "I had no idea that Lord Mallory's affairs were a matter of such consequence to you, Elizabeth."

Elizabeth, her hand still on Lord Dabney's arm, stared up at him. Before he could continue, their conversation was interrupted by yet another rider. This time it was Mr. Norville, who looked down at them from the back of a handsome bay. If he were pleased to see them, he concealed that emotion admirably. Indeed, he looked more formidable to Elizabeth than he did in their first encounter in the inn.

"My apologies for interrupting your tête-à-tête, Lord Dabney," he said coldly, looking not at all sorry and merely nodding to acknowledge Elizabeth's presence, "but I have a question that I need to address to Miss Harrington."

Elizabeth, irritated by his coldness and distressed by the fact that they could both see Nora and Mallory playing with Rufus, a cozy sight unlikely to please him, nodded icily in return.

He dismounted in one fluid motion, and, handing the startled Dabney his reins, took Elizabeth's arm and led her to one side. Ignoring Dabney's spluttered protest at this cavalier treatment, he asked in a cool voice, "Holding court, Miss Harrington?"

Before she could reply indignantly that she was doing no such thing, he said in a lowered voice, "You told us one evening that your mother kept a journal about jewels. Would you allow me to borrow it?"

Again stopping her before she could speak, he added, "I assure you that I would be most careful with it and return it within a very few days. This is more than a whim, Miss Harrington. It could be more important than you can possibly imagine."

Elizabeth, who was burning to ask him why he needed it and what he was looking for, gathered her thoughts quickly. "I know quite well that it would be useless for me to ask why you wish to see it, and I am trying to decide why I should allow you to read it."

He looked at her intently. "I am not in a position to tell you why I need it, Miss Harrington—and, in fact, I may well be wrong in what I am thinking. It is possible that your mother's journal will not help me at all."

"Help you in what way, Mr. Norville? In solving the riddle?" She looked at him curiously.

He did not reply for a moment, but his steady gaze never wavered from her face. "In solving a larger riddle, Miss Harrington. I can tell you no more than that. Nor, I assure you, would I ask to borrow something I know is dear to you without good reason."

Despite herself, Elizabeth agreed to allow him to see it, and, bowing low over her hand, he told her that he would call for it the next afternoon. Retrieving the reins from Lord Dabney, Mr. Norville sat once more astride his mount. He bowed to both of them.

"My thanks," he said, raising his hat.

As he cantered away, Lord Dabney stared after him and then down at Elizabeth. "What *is* going on, Elizabeth? How very peculiar your friends are coming to be!"

Elizabeth, too, was puzzled. "I can only agree, Gervase," she replied slowly. "I can only agree."

Chapter Eleven

The next day Elizabeth, Nora, and Sir Edmund attended morning service at St. George's in Hanover Square. Nora looked about her, wide-eyed at the elegance of the congregation. "They all look so important," she whispered to Elizabeth, who murmured back, "Toss a pebble in any direction and you will strike a peer." Nora could scarcely concentrate on listening to the sermon, so busy was her imagination reconstructing the many weddings that had taken place before those very altar rails, for St. George's was a very fashionable site for a wedding.

"I normally attend Grosvenor Chapel," Elizabeth told Nora after the service, "but I thought perhaps you would like to see St. George's."

"Oh, yes—although I did think I would be able to see it a little more clearly. The buildings are so close that I could not get far enough away from the front of St. George's to truly see it."

Elizabeth chuckled. "That is definitely a problem. In fact, I expect that is why they never put up the statue of King George I, in whose honor the church was built, on the pediment over the portico. No one would be able to see it except those in the first-floor windows of the buildings across the street. It is too bad that Sir Richard Grosvenor's plan did not work out, for he had intended that St. George's be at the end of a long vista from Park Lane down Grosvenor Street. That would have been a magnificent view."

Nora agreed, and they lapsed into silence for the rest of the trip to Hyde Park, Sir Edmund riding quietly alongside them.

This ride was uneventful, Nora's attention being focused on the fashionables they were passing, Sir Edmund's on their horses, and Elizabeth's on her mother's journal.

Luncheon was also a peaceful affair, with Sir Edmund regaling them with tales gleaned from his evening in the coffee room at Limmer's, a hotel patronized by the sporting world. Sampson and Rufus were draped across his boots, gathering their strength for the evening. When Sir Edmund tired of horse stories, he turned to the war.

"Well, Lizzy, that Prussian fellow Blucher defeated the Frogs at Laon, and Castlereagh has signed a treaty to continue the war until our objectives are attained. Keeps us all together for the next twenty years."

"I wonder how long it will really last," mused Elizabeth. "England, Russia, Austria, and Prussia—twenty days seems like a long time for that group to work together—twenty years seems ridiculous."

Glancing down the table at Nora, she saw that her charge's attention was fading rapidly. Before Sir Edmund could open his lips to respond to Elizabeth's comment, Nora spoke plaintively. "What time will we be going to see Lady Gregory this afternoon, Elizabeth?"

Thinking of Mr. Norville coming to pick up the journal, Elizabeth replied, "I think it would be best to wait until tomorrow, Nora. Today is rather an awkward time."

Since Nora was inclined to take exception to this ruling, it was fortunate that Mr. Scott and Mr. Keeley chose that moment to call. Nora hurried to the drawing room to receive them, and Elizabeth, grateful for the diversion, happily abandoned her luncheon to join them. She was, however, slightly less pleased when she realized that Mr. Stanton Scott had brought a sword which he proposed to use to demonstrate some of the basic rules of swordsmanship for Nora. Elizabeth firmly removed the sword from them, explaining patiently that the drawing room was no place for an unsheathed sword and that swordplay was not a suitable pastime for a young lady. Mr. Scott was abashed, Nora sulky, Mr. Keeley amused.

"Miss Kelly can use a sword," pouted Nora as Elizabeth

handed the offending item to Burton, who carried it gingerly from the room with the air of one removing a snake.

"Yes, but that is because Miss Kelly is an actress," Elizabeth replied in a damping tone, "which is certainly not what you are, my dear, nor is it what your mama would ever wish you to be." Elizabeth had a fleeting vision of Cecilia's expression if she discovered that her eldest daughter aspired to the stage.

It appeared that at least one of her callers shared that vision. "C-certainly not, Miss Lane," exclaimed Mr. Stanton Scott, horrified that the object of his devotion might consider such a possibility. "W-when you asked me to bring my sword, I t-thought that you merely wished to see it as a matter of curiosity, *not* because you truly wished to use it. Why, you could be injured!" And he paled at the thought.

"Not up to snuff, are you, old thing?" inquired his companion, Mr. Keeley, mockingly.

Mr. Scott turned upon his companion fiercely. "Miss Lane didn't ask *you* to bring your sword, Keeley. She asked *me!*"

"That's because she knew that *I* would never do so mutton-headed a thing, Scott," replied Mr. Keeley with a tone nicely calculated to infuriate his friend.

"More likely it is because she knew you wouldn't know one end of a sword from the other!" said the harried Scott scathingly. Turning to Elizabeth, he said meekly, "I do beg your pardon, Miss Harrington, for being so thoughtless."

Then, as he looked at Nora, his nervousness overcame him again. "M-Miss Lane, please forgive me for promising to do something it was n-not in my power to do. P-perhaps I can serve you in some other way."

Nora smiled sweetly. Too sweetly, thought Elizabeth suspiciously. Extending her hand to Mr. Scott, she said, "I am certain that I can rely upon you, Mr. Scott, and I shall certainly call upon you first should any need arise."

Throwing Mr. Keeley a scorching glance, her gratified admirer seated himself beside her.

Mr. Norville, who had stood unobtrusively in the doorway as Burton removed the offending sword, called attention to his presence by a discreet cough.

"I hated to disturb you, Miss Harrington," he said pleasantly, "for I saw that a lesson was in progress."

It would have been difficult to determine who in the room was least pleased to see him. Neither Mr. Scott nor Mr. Keeley was eager to welcome an older gentleman, particularly one who was acquiring something of a reputation as a sportsman, having been seen in Gentleman Jackson's Boxing Saloon going a round with the Gentleman himself, in Manton's Shooting Gallery in Oxford Street hitting the wafer nineteen times out of twenty, in Rotten Row riding a handsome, mettlesome bay that he handled to perfection.

Looking at Norville in his trim buckskins and shining Hessians, his coat of blue superfine molded to his broad shoulders, Mr. Scott was suddenly keenly aware that he was a slender, callow youth, while Mr. Keeley was acutely conscious of the fact that Norville needed no padding for the shoulders of *his* coat. Nora, already annoyed with him because of the condescending and unromantic nature of his proposal and now because of his secrecy about the riddle, could scarcely speak to him in a civil tone. Elizabeth, unpleasantly aware of the fact that he had witnessed the sword incident and doubtless was again questioning her ability to chaperone Nora, was no better pleased by his untimely appearance, but she managed to greet him with a reasonable show of politeness.

It remained for Sir Edmund, who entered the drawing room almost immediately after Norville, to extend a sincerely warm welcome. "Norville, good to see you!" he exclaimed, bustling into the room with his *Morning Chronicle* under his arm and the livestock at his heels. "Have a chair and let's discuss the happenings in France."

And, nodding to the other occupants of the room, he settled himself to do so. As Norville joined him, Elizabeth excused herself to hurry upstairs and get the journal. When she returned to the drawing room, she placed it on the Pembroke table by the door so that she could give it to Norville inconspicuously as he left.

In spite of Sir Edmund's desire to talk about France, the conversation had turned to the Duke of Diamonds, the young people firm in their opinion that the Duke was a romantic figure, Sir Edmund taking issue with them.

"No, by gad!" he exclaimed as Elizabeth opened the door. "The fellow is a *thief,* not some figure from a poem! He *steals* things!"

Nora would not allow it to be so. "He does not steal, Sir Edmund," she maintained firmly. "He does take the jewels, but he *returns* them. A thief does not return things, he keeps them."

"Of course, what a sapskull I must be," said Sir Edmund caustically. "I'd rather not have some fellow I don't know tiptoeing through my house with a dratted Easter egg in one pocket and my belongings in the other! I suppose I should be overjoyed and invite him to sit down and take a glass of port with me for his trouble!"

Mr. Scott, who had an unfortunate tendency to be somewhat literal in his understanding, considered Sir Edmund's comment with a furrowed brow. "I don't believe you would see him, sir," he objected. "I don't think anyone has actually seen the fellow returning the jewels. Only his victims have seen him as yet—and even then he was wearing a mask."

Sir Edmund stared at him. "Naturally, that would make the difference," he agreed in a disarmingly affable tone. "If I didn't see him, that would make everything as right as a trivet. I shouldn't mind so much then to have some stranger padding about the house."

"I don't think he could be a stranger," said Nora, taking up a new thread. "I believe he must be someone that people know and that's how he can manage this so well."

Sir Edmund was not prepared to yield any ground, however. "Drat it all, Nora," he said firmly, "if I found someone wandering about in my bedchamber—even if he were a friend—I'd dashed well think there was something havey-cavey afoot."

"Not if you were giving an entertainment of some sort, Edmund," Elizabeth maintained stoutly. "Or even if it weren't a large affair, just friends calling as they are at this very moment. The presence of, say, Mr. Scott in your bedchamber could be explained away in any number of ways."

Before Mr. Scott could blushingly disclaim any desire to put in an appearance in the more private portions of Sir Edmund's household, a diversion was created by the entry of Lord Mallory and his sisters and the attack of Rufus upon Mallory's boots in an attempt to welcome him to the drawing room.

Mr. Scott and Mr. Keeley politely took their leave at this point, reluctantly leaving Mr. Norville and the Grahams in full possession of the drawing room. Anne promptly scooped up Sampson, and she and Marie settled themselves on either side of Nora, who watched with irritation as their brother joined the others. *Leaving me with the children,* she thought to herself in annoyance as he pulled his chair close to Elizabeth. *And trying to turn Elizabeth up sweet.*

Sir Edmund had been unable to abandon the subject of the highwayman so suddenly. After greeting their new guests, he said abruptly, "Well, I still wouldn't want the fellow padding about my house without so much as a by-your-leave, no matter if he was returning my property!"

"I take it you have been discussing the Duke of Diamonds," remarked Mallory, his eyes twinkling at the disgust in Sir Edmund's tone.

"Duke!" snorted Sir Edmund. "Gives himself airs and so they call him a duke!"

"I understand that he takes only the choicest bits of jewelry, too," remarked Mallory, adding fuel to the fire of Sir Edmund's wrath. "Surely some discernment shows nobility of taste."

"Don't tease him," laughed Elizabeth before her outraged brother could reply. "We shall never have any peace if you do."

Obediently, Mallory promptly turned the course of the conversation by asking Sir Edmund his opinion of a horse he planned to put up for sale at Tattersall's. His attention immediately engaged by this much more important topic, Sir Edmund put aside the ethics of the Duke of Diamonds and listened attentively to Mallory's description of the animal.

Elizabeth took advantage of the distraction to take Norville to one side and give him the leather-bound journal. She had sat for some time the evening before, reading over its pages carefully for anything that could give her a clue as to why he might wish to read it but had discovered nothing.

"I am grateful, Miss Harrington," he said formally, taking it from her. "I will indeed guard it carefully and return it as soon as I possibly can."

"I'm sure that I hope it helps you, sir," she replied coolly, "although I cannot imagine how it could be of service, particularly since you have not seen fit to share your thoughts with me."

"What a Rudesby you must think me," he said, giving voice to her precise thoughts, "taking your journal with no explanation at all. Please believe that as soon as I am able to do so, I will tell you why I needed it."

Bowing briefly to her and then to the others in the room, he departed.

"What a very strange man he is," said Nora disapprovingly as soon as the door had closed after him. "What did he take with him?" she asked Elizabeth curiously.

"Nothing of consequence," said Elizabeth hurriedly, eager to avoid questions. "Just something he wished to read."

She flushed when she saw that Mallory was watching her closely. "He is an unusual man," he commented, "but I know from my brother's letters that he is an extremely capable one and — as they say — up to every rig in town. I'd give a monkey to know what's on his mind."

"A good man on a horse," said Sir Edmund approvingly, bestowing his highest accolade and recalling Mallory to their discussion.

By the time the Grahams took their leave, Nora had promised to go to see the Tower lions with them later that week.

"The children love it," explained Maria in her most grown-up voice. "George and Anne love to go. Miss Stevenson and I will take them, of course, and we thought you might like to go because the Tower is a London landmark and because we would enjoy your company, of course."

Approached in such gratifying terms, Nora was willing to honor their outing with her presence, and both parties were quite in charity with one another at their departure. Lord Mallory and Elizabeth each went their separate ways to mull over the curious behavior of Mr. Norville. And if Nora happened to be following an idea of her own concerning Lord Mallory, it was a thought she shared with no one except Rufus and Sampson.

The next day found Mallory, Nora, and Elizabeth on their way to see Lady Gregory once more, eager to share their new insight into the riddle with her. To their disappointment, they found that she had already worked it out.

"Please don't be so cast down," she said, looking at their faces. "Remember that Sir Howard enjoyed riddles greatly and so I have been exposed to any number of them."

"Did you notice that this one is not truly an acrostic?" inquired Mallory, returning to his earlier complaint.

Lady Gregory nodded. "I noticed something else as well." Taking a slip of paper from a drawer, she beckoned to them to come closer. "Look at this." On the paper were the answers.

EGG
LOCK
SPRING
AUTUMN

"Across the top, you have the word *egg* and on the third line is the word *ring.*"

"Do you think that is important?" asked Nora eagerly.

Their hostess nodded again. "I'm not sure what it all means, but after I worked it out last night, I wrote a letter to one of our old servants, Elsa Briggs."

"Elsa?" they exclaimed in chorus.

Lady Gregory smiled. "She is the only Elsa that I know. She was the nanny for our children and lives retired in the small village of Malden near our country home."

"Perhaps your husband sent the egg to her," said Elizabeth, musing over the information. "But wouldn't she have let you know?"

"Perhaps not, if she thought that the egg was for her. My husband sends her gifts occasionally, and of course all of our people know of his fondness for Easter eggs. So it is possible that she received one and thought that it was intended for her."

"Well, we must go and find out," said Nora, ready to pack her bandbox and depart.

"I quite agree that we must find out," said Lady Gregory, "but I think it would be best if we did not all go."

"Please allow me to take your letter, Lady Gregory," responded Mallory, stepping forward. "Unless you feel that this is something that you must do, in which case I would be happy to escort you."

She smiled at him. "I would be grateful to have you take the letter, Lord Mallory, and to bring back the egg, if there is one."

On the ride home, Nora was torn between excitement at the prospect of solving the puzzle and sulkiness at being denied permission to make the trip to see Elsa Briggs.

"I don't see why you get to go and we must stay here and be pokey," she complained, glaring at the offending Mallory, who smiled back at her in an aggravatingly smug manner.

"Lord Mallory can go much more quickly on horseback than he could if we went down in a carriage, Nora," explained Elizabeth patiently. "And aside from that it would be quite improper for us to accompany him."

"Fiddlesticks!" muttered Nora, consigning propriety to the winds.

"Have you no engagements, Miss Lane?" inquired Mallory. "I cannot imagine that you and Miss Harrington will be 'pokey.' I should imagine that you will be on the go every day."

This proved a happy diversion, for Nora was able to expound happily on the prospects of attending a breakfast, three routs, an evening party, and the theatre in the course of the next few days.

"And pray don't forget," Mallory reminded her, "that you agreed to visit the Tower this week. George and the girls would be dreadfully disappointed if you did not allow them to take you."

Nora assured him that she would be happy to go and, wearing her best grand-lady air, chatted in a very grown-up manner for the rest of the ride to show him that she was indeed out of the schoolroom. Elizabeth threw him a grateful smile and relaxed.

Sir Edmund had magnanimously agreed to escort Nora and Elizabeth to the parties they were to attend that evening, and he greeted them as one being led to the sacrifice.

"You look magnificent, Edmund!" announced his appreciative sister, surveying him with an admiring eye.

Sir Edmund was fingering his cravat fretfully. "Fish says that he arranged this in the Oriental style and that it is all the kick, but I must say that it is damnably uncomfortable and that it is of no particular concern to me whether I am fashionable or not."

"Ah, but think of poor Fish's feelings," remonstrated Elizabeth. "How often does he have the opportunity to display his handiwork? And besides," and here she swept her blue silk skirt into a curtsey, "tonight you are escorting two ladies who will do their utmost to be a credit to you."

"Yes, well, I suppose I must give way," he sighed, adjusting his quizzing glass to survey them. Elizabeth's gown of Geneva velvet and silk was of a deep blue that exactly matched the blue of her eyes, a color that was emphasized by her hair ornament, a gold ferronnière which held a single amethyst of the same blue in the center of her forehead. Nora was attired in a gown the color of summer sunshine, threaded with the everpresent black ribbons, her hair dressed *à la Psyche*.

Sir Edmund raised his glass to survey Nora's hair. "What is that in your hair, Nora?" he demanded, looking more closely.

Nora patted her chignon complacently. "It is a golden hairpin, Edmund."

"Well, it looks like an arrow!" said Edmund unappreciatively. "It looks like you have been attacked by some of the wild Indians that we hear about in the Colonies."

"But it looks stunning," Elizabeth hastened to assure her, seeing that Nora was beginning to bristle.

Elizabeth was aided by the unannounced arrival of Sampson and Rufus, who had taken advantage of an unwary maid opening the door of Nora's chamber to join them. As they departed down the front steps to the carriage, Burton stood at the open door, an animal under each arm.

"Poor Burton," Elizabeth laughed as the carriage pulled away. "Having animals in the house has been a terrible ordeal for him."

"For him!" snorted Sir Edmund. "It isn't his room that they make a run for whenever the opportunity presents itself, nor is it his boots that have been chewed to ribbons!"

"They have really been very good," insisted Nora, defending her pets.

"I suppose they have been better than, say, a lion and wolf

140

would have been," replied Sir Edmund with awful sarcasm, "but I do not call that *good*. I trust you will not bring home anything from the menagerie at the Tower when you go to visit."

"Don't the gaslights look splendid, Nora?" interjected Elizabeth hastily.

Nora looked out the window obediently as the carriage rolled down Pall Mall on the way to Warren House and their first party.

"It looks quite splendid," agreed Nora. "So much brighter than oil lamps."

Their first call was a terrible trial to Sir Edmund's already ragged nerves. Not only did they have to wait for some thirty minutes after reaching Warren House before they had an opportunity to even step down from the carriage, but they also had to wait for ten more before the crush of people would allow them more than a bare entrance into the building.

"If it were snowing, we'd catch our death standing here where the cold rushes in each time the door opens," he complained.

"Hush, Edmund," his sister whispered in a command. "It has been an age since you have attended anything like this. The crush merely means that their rout-party is a success."

"Well, I wish it *weren't* a success! If it were a failure, we'd be in and out in the wink of a cat's eye instead of standing here staring into the backs of total strangers."

They made their way up the great staircase of Warren House at what Sir Edmund peevishly termed a snail's pace. Elizabeth tried to distract him by pointing out the magnificent steps of Italian marble, each one twenty feet in length, but he remained unimpressed.

"Can't even see the damned things, Lizzy. There are people all over 'em. Could be made of solid gold for all I know."

At the top of the stairs they were greeted most graciously by Lady Warren, who knew Elizabeth slightly, Sir Edmund more slightly still, and Nora not at all. To Elizabeth's relief, Sir Edmund managed a civil comment or two before moving on. She found herself staring down over the crowd below, searching for Mr. Norville. It was of course impossible that such a man should be at an affair like this, for he would hate it even more than Edmund. Nonetheless, she searched for and suddenly found him.

141

He was descending the staircase, obviously on his way out. To her chagrin, she could see Lady Brill beside his upright figure as they left the party together. It mattered not at all, of course, except that it did appear that Mr. Norville was rather more susceptible to the charm of London life than he had indicated and that his marital interest in Nora seemed to be abating.

Together, the three of them made their way through the crowds in the Green Saloon, the Red Flowered Saloon, the Yellow Saloon, and the State Drawing Room, and so down the staircase. They nodded occasionally to a familiar face across the room, but conversation in the crush was impossible. At the hall door they waited for their footman to go and fetch the carriage, an errand which took no small amount of time, for the carriage had to be parked at a distance because of the crowd, and they had to wait their turn for the carriage to pull up in front to fetch them.

"And this is your idea of a delightful evening?" Sir Edmund demanded indignantly of his sister as they stood among other guests who were awaiting the arrival of their carriages. "No cards, no conversation—just parading from room to room? I have had a better time at funerals!"

It was in vain that she attempted to soothe him; every feeling had been offended, and he was compelled to share his outrage, providing general amusement for everyone except Elizabeth and Nora.

A sudden explosion of sound from the outside interrupted all attempts at conversation among those waiting, and the press grew greater as everyone tried to see what had happened in the street. An excited footman at the open door turned and relayed information to the one standing just behind him.

"What are they saying, Edmund? Can you tell?" asked Elizabeth, pulling at his coatsleeve. She could see nothing outside save glimpses of torchlight and shadows, and Nora, being much shorter, had no view at all.

"Just a moment, m' dear, let me listen. I can't have heard this right the first time."

After a minute or two he turned back to them, his expression stunned.

"Well, Edmund, do tell us!" demanded Nora. "What is happening?"

"A fellow just came clattering down the street, cutting through the carriages and running his horse along the pavement, never minding if anybody was walking along there—they say he was riding a fine black horse," he added, digressing.

"Never mind his horse, Edmund! What else was happening?"

"They said that the fellow was dressed up for a masquerade. He was all in black with a black mask covering his face and a black chapeau bras on his head. There were several riders hard on his heels."

"And why was he galloping, Edmund? Why were the other riders following him? Were they in costume, too?"

He shook his head. "It seems the masked man held up a coach on Piccadilly. On Piccadilly, of all places! Whoever heard of a highwayman on Piccadilly?"

"A highwayman!" exclaimed Nora, her eyes bright. "Was it the Duke of Diamonds?"

There was a murmur of excitement among the other listeners, for those farther back from the door had been listening eagerly to Edmund's account.

"The fellow that stopped don't know who he was. Said he held up a lady's carriage and took all of her jewels."

He paused a moment and turned back toward his source of information closer to the door. Their carriage arrived just then and they threaded their way through the crowd to reach it.

Taking pity upon Sir Edmund's misery, Elizabeth told him that they need not attend Mrs. Gooding's rout and could instead take themselves directly to the home of Sir Lawrence Lucas and his wife, who had invited them to an intimate supper.

"We will be a trifle early, but Lady Lucas will not mind it, I am sure," said Elizabeth.

"And there will be food and cards," ventured her brother hopefully, beginning to make a recovery.

"I am certain of it," she replied reassuringly.

And supper and cards they did indeed have. Sir Edmund found himself at peace with cold chicken and champagne, whist and piquet. The intimate supper was a modest gathering of about fifty friends, among whom Sir Edmund found one or two kindred

143

spirits with whom he could play cards and discuss horses, Nora discovered Mr. Stanton Scott and Mr. Keeley, and Elizabeth found herself looking about, half expecting Mr. Norville to appear and criticize her for bringing Nora.

There was no sign of him, of course, but he was soon driven from her mind by the arrival of Lord Dabney, who brought with him an account of the Piccadilly robbery.

"*Was* it the Duke of Diamonds?" Nora asked him.

"Indeed it was, Miss Lane," he replied. He inflated his chest slightly as he realized that he was the first to arrive with a reasonably full account of the evening's excitement and was therefore the center of attention.

"He stopped Lady Brill's carriage on Piccadilly and—"

"Lady Brill's carriage?" exclaimed Elizabeth. "Was she alone?"

Radiating disapproval at this interruption of his story, Lord Dabney nodded his head. "Lord Brill was not with her. She was accompanied only by servants, who were naturally of no use in the face of such danger."

Sir Edmund snorted inelegantly. "Danger? The fellow hasn't done anything dangerous yet. He's dashed unpleasant, of course, not at all the thing—but not dangerous!"

"As I was saying," Dabney continued, pointedly ignoring Sir Edmund, "her servants afforded her no protection, and so the highwayman escaped with all of the jewels she was wearing. He galloped his horse down Berkeley Street, creating havoc among the carriages and pedestrians—"

"Know that for a fact," affirmed Sir Edmund. "Saw it. Must have been a dashed good rider to make it through that crowd without an upset," he added thoughtfully, considering the situation from a new and interesting angle.

"—and cut through Lansdowne Passage—" continued Dabney doggedly.

"Lansdowne Passage! You don't mean it!" exclaimed Sir Edmund. "Down the steps and into Lansdowne Passage?"

"—and so came out in Curzon Street and must have doubled back onto Piccadilly. Somewhere along the way he got rid of his mask and black outerwear so that he would blend with the normal traffic on Piccadilly. Needless to say, they did not catch him."

"A real neck-or-nothing rider and a clever one, too," mused Sir Edmund aloud, much impressed. "There may be more to this fellow than I suspected."

"Well, it is perfectly clear that if they want to catch him, all they need do is post a watch at Lady Brill's home. We all know what the next step will be," announced Lord Dabney. His tone made it clear that that was exactly what he would do if the problem lay in his capable hands.

Nora's forehead creased in anxiety. "But you don't think they will do so, do you, Lord Dabney?"

Pleased to be consulted, he assured her that not everyone was so farsighted as he, and that Lord Brill, as well as the authorities, would probably overlook this vital precaution. Nora's expression relaxed slightly, but she was still thinking about the problem on their drive home.

"I know who the Duke of Diamonds is," she announced to Elizabeth and Edmund. "Or at least I think I do," she qualified hurriedly, seeing their startled expressions.

"How could you know, Nora?" asked Elizabeth.

"I believe that it is Lord Mallory."

"Nonsense!" responded Sir Edmund promptly. "The boy is a good rider, no question of that—excellent bottom, in fact. But this is something more than young Mallory could handle." He thought about it a moment. "And why should he be doing such a dashed queer thing, anyway?"

"Nora, you know that Mallory isn't even in London right now," Elizabeth reminded her.

"We don't know that is absolutely true, Elizabeth. And think of his hoaxes. Remember the story about moving his friend's rooms?"

"Yes, of course I remember, but that is hardly reason enough to suspect him of—" began Elizabeth.

"And even Edmund says that he is a good rider."

"But not good enough," said Sir Edmund. "Dash it all, Nora, that's what I just said. Young Mallory is a good horseman, but he couldn't do that sprint tonight without landing in the basket."

"You can't be sure of that," retorted Nora. "You just don't want to think I might be right."

"Can't see why you hope he's the one," said Sir Edmund frankly. "Not the kind of thing that you encourage your friends to do."

After thinking a moment, he added, "They say he was riding a big black horse . . ."

Conversation faded and the three were left alone with their private thoughts: Nora wondering how she could find out if Mallory was the Duke, Sir Edmund wondering where the Duke had found such a fine horse, Elizabeth wondering why Norville had not been with Lady Brill when the robbery occurred . . . and indeed why he *had* been with her earlier at Warren House.

Chapter Twelve

Morning brought no answers to any of their questions, but fortunately there was much to occupy them. Nora and Elizabeth attended a breakfast at Montclair House, and Sir Edmund departed for Tattersall's. Montclair House, which had been recently transformed by the interior decorator Walsh Porter, came as a revelation to Nora. She was accustomed to elegant homes, but never had her senses been assaulted as they were at Montclair House. The principal rooms were vivid with crimson velvet and damask, heavily trimmed with gold lace and tassel fringe, and everything that could be gilded had been. She was, in short, astonished. Elizabeth, however, had been prepared by hearing accounts of the refurbishing for months, so she was more equal to the occasion and was able to admire the paintings, the statues, the new furnishings, and to enjoy the breakfast.

They were scarcely home in time to dress for the dinner party, the breakfast having begun at three in the afternoon, and the dinner party scheduled to begin at eight. The change in parliamentary procedure over the years had occasioned a corresponding change in the hours kept by fashionable London society. Since Parliament did not begin sitting until late in the afternoon, all social occasions, dinners, parties, balls, began at later times than they once had, and all of the members of the *haut monde* slept later in the mornings. Nora had begun to adjust to London hours, and Elizabeth, of course, was already fully accustomed to them.

As they awaited the arrival of Lord Dabney, who was to be

their escort, Nora said hesitantly, "Does it not seem curious to you, Elizabeth, that we heard nothing of Lady Brill at the breakfast?"

Elizabeth looked at her in surprise. "Why, it was widely talked of, Nora. You were at my side when Mrs. Worth and Mr. Dudley described the highwayman's escape down Berkeley Street. Mr. Dudley said that his carriage was passing at that very moment."

"Yes, I don't mean the robbery, though. There has been no mention of her discovering the little Easter egg with the riddle to guide her to her jewelry. Is that not strange?"

Elizabeth smoothed her silk skirts and walked to the drawing-room window to stare down at the lighted front steps below. "It is true that the other two victims heard from him almost immediately," she agreed.

"You don't think that they did as Lord Dabney suggested and set a watch to catch him?" asked Nora anxiously.

"Had they caught him, we would surely have heard of it," was the reassuring reply. "And if they had set a watch and had seen him, even if he escaped, we would surely have heard of that. There is too much interest in the Duke of Diamonds to allow any of his movements to go unremarked."

Nora released a grateful sigh, and Elizabeth looked at her curiously. "Surely you do not still think that Mallory is the highwayman, Nora."

Nora failed to meet her eyes. "I'm not certain what I do think."

"But I don't understand what reason you have to suspect him, Nora—beyond the hoaxes, of course. Is there anything else that has occurred to make you think this is possible?"

Nora shrugged in affected carelessness. "Not really. I suppose that you are right and that he was already on his way to Malden and Elsa Briggs."

Elizabeth agreed. "Hopefully, he will return tomorrow and we will know whether or not Sir Howard corresponded with her before his disappearance."

Lord Dabney's entrance into the drawing room put a period

148

to further conversation on that topic, and Elizabeth put aside the teasing question of Nora's suspicions about Mallory. She also resolutely put aside the even more teasing question about Mr. Norville and Lady Brill, giving her attention politely to her escort, who was giving a detailed account of his mother's most recent illness.

The dinner party was at the home of Gerard Thornbridge and his wife Evelyn, a couple with whom Elizabeth had been acquainted for several years. Great was her amazement to discover that Mr. Norville was also one of the guests.

"Thornbridge and I are friends of long standing, you see," he explained, clearly amused by her discomfiture upon seeing him. "Astounding as it may seem to you, Miss Harrington, I do indeed have friends, even in London."

"I am sure that there is no reason you need not have friends, sir. Although I must admit that I suspect you are here to see how Miss Lane and I go on together."

He bowed, his eyes glinting. "And you would, of course, be quite right. I feel that I owe it to Mrs. Lane. She has written to me of her concern for her daughter."

"Cecilia has written to you?" Elizabeth asked sharply, her cheeks flushing. Lord Dabney, who had been conversing quietly with Nora and their hostess nearby, looked up, attracted by the tone of her voice.

"Is there anything amiss, Elizabeth?" he asked, frowning at Norville. He had not yet recovered from the indignity of being obliged to hold the reins for Norville in the Park.

Elizabeth shook her head and attempted a smile, anxious to avoid having him join them until she had finished speaking with Norville. Accordingly, she lowered her voice and carefully donned a pleasant expression that was in decided contrast to her words.

"And why should Cecilia be concerned about the welfare of her daughter, Mr. Norville? She is with me, is she not?"

"That, I believe, is the wellspring of her concern, for she is aware that you live a very fashionable life, and as I pointed out to her when I arrived at Braxton Hall to discover that Miss

Lane had departed with you, a fashionable miss is *not* what I wish to marry."

Elizabeth managed to maintain a cool smile, mentally berating Cecilia for toadeating this overbearing man. Whether or not Nora became a "fashionable miss" was a matter of concern to Cecilia only because it was important to Norville, who held the keys to Braxton Hall. She could have gladly boxed her lovely cousin's ears had she been present. Since she could not, she smiled in a deceptively pleasant manner at the root of the problem.

"I was amazed to see that you did not walk behind us at Warren House last night, Mr. Norville, so that you could keep watch over Miss Lane. I saw you leaving much earlier with Lady Brill, who is, I believe, quite a fashionable woman herself."

Norville paused a moment before replying. "As you say, Miss Harrington, I believe that Lady Brill is indeed very fashionable, and as I said, I do not wish to marry a fashionable woman." And, bowing stiffly, he moved away to speak with a silver-haired gentleman on the other side of the saloon.

When they went in to dinner, Lord Dabney escorted Elizabeth, and she had the dubious pleasure of seeing Mr. Norville offering Nora his arm. It was obvious to Elizabeth from Nora's manner that Norville's attempts to make himself more acceptable to her were meeting with success, and she had ample opportunity during dinner to have this observation confirmed. She was, she told herself, pleased that he had used some degree of good sense; nevertheless, he did not seem to her the man for Nora.

The dinner began with a surprise, for Evelyn Thornbridge had placed a small gilt egg at each place.

"I saw them in a shop on Oxford Street yesterday, and I couldn't resist," she commented as her guests were being seated. "It seemed so timely, what with the Duke of Diamonds making his rounds. The proprietor of the shop told me that there has been a sharp increase in the demand for Easter eggs since he made an appearance."

150

"And do they contain riddles that will lead us to our own treasures?" inquired Mr. Henry Snowdon, a tall, slender gentleman seated across the table from Elizabeth.

"No, no, they don't open I'm afraid," laughed his hostess. "But it is amazing, is it not, that he seems to know his victims so well?"

The remainder of the dinner was devoted to the discussion of London's latest sensation and speculation about his identity. Elizabeth was amused to hear the candidates proposed: everyone from their host, Gerard Thornbridge, to the Prince Regent himself was suggested and discussed.

"No, I am *not* the one!" exclaimed Thornbridge. "Why, you would not find me facing the pistols of a coachman."

"And I don't believe His Royal Highness could have made that dash down Piccadilly," remarked another. "Too hard on his stays," he added irreverently.

It was inevitable, Elizabeth thought, that Mallory's name would come up. As they cast about for more likely suspects, Lady Rosenby remembered the Hill Street hoax and recounted it.

"You could be onto something there," agreed Thornbridge. "Young Mallory is one of those hey-go-mad fellows, and he can ride like the very devil."

"*And* he is welcomed into all of the best homes," added someone else.

Elizabeth finally brought herself to look at Nora, who was sitting very still, her face pale, studying her plate attentively. Mr. Norville, too, had noticed her preoccupation and caught Elizabeth's eye with a glance fraught with meaning. Sure that he was thinking that she was responsible for allowing Nora's all-too-obvious attachment to Mallory, she sat in seething silence, prepared to do battle when the occasion arose.

As it happened, however, she did not have to confront Norville that evening. When the gentlemen joined the ladies in the drawing room for coffee, Mr. Norville had already made his departure, sending his regrets to his hostess.

"I am sorry that Norville could not join us," said Mrs.

Thornbridge. "He is such an asset to any hostess, and we so seldom see him in London."

Elizabeth chuckled when she saw that Nora was staring with wide, disbelieving eyes at her hostess. It certainly did not seem to two of the ladies present that he was an ornament to any social gathering. Even though he had made some progress with Nora, this was a bit too strong for her.

"Such a fine-looking man," agreed Lady Rosenby, a tall, striking brunette. "It was a pity to waste him on Caroline Sale. I was very hopeful that he would come back to London after she married Brill, for I certainly had my eye on him, but it was of no use. It was off to the wars with him."

"What did happen with Lady Brill after her robbery?" inquired someone else. "Did she find her Easter egg and her jewels?"

Lady Rosenby, who seemed to know everything, shook her head. "She has not found them yet, I understand. Of course, from what I know of Brill, those jewels that the Duke took from her were probably paste and not worth the price of the Easter egg. Perhaps he knows that Brill is all to pieces and decided that the jewels weren't worth the trouble of returning them."

She chuckled and turned to Nora, who was sitting next to her. "*I* wouldn't mind being robbed by the Duke, my dear, would you? Particularly if he is young Mallory."

It was fortunate that she did not truly expect an answer and that the conversation flowed on, for Nora sat as one transfixed, oblivious to Lady Rosenby and, thought Elizabeth unhappily, to all else save her own thoughts. She had Lord Dabney take them home at the first possible moment after tea had been served, eager to remove her charge before she betrayed her intense interest in Mallory.

Elizabeth was grateful that the next day brought the Graham girls and Miss Stevenson to bear Nora away to see the lions.

"You will love the menagerie, Nora," Anne assured her confidently as she sat on the carpet of the drawing room with Rufus in her arms, ignoring Miss Stevenson's clucking reminder

152

that young ladies seated themselves upon chairs. "What is your favorite animal?"

"Elephants," Nora responded promptly. "I have a great affection for them because they are so clever." Elizabeth felt that it was as well that Edmund was not hearing this. He would have immediate visions of an elephant arriving on the doorstep, probably harboring plans to sleep at the foot of his bed.

Elizabeth was relieved to see that Nora was being attentive and could respond promptly to Anne. She had been wandering about in a fog during the earlier part of the morning, oblivious to anything going on about her, so absorbed was she in her own thoughts. At least she was now paying attention to someone outside herself, even though they had not yet heard from Mallory.

"How is your brother?" asked Nora diffidently.

"Oh, George is fine," responded Anne. "He is waiting for us in the carriage."

"Oh, well, I am glad of that, of course." She paused a moment. "How does Lord Mallory go on?"

"He told Mama that he had to leave London on a business trip," responded Maria, "and I don't think he has yet returned."

Her curiosity satisfied, they departed for the Tower, Anne promising Rufus a treat upon their return.

The Tower was an impressive sight, and Maria pointed out to Nora the White Tower, built by the Normans over seven hundred years ago. She was astounded by the sheer size of the Tower, for it covered eighteen acres and was still in use as an arsenal, garrison, state prison, mint, repository for the Crown jewels, and zoo. A great wall in which were built thirteen towers surrounded the White Tower.

Together the little group ventured across the stone bridge that spanned the moat. Within the walls were several streets and a host of buildings, presided over by an officer of the army called the Constable of the Royal Palace and Fortress of London. The forty warders were dressed in scarlet coats with large sleeves and flowing skirts, edged in several rows of gold lace, and bound with a broad girdle around the waist. On their heads they wore round, flat caps.

They rang the bell for the keeper of the menagerie and paid him a shilling to show them the animals and tell about them. To Nora's disappointment there was no elephant, but she was comforted by the presence of lions, tigers, leopards, panthers, hyenas, a Spanish wolf, an ant bear, and assorted mountain cats and raccoons. She was pleased to see that their dens were clean and well-cared for, each having two stories and being separated from the public by iron gratings.

The irrepressible George had joined them by the tigers, prepared to offer them biscuits from his pockets.

"Don't do that, George," scolded Anne. "They don't like for you to bother the animals."

"Or for the animals to bother you if they are especially hungry," cautioned Miss Stevenson.

"Then I'll eat them. I need them to keep up my strength, Annie girl," said her unrepentant brother.

She sniffed. "What do you use your strength for, George? Certainly not for your studies. I heard Mama say so."

"Well, you shouldn't have been listening, for I'll wager she wasn't saying it to you."

"No, she was telling Trevor," said Anne, hoping to discomfit him at least a trifle.

"That's all right then. Trevor is a great gun! He won't mind. Why, he even gave me a guinea when—"

"Yes, we know, George," said Marie hastily, cutting him off before he could give them his twentieth account of the Pancake Greaze. "And we're all glad that Trevor gave you the money."

"Do you ever go riding with your brother?" inquired Nora of George as they made their way back across the bridge to the outside world.

His small face lighted up with pleasure. "Sometimes—mostly at Chanderley though and not here."

"Does Lord Mallory sometimes ride a fine black horse?" she asked artfully.

"That would be Midnight!" exclaimed George. "Michael used

154

to ride him, but Trevor says that he's dangerous. Why, Trevor says—"

Before George could continue his cataloging of Trevor's comments, Lord Mallory himself rode up next to them. As he dismounted amidst a clamorous greeting, he smiled across the heads of his family at Nora. As soon as the opportunity afforded, she whispered, "Did you discover anything?"

He nodded grimly. "I have already been to Lady Gregory. I will tell you about it later this afternoon."

Before she could restrain herself, Nora asked tartly, "And have you already told Elizabeth?"

"Ah, the radiant Elizabeth!" He smiled, his eyes alight. "How could I stay long away from her?" he asked teasingly.

Her eyes darkened, but before she could reply, he said soothingly, "Never mind. I have not yet been to Grosvenor Square. I will escort you home and stay when the children leave to tell both of you what has happened."

With that Nora was compelled to be satisfied, but it seemed a very long while before they all had their ices, were set down in Grosvenor Square and visited politely in the drawing room, then escorted Miss Stevenson and the children to the door. Not until then could she and Elizabeth be allowed the satisfaction of learning Lord Mallory's news.

Chapter Thirteen

When they were left alone, both ladies turned to him eagerly. "Well?" Nora demanded. "What happened in Malden? Did you find Elsa Briggs?"

Lord Mallory shook his head. "She no longer lives there with her sister," he replied. "It seems that her sister was taken ill, and they both moved to be closer to their brother and his family. I learned all of that from the family that moved into their cottage."

"And did you discover their direction, Lord Mallory?" cried Elizabeth. "How dreadful to come so close and to miss her!"

"I was not the first one to come so close," said Mallory grimly. "There had been three others there before me—two gentlemen and one lady."

"Three others!" exclaimed Elizabeth, and she and Nora stared at him in disbelief. "Why would so many be looking for Elsa Briggs?"

"It would seem that there are several people who not only have heard the riddle, but have also worked out its answer," replied Mallory.

"And did all of them learn her new address?" demanded Nora.

Mallory nodded. "And I would remind you that there may have been others who came to call on her before she moved away."

"That is so!" exclaimed Nora, collapsing onto a dainty sofa in an unladylike heap. "The egg could have been found before she moved."

156

"But I don't think it was," replied Mallory. "I asked whether Miss Briggs had received any packages since they had been living there. Mrs. Dobbins, the new tenant of the cottage, told me that a package came for Miss Briggs about six months ago, apparently from 'foreign parts,' as she put it. It had been greatly battered during its journey, and she decided to send it to Miss Briggs by hand when her eldest son was making a trip in that direction, so the package wasn't delivered until about three months ago."

"How clever of you to ask about the package, Trevor!" crowed Nora, forgetting propriety in the excitement of the moment. "Had any of the others—the two gentlemen and the lady, I mean—had any of them asked about it?"

"I'm afraid so. One of the men and the lady had inquired. The lady called upon them about a week ago, the gentleman shortly afterwards."

Elizabeth had been sitting quietly, trying to fit together the bits of information. "Did Mrs. Dobbins learn the names of any of the other callers?" she asked.

Mallory shook his head. "All that she could tell me was that one of the men was dark, one *quite* fair, and the lady *very* fair and *very proud.*" He grinned. *"And she said that they were all nip-farthings* save one, who did offer her something for her trouble. I don't believe she thinks highly of the gentry."

Entertained by this bit of news, Elizabeth responded, her eyes dancing, "I certainly hope that you took the hint, Lord Mallory, and gave Mrs. Dobbins something for her pains."

Mallory assumed a serious tone. "I'll have you know, Miss Harrington, that I am no cheese-paring fellow. By the time I left Malden, Mrs. Dobbins was convinced that I was a gentleman of the first rank."

Nora regarded him disapprovingly. "This is no time for making a cake of yourself with Elizabeth, Lord Mallory."

"How is it that I was Trevor a few moments ago, and now I am again Lord Mallory?"

Nora flushed. "I have merely been in company with your sisters," she said hastily, "and had grown accustomed to hearing them speak of you so."

He bowed. "Please continue to do so. When you call me Lord Mallory now, I feel that you are displeased with me."

"And so I am!" she replied petulantly. "Why, here we sit like ninnyhammers, wasting time when the others may be seeking out Miss Briggs this very moment!"

"Ah, but I am not so paperskulled as you seem to think, Miss Lane. At this very moment Lady Gregory is calling upon Miss Elsa Briggs."

Both ladies leaped up from their places, Nora catching at his sleeve. "Do you mean that Miss Briggs resides in London?"

"I mean precisely that," he laughed, smoothing his sleeve with a reproving glance at Nora. "If Miss Lane will leave my jacket intact and if you ladies will put on your pelisses, we will adjourn to Lady Gregory's drawing room where we will await her return."

And so it was that when Lady Gregory arrived home, she had an attentive audience awaiting her. They noticed with sinking hearts that she was empty-handed.

Seeing their expressions, she shook her head. "I'm afraid that we don't have it. It is true that my husband did mail Elsa an Easter egg. It was very slow in making its way to Malden, however, and by the time it reached her cottage, she had moved here to London."

Mallory nodded. "I have told Miss Harrington and Miss Lane about that part of the story."

She looked at the other ladies. "You know then that it did not finally reach Elsa until just before Christmas. By that time, poor Elsa had fallen ill herself after months of nursing her sister, who was still in poor health. Their brother has a large family, and life in London is quite expensive, so they were growing desperate when Sir Howard's gift arrived. The egg, it seems, was quite a lovely one, and her oldest nephew told her that he had seen some like it before in the shops along Ludgate Hill and on Bond Street. It seemed the most practical thing to the old lady to send him along to see if any of the shops would like to purchase it so that she and her sister might live on the proceeds for at least a while."

She paused a moment. "I am quite sure that Elsa did not fully realize how valuable it might be, so I am sure that she did not receive what she should have for it. I must do something for her."

"But did her nephew sell it?" asked Nora, leaning closer to Lady Gregory in her anxiety.

"Oh, yes, I'm afraid that he did. Just at Christmas, too, although of course it was not nearly so likely to sell then as it is now."

"To which shop did he sell it?" inquired Elizabeth. "We must go immediately to see if we can trace it."

Lady Gregory shook her head. "I'm afraid not. We don't know which shop the nephew sold it to, and he went to sea some six weeks ago."

They all sat in silence for a few moments, mulling over this latest bit of bad news. Finally Elizabeth, remembering how important this matter was to Lady Gregory and Lord Mallory, sat up and straightened her shoulders purposefully. Nora, who had been watching her hopefully, sat a little straighter, too.

"Then we must take down a description of it and visit all of the shops we think likely ones for her nephew to have visited. What did Miss Briggs say the egg looks like, Lady Gregory?"

Lady Gregory looked more hopeful herself. "From Elsa's description, I believe it is an enamel egg of red and gold, more the size of a goose egg than a hen egg, and it is decorated with colored stones. I should imagine that the colored stones are real jewels, although Elsa didn't appear to realize that."

"Is there any pattern to the stones?" asked Mallory.

"Elsa said that they were arranged to look like flowers," she replied.

Nora could not bear being left out. "Does the egg open like a jewel case or is it solid?"

Lord Mallory looked at her approvingly as he listened to Lady Gregory's response. "It opens and is lined with red velvet, although there was nothing found inside it."

159

"Are the stones arranged all around the egg, or just on the top?" asked Elizabeth.

"They are crusted all around," she replied, "and the colors of the stones vary."

"Is there anything else, any mark, to distinguish it?" asked Lord Mallory.

"Elsa said that there was a tiny *G* engraved just above the clasp, which she of course thought stood for Gregory."

"Well, now that we have some idea what we are looking for, we had best begin," said Elizabeth, "for we may be sure that the others are looking, too."

"Had the others visited Miss Briggs, too?" asked Nora.

"Her sister had told the gentleman who called first, but Elsa was frightened by that and told her sister not to discuss the matter with anyone else."

"So we have one other party searching for the egg," mused Elizabeth.

"We will begin this very afternoon," announced Nora firmly.

And so it was that they found themselves at Ludgate Hill within the hour, prepared to begin their search at Rundell and Bridge, the celebrated goldsmiths and diamond merchants. Although their display cases did contain some jeweled eggs in honor of the season, there was none answering the description of Elsa's egg. Mr. Rundell was delighted to welcome them to his store, but when questioned by Lord Mallory, he had no recollection of such an egg as they described to him. When they evinced no interest in any of those he had available, he regretfully accompanied them to Lord Mallory's carriage, urging them to visit again.

They paid two more calls that afternoon, neither of which was fruitful. Discouraged, they returned Lady Gregory to her home, agreeing to meet again the following afternoon, and then made their way to Grosvenor Square.

"At least it was not a complete waste of an afternoon," remarked Nora, patting the small package she carried. She had purchased a pair of small gold earrings for Cecilia at their last stop, for Mothering Sunday would be coming soon, and she intended to mail her mother the gift. "I wonder how Sir Howard's egg fits the riddle," she wondered aloud. " 'I am the beginning' was the egg itself. 'I hold the key' makes you think that it has something in it, but I have no idea about the other two lines."

They all sat silently, thinking over their problem as the carriage rolled along Grosvenor Street. Finally, Elizabeth said, "And Lady Gregory pointed out that the word *ring* appeared in the answers to the riddle, but there was no ring in the egg that came to Elsa."

"Or at least there was no ring in it when it reached her," said Mallory morosely. "I wonder what Chawton thinks was in that package that Michael carried."

Since the ladies had no answer to his question, they continued to ride in silence until they reached Elizabeth's door, at which time Lord Mallory, remembering his manners, attempted at least the appearance of good-humored attentiveness.

"Will I see you at the Binghams' rout tonight?" he asked as he showed them to the door.

Informed that they would indeed be present, he bowed to them as Burton ushered them into the house. There they found Sampson stalking Rufus, who was lying comfortably in a patch of sunlight, oblivious to his peril.

"Miss Lane's pets have been taking their exercise indoors this afternoon, Miss Elizabeth," Burton told her stiffly, his tone indicating that their exercise had afforded little pleasure to other members of the household.

"Miss Lane will take them upstairs with her now, Burton," Elizabeth said hastily, preparing to scoop up Sampson.

She was unfortunately too late, and Sampson alighted upon his quarry. Rufus sprang from the floor and raced from the entrance hall, Sampson still clinging to his back. It appeared that his nap had renewed his strength, for he ran as one possessed, describing a large circle that took him through all of the rooms on that floor, and finally collapsed in a heap at Elizabeth's feet. Not daring to look at the outraged Burton, she picked up Rufus and Sampson and handed them both to Nora, then escaped to her own room.

The evening party at the Binghams was a pleasant one. There were enough couples for dancing, and Lord Mallory appeared to have recovered his spirits enough to make one of the company, offering his arm first to Elizabeth and then to Nora for dancing. Nora was somewhat affronted to be second choice, but as she was called upon to dance every dance, there was no danger of her taking her place in one of the chairs by the wall where the older people sat. Elizabeth chose not to dance most of the dances so that she could better keep an eye on her young charge, so she was pleased to have Mallory join her. Sir Edmund, having already made the supreme sacrifice in escorting them, had been freed of further duties to retire to the card table.

"Did you hear about Lady Brill?" Mallory asked her as they watched Nora whisk by on the arm of Sir Adrian Mayhew.

"That she was robbed in her coach on Piccadilly? Yes, indeed."

"No, no—the most recent news is that our Duke revisited her at her home. When she awoke this morning, she found the Easter egg and the note just beside her on the pillow."

"And did she find everything that had been taken?"

"So it would seem—and I understand that she was quite charmed by the whole thing. They say that the Duke wrote her a very pretty note. But Lord Brill is in quite a pelter over the robbery. Says he will call out the Bow Street Runners and drag the Duke before the magistrates by his heels."

"But why is he still so distressed if Lady Brill recovered all of her jewels?"

Mallory chuckled. "Brill says his privacy has been invaded and he won't have it! Adrian says he was cutting up pretty stiff at Tattersall's. The talk there was that Lady Brill's jewels are probably paste, and he was afraid that the Duke would bandy it about."

"The Duke doesn't seem to be too worried about being caught," remarked Elizabeth casually, thinking of Nora's suspicions and watching Mallory carefully from the corner of her eye.

"What does he have to fear?" he asked in amusement. "As yet he hasn't really stolen anything—just made a sort of May-game of his victims."

"Indeed he has," agreed Norville, appearing suddenly on the other side of Elizabeth. Mallory rose to greet him, and Norville, looking down at Elizabeth, remarked, "I would not have thought to find you merely watching the dancers, Miss Harrington. You never lack for willing partners, I have noticed, so it must be that you find the company very pleasant." And he raised one dark eyebrow in Mallory's direction.

Before Elizabeth could make the sharp retort that she felt rising to her lips, Mallory smiled good-naturedly and said, "Naturally she does, Norville. Join us and you will find just how charming our company is."

To her surprise, Norville gazed intently at the two of them for a moment and then replied, "I believe I shall." And to Elizabeth's annoyance and delight—and she could not determine which was uppermost—he did just that, drawing up a chair beside her.

Ignoring him rather pointedly and returning to her topic, she said to Mallory, "And so you think the Duke has nothing to fear?"

He shook his head decidedly. "Not in the least. No one but a sapskull like Brill would talk of Bow Street."

"I would not underestimate Brill," said Mr. Norville. "He may not be a gentleman that you would welcome in your drawing room, but that does not mean that he is caper-witted. He is, in fact, quite clever, I believe." He looked very hard at Mallory. "It would be a serious mistake to underestimate him," he repeated.

Mallory waved it off. "Well, Brill is nothing to me, and I am certain that the Duke can take care of himself if he will but give up Piccadilly as one of his haunts. He seems a most capable fellow."

Then, rising from his place, he bowed to Elizabeth. "I know, ma'am, that you dance no more this evening, but as Mrs. Bingham informed me earlier that she is short of gentlemen,

163

I must go and do my duty. So, if you will excuse me."

Watching him lead out a quiet young girl who had not yet danced that evening, Norville remarked, "He seems a pleasant enough young man. Steadier than I would have thought after hearing some of the stories about him."

"Oh, he is indeed a very charming young man," agreed Elizabeth warmly, for Mallory had found a place in her affections.

"But, as you say, ma'am, he is quite a *young* man—a trifle young for you, is he not?"

Elizabeth turned to glare at him, her color rising quickly as it always did when she was angry. "Just what do you mean by that, Mr. Norville?" she demanded.

His amused expression did nothing to soothe her. "I mean just what you think I mean, Miss Harrington," he responded genially, quite as though they were discussing the weather or some other innocuous topic. "I would have expected you to cast out lures for someone a trifle older and more experienced than young Mallory, and, indeed, I feel quite responsible since—"

"Cast out lures?" she gasped in disbelief. "Do you truly think that I am *casting out lures* for Lord Mallory? I assure you, Mr. Norville, that I have no need to do so."

"Is he as far gone as all that?" inquired Norville in a serious tone. "I did not realize that he was that smitten. Had it not been for the presence of Miss Lane, I feel that this situation would not have arisen, so I do feel—"

But Elizabeth did not care to know what he felt. Standing up so abruptly that she almost lost her balance and he had to take her arm to steady her, she said through clenched teeth, "You have the most abominable manners of any man that I have ever met! I would advise you to take lessons in gentlemanly behavior from Lord Mallory!" And jerking her arm away, she started to march from the room.

Before she could take more than a step, however, Mr. Norville had reclaimed her arm and had turned her firmly toward the refreshment table.

"What do you think you are doing, sir?" she demanded in a low voice. "Let go of me at once!"

He smiled down at her in an irritatingly superior manner. "I am keeping you from making a spectacle of yourself, Miss Harrington."

Startled, Elizabeth glanced up and saw that they were indeed being watched by several interested spectators. Although inwardly berating Norville for placing her in such an awkward position, she forced herself to smile pleasantly up at him.

"I realize, of course, that as Nora's chaperone you think I must be above reproach," she said, her acid tone in sharp contrast to her sweet smile.

He stopped beside an artfully arranged group of potted palms that offered them a degree of privacy and looked down at her with a serious expression. "I owe you an apology, Miss Harrington," he said somewhat stiffly. "I realize that I have no right beyond my connection with Miss Lane to interest myself in your affairs."

Elizabeth, surprised by his apology, gave a brief, angry nod to acknowledge her agreement. Then, aware that prying eyes still watched them, she resumed her smile to continue the conversation. "Indeed you do not, sir. And you were most insulting as well."

He smiled ruefully. "I realize, too, that you have no need to cast out lures, Miss Harrington. I merely said that because—" But here he stopped abruptly.

"Because of what?" she inquired curiously, studying his dark countenance. A most unaccountable man, she thought to herself, quite unlike any that she had known. His expression revealed nothing of his thoughts. Undoubtedly his years of service as a secret agent had caused this, and she found herself wondering what he had been like when he was young and madly in love with Caroline Sale. She was shaken from her brief reverie when his dark eyes met hers.

"I seem always to be at my worst with you and Miss Lane," he said softly. "I suppose that you would not believe that this is not my manner with everyone."

"I have heard that it is not. Lady Rosenby, for instance, appears quite taken with you."

A glimmer of a smile touched his eyes. "Lady Rosenby is a charming woman," he acknowledged, "although she is most definitely—"

"A flirt?" inquired Elizabeth innocently. "I believe that she is called so. How curious that what you find a charming quality in Lady Rosenby you consider somewhat less captivating in me."

He was silent for a moment, and she found herself flushing under the intensity of his gaze. "You are mistaken, Miss Harrington. I find you far more captivating than Lady Rosenby."

Elizabeth was caught off her guard, but she rallied quickly. Infamous man, she thought to herself. Doubtless this was another of his delightful little tests.

"How well you have concealed it, Mr. Norville," she replied tartly. "I assure you that no one, myself least of all, would have suspected it."

It was as though she had not spoken. He continued to regard her intently. "And do you mean to accept Mallory when he offers for your hand?"

Elizabeth was staggered by his question, but she refused to let her confusion show. She raised her chin, and her tone became glacial. "I cannot see that that is any affair of yours, Mr. Norville."

He bowed stiffly. "Forgive me, Miss Harrington. As you say, it is indeed no affair of mine. I must apologize again for my lack of address."

He turned quickly and walked from the room, leaving Elizabeth's thoughts in a whirl. He had behaved for a moment as though he had a personal interest in her. Whatever had caused the man to behave in such a manner? Then she reminded herself that his work had made him a gifted actor and that this was doubtless one of his little tests for her as Nora's chaperone. Glancing about her, she saw that she was still the subject of some interest, so she smiled nonchalantly and strolled casually to her seat to watch the dancers.

The rest of the evening did nothing to restore Elizabeth's opinion of Mr. Norville. After a brief interlude, he returned to the party and solicited Nora's hand for the next dance. He made himself so agreeable that Nora was completely in charity with him. The final straw came when Sir Edmund informed her that he had told Norville that they were sorry not to see more of him in Grosvenor Square and that he had invited him to dinner the following evening. "For you know that we're at home tomorrow night, Lizzy," he reminded her. "You told me I must be there to escort you and Nora to the theatre."

"And I suppose you invited Mr. Norville to attend the theatre with us as well," said Elizabeth bitterly.

Missing the tone of her voice entirely, her brother returned blithely, "Well, I'm not so rag-mannered as to leave him here in our drawing room while we go off to the Drury. I'll just step round and pick up the tickets at Mitchells' tomorrow morning."

Sir Edmund was so obviously pleased with himself in making this contribution to their amusement that Elizabeth did not have the heart to tell him just what she was thinking. Nora, however, noticed her irritation and approached her about it later when they were alone.

"Do you not think, Elizabeth, that Mr. Norville improves upon acquaintance? I still do not wish to marry him, of course, but he is not the ogre I thought him at Braxton Hall."

Elizabeth forced herself to swallow all of the extremely uncomplimentary observations she longed to make about Mr. Norville. It was still possible, after all, that Nora might marry him, in which case it would be too bad of her to abuse him now. So she smiled as pleasantly as she could, and said, "It is merely that Mr. Norville and I view some matters differently, Nora, and sometimes it is difficult for us to be easy with one another. But of course he is not an ogre." She mentally toted up a list of things that she could call him that would be much more appropriate and felt somewhat better. Nora, too, looked relieved and retired happily to bed.

The next morning, as they were sipping their chocolate and looking over their mail, Nora gave a sudden crow of excitement that caused Rufus to bolt upright from his postbreakfast nap.

"Look, Elizabeth! It is an invitation to a masked ball! Find

167

yours quickly—it is in a large blue envelope like this one!" she cried, waving hers in the air. "Can we go? Oh, do say that we can!"

"Yes, of course we can, Nora, Perhaps we can have Lord Dabney escort us."

Nora's face fell, and Elizabeth chuckled.

"All right, I give in—*not* Lord Dabney."

"Do you mind very much, Elizabeth? If it will distress you, of course we will ask him."

"No, it won't distress me at all, but I think that we will have to do a little planning and determine how we will ensnare Edmund. He detests masquerades."

"Edmund need not go if he doesn't wish to, Elizabeth. Why, Sir Adrian or Mr. Scott or even Lord Mallory would escort us. They have offered ever so many times to squire us anywhere we wish to go."

Mindful of Mr. Norville's strictures, Elizabeth demurred, saying that they would simply have to use their wiles on Edmund.

"Well, what of Mr. Norville? He has offered to be of service, too."

"No!" said Elizabeth hastily. "We will make it a family party, and you may dance with all of the gentlemen once we are there."

"What will you go as, Elizabeth? Have you thought about it?"

Elizabeth laughed. "Not yet, Nora. I just received the invitation."

"Well, I know what I wish to go as," announced Nora. "I have been hoping and hoping that we would be invited to a masquerade."

"And what will your costume be?"

Nora arched her brows mysteriously. "Wait and see. I daresay you would not even recognize me."

Before Elizabeth could pursue this line of conversation to see what her charge was up to, Sir Edmund entered the room in an innocently carefree state of mind.

"Going to help young Mallory pick out a hunter today," he

announced brightly, attacking his beefsteak with gusto. "I'd like to take a peep at those cattle of his brother's, too, to help him decide what to do with them." If Sir Edmund had announced that he had received a gift of fifty thousand pounds, he couldn't have sounded more pleased. He didn't notice when Nora moved her chair slightly closer to his.

"Edmund, have you ever wished that you were someone else? Have you ever longed for a more exciting life?"

He looked at her blankly. "Eh? Why would I wish a thing like that?"

"Wouldn't you love to be a gypsy and take to the open road?" she asked in a burst of romantic fervor.

Edmund looked indignant. "Well of course I wouldn't want to!" he replied. "Deuced uncomfortable living under a hedge on that open road."

"Oh, no, Edmund, they live in gaily painted little wagons that would be *very* cozy, and they sing and dance around the open fire at night . . ."

Edmund would have none of it. "Dance round a fire? What sort of cork-brained notion is that? I should like to see me making a cake of myself by hopping around some fire. Why, I'd have to wear earrings, too, I suppose, and let them make little holes in my ears."

He looked closely at Nora's eyes. "It's my belief, my girl, that you're running a fever and should be got to bed as soon as possible."

Elizabeth pushed her invitation in front of her brother, laughing. "You need not worry about Nora, Edmund. She is just excited about going to a masquerade. This will be her first."

His expression relaxed, but he was still wary. "Living in a pretty little cart don't sound a farthing better than camping under a hedge," he noted, returning to the consolation of his beefsteak. Elizabeth signed to Nora to leave him in peace, but as they left the dining room, they heard him murmur, "Damned good with horses, those gypsies . . ."

Feeling that they had made their first inroads with Sir Edmund regarding the masquerade, the ladies joined Lord Mallory and Lady Gregory to continue the search for Sir Howard's egg. Their search that day carried them to Oxford Street, which offered so many diversions that they could scarcely keep Nora from entering each shop they passed. Having lost her to a shop filled with slippers that displayed a pair just the right size for Cissy's doll at home, Elizabeth left Lady Gregory and Mallory to retrieve her and walked back down the street to Teasdale's, the last goldsmith that they planned to visit that afternoon.

Pausing at the window, she stared intently at the displays. There, elegantly arranged on a piece of black velvet were several jeweled eggs, each one on a delicate little stand. She scrutinized each one carefully and was delighted to see that one was a red enamel egg decorated with gold and jewels. Bending closer, she tried to see if there were a *G* engraved above the clasp.

"Good afternoon, Miss Harrington. It is, as always, a pleasure to see you."

Elizabeth straightened immediately and turned to face Mr. Norville, who politely doffed his hat to her. "Good afternoon, Mr. Norville," she replied coolly, "I am afraid that honesty prohibits my saying that it is always a pleasure to see *you.*"

He smiled disarmingly. "Delivering a few home truths, Miss Harrington? You encourage me. I had no notion that young ladies reared in Mayfair honored truth above the social pleasantries."

Elizabeth did not allow herself to respond. She merely smiled frostily and turned back to the window, admiring a necklace and earrings at the side opposite from the eggs.

"It is astonishing how one keeps tripping over eggs these days, is it not?" he inquired, keeping his place beside her and looking down at the egg she had just been inspecting. "I believe that Miss Lane is quite right—there are eggs and riddles everywhere."

At that point, Nora and Lord Mallory strolled from the slipper shop out onto the pavement, Lady Gregory still lingering

170

inside. Mr. Norville looked down at Elizabeth, his eyes suddenly hard.

"Not troubling yourself to chaperone your charge, Miss Harrington? Mallory must find it most convenient to have you turn a blind eye to Miss Lane's activities, but I doubt that her mother would approve."

She glared at him. "You cannot have it both ways, Mr. Norville. Last night you ridiculed me for setting my cap for Lord Mallory, and today you have me throwing Miss Lane at his head. If you were this inconsistent during the war, it is astounding that we drove the French from Spain while you were present!" And she entered Teasdale's, closing the door smartly behind her.

Norville, left standing by the window, watched ruefully as Lady Gregory emerged from the shop down the street to join Nora and Lord Mallory. His chagrin was greater still when he turned back to the goldsmith's window as that gratified gentleman was removing the jeweled egg from its stand and handing it to Elizabeth.

Chapter Fourteen

Five heads bent closely over the egg, and it was Nora who exclaimed, "This is Sir Howard's egg! There is a *G* above the clasp!" Triumphantly, she pointed to the delicate letter etched above the egg's dainty clasp. Opening the egg, Mr. Teasdale proudly displayed its red velvet interior, and then pointed out the interesting variety of the stones that crusted its surface: emeralds, amethysts, rubies, chrysoberyl, chalcedony, lapis lazuli.

Lady Gregory reached a satisfactory arrangement with Mr. Teasdale, and the group retired to her home to examine the egg in privacy. To the annoyance of Elizabeth and Nora, Norville made clear his intention of accompanying them and followed their carriage on horseback.

"To think that he should come along just when we found it!" remarked Nora with irritation. "It is the most infamous thing!"

"Actually, it is quite interesting," remarked Elizabeth, who had been thinking about that remarkable coincidence. "I wonder if he has been looking for the egg, too."

The others stared at her. "Well, of course, he knew about Sir Howard's egg from Lady Gregory," said Lord Mallory slowly, "but do you mean that Norville might have known about Elsa Briggs as well? That he might have been one of her callers?"

Elizabeth nodded. "I mean precisely that. Mr. Norville seems to have an unusually strong interest in this egg."

"I expect he's trying to be of help," said Mallory, thinking of Norville's connection with Michael.

"Well, he doesn't appear to be trying to help *us*," responded Elizabeth tartly.

In Lady Gregory's drawing room, everyone watched anxiously as she took the egg from its box and opened it gently, running her finger along the velvet lining, searching for an opening.

"There doesn't appear to be an opening here," she said ruefully. "I suppose I'll have to take the lining out." And, using a dainty pair of gold scissors, she worked carefully at the lining until she could lift it out. Nestled below the velvet was a diminutive brass key, attached to a brass circlet.

" 'I hold the key'!" crowed Nora jubilantly. "And the flowers made by the jewels on the cover must mark the end of winter!"

"And what of the last line: 'From summer I flee'?" asked Mallory.

Nora paused in her celebration. "I don't know that yet, but perhaps the key will unlock the answer to that."

"The question is," remarked Norville dryly, "What *does* the key unlock?"

There was a moment of silence as they all sat and stared at the key.

"It is a small key," remarked Elizabeth, giving voice to the obvious. "It couldn't unlock a door. What things are small enough to have a lock for a key that size?"

"It could unlock a cabinet door or a desk drawer," said Nora, studying it.

"Or a small chest . . . or jewel box," added Mallory.

"Do you recognize it, Lady Gregory?" asked Elizabeth, picking up the key and fingering it.

Lady Gregory shook her head. "I've never seen it before. Sir Howard had a set of keys in the drawer of his desk in the library, but I am certain that not one looked like that that."

Nora peered at it and then lifted it from Elizabeth's cupped palm. "How curious," she remarked. "It almost looks like a ring." Slipping the brass circlet on her finger, she exclaimed, "Look at this! It *is* a ring! It is too large for me, but here is the ring from Sir Howard's riddle!"

The others crowded about her, and she handed the ring to Mallory. "Here, Trevor, you try it on," she said, lapsing again into informality in her excitement. The lapse was not lost upon

173

Mr. Norville, Elizabeth noted ruefully. Here would be something else for him to upbraid her about.

Mallory slipped the ring onto his index finger, which it fitted snugly, projecting the key at a right angle from his finger. "One wouldn't be apt to forget a key if it were fitted to a ring," he remarked. "A clever idea."

"A Roman idea, I believe," responded Elizabeth. "My mother's journal had a brief note about such a ring, but I had forgotten about it. They were reasonably common then."

"Well, that's all very interesting," sighed Lady Gregory, sinking onto a couch, "but I don't see that it takes us any closer to an answer to our problem, for we don't know what it unlocks."

Norville turned to Lord Mallory. "Have you everything at home that your brother sent from Spain?"

Mallory nodded. "My mother kept his room as it was, both here and at Chanderley. His batman brought home all of his belongings after his death."

"You must go through everything very carefully, examining anything that might require a key such as this. Michael was one of the last people to see Sir Howard, and there is the chance that he might have sent something with him."

Mallory flushed. "Thank you for not saying that Michael might have taken something that didn't belong to him," he said gruffly. "I will examine everything."

"What about us?" demanded Nora, affronted. "Is there anything that we can do?"

Norville smiled. "I'm afraid that the other action that we need to take is one that Lady Gregory may not find desirable."

"Yes, I know what it must be, Mr. Norville. All of my husband's possessions must be carefully examined also."

"I don't wish to be presumptuous, Lady Gregory, nor do any of us wish to intrude," said Elizabeth gently, "but if you would like our help, you may certainly have it."

Lady Gregory smiled wearily. "If it will lift the cloud from my husband's name, I am certainly willing to attempt it. And I would be grateful for your help," she said to Elizabeth. "It is kind of you to offer."

"We will not trouble you any more today," Elizabeth responded, frowning at Nora, who was obviously ready to take immediate action. "I know that you need to rest and to consider how to approach this problem. Tell us what time you would like for us to call and we will be at your service tomorrow."

The unfashionably early hour of noon was set for meeting at Lady Gregory's the following day, and with that Nora was obliged to be content. It was with some difficulty that Elizabeth restrained her from offering to help Lord Mallory, and she was forced to point out the impropriety of helping a young gentleman go through his brother's bedchamber and study. It was not truly a sense of propriety that finally won her over; instead, she happened to recall that they were attending the theatre that evening and that she had agreed to be at home in the late afternoon to receive a caller.

"Who is the caller?" inquired Elizabeth.

"Just Mr. Scott and Mr. Keeley and one or two of their friends," she replied airily.

"That sounds like rather more than 'a caller,' " she commented dryly, grateful that Mr. Norville would not be present and hopeful that Lord Dabney would not be. Her hopes, however, were soon dashed, for they found that worthy gentleman about to ascend the porch steps as Lord Mallory's carriage set them down in Grosvenor Square. She had wished more than once in recent days that Lord Lacey were still in London. His presence helped to keep Lord Dabney's informal visits to a minimum.

"It seems to me that you spend an inordinate amount of time with that young man. You should always be conscious of appearances, Elizabeth," he remarked sententiously, puffing up his chest "exactly like one of those foolish pigeons in the Park," as Nora later described it.

Elizabeth spoke hurriedly before Nora could say something tactless. "Lord Mallory was kind enough to see us home after we had called upon a friend," she explained.

"I would certainly have been happy to see you home, Elizabeth. You know that I am always at your service. At whose home were you calling?"

"We had called upon Lady Gregory," replied Elizabeth reluctantly.

His eyebrows lifted. "Lady Gregory? I had thought that she removed to the country after the contretemps Sir Howard was involved in."

"Why should she retire to the country?" asked Nora hotly, ready to take up the cudgels on Lady Gregory's behalf.

Lord Dabney looked somewhat taken aback. "Merely because things were somewhat awkward for Sir Howard's family after his . . . disappearance last year."

"And you needn't say 'disappearance' as though you didn't really believe it," Nora continued. "His family has quite enough to bear without having people looking down their noses and acting niffy-naffy about his death!"

Lord Dabney raised his quizzing glass and stared at Nora as though he had just encountered an aborigine in Bond Street. "Well, upon my word, Elizabeth! I had no idea that you and Miss Lane and Rachel Gregory had become such bosom-bows. And I do think that Miss Lane is in need of a little more town bronze," he added in a lower tone, unwilling to bring down Nora upon him again. "She gets on her high ropes a great deal too easily."

"Well, I am sorry, Gervase, that she nipped at you like that, but we are quite tired. Perhaps it would be—" Elizabeth had no opportunity to politely send Lord Dabney on his way, however, for, after admitting them into the entrance hall, Burton opened the drawing-room door and revealed a coterie of young dandies. Nora's greeting made it all too clear that she was not at all weary.

"I must say, Elizabeth," he remarked in irritation, disapprovingly examining the guinea-size buttons on Scott's dashing new coat through his glass, "these fellows are underfoot far too much. I wonder that you allow it."

"They are perfectly harmless, Gervase, and they never overstay their welcome," she replied, thinking that it would be a relief if Lord Dabney would follow their lead in that respect. Once he became firmly ensconced in the drawing room, he seemed to consider himself a fixture, quite one of the family

176

party, in fact. He had been quite a help to Elizabeth at one point, for his presence had deterred some of her more dashing suitors from overstepping themselves. Now, however, his air of ownership where Elizabeth was concerned was often annoying, and Nora all too frequently clashed with him.

The drawing-room chatter was all of the masked ball to be held the next week, and the suggestions for costumes were generally abused, giggled over, and discarded.

"Well, I dashed well *won't* go as Caesar!" announced Mr. Scott upon being chivied by Mr. Keeley.

"Whyever not?" inquired Sir Adrian with becoming gravity. "I believe that it is widely agreed, Scott, that you would display to advantage in a toga." The unfortunate Mr. Scott, acutely conscious of the buckram wadding in the shoulders of his new jacket, blushed hotly.

"Well, I should like to see *you* in that getup, Adrian!" retorted the victim.

"You are quite right, young man. The figure of Caesar requires a more mature form." He turned to Elizabeth and confided gravely, "I have been thinking of going as the great man myself."

He had lowered his voice to make this confidence, but it was still clearly audible to the rest of the group and a stunned silence ensued. Elizabeth directed a quelling glance at the graceless group across the room, who were showing signs of irrepressible mirth. Her glance sufficed to hold them within reasonable bounds of good taste, although Sir Adrian was obliged to retire briefly to the hallway to compose himself.

"And what will you go as, Miss Lane?" inquired Mr. Keeley. "Will you be Juliet to my Romeo?"

Nora laughed and shook her head, but although Elizabeth strained to hear her choice of costume, the pompous tones of Lord Dabney describing his own regalia served to drown her response. The voices of the young people grew softer, and it seemed to Elizabeth that there was an inordinate amount of merriment.

Before she could bring Lord Dabney's monologue to a close and discover the reason for their laughter, Lord Dabney caught her unawares by announcing that he would be happy to escort both Elizabeth and Nora to the masquerade. "For, as you know, Elizabeth, such affairs sometimes become too sportive, and ladies should attend with a gentleman who will watch over them."

"I am most grateful for your kind offer," Elizabeth began, but he waved her gratitude aside, not giving her a chance to explain that she had other plans.

"Not at all, Elizabeth. It will be my pleasure."

"Be your pleasure to do what, Dabney?" asked Sir Edmund, entering the drawing room abruptly from the small study that adjoined it.

"It will be my pleasure to escort Miss Harrington and Miss Lane to the masked ball at Lady Seaton's next week."

Sir Edmund was a mild, good-natured man, but he had an abiding dislike for Lord Dabney. "Thinks himself at home to a peg on a horse," Sir Edmund had been known to remark, "and he ain't. What's more, I've seen him leaving his cattle standing in the cold for an hour at a time with no groom to walk 'em."

"Good of you, Dabney," replied Sir Edmund briskly, "but there's no need to put yourself out. I'll be escorting my sister and Miss Lane to the ball."

Elizabeth and Nora looked at each other with mingled astonishment and relief.

"Have you chosen your costume, Sir Edmund?" inquired one of the bantlings.

He nodded firmly. "Plan to go as a gypsy," he responded. "Devilish good with horses, those gypsies."

Nora and Elizabeth had been profuse in their thanks to Sir Edmund, but he waved them aside, saying that he couldn't have them attended by a Jack Pudding like Dabney. So pleased was Elizabeth by the turn of events that she could face an evening spent in Norville's company with equanimity.

She was forced to admit to herself that he looked particularly arresting when he entered the drawing room that evening. Dressed in a black jacket and trousers and a white pique waistcoat, his neckcloth impeccably arranged, his attire would have done credit to Mr. Brummell himself. Sampson and Rufus seemed to approve of him, also, and bestowed tokens of their esteem in the form of a multitude of tiny hairs intricately arranged upon the tidy black expanse of jacket and trousers. Sir Edmund stood in the doorway of the drawing room, shaking his head at the scene before him.

"It's no good, you know, Norville. Can't be a dapper fellow and keep livestock in the house. The two don't mix." He glanced down at his own once-immaculate clothing ruefully. "Fish has threatened to give his notice. Says that it's taking years off his life trying to keep me presentable and that he can scarcely hold up his head in public anymore. Took to his bed for a day when I went out to White's with cat hairs all over my jacket."

"What made him get up again?" asked Norville in amusement.

Sir Edmund chuckled. "The pup chewed a hole in one of the new Hessians Hoby had just delivered. Fish decided he had to get up to defend my belongings and his honor."

Sir Edmund gallantly led Nora in to dinner, leaving Elizabeth to come with Norville. "It seems I must apologize again, ma'am, for my too-hasty remark this afternoon. I trust you will forgive me."

Elizabeth inclined her head slightly to acknowledge his apology and met his eyes coolly. "A hasty temper can be an unfortunate encumbrance in life, Mr. Norville—more unfortunate for those about one than for oneself, perhaps." She smiled up at him sweetly. "It is so much easier to possess a defect in character that makes others uncomfortable rather than oneself. Have you not found that to be true?" she inquired in an innocently conversational tone.

"Since delivering home truths appears to be a specialty of yours, Miss Harrington, I must bow to your superior knowledge in that area."

She chuckled, acknowledging a hit. "Very well, Mr. Norville. We will, for the moment at least, cry quits."

Dinner was, from that point, a pleasant affair, although Elizabeth felt something very akin to regret as she watched Mr.

179

Norville making himself agreeable to Nora. It was a good thing, of course, for should the marriage take place, it would be infinitely more acceptable to poor Nora if she found him charming. For herself, of course, it was quite otherwise, for his peremptory manner and hasty temper could scarcely suit a young woman long accustomed to ruling herself and those about her. But it was Nora that he wished to win, and, if he were determined to make a sincere effort, Mr. Norville might succeed in winning a place in her affections.

The play that they were to attend that evening was a sprightly comedy entitled *Love's Young Dreams* and starred that charming ingenue, Miss Amelia Jackson. No sooner had they arrived and made themselves comfortable in their box than they were joined by Sir Adrian, Mr. Scott, and Mr. Keeley. If Mr. Norville were somewhat less than delighted by their appearance, he concealed it admirably, and Nora was able to reign over her small court without black looks from him. Sir Adrian was still in their box when the curtain rose again, and when Miss Jackson stepped onstage and was duly applauded, he whispered to Nora under cover of the noise, "You outshine her in every way, Miss Nora." Elizabeth let this bit of gallantry slip by unremarked, but determined to keep her eye upon Sir Adrian.

Under cover of applause a few minutes later, Nora leaned close to Elizabeth and whispered. Glancing at the crowd below them, Elizabeth encountered Lord Chawton's gaze, his quizzing glass to his eye as he stared at them. When he realized that she had noticed him, he smiled mockingly and bowed. Without acknowledging his presence, she directed her gaze again to the stage and did not glance his direction until the next interval, at which time his place was empty.

"Why was he just sitting there *staring* at us?" whispered Nora, shivering. "He is a most unpleasant man."

Elizabeth had hoped to discuss the problem of the key with Mr. Norville during the interval, but he excused himself as the younger gentlemen again took over the box. Elizabeth sat quietly, listening absently to the banter of the youngsters and mulling over the matter of the key. Suddenly, her eye was caught by a familiar upright figure across the theatre from them. Mr.

Norville had entered another box and seated himself quickly beside the sole occupant of the box. He had joined Lady Brill.

She acknowledged to herself that it was no great surprise to see them together. He had loved her long ago and apparently loved her still—she was a beautiful woman. Elizabeth wondered absently if he would be able to convince himself that he truly could marry a miss as young as Nora. Of course, he had no choice if Nora decided that she wished to accept his offer, for he *had* offered for her and had done so in writing. Perhaps it will work out, she thought. Perhaps Nora will come to love him—or at least to be charmed by him—and perhaps he will find her biddable enough to live with—and perhaps Braxton Hall and Cecilia will be saved. Perhaps. Then she looked back at Mr. Norville, who was seated very close to Lady Brill and talking earnestly.

"And what will your costume be for the masked ball, Miss Harrington?" asked Sir Adrian, interrupting her reverie.

"I haven't yet decided, Sir Adrian—perhaps a shepherdess."

He bowed courteously. "You would be lovely," he said pleasantly.

Mr. Keeley agreed, adding, "And Scott would be more than happy to be your lamb, should you need one."

The unfortunate Mr. Scott denied this vehemently, only to have Sir Adrian say, "Scott, your lack of gallantry shocks me. What must Miss Harrington think of you?"

Turning scarlet, Mr. Scott denied any intention of offending Miss Harrington and assured her that if she needed him as a sheep, then a sheep he would be. Reassuring him that he need not make such a sacrifice, she sat quietly, listening to the careless banter of the others and wondering what Mr. Norville and Lady Brill had found to talk about.

The next act of the play was a highlight for Nora, for Miss Jackson appeared in a gentleman's attire. She was rapidly becoming known for her light comic style and for her breeches roles, which she played with great verve. *Love's Young Dreams* even included a brief but dramatic bit of swordplay for Miss Jackson, during which Elizabeth noted that Nora suddenly pulled at Sir Adrian's sleeve and whispered. Elizabeth frowned and found herself hoping that Miss Jackson had not revived Nora's desire to become an actress herself. Her hope was short-lived, however, for soon Nora clutched her arm and whispered, "Isn't she *splendid?* Wouldn't you love to play that role?"

She had not counted it fortunate that Mr. Norville had remained in Lady Brill's box, but after listening to Nora's effusions, Elizabeth could see that there were certain advantages to having Mr. Norville completely across the theatre from them. When the curtain came down, Nora could talk of nothing else.

"Do you recall, Elizabeth, when we saw Lord Byron giving Miss Kelly pointers on her swordsmanship? Do you suppose that he helped Miss Jackson or do you suppose that she has an actual teacher and takes lessons?" She sighed. "I should *so* love to wield a sword."

Before anyone else could respond, Mr. Norville, who had quietly entered the box in time to hear her final exclamation, replied promptly, "Perhaps I could give you some pointers, Miss Lane."

"I would be very grateful, Mr. Norville." She turned such a glowing face to him that it was not remarkable that the other gentlemen began to feel themselves ill-used.

"I would be happy to be of assistance, Miss Lane," announced Sir Adrian. "You have only to call upon me."

Mr. Scott and Mr. Keeley, not to be outdone, made known their desire to be of service to Miss Lane in her new course of study. If Mr. Scott thought it was most unusual for all parties to act as though this was de rigueur when only a few days earlier he and his sword had been sent from Grosvenor Square in disgrace, he did not comment upon it. Elizabeth, however, was astounded at Mr. Norville's high-handed manner and his acquiescence in such a scheme.

Sir Edmund, who had been chatting with a man in the box next to theirs, rejoined the group in time to hear that Nora was about to undertake a new study. He regarded her with some amazement. "Thought you had done with lessons, Nora," he commented, remembering her urgent desire to leave the schoolroom behind. "What's it to be—lessons in watercolors or dancing?"

"I am going to learn to use a sword, Edmund," she announced happily. "Mr. Norville—and the other gentlemen—have agreed to teach me."

He stared at his sister blankly. "I'd no idea that handling a sword was one of the accomplishments of a young female today."

Mr. Norville, who was watching Elizabeth rather than Sir Edmund, replied. "Not one of the usual accomplishments a young woman is taught, Sir Edmund. But then, it is important to learn to be oneself, is it not?"

His explanation might have left Sir Edmund still at sea, but it cleared matters for Elizabeth, who understood that he was making an effort to honor Nora's individuality rather than being concerned entirely with his own wishes. Such an effort made their engagement look more promising, and for that, of course, Elizabeth was grateful.

Chapter Fifteen

The search for something requiring their key to unlock it resumed the next day. When the ladies had drunk their chocolate
and arrayed themselves in their oldest, most serviceable gowns,
they departed in Elizabeth's chaise for Curzon Street, where
they met Lady Gregory and Mr. Norville. Lord Mallory had
sent a message to Lady Gregory, assuring her that he was con-
ducting his search through Michael's things and would inform
them immediately should he make any discoveries.

They began their work in Sir Howard's library, dividing the
room into sections, with Lady Gregory taking Sir Howard's
desk.

"I have of course already looked through most of his papers,"
she explained. "Sir Howard was a very orderly person, so it
was not a difficult matter to discover those papers that our solicitor needed. I fear that I was in no state to go over everything carefully, however."

"Be certain that you examine the drawers with great attention," Mr. Norville cautioned her. "It is very possible that there
is a false bottom in one of them or one that may have a compartment hidden in the back. It is not unusual for a desk to
have such a hiding place for valuables."

All of them set to work, Lady Gregory retiring to the desk,
the others carefully removing each book from the shelf, flip-
ping through its leaves, checking its spine, and examining the
bookshelf itself. They had worked steadily for two hours when
Nora collapsed in a disconsolate heap.

"I can't believe that there is anything here!" she cried, looking down at her hands. "I am all over dirt and paper cuts!"

Elizabeth stared down at her own hands ruefully. "It is fortunate that gloves are so much in vogue," she agreed. "We shall have to send Silvers to the herbalist for a special preparation for our hands and get out our chickenskin gloves."

Norville, who had not paused in his methodical inspection of the volumes before him, glanced at Nora. "You must have a little resolution, Miss Lane. Did you truly expect to walk into Sir Howard's library and discover the answer to our questions within the first hour or two?"

It was only to be expected that Nora, who had thought that very thing, should be a little put out with Mr. Norville. "Of course I did not!" she exclaimed mendaciously. "But I did not realize that handling books would be such dirty work!"

When there was no response to this plaint, other than a quiet chuckle from Elizabeth and an offer of tea from Lady Gregory, Nora grudgingly began her work again.

"I do hope that Trev—that Lord Mallory has been more successful," she said, quickly catching herself. Mr. Norville flicked a single dark glance in her direction, but, to Elizabeth's relief, made no comment.

It was almost an hour later when Elizabeth came to the *Discourses* of Epictetus and found that next to it there was a space. "Have you been reading Stoic philosophy, Lady Gregory?" she inquired, for Sir Howard had been very orderly in the arrangement of his library.

Lady Gregory raised her head quickly from her papers. "No, but Sir Howard was very fond of the *Meditations* and frequently read from it, particularly when he was distressed. Is there a volume missing among the Stoics?"

Elizabeth nodded, and Lady Gregory hurried to her side. "Yes, it is Marcus Aurelius that is missing. It is a slender volume bound in red morocco leather."

Nora and Mr. Norville had stopped their work and come to stand by Elizabeth. "Was that book among Sir Howard's possessions that were returned to you, Lady Gregory?"

"No—or at least I am almost certain that it was not. None of his papers were sent home to me, nor was his travel desk, nor were there any books in his trunk. I inquired about them, but I was told that some things were kept for governmental purposes and that because of the war I could not have them. They indicated that perhaps at the end of the war I might reclaim his possessions."

She paused a moment, then added bitterly, "I cannot say that there was anyone who was particularly interested in answering my questions. They were more interested in asking them, as though I knew something that I was not telling them."

"You did not mention that to us earlier when you told us about the missing Easter egg," observed Mr. Norville.

"I could understand that the government might feel that any papers or books—and perhaps even the case in which they were kept—should be retained for examination. But the Easter egg was a purely personal item. I couldn't understand why they had kept that, and they wouldn't give me any reason for doing so."

"I can certainly think of no reason," agreed Elizabeth.

Mr. Norville's brow was creased in thought. "But you did tell them that Sir Howard took a travel desk with him and that it was missing?" he asked.

"I most certainly did! I described it as specifically as I could and told them that I would like to have it for my son, but I could tell even as I was speaking that it would do me no good at all to ask for it."

"To whom were you speaking, Lady Gregory?" he asked.

"I was speaking then with Sir John Radmore. I had small use for him before my husband's disappearance, and I have none at all now. Although he had been a guest in our home countless times and a friend of Sir Howard's for some twenty years, he gave not the slightest sign of it after my husband disappeared. Nor has he since that time. I wonder that he can face himself in the mirror each morning, but he seems to have had no problem with cutting old ties."

Nora was indignant. "You should have made your displeasure known to his superiors, Lady Gregory! He should not be allowed to treat you in so dishonorable a fashion!"

"I am afraid that his superiors evinced no interest in me un-

186

less I confessed to knowing about Sir Howard's plans. In their own minds, they had already tried him and found him guilty."

Elizabeth was touched by the despair in her voice and impulsively took her hand. "I am sure that Sir Howard's name will be cleared. We will most certainly find something in our search that will be helpful."

Norville pulled a chair close to Lady Gregory. "Tell me, please, as nearly as you can, what Sir Howard's desk looked like."

She looked a trifle surprised by his question but detailed it for him as well as she could. "It was lap-size, of course, and it was made of rosewood inlaid with satinwood and claret-colored leather. Inside were compartments for papers and writing utensils and ink—and there *was* a compartment that locked. Perhaps the key unlocks that compartment."

Nora's face fell. "Yes, but we don't have that compartment."

"I wonder if we might," said Norville slowly. "What of Michael Graham?"

Elizabeth stared at him. "Lord Mallory's brother? Lord Mallory would surely have told us if he had Sir Howard's travel-desk."

"I am quite certain that he would have," agreed Norville, "if indeed he were aware of the fact. Perhaps he would not know if his brother had such a desk or not. It could have been put away with Michael's other possessions without question."

"Then we have to speak to Lord Mallory at once!" exclaimed Nora, leaping to her feet and trying to dust off her grimy hands.

Elizabeth laughed. "I do not think that Lady Mallory would thank us for descending upon her en masse and in all of our dirt. Why not return home, remove some of the grime, and send round to Lord Mallory, asking him to meet us in Grosvenor Square?" She turned to Lady Gregory. "Or would you prefer that we all return here?"

Norville spoke before Lady Gregory could answer. "Miss Harrington, I certainly agree that we should not all troop round to Mallory's, but I fail to see the necessity of allowing time for you to make your toilette before meeting with him." His tone indicated his strong disapproval of what he obviously considered vanity on her part.

Turning to Lady Gregory, he made a brief bow. "If it meets with your approval, ma'am, I believe it would be best if one of your footmen carried a note to him, asking him to come immediately to speak with us."

"Of course," she responded. "I will write it this moment." And so saying, she seated herself at Sir Howard's desk and quickly penned a note and dispatched it.

They waited impatiently, despite Lady Gregory's hospitable attempt to distract them with tea, and Lord Mallory was somewhat startled to find himself so eagerly greeted when he was shown into the library.

Before he could say anything, Nora had pounced upon him. "Did you see a travel-desk among your brother's things, Lord Mallory? Oh, do say that you did, for the key may belong to that!"

Mallory looked at the others, thrown slightly off balance by the abruptness of the attack. Norville looked at his expression and smiled.

"Miss Lane has just stated the essence of the problem, Mallory. It seems that Sir Howard took his travel-desk with him, which disappeared along with his papers and his copy of Marcus Aurelius. Do you remember seeing such an item among your brother's possessions?"

Mallory had stiffened perceptibly. "What are you implying, Norville? Do you believe that my brother 'accidentally' took Sir Howard's desk, believing that it was his own?"

"Don't be such a clunch, Mallory!" said Norville impatiently. "Of course he would not have done so. But it is within the realm of possibility that Sir Howard might have entrusted him with the desk."

Mallory relaxed a trifle. "Then why would Lady Gregory not have it?" he inquired.

"You know quite as well as I that Michael had scarcely arrived back in Spain after his journey to St. Petersburg when he was killed during his reconnaissance mission. He could have intended to send it back to London by packet, or it is possible that he was instructed not to let it leave his hands and to present it to Lady Gregory in person."

Mallory nodded. "That is possible, I suppose. But I don't believe there was such an item in any of his trunks or valises."

Lady Gregory had been listening intently, but now she interrupted. "But why would my husband do such a thing?" she asked. "What could there possibly be in that desk that would merit such secrecy?"

"We cannot be certain of that," replied Mr. Norville, "but we know of the precautions that were taken in delivering the package to Sir Howard. We know that something of great value was at stake."

"Well, why do we stand here?" demanded Nora. "Let us begin immediately to look for it!"

"I give you my word that we will not find it at our home here in London. I have been through everything of Michael's here," he said ruefully.

He thought a moment, then added, "When I first encountered you, Norville, I told you that I had been to Chanderley, our country home, to see if Michael had mailed anything there—but of course he had not. I did not, however, go through everything of Michael's that has been packed away there in his old room."

"We must look through his room!" said Nora decisively, ignoring Elizabeth's attempts to silence her.

For a moment there was no response, then Lord Mallory smiled. "Do you know, perhaps Miss Lane is right. My mother is taking the children to Chanderley on Monday, both to give her an opportunity to check on things there and to allow the children to go searching for the leaves and odds and ends they need to make their pace eggs. She would not mind if I came along and brought some guests. I expect it would serve to cheer her up a bit."

Oddly enough, Nora's face had fallen as he spoke, and Elizabeth could not understand why Nora wasn't demanding that they leave immediately.

"Must we go Monday?" she asked weakly. "Could we not wait until Tuesday?"

The others stared at her. "Why do you wish to wait, Nora?" asked Elizabeth. "I thought that you were anxious to know whether or not the desk is there."

"Oh, I am, I am!" she insisted, staring down at her feet. "It is just that. . . ." and here her voice trailed away.

"It is just that *what?*" asked Elizabeth.

"That the masked ball at Lady Seaton's is on Monday night," she said in a whisper. "And I shall probably never have another opportunity to attend one."

"Why, of course you'll go to others," said Mallory. "During the height of the season, I daresay you'll be invited to one or two a week."

Nora's head hung lower still, and her voice grew fainter until she could scarcely be heard. "I won't be here to go. This will be my only opportunity."

Mallory yielded. "I daresay that one day won't make any great difference." He turned to the others. "If that will be agreeable to you?" he inquired.

Norville nodded briefly, made his farewells, and departed quickly. As Nora was helping Lady Gregory restore order to Sir Howard's desk, Mallory looked down at Elizabeth.

"What did Miss Lane mean about not being able to attend other masquerades?" he asked quietly. "Is she indeed leaving?"

Elizabeth nodded. "She may stay until Eastertide, but then she must go home."

"I see. Then I am glad that I gave way to her. It would be too bad to spoil her treat. After all, if that desk is at Chanderley, it will still be there on Tuesday."

Further searching was thus postponed until Tuesday and their trip to Chanderley, and Elizabeth and Nora rode wearily home. They were not allotted much time for rest, however, for very soon after they had bathed and changed, Burton announced that they had callers, and Nora's court began to assemble. Sir Adrian of the bright eye and ready wit led the way.

"Have you decided, Miss Lane?" he asked in a mock heroic voice. "Tell me my fate. Will you or will you not play Cleopatra to my Antony at Lady Seaton's ball?"

Nora dimpled and shook her head demurely. "I am afraid

not, Sir Adrian, although it was charming of you to ask me."

Sir Adrian turned to Elizabeth with the back of his wrist pressed to his forehead and said in a low—but still audible—voice, "This is the posture that Mr. Garrick used to suggest an attitude of Despair, is it not, Miss Harrington?"

She nodded, chuckling, and he turned back to Nora, having added a languishing expression to his posture of Despair. "I do not know, Miss Lane, if I shall be able to withstand the blow that you have dealt me. I—"

"Oh, do stow it, Adrian!" interrupted the insensitive Mr. Scott, pleased to avenge himself. "Miss Lane has saved you from humiliation. With your legs, you would have made a cake of yourself in that costume."

Sir Adrian appeared affronted and glanced down at his maligned limbs. "I believe that it is widely acknowledged that I have a very trim ankle and splendid legs."

"Spindle-shanks!" commented his friend rudely.

Elizabeth, eager to put an end to the inelegant bickering before it escalated, smiled at Nora. "I have not heard you say what you have decided about your costume, Nora. Do tell us."

The gentlemen added their entreaties with such force that Nora was obliged to give way. "I shall go as an egg-dancer," she announced. "I shall wear gypsy clothes and carry a basket for my goods."

Her court loudly applauded her decision and appeared inclined to demand a rehearsal of the dance. Fortunately, there was another caller before she could begin. Mr. Norville entered, wearing a sword.

After acknowledging Elizabeth and the gentlemen, he turned and bowed to Nora. "I have come, Miss Lane, to give you your first lesson in swordsmanship."

This announcement brought a glow to Nora's cheeks, but unfortunately it did not draw a similar response from Elizabeth and the gentlemen.

"I say! We weren't even allowed to have a sword in here!" exclaimed Mr. Keeley, having had time to recall Mr. Scott's grievance. "Do you remember, Miss Harrington?"

Elizabeth had no time to deal with complaints, however, for

191

Mr. Norville, taking a leaf from Nora's book, was obviously about to begin the lesson with no waste of time.

"We will begin with the foil rather than the smallsword," she could hear him saying as he drew the weapon from its sheath. "This is used for dueling . . ."

Excusing herself to the other gentlemen, Elizabeth hurried over to him. "I believe, Mr. Norville, that she had best take you to another room and have Burton clear the area for you."

He nodded, and Elizabeth noted with some alarm that he had certainly come prepared: there were two foils and two wire-mesh masks. After apologizing to Sir Adrian and the others as they departed, she hurried to the morning room in the back of the house where Burton was rearranging the furniture, his countenance clearly expressing his disapproval of such activities within a well-regulated household. Elizabeth felt that she quite agreed with him.

Norville was showing the foil to Nora, and explaining a little about parries and thrusts, Nora listening eagerly. He had just begun to demonstrate a low-line parry when the door opened and Sir Edmund strolled in, preceded by Sampson and Rufus. Norville looked down at them and stopped abruptly.

"We will have to call a halt," he said to Nora. "It is too dangerous to try this with the two of them underfoot."

Sir Edmund was still looking askance at the foil. "Norville!" he remonstrated, shocked. "You can't quarrel with a young woman like Nora!"

"No, they are not quarreling, Edmund," said his sister soothingly. "Do you not remember that Mr. Norville was going to show Nora how to fight with a sword?"

Sir Edmund's brow cleared slightly, but clouded again almost immediately. "No, now really, Norville! That is not at all the thing either—teaching a young girl that she can fight like a man."

Norville grinned at him. "Worried, are you, Sir Edmund? I would be, too, if I lived with your sister. Just a bit of a temper, hasn't she? I doubt it would be wise to put a sword in her hand and teach her to use it. I feel much more secure with Miss Lane."

Elizabeth smiled pleasantly. "You are too kind, Mr. Norville," she replied smoothly, and wished fervently for the sword. "Perhaps I will learn soon."

Sir Edmund lowered his voice a trifle to speak privately with his sister. "Don't like to interfere, dear girl, but I don't believe he meant to be kind—and from what I hear of him, he could teach her how to use that sword very well."

He studied his sister for a moment, then looked back at Nora and Norville, still deeply involved in conversation. "And I don't believe it's the thing to have Nora learn to fence," he repeated. "Don't think Cecilia would think it was the thing, either. Need a tighter rein with Nora, my dear. Take that foil away from her before she hurts herself—or someone else."

Having a sudden vision of Cecilia's horrified expression had she known of her daughter's newest pastime helped Elizabeth have enough starch to call a halt to the lesson and to tell Mr. Norville that they would have to reconsider the lessons.

Norville received the news graciously and, as he turned to leave, Elizabeth could not resist adding, "I thought that I would call a halt to things before you asked me why I was not doing my duty."

He turned and smiled. "How very quick you are, Miss Harrington." And bowing once again, he took himself away, leaving Elizabeth to be deeply grateful to Edmund and the vision of Cecilia.

"I can't believe that you stopped us just as we were beginning!" fumed Nora as the door shut behind Mr. Norville. "How am I to learn to duel if you will not let me practice?"

"I don't believe that dueling will be one of your activities for some time to come, Nora. I know that you wish to learn to handle a sword, but I will have to think more about this. You must remember that I stand in your mother's place during this time, and I must think of your own best interests."

Nora was unimpressed by this explanation. "Then you mean that you would go ahead and marry me to Mr. Norville," remarked Nora.

"No, I would not. Pray do not be difficult, Nora. Some things must be my decision."

Nora tossed her head. "I believe that it is high time that *I* begin to make some of the decisions that affect me," she announced. And with that ominous observation, she turned on her heel and left Elizabeth to worry about what she might do next.

Elizabeth was not left to worry for very long, however. She was surprised when Nora did not come down to breakfast the next morning, but not disturbed. She was, in fact, enjoying the peacefulness of her chocolate and toast without Nora's chatter. Sir Edmund had joined her, but was engrossed by his beefsteak and *Morning Chronicle*. Burton brought in her mail on a silver salver, and she settled herself to look over the invitations that inevitably came the way of a young lady who was lovely, charming . . . and wealthy. Laying aside an invitation to another breakfast and a sonnet written about her eyebrows by a young puppy desperate for her attention, she noticed a square pink envelope addressed in bold violet ink. Elizabeth held it to her nose and inhaled the fragrance gently.

"Cecilia!" she said, slitting the envelope with her silver letter knife.

"Where?" demanded Sir Edmund, putting down his paper and looking around him desperately, ready for instant flight.

"Here, Edmund," she chuckled, waving the missive at him. "I recognized the scent she wears. I noticed that she hadn't given that up even when she was telling us that the wolf was at the door."

He relaxed immediately, disregarding his sister's comments about the perfume. "Oh! Well, you needn't startle me so early in the day, my dear." He patted his middle cautiously. "Caused my beefsteak to rise a good three inches."

Elizabeth did not answer him immediately, being already absorbed by the contents of the letter. She read it quickly, then read it once again before placing it on the table before her with a thump.

"Well, of all the old cattish—!" She shook her head angrily, and Edmund, reacting to the thump, looked up to see his sister's lovely countenance looking ominously flushed.

"Now don't fly up into the boughs, Lizzy," he cautioned.

"What's to do?"

"She is forever pinching at me! Why must Cecilia be a family connection of ours?"

Since Sir Edmund devoted as little thought as possible to Cecilia, he was unable to enlighten her, although he felt strongly that she had brought up a valid point.

Elizabeth waved the letter at him. "She says right here, Edmund, in black and white—or at least in pink and violet—that she is not certain that I am capable of taking care of 'her Nora.' 'Her Nora,' indeed! It was 'her Nora' that begged to be taken away from the mother that was about to sell her into marriage!"

Edmund had folded his paper neatly and was listening to her sympathetically. "Here's the thing, though, Lizzy: who told her that you're not capable of taking care of the chit? *I* never did."

Elizabeth paused in her tirade, her forehead creased in thought. "I don't know who could have told her, Edmund." She smoothed the crumpled letter and tried to read over it. "She knows about staying at the inn, though, and sitting in the kitchen with the others, and she knows about Lord Mallory and his sisters and all of the young men who come to call on Nora."

"Well-informed, ain't she?" her brother inquired. "Looks to me as if we have a spy among us."

"A spy! Surely not, Edmund! Who would have any interest in doing such a thing?"

Sir Edmund shrugged. "Could just be some tattle-monger friend of Cecilia's. Nora can't be still for longer than a minute, any more than she can hold her tongue. Some friend of her mama's may be hearing about her highflights second-hand from one of those young cubs that hangs about here."

Elizabeth, while not happy with this thought, was better pleased than she had been with the idea that they were harboring a spy. While she was mulling it over, Burton appeared in the doorway to notify his mistress that she had someone to see her. Before he could announce the callers, however, they had already entered the dining room, and Burton, his dignity outraged, withdrew. Mr. Norville, his face a thundercloud, stood beside Elizabeth with Nora in tow.

Elizabeth stared at the latter in shock, for Nora was wearing a walking dress and cape, and had obviously been outside, for her cheeks were pink with cold – and with mortification.

"Why, Nora! Where have you been!" asked Elizabeth.

"That is a reasonable question, Miss Harrington," conceded Norville, speaking in a tone that boded no good for anyone. "And I can certainly answer it for you. My man announced to me about thirty minutes ago that a young lady had come to call."

Elizabeth and Sir Edmund stared at Nora, who looked resolutely down, refusing to meet their eyes.

"By Jove, Nora, that's not at all the proper thing to do!" exclaimed Sir Edmund, his eyes goggling. "You'll set all the tattle-mongers talking!"

"Exactly so, Sir Edmund," agreed Norville. "But Miss Lane appears to have not the slightest idea that she has done anything improper by coming to my home, coming unchaperoned, and coming at such an hour!" His eye caught Elizabeth's in a meaningful glance.

"I suppose that you think I should be sleeping outside her door to keep her from sneaking out of the house!" exclaimed Elizabeth angrily. "Why would I expect a young girl to go sneaking away in the early morning like this?"

Another thought had occurred to Sir Edmund. "Just how did you get out, missy?" he asked Nora. "Wasn't the front door locked?"

She nodded, still staring at the toes of her small half-boots.

"Well, what did you do, my girl? Climb out a window?"

Nora shook her head, but remained mute. Sir Edmund, however, persevered. The question had taken firm hold of his mind, and he was anxious to confirm the security of his household.

Another thought shook him. "Did someone let you out and then lock the front door back again?" he asked.

The culprit failed to respond for a moment, then shook her head miserably. "I promised Robert, the footman, my new silver earrings for his sweetheart if he would let me out and not say anything about it," she said in a very low voice. "But it wasn't his fault! Truly it wasn't!" she added hastily as she looked up and saw Sir Edmund's face.

The unfortunate Robert was called in upon the spot, the earrings in question were returned to their rightful owner, and Robert was made to understand that his continued service in that household was contingent upon his walking the straight and narrow path of virtue in the days to come. It was a path that he assured Sir Edmund that he would walk carefully in the future, for Sir Edmund was a kind master and paid his people well. Nora saw clearly that she would receive no more assistance from members of the household staff.

"Whatever possessed you to do such a shatterbrained thing?" asked Elizabeth in disbelief after Robert had made his exit.

Nora lowered her eyes again and examined her hands with an appearance of interest. "I wished to take my fencing lesson," she said in a low voice.

Sir Edmund gave a shout of laughter. "Serves you right, Norville!" he chortled. "You said my sister was too dangerous a one to teach and that you'd rather teach Nora because she was safer!"

This elicited a flitting smile from Norville, and he sat down to partake of breakfast as Sir Edmund bade him do. Sir Edmund was still chuckling. "Sometimes it's hard to tell the difference between a kitten and a lion cub, Norville," he commented adroitly. "Have you read the latest from France?" He patted the newspaper significantly. "We're moving in on the Frogs. We'll get Boney this time, sure as check."

The ladies, not particularly interested in the conversation, adjourned to Nora's room to discuss matters of etiquette and discretion. Nora was unusually subdued, which Elizabeth took as a sign that she understood the enormity of her offense and was sorry for it. Her state of withdrawal lasted until the arrival of Sir Adrian and the rest of her admirers, at which time the excitement of their news brought the brightness back to her eyes.

"The Duke has struck again!" announced Mr. Scott dramatically as soon as they had arrived.

"Who did he rob this time?" asked Nora eagerly, once more her lively self.

"Lady Radmore," contributed Mr. Keeley. "They say that Sir John is in a rare taking about it, only he ain't making a show of it like Brill did. They say his color drained straight away when he heard of it. He was playing at Boodle's late last night when it happened. Spoiled his game for him, the others said."

Sir Adrian was unwilling to be left out. "Freddie Burgess was there when they told him. Freddie says that Sir John never said a word—just sat and stared at the footman that brought him the news. Then he stood up suddenly, folded his cards, and said, 'I believe you can deal me out, gentlemen' and walked out. He never even paid what he owed."

"Strange," said Elizabeth thoughtfully. "Sir John must know that the Duke returns everything he takes and that he doesn't harm anyone."

"Where was Lady Radmore when she was robbed?" asked Nora.

"She was just returning from a visit to her grandchildren in Bath," returned Mr. Scott. "She was stopped out on the road well before London, but it was the Duke, all right. She was frightened at first, because she has been away and had heard nothing about him. But he was so courteous, she said, that it was almost a pleasure to be robbed, even though he took all of the jewels she was wearing, as well as her jewel case from her luggage. He even took the gold case with her grandchildren's miniatures in it, although he apologized profusely for doing so."

Nora frowned. "Why would he take the pictures?"

Mr. Scott shrugged. "Perhaps because of their frames. At any rate, we know that she will get them back again."

When the gentlemen departed, Nora and Elizabeth sat together for a while without exchanging a word.

Finally, Nora said, "I don't know Lady Radmore, Elizabeth, but isn't that the name that Lady Gregory mentioned yesterday? Or is there perhaps another?"

Elizabeth shook her head. "Sir John Radmore is the person that Lady Gregory was speaking of."

Silence descended again, a more profound one this time.

"You don't suppose—" began Nora.

"No, of course not, Nora," responded Elizabeth before she could finish her thought. "There is not the slightest possibility of such a thing."

Nora went to her bed that evening quite certain, however, that Lord Mallory was the dashing Duke. Elizabeth, on the other hand, retired to her pillow wondering if the inscrutable Mr. Norville had any part in all of this. And if so, what role did he play?

The evening had been a quiet one for a Saturday, for they had attended only one evening party and arrived home early from it, Nora out of spirits, Elizabeth thoughtful, and Sir Edmund weary of drawing-room chatter. They all retired gratefully to bed, but their peaceful sleep was destined to be short-lived.

It was at approximately three in the morning that Sir Edmund awakened. Rufus, who had found his way in with Fish just before Sir Edmund retired, was growling in a fearful way that made him sound ten times his size.

"Dash it all, dog, do go back to sleep. No one is going to see to you in the middle of the night!" And Sir Edmund pulled his nightcap down firmly over his ears, plumped his pillow, and snatched his covers up over his head. Rufus remained oblivious to his command, and the rumblings in his throat grew so intense that Sir Edmund could finally stand them no longer. Lighting the candle at his bedside, he held it up so that he could see the pup. Sampson, who had been curled up at the foot of the bed, looked up in irritation at the rearrangement of his covers. Rufus was standing intently at the chamber door, his nose pressed to the narrow opening at its bottom.

"Come now, Rufus! That will be enough!" said Sir Edmund imperiously, hopeful that his tone and the light combined would have their effect, but it was to no avail. Rufus continued growling with intense concentration.

Sir Edmund shrugged himself unhappily into his dressing gown. "I'll give you to Fish, that's what I'll do. Then I can get back to sleep. I'll—" He broke off abruptly from his monologue, for he heard a soft thud in the hallway.

Marching to the door, he threw it open, holding the candle

high over his head, at which time several things occurred almost simultaneously.

"Who's there?" he demanded. "Is that you, Fish?" As Sir Edmund spoke, a shot rang out, causing the candle to gutter and go out. Just before that happened, however, Rufus, now free, charged into the hall, barking ferociously, with Sampson bolting out like an orange shot behind him. In the darkness that descended so suddenly, Sir Edmund could hear scuffling and growls and the voices of Elizabeth and Nora calling out in alarm. There was a tearing of cloth and then the soft thudding of stocking feet on the stairs.

"Stop thief!" shouted Sir Edmund. Rufus barked, and Sir Edmund could hear the scrabbling of his toenails on the hardwood steps.

In a matter of moments both ladies arrived with their candles, and they were joined quickly by Burton, regal even in his dressing gown, and two of the footmen, one of them the unfortunate Robert.

"After him!" commanded Sir Edmund, pointing to the stairs. The two footmen bounded down the steps with Robert in the lead, determined to redeem himself. Burton followed at a more sedate pace as became his age and the dignity of his position.

"Edmund, are you all right?" demanded Elizabeth. "What happened?"

Edmund was occupied in examining the wall behind his head where the bullet was embedded. "A damned good shot," he observed critically. "*If* the fellow was aiming for the candle."

Elizabeth, who had been awakened from an extremely sound sleep by the shot, could not decide whether to be exasperated or amused. "Edmund, will you please turn around and explain to us what took place?"

He looked up in surprise, having been deeply absorbed in his own line of thought. "Rufus made such a fuss that I got out of bed. When I heard something in the hall and opened the door, the fellow shot the candle out of my hand. Could have killed me," he mused.

"Well, it wasn't the Duke of Diamonds," announced Nora.

"Eh?" asked Sir Edmund, startled.

"The thief," Nora explained. "He couldn't have been the Duke of Diamonds."

"Why not?" he asked. "Fellow broke in without so much as a how-do-you-do."

Nora grew impatient. "He didn't take our jewels, or at least he didn't take Elizabeth's, since I don't have any, and he didn't talk to either of us. He hasn't committed any robberies in the middle of the night. That's just when he returns things."

Elizabeth stared at her. "But, Nora, what was he doing here?"

Before she could reply, Burton and the footmen rejoined them. Burton was cool and unruffled, but the two footmen were panting with the exertion of their chase, and Robert had Rufus, still growling threats, tucked under one arm.

"I believe, Sir Edmund," Burton said clearly, "that the intruder must have escaped in the same manner that he made his entrance, through the door which leads to the mews. It was closed, but unlocked, and that is where we found your two animals, one of them causing an ungodly din."

"He was on horseback, Sir Edmund," panted Robert. "We could hear the sound of hooves on the pavement as he galloped away." Burton looked pained by this interruption of his subordinate, but he picked up the story again without comment.

"We were not able to catch sight of him, but," and here he glanced at Rufus, "the young animal had this in his teeth." And he gingerly held out a soggy strip of fine black wool.

Sir Edmund and the ladies examined it, ignoring Rufus, who showed unmistakable signs of wanting to recapture his trophy. "It is a good-quality fabric," said Elizabeth.

"And it is black—like the Duke of Diamonds wears," added Nora. They stared at one another for a moment.

"Elizabeth, go and check your jewels," commanded Sir Edmund. Silvers, who had been hovering in the background in her wrapper, shrieked and fled to Elizabeth's dressing room. The housekeeper and maids, who had been waiting with her, fluttered and chattered outside the door while Elizabeth and Silvers, accompanied by Nora, opened the wardrobe which contained Elizabeth's chests of jewelry. All three of them were gone, including the box containing her mother's collection of rings. Elizabeth sank down on the little blue daybed, and Silvers rushed to her room to fetch her vinaigrette.

Finally, acknowledging that sleep in that household was a lost cause until everyone calmed down, Sir Edmund escorted the ladies to the library, where they were plied with tea and toast while Sir Edmund recruited his strength with something slightly stiffer. At his orders, the housekeeper was serving the staff in the kitchen, for by now even Sir Edmund's stablehands had been awakened by the fuss. Robert had been sent round to report the robbery to the authorities.

"Although no good will come from that," said Sir Edmund in annoyance. "Haven't caught the fellow yet—won't now."

"But it *couldn't* have been the Duke of Diamonds," insisted Nora. "He never uses violence, and he doesn't rob ladies while they're sleeping."

"No, he just creeps about the house planting Easter eggs and scattering their jewels with riddles while they're sleeping," said Sir Edmund dryly. "I fail to see the distinction, Nora."

"Well it *is* different, Edmund!" She brightened a little. "Although, Edmund, he could have shot you had he wished to, so he didn't truly use violence."

"Let's part your hair with a bullet, young lady, and see if you think it's violent."

"Oh, come now, Edmund, don't be so hen-hearted. You said yourself that he was a very good shot. So if he had wanted to hurt you, he could have."

"Did seem a good shot," mused Sir Edmund. "Wonder why he shot the candle out though?"

"So that you wouldn't see his face, Edmund," Nora explained impatiently. "He must have been someone you know."

"Dash it all, Nora, my friends don't creep around my house in the dead of night—" He broke off suddenly as understanding dawned. "You're still thinking it's young Mallory!" he exclaimed.

Before she could make any disclaimer, Sir Edmund was pursuing his thoughts. "Told you before that he's a good horseman, but not good enough for the run down Berkeley. And if he's as

202

good a marksman as the fellow tonight, I've yet to hear about it."

Rufus was reclining across Sir Edmund's slipper, and the sudden movement as he made his home point to Nora caused the pup to sit upright and look at the speaker reproachfully.

Called to order, Sir Edmund stared down at him for a moment. "Wouldn't have even known about the fellow if it hadn't been for you, boy." He reached down and gave the pup a tentative pat. "We don't like fellows creeping about our houses, do we?"

"This is so different a style of robbery from his usual one," said Nora, still clinging to her theory. "Do you suppose he'll come back to return the jewelry?"

Sir Edmund sat bolt upright, his nightcap at attention. "Come creeping back into my house *again?*" he demanded. "No, by gad, that's too much! I won't have it! If he sets foot in this house again, I'll have him by the heels!"

"But, Edmund, what about Elizabeth's jewels? Don't you want her to have them back?"

"Well, of course I want them back, but I don't want some curst sneaksby back in here! Makes my blood boil just to think about it!" He looked down at the pup and patted his head again. "We won't stand for it, will we, boy?"

In token of his complete agreement, Rufus fell over on his side, his chin on Sir Edmund's slipper, and went back to sleep.

Chapter Sixteen

Everyone in Sir Edmund's household, even the humblest maid and stableboy, slept late, exhausted by the excitement of the night before, and when they finally did arise, the robbery was unquestionably the favored topic of conversation. Robert, who had almost caught a glimpse of him, averred that he was undoubtedly the Duke of Diamonds. Jackson, Sir Edmund's groom, held that he was one of a group of thieves that had been working some of the big houses just to the north of Mayfair.

"And what would bring him here?" asked Robert with a knowing look. "Why would he pick out Sir Edmund as his mark? Why change his territory? And how did he know about the rings?"

"Ah, but it wasn't Sir Edmund what was his mark, now was it?" interposed Mrs. Washburn, the housekeeper, who, although she belonged to Robert's party, believed in pound dealing. "It was Miss Elizabeth what had her jewels stole. And it was that, Mr. Jackson, what made us believe it was the Dook."

With that masterful piece of reasoning, the lady took herself proudly to a table in the corner to superintend the preparation of the tea trays that would be carried upstairs.

Robert, who obviously shared Sir Edmund's sentiments, muttered into his mug of beer, "Well, he better not show his face around here again, that's all!"

Burton, who had maintained a stately silence and declined to take sides, said majestically over his mug of tea, "I'm sure that we all know our duty and will do it tonight." A general murmur of agreement swept round the kitchen, and it was clear that Rufus would be ably assisted that night. Whether they were dog fanciers or not, the servants now one and all approved of Rufus. Even those like Mrs. Washburn and Burton, who had taken the dog in dislike, had changed their tune. Mrs. Washburn had, in fact, just prepared a small dish filled with delicacies to tempt a small dog's appetite.

"Could have all been murdered in our beds," observed Martha, the upstairs maid, "had it not been for that pup." Again the murmur of agreement swept round the group. Rufus had clearly found his place in life.

The drawing room was filled with callers that afternoon, all eager to hear the details of the Duke's latest feat, for such they judged it to be.

"He must have been a very busy gentleman last night," observed Miss Tillsbury archly. Miss Tillsbury, who could not bear to hear her gossip secondhand, was noted for arriving upon the scene of notable society events at the first possible moment. Anything said before her would be common news in every household of the *ton* by nightfall, for she would move from drawing room to drawing room, earning her way with her stories.

"What do you mean?" asked Nora, suddenly alert.

"Why, hadn't you heard, my dear? He also visited Lady Gregory's, although I understand they're trying to keep that very hush-hush." She lowered her voice and nodded her head knowingly. "She doesn't mix much at all since the unfortunate occurrence with Sir Howard."

Burton entered the room at that point and caught Elizabeth's eye, glancing significantly to the hallway behind him. Elizabeth rose immediately and excused herself from her guests, leaving Nora to fend for herself with Miss Tillsbury.

"What is it, Burton?" she asked, closing the drawing-room door securely behind her to prevent Miss Tillsbury from gleaning any other tidbits of news to carry along her way.

"Lady Gregory would like to see you, Miss Elizabeth. Since she did not wish to see anyone else, I took the liberty of showing her to the morning room."

"Thank you, Burton. You were quite right to do so."

Elizabeth entered the morning room to find Lady Gregory, who was normally so calm, pacing back and forth across the carpet. When she looked up, Elizabeth could see that she could scarcely have slept at all, for the circles under her eyes were very dark.

"Miss Harrington! I understand that you too were robbed last night!"

Elizabeth nodded and came closer so that she could take Lady Gregory's hands. "I have just heard that you were also a victim."

Lady Gregory laughed bitterly. "So the gossips already know! I suppose I mustn't be surprised by that."

Alarmed by her appearance, Elizabeth led her to a sofa. "Please sit down, Lady Gregory, and allow me to ring for some tea."

"No tea for me, please. It would not calm me."

"What was taken, Lady Gregory?" Elizabeth asked, and just as quickly she answered her own question. "Was it the egg? Sir Howard's egg?"

Lady Gregory nodded. "He took nothing else—and nothing was damaged. My butler isn't even certain how he gained admittance to the house."

"You say 'he.' Did you see the thief?"

She shook her head. "I am merely doing what everyone else is doing and attributing my robbery to the Duke of Diamonds. That is what the magistrate thinks."

"Did you describe the egg to him?"

"I did, but it will do no good. There are too many things that could happen to it now."

"If only we had the key!" cried Elizabeth. "How will we know when we have found what we are seeking without the key?"

"We wouldn't know," agreed Lady Gregory, "which is why it is so very fortunate that I decided to remove the key from the egg and to hide it elsewhere." And she slipped a fine chain from inside the bodice of her walking dress. At the end of it dangled the key.

"How splendid!" cried Elizabeth. "I never would have thought to remove that key. That was very clever of you, Lady Gregory."

"I have been congratulating myself," she admitted, "but I confess that I am deeply troubled by the robbery. There is nothing to prevent his returning and taking the key now—or anything else he wants for that matter."

She paused a moment and then looked directly at Elizabeth. "And I have been very troubled by another thing. Very few people knew of that key, Miss Harrington. How did the Duke of Diamonds learn of it?"

Elizabeth's thoughts flew immediately to Mr. Norville and then to Lord Mallory. Reluctantly, she replied, "It appears that you are correct, Lady Gregory. We must hope that we will find a reasonable explanation for this." She smoothed her skirts and added, even more reluctantly, "Would you like for me to send notes to Lord Mallory and Mr. Norville, asking them to pay you a call?"

Lady Gregory shook her head. "No, I am too weary for callers. I was truly too tired to come to you, but I had to tell someone about the key, and I felt that I could trust you."

"You may indeed," she assured Lady Gregory. "Do you wish for me to keep the matter of the whereabouts of the key a secret?"

Lady Gregory considered the matter for a moment or two, then shook her head. "You may tell the others—Miss Lane and Lord Mallory and Mr. Norville. It could prove interesting."

Elizabeth was not certain in what way telling the others would be interesting, but she did not pursue the subject, for Lady Gregory appeared close to collapse. "Is your carriage outside, or should I have mine brought round for you?" she asked.

"Mine is waiting," Lady Gregory replied.

"Please go to bed when you arrive home," Elizabeth said as she helped her to the door. "You need to rest."

"Yes. Yes, I do," she agreed. "I seldom feel this way, but I know today how old I am coming to be."

Elizabeth watched her uneasily until Burton had seen her safely into her own carriage and the horses had pulled away. How had someone known of the key, if not from one of them? Did the others, the gentlemen and the lady who were pursuing the egg, know of it? If not, which one of their own small circle had given away the information? Or, perhaps, used it to his own advantage?

Lord Mallory and Mr. Norville, having heard of the excitement in Grosvenor Square, both put in an appearance during the course of the afternoon. The former grinned down at Nora and observed that she would have done better to practice her shooting than her fencing had she known what lay in store. Nora tossed her head. "You wouldn't have thought it such a lark had you been here, Lord Mallory! Hearing the pistol go off was a terrible shock! I expected to find Sir Edmund dead!"

"He seems to be in remarkably good form," remarked Mallory, nodding across the room at Sir Edmund, who had come in searching for his *Morning Chronicle*. "It must not have overset *his* nerves."

"My nerves were not overset, Lord Mallory," Nora returned stiffly, judging correctly that he was making sport of her. "But one scarcely expects to hear a pistol shot in the middle of the night in one's own house."

Recognizing the peril of too many *one's,* she retired to the safety of conversing about Sir Edmund. "And if you think that Sir Edmund was entirely unaffected by last night, you would be wrong. He plans to catch the Duke when he returns tonight."

"Oh, he does?" said Mallory, his eyes alight. "How does he propose to accomplish that?"

"I don't know precisely what his plans are, but I do know that most of the servants are planning to stay up and help him, too."

"Then, if the Duke is a clever man, I daresay he won't return tonight."

Nora looked at him searchingly. "And do *you* think that he is a clever man, Lord Mallory?"

"He certainly seems so to me—although I must admit that popping off that pistol seems a paperskulled thing to have done."

"Edmund thought that the Duke was afraid that he would be recognized, and so he shot out the candle."

Mallory looked interested. "Afraid Sir Edmund would recognize him? Now that would have been interesting. What would Sir Edmund have done?"

Nora shrugged. "It would depend very much on what Edmund thought of him as a person, I should imagine. That, and how well he rides—and the Duke has already received a favorable review from Edmund in that respect."

"Now that is a compliment indeed," returned Mallory. "The Duke should be gratified."

"I'm sure that he is," retorted Nora pertly, certain that she was speaking with the Duke himself. "And I hope that you are correct about his being a clever man, for tonight could be a night of reckoning for the Duke."

As it happened, however, the Duke did not put in an appearance during the night. This did not surprise Nora in the least, for she was certain that Mallory, once forewarned, would be cautious. The rest of the household was prepared. When the lights went out that night, Sir Edmund lay in his bed with his pistol at the ready, Rufus stationed at the door. Robert and two of the other footmen were stationed downstairs in the kitchen, prepared for an assault from that direction. Burton, armed with a candlestick, was lying in wait in the hallway outside Elizabeth's room. Mrs. Washburn and Silvers sat on the daybed in Elizabeth's dressing room, quivering with excitement and fear. Mrs. Washburn was prepared with a rolling pin and Silvers with a cane. It was not a normal cane, however, for as she had demonstrated dramatically to Mrs. Washburn, once the handle was removed, a wicked-looking stiletto was ready for use. Mrs. Washburn had shrieked and had palpitations, and Nora had been forced to seek Elizabeth's vinaigrette before she could be restored.

Nora, afraid that she might be left out, had crept into Elizabeth's room, and they both lay there under the covers, watching the door and expecting their visitor. In the mews Mr. Jackson and two of the stableboys were waiting, watching like hawks. The household was ready.

Their preparation was for naught. Dawn broke, and there was no sign of the Duke. The eager protectors faded with the light, and once again Sir Edmund's household slept late. Imagine their consternation when Nora awoke and, glancing at Eliz-

209

abeth's pillow, shrieked. There, nestled next to Elizabeth's red hair, lay a blue enamel egg, inside it the expected scroll, bound with a scarlet ribbon. Nora's scream having awakened her, Elizabeth hurriedly opened the egg and read the message, Nora looking over her shoulder.

> *Lady dear, you cannot know*
> *How my heart is beating so.*
> *Your copper hair, your deep blue eyes,*
> *Only a fool would fail to prize.*
>
> *Thus, although my pain is great,*
> *And although you have lingered late,*
> *I cannot give your jewels to you*
> *Until your heart to mine is true.*

"Well!" exclaimed Nora. "How very bold of him! Imagine not returning your jewelry and expecting you to be true to him without even knowing who he is!" In her heart, she was preparing the searing speech she would make to Lord Mallory when next they met. Who would have thought that he was really head over heels in love with Elizabeth!

Sir Edmund came hurrying in, followed by Silvers and Mrs. Washburn, who had also been awakened by Nora's scream. Burton still sat dozing gently in the hallway, clutching his candlestick to his chest.

Sir Edmund read the note and snorted. "I suppose the fellow thinks this doggerel verse is poetry! What fustian!" He stared at Elizabeth. "And what infernal nerve to say that he won't give you back your jewels until you are true to him! As though you would have anything to do with some highwayman!"

He looked down at Rufus and Sampson, who had followed him into the room. "And where were you while he was sneaking about the house? I'll tell you where you were—snoring in my room, that's where!" The pair of them looked properly abashed and crept into a corner of the room.

His forehead creased as he thought about what he had just said. "Why did the dog growl the first time and not now?" he inquired thoughtfully.

"Perhaps he was worn out from the excitement of the first visit," volunteered Nora.

The creases grew deeper. "And that fellow came right into your room with all of us sitting here waiting for him! I can't say that this makes me easy in my mind."

Mrs. Washburn and Silvers seemed strongly inclined to agree with him, for the vinaigrette was not sufficient to restore the housekeeper, and one of the maids was obliged to resort to burnt feathers as a restorative. Elizabeth herself was not much happier. If Mallory really were the Duke, then why did he want her jewelry? And Nora would certainly not be pleased with this apparent partiality for Elizabeth. If Norville were the Duke, the same observations still held. And he, at least, had certainly not indicated that he felt a *tendre* for her—quite otherwise, in fact. Mr. Norville obviously regarded her with contempt, making himself pleasant only when he intended to entrap her into revealing herself an incompetent chaperone for Nora. And, whoever he was, what could be the true purpose of retaining her jewelry? Elizabeth did not for a moment believe the foolish reason given in the note. There must be some genuine reason for keeping it.

Suddenly she thought of Lady Gregory. Could the egg have been returned? Had the Duke paid a second call that night? Hurriedly she scribbled a note for Robert to take round to Curzon Street and then waited impatiently for a reply. She had a good deal to occupy her attention during this time, for the household staff had to be restored to working order and the business of the day set in motion. It was also the day of the masquerade ball, and there was much to be done to prepare the costumes for the three of them.

When Robert finally arrived with Lady Gregory's reply, she ripped it open and read it where she stood, the envelope fluttering unnoticed to the hallway floor. The Duke had indeed paid a call at the Gregory home and had left his calling card in the case where Sir Howard's egg had rested. The egg had been returned. Her brief note from the Duke had read:

211

To the riddle now you hold the key—
The answer will set Sir Howard free

Elizabeth folded the missive into a tight little screw and slipped it into her pocket. Set Sir Howard free? What could that mean? It must of course mean that his memory would be cleared, for surely Sir Howard was not still alive.

It was fortunate, perhaps, that they had the ball to look forward to that night, for it kept their minds and fingers occupied. Sir Edmund had grumbled the entire evening as Elizabeth and Nora had worked on putting together his costume.

"It is so fortunate that you have dark hair," commented Elizabeth cheerfully. "At least we don't have to dye it."

Sir Edmund had stared at her in wild-eyed disbelief. "Dye it! I should like to see you try to do it, my girl!"

"But I won't have to, Edmund. All we need do is provide you with a moustache. And I have the perfect one right here." And she held up a dark curling moustache.

Sir Edmund's eyes almost started from their sockets. "You don't expect me to put on that thing, Lizzy!" he exclaimed in horror.

"Well, of course you must, Edmund. You need to look your part, and this will be the finishing touch." She and Nora regarded their handiwork admiringly. Edmund was attired in black pantaloons and a white cambric shirt with full, loose sleeves tightly cuffed at the wrists and open at the throat. He had been permitted to retain his highly polished black topboots in exchange for wearing a large medallion on a golden chain around his neck. An open vest of peacock blue and a kerchief of scarlet knotted around his throat completed his costume. Fish could only stand at one side and wring his hands as the ladies worked.

Elizabeth scrutinized him carefully and then took out a heavy gold ring set with a red stone. "Here, Edmund, put this on. They say gypsies are always fond of jewelry."

Sir Edmund slipped it on reluctantly, staring at it and then at her. "Don't worry about it, Edmund. It isn't a real ruby; it's just a trumpery piece for tonight."

"Just as well," her brother grumbled. "I'll be lucky if the Duke doesn't decide to hold me up for my jewelry. Fish, tell Burton to bring some brandy to my study."

And Sir Edmund departed to fortify himself for the agonies to come while he waited for the ladies to join him. Nora was a vision of bright gypsy splendor in a full skirt of vivid purple and a bodice of the same peacock blue found in Sir Edmund's vest. Her waist was bound with a long scarf of brilliant colors, and her arms were hung with countless gold bracelets, her slender neck with a necklace of golden spangles. She had loosened her dark hair and let it hang free, glad now that she had feathered only the sides when she had had it cut. Large golden hoops hung from her ears, and small slippers of scarlet velvet peeped from beneath her skirt. Elizabeth strongly suspected that she had used lampblack to darken her lashes and rubbed a damp red ribbon on her cheeks for color. All in all, she was grateful that Cecilia could not see her at the present moment.

Elizabeth herself had discarded the idea of the shepherdess as too mundane and had elected to go as a sea nymph. She wore a slender gown of blue-green satin, whose color shifted according to the light, and a diaphanous overgown of seafoam green with cream-colored lace ruches to represent the waves. On her hair she wore a garland of woven green, like seaweed, crusted with tiny seashells. The clever Madame Devereaux had stitched into her costume tiny brilliants that would catch the light and sparkle like sunlight on the sea. Seashells adorned her wrists and neck and hung from her ears. Even her mask was of seafoam green and was edged with lace.

Although forced to prepare for the masquerade on such short notice, Elizabeth had taken great pains with her costume. She was not certain why she had taken such trouble, and if, from time to time, she pictured a certain dark gentleman staring at her with an admiration untainted by criticism, it was no more than natural. Unaccustomed as she was to disapproval, it was only to be expected that she would wish to overcome Mr. Norville's objections to her.

Nora was in a fever pitch of excitement by the time their carriage arrived at Lady's Seaton's home that night for the masked

213

ball. Elizabeth was pleased, although not surprised, to see that her charge was called upon to dance from the moment of her entrance. Elizabeth herself was engaged immediately by a charming harlequin. As they glided across the floor, she caught a glimpse of a lovely woman dressed as a queen, a golden coronet crowning her shining hair. Tall and stately, she laughed up into the face of her partner, a square-shouldered man with dark hair, attired as a pirate. It was Mr. Norville and Lady Brill! Elizabeth felt her heart sink, but she smiled more brightly at her harlequin.

Dance followed dance until she was approached by an admiring Lord Mallory. Even though he was masked and in costume, she had no trouble identifying him. His height and easy grace, his golden hair and ready smile, gave him away. To her amusement she noted that he was dressed all in black, including a black cape and black tricorn, which he removed to make her a sweeping bow.

"And so I have the pleasure of dancing with the Duke of Diamonds?" she inquired, laughing.

"At your service, ma'am. And should you find yourself in need of a diamond, just mention it to me." And he held open a pocket of his jacket to reveal a mass of shining stones that made Elizabeth gasp.

"Don't allow yourself to be overcome, Miss Harrington," he cautioned her. "These are not real, but I thought that they would make me seem more authentic."

He smiled down at her. "I understand that the Duke feels a *tendre* for you. I must admit that I am not surprised."

Elizabeth felt herself flushing and said hurriedly, "How did you recognize me, Lord Mallory?"

He glanced at her bright, feathery curls. "If I had not recognized your titian hair, I would certainly have known you by your bright eyes." He raised the fingers of her lacy mittens and pressed them to his lips.

"Very pretty," said a dry voice. Both Mallory and Elizabeth glanced up, startled.

"I hate to intrude upon this touching scene, Miss Harrington," said Mr. Norville—and Elizabeth had no doubt that it was he, disguised though he was as a pirate, "but were you aware that

Miss Lane is performing in one of the small saloons?"

"Performing?" blinked Lord Mallory. "Performing what?"

Elizabeth pressed her fingers to her cheek. "Oh, dear heaven! The egg-dance!"

Mr. Norville bowed. "Just so, Miss Harrington. And since it is scarcely my place to put an end to it, I thought perhaps you might do so."

"Well, of course I will!" exclaimed Elizabeth. "If that isn't just like the child!" And she hurried away behind Mr. Norville with Lord Mallory bringing up the rear, chuckling.

The scene that greeted Elizabeth's eyes was as distressing as she was afraid it would be. Nora had discarded her slippers and, blindfolded, was stepping lightly among the eggs scattered on the lovely Persian carpet. As they entered the room, the pace of the music supplied by a fascinated violinist accelerated, and Nora's skirt whirled about her, her small feet keeping the rhythm perfectly. Her audience, primarily young gentlemen with a scattering of disapproving young ladies, stood in a semi-circle about her, a few of the gentlemen beginning to clap with the beat of the music.

"She's quite good, you know," said Mallory approvingly.

Elizabeth shot him a glance of disbelief. "You know that she must not do this sort of thing, Lord Mallory. It sets all the tongues to wagging when a young girl behaves in an irregular manner. She should not be dancing alone in front of a group just as though she were on stage."

Mallory settled his tricorn firmly on his head. "Then we must stop the tongues from wagging. Miss Lane will not dance alone."

And before Elizabeth realized what he was doing, Mallory had stepped in among the eggs, catching Nora's hands in his own, and deftly danced her away from the eggs.

"I am the Duke of Diamonds, gypsy maiden, and I have come to rob you of your gold."

Nora recognized his voice and laughed. Freeing her hands from his, she took the blindfold from her eyes and looked up at him, her audience still watching, fascinated, although neither Nora or Mallory seemed at all aware of them. Even the violinist was fascinated, and he switched his melody to a lilting, romantic air to match the mood of the little scene before him with the handsome highwayman and the dainty gypsy girl.

Slipping the bracelets from her wrists, she cupped them in both her hands, forming a small mound of gold. Curtseying, she offered them to him. "Take my gold if you will, sir."

He reached out as though to take it and then, looking down into her eyes, stopped, and his voice grew serious. "No. I cannot take the gold from you, little one. Not from you."

He smiled, his eyes suddenly bright with laughter in the candlelight. Reaching into his pocket, he plucked out a diamond the size of a robin's egg and presented it to her with a dashing bow. "Allow me instead to present you with this token of my esteem, my lady." And he dropped the stone into the palm of her hand. "And with this." He reached into the pocket of his waistcoat and drew out an Easter egg pendant, strung on a blue ribbon, and placed it around her neck.

The strains of the violinist, who was becoming more and more caught up in the scene before him, had become increasingly tender and vibrant. As Lord Mallory moved lightly to the door and turned to wave to Nora, his melody reached a crescendo and then faded as he disappeared from sight.

There was a slight pause and then the audience began to buzz among themselves about the strange little scene they had just seen enacted. Nora, fingering her necklace with one hand, stood looking silently at the diamond in the palm of the other.

Mr. Norville turned to Elizabeth. "I must compliment you, Miss Harrington, upon your deft handling of that situation. I had been worried that Miss Lane might draw undue attention to herself, but now I need worry about that no longer. All that was lacking here was the stage of the Drury." And nodding curtly to her, he turned and walked away.

"Quite as though it were my fault!" gasped Elizabeth to herself. "As though I had told Mallory to make a spectacle of himself. Why did he not do something himself instead of complaining about me?" In such terms did Elizabeth angrily talk the situation over with herself. As her anger faded, she realized that her sea nymph costume had not had the desired effect upon Mr. Norville. In fact, she felt that it was doubtful that he had even noticed how becoming her costume was.

216

She was able to take herself in hand well enough to walk over to Nora and say in a relatively calm voice, "You knew, Nora, that you should not have been dancing. We had talked about this beforehand."

"I know that we had, Elizabeth. But I truly wanted to. I did not feel that I had a right to be in the costume unless I did the egg-dance."

Elizabeth ignored this sally as unworthy of comment and continued. "The people who were in here watching, Nora, will delight in telling the story to everyone else that they meet to-night."

Nora shrugged. "Why should I be bothered by them?"

Elizabeth took a deep breath. "To make a creditable marriage, one must have a good reputation, Nora, and it takes very little to undo a reputation in London. People do not know you well as yet, and you don't want to make them think poorly of you."

Nora's eyes kindled with anger. "A little thing like this could overset them then?"

Elizabeth nodded.

"Then I care even less about what they think! And at any rate, I am already about to be married, am I not? So surely I need not trouble myself!"

She stared down at the diamond that still lay sparkling in the palm of her hand. "Look at this, Elizabeth. Lord Mallory gave me a diamond."

Elizabeth hastened to explain. "He has a whole pocketful of them, Nora. They are paste, not real ones."

Nora went on as though she had not heard her. "And what do you think, Elizabeth, of his dressing up as the Duke? And having the diamonds and the Easter egg in his pockets? Does that not show that he *is* the Duke of Diamonds?"

Elizabeth chuckled. "If dressing up as the Duke means that he *is* the Duke, then we have at least half a dozen of them present tonight. I have never before seen so many gentlemen arrayed in black."

Nora was undeterred. Lowering her voice, she whispered, "I think, Elizabeth, that he is going to strike again tonight. Lady Seaton must be his next victim."

Before Elizabeth could reply, their conversation was interrupted by the arrival of a newcomer. To their dismay, Lord Dabney, arrayed in a Roman toga, tights, and gaiters had been lingering among the members of Nora's audience and had chosen this moment to join them.

"I trust, Elizabeth, that you have been able to impress upon Miss Lane a sense of the impropriety that she was guilty of tonight. My heart went out to you when I saw her behaving in so indecorous a manner."

Elizabeth, who had been very angry with Nora and had felt the impropriety of her behavior keenly, bristled. "She is very young, Gervase, and so may be forgiven for acting without thinking."

Lord Dabney looked shocked. "I cannot believe that I can be hearing you properly, Elizabeth! Surely you are not condoning such behavior! And with Lord Mallory, too, who is notorious for his pranks!"

"It was all quite innocent, Gervase, so please do not be taking on about it in this manner! It is, after all, my affair!"

Lord Dabney drew himself up and looked as dignified as his costume would allow. "As you wish, Elizabeth. I'm sure that I do not wish to intrude. I merely have the interests of an old friend at heart."

Elizabeth relented. "Oh, very well, Gervase. I know that you have my interests at heart, but you cannot be pinching at Nora like that."

It suddenly occurred to both of them that they had been speaking of Nora as though she were not present, and they turned to where she had been standing. She was there no longer, however, and a quick survey of the small saloon in which they stood told her that she was no longer in that apartment. Elizabeth hurried back to the ballroom with Lord Dabney in her wake, but she was no more successful there. Together they scoured the other rooms into which the ball had flowed, but Nora was not to be found. This would have been disturbing to Elizabeth in any circumstances, but tonight, with the addition of the strange sense of anonymity that the masks gave to the merrymakers and the realization that Nora must have been very upset by their conversation, she found that she was growing almost panic-stricken.

She surely would not have tried to leave the party, Elizabeth consoled herself. Accordingly, she turned to Lord Dabney and gave him his instructions firmly.

"Gervase, you go back through the ballroom and the other first-floor apartments again. I will go upstairs. If she were very upset, she might have tried to find a place to be alone to compose herself." She actually considered it quite unlikely that Nora would have become that discomposed, but it would at least keep Gervase from accompanying her.

In the first two chambers she entered on the next floor, she found young ladies giggling and adjusting their costumes and hair. Apologizing for her intrusion, she had just withdrawn from the second one when she caught a movement from the corner of her eye. Glancing up quickly, she saw a young man disappearing around the corner of the hallway in the most furtive manner imaginable. Overcome by curiosity, she followed him.

When she turned the corner, there was no sign of him, but a door standing ajar led to a back staircase. She heard a slight noise from above and decided to follow it. It seemed very unlikely that this all had anything to do with Nora, but she could not resist the impulse to find out what was causing the young man to be so secretive. She could see no one when she emerged from the stairwell into the hallway of the next floor, and so she stood very quietly and listened. At first she could hear nothing at all, but then there was a rustling, followed by a thud and the sounds of a struggle.

Rushing to the room from which the sounds were issuing, she threw the door open and entered. Two men, both in black and masked, were locked in combat. At the sound of her entrance, one of them looked up and the other took advantage of his wavering attention to raise a dagger and strike down with it. Then, turning, he plunged through a door into an adjoining chamber, leaving his victim on the floor.

Elizabeth ran over to him and turned him onto his back. A bright red stain was spreading across the shoulder of his jacket. Quickly she lifted her skirt and tore away a portion of her petticoat with which to stanch the wound. She heard a gasp as she bent over the injured man and looked up to see the young man she had followed standing in the doorway, holding his hand to his lips.

"Elizabeth! What have you done?" he exclaimed.

Elizabeth continued working, opening the shirt to place the pad on the open wound. "Nora! What are you doing in that regalia?"

Nora was confounded and hung her head. "Sir Adrian brought it for me. And after you gave me such a scold about the egg-dance and talked in front of me as though I wasn't there, I thought perhaps I would go ahead and play this joke. I was just to go down to the ball for a while, masked of course, so no one would know who I was."

"Not until you were trapped into asking some young miss to dance and giving yourself away. Or until one of the gentlemen tried to make conversation with you or take you to the card-room. Nora, you have no more sense than a goose!"

Nora nodded in agreement, and Elizabeth continued applying pressure to the wound.

"After I changed, I heard a noise in the hallway," Nora said. "I looked out and saw Lord Mallory disappearing around the corner, so I followed him. He went into one of the rooms in this corridor, so I was looking into all of them when I found you."

Elizabeth was startled. "Lord Mallory?" She looked down at the figure she was tending. "This isn't Lord Mallory!"

"How observant of you, Miss Harrington," the figure said weakly.

Elizabeth almost dropped the bloody pad in her hands. "Mr. Norville!" she exclaimed and stared at Nora.

Nora's voice was scarcely more than a whisper. "Was it—was it Lord Mallory who stabbed you, Mr. Norville?"

There was no answer as Mr. Norville took the pad from Elizabeth and, pressing it against his shoulder himself, struggled to arise.

"You should not be moving yet, Mr. Norville," she scolded.

"I'll be quite all right, Miss Harrington. The wound is not a bad one. I believe that I must have hit my head on the edge of that table as I went down."

Elizabeth surveyed him from head to foot as he eased himself down on the nearest chair.

"What, may I ask, Mr. Norville, are you doing in that costume? When we last saw you, you were dressed as a pirate, not as the Duke of Diamonds."

"Very true. Again, you gain points for being observant, Miss Harrington."

"But you are avoiding my question, Mr. Norville. Why did you change your costume?"

He pushed back his mask and looked at her with irritation. "You are being overly inquisitive. Why should I not change my costume?" He surveyed Nora with interest. "It is apparent that Miss Lane did."

Nora blushed and stammered, "That's quite different, Mr. Norville. I was just going to play a joke."

She stared at the floor for a moment to compose herself, then looked back up at him. "What of you, sir? Were you going to play a joke? And was it Lord Mallory with whom you were fighting?"

Norville rubbed the bump that had formed on the side of his forehead. "I might as well be in the hands of the Spanish Inquisition," he murmured. The pad he was holding to his shoulder with his other hand slipped, and as he reached for it, a diamond necklace and bracelet slipped from his pocket. He snatched for them, but they fell to the floor.

Nora picked them up and looked first at them and then at her cousin. "These aren't paste, are they, Elizabeth?"

Elizabeth picked up the necklace and held it to the light. Before she could answer, Norville sighed and spoke. "I will save you the trouble, Miss Harrington. No, they are not paste, and yes, they are diamonds. No, they are not mine, and yes, I did take them."

Nora's eyes grew wide. "Are *you* the Duke of Diamonds?" she asked in disbelief.

Norville nodded. "I am afraid that I am—and I would like it very much if no one else came to know of this."

"I'm sure you would," replied Elizabeth tartly, "but I can't think of any particularly strong reason why we should keep it a secret. I might point out, Mr. Norville, that this makes any of

221

my peccadilloes seem truly mild by comparison. I wonder that you could have taken such a high-and-mighty air with me, knowing that you were trotting about collecting other people's jewels."

"I did not think that you would be slow in pointing that out," he sighed.

"Indeed not! But I am amazed, Mr. Norville, that so proper and upright a gentleman could have done such a thing! And then to criticize poor Nora for dancing her little dance! It is really too bad of you, sir!"

Before he could defend himself, the door to the adjoining chamber, through which Norville's attacker had escaped, swung open, and Lord Mallory entered, his mask up.

"Whatever has happened here?" he asked in amazement, staring at Norville's bloody shoulder. "Did the ladies set upon you, Norville?"

"Of course not," replied Nora shortly. "What, may I ask, Lord Mallory, brings you to this part of the house?"

"Although I could ask exactly the same thing of you," he pointed out in the tone of a reasonable parent explaining things to a particularly slow child, "I will not. When I could not find Miss Harrington or you, I asked Lord Dabney if he had seen you. He pursed up his lips and said that Elizabeth—that Miss Harrington had come upstairs to search for you. Quite reasonably, I decided that I too would come."

A noise in the hallway caught their attention, and Norville looked about him in alarm. "Did anyone else come with you, Mallory?"

Mallory nodded. "I fear that Lord Dabney is bringing up the rear."

All three of them groaned, and Norville said, "Go out and get rid of him, man! He mustn't know that I am here."

Mallory obeyed with alacrity and reentered the room smiling a few moments later. "Told him that Miss Lane was in great distress because she had realized the seriousness of her error in doing the egg-dance. Told him that Miss Harrington had to stay with her to take care of her."

"You told him what?" cried Nora, outraged.

He grinned more widely. "Told him that you weren't a bad

little thing, but too hot at hand. A little more town polish and you'll do."

Nora could not think of anything scathing enough to say in retort, so she was forced to sit and seethe while the others talked.

"Now, what has happened to you, Norville? Do you need a surgeon?"

Norville shook his head. "My man will take care of me when I get home. He took care of far worse wounds than this in Spain. And Miss Harrington has already taken steps to stem the bleeding."

"Is this what did the damage?" Mallory drew a dagger from under the bed and looked at it. "I would say so," he said, answering his own question as he pointed at the blood on the blade.

Mallory held it up to the light. "Quite a fancy piece," he commented, looking at the hilt. "Will you tell me now who used this and why?"

Norville sighed again. "I suppose I must tell you at least a part of it. But in reply to your questions, I don't know who my attacker was, although I think I may know why he attacked."

"Could it be that he was someone who took exception to your taking Lady Seaton's jewels?" asked Elizabeth sweetly.

Mallory stared at him in amazement. "You don't mean that *you're* the Duke of Diamonds, Norville?" He chuckled. "Half of London must think that I'm the Duke, but I'd lay a monkey that nobody has considered you as a possibility."

There was a silence while he thought it over, then frowned. "They think I am the Duke because of the pranks I've played in the past, but you're not a prankster, Norville. What made you do it? What are you up to?"

Norville had grown progressively more pale as Mallory was talking. Finally, he said, "I know that I must explain to you all if I expect you to keep my secret, but may I ask you to wait until tomorrow? I think that it would be best if I got home as soon as possible. I would prefer to be able to make my departure without help, and I think I should move quickly."

"I won't hold you up and make a spectacle of you, Norville, but I will see you home," said Mallory, moving to bind a fresh pad of cloth in place, Elizabeth having retired to the next room and ripped off another portion of her petticoat.

"I must get back into my pirate costume, Mallory, if you would help me."

"Of course I will. Where did you leave it?"

Norville directed him to a room at the end of the hall. Mallory, glancing quickly at Norville and then at Elizabeth, turned to Nora and said firmly, "And you must resume your gypsy costume if we are to remove Norville without attracting undue attention." And, ignoring her protests, he guided her to the door and closed it firmly behind them.

"A very persuasive young man," Norville commented weakly. "He seems to have Miss Lane very well in hand." He studied Elizabeth's face for a moment as she knelt beside him and then asked quietly. "And do you mind?"

She finished pinning his bandage firmly in place and then stared at him blankly. "Do I mind what?"

He took her hand gently. "Remember that I saw them dancing together downstairs. Do you mind that Mallory is so taken with Miss Lane?"

"It seems to me, sir, that you are the one who should mind," she said crisply. "Do you not remember that you are the one who wishes to marry Nora?"

In the brief silence that followed, Elizabeth appeared to forget that he was holding her hand, for she left it quietly in place and carefully pushed his tumbled hair from his forehead with her free one.

"And *do* you mind, Mr. Norville?" she asked softly, looking into his dark eyes.

He smiled, and she felt his good arm drawing her down to him, his eyes never leaving hers until she was crushed against him. Elizabeth, sharply aware of his warmth and his strength, could feel his lips against her hair and hear his voice murmuring her name.

"Look at me, Elizabeth," he whispered. "Lift your head and look at me."

Slowly she did as she was bidden and found herself once again looking into those disturbing dark eyes. He traced the outline of her lips gently and then, noticing the seashells at her throat, chuckled.

"A sea nymph, are you?" he inquired. "How very fitting a choice . . . forever young and bewitching . . ."

His voice trailed away as he drew her lips down to his, and for a few fleeting moments Elizabeth forgot everything else, even the necessity of breathing. An unfamiliar exhilaration, headier than any champagne, washed over her, and for a moment she gave way to it.

The spell was broken abruptly, however, when Norville attempted to move his other arm too suddenly and began the bleeding afresh. Elizabeth sat up quickly and hurried to stanch the bleeding, reminding herself as she did so that she had no reason to trust this man. When the wound was cared for, she deftly removed Norville's black cape.

"If you will excuse me, sir, there is something I must see," she commented, spreading his cape out on the bed.

He watched her with a puzzled expression. "What do you expect to see there, Elizabeth?"

Ignoring his use of her given name, she replied briskly, "I thought perhaps there might be a piece of cloth missing, but I see that your cape is intact. It was not you, then, that Rufus attacked when my jewels were taken."

He shook his head. "No, that was not I."

"Then it was not you that came the next night and left the egg and the note."

There was the briefest of pauses and then he smiled. "Oh, yes, Elizabeth. I left the note. It was an irresistible temptation."

"An irresistible temptation to make sport of me and further upset my household?" she demanded angrily. "You are the most arrogant, rag-mannered—"

She broke off as Mallory and Nora returned with the pirate costume. There was no chance to say anything further, for the ladies were dismissed while Mallory helped him to change. Norville promised that he would send them a note the next day as to when he could meet with them and give them an explanation. They had planned to leave for Chanderley, but their departure would now be delayed until they had an opportunity to look into this new turn of events.

Nora could not say enough about Mr. Norville. "Isn't he

wonderful?" she asked Elizabeth. "Who would have believed that he would do anything so dashing as this?"

"I would rather like to know *why* he has been doing this," returned Elizabeth tartly, all of her old suspicions returning now that she was safely removed from his very disturbing physical presence. "It appears to me that he has indeed been making a May-game of us all."

Nora could not agree, however, and her conversation made it quite clear that Mr. Norville had risen greatly in her esteem. As Elizabeth said good night to her at her bedroom door, she could hear Nora murmuring, "Nora Norville . . . the Duchess of Diamonds . . ."

What a puzzle the man was, Elizabeth thought again in exasperation. If Sir Howard had been truly fond of paradoxes, he would have been enraptured by Andrew Norville. One never knew what to expect. What could he have meant by that note? She answered her own question bitterly. Undoubtedly he thought her such a light-minded flirt that she would be untroubled by any concern for loyalty to Nora or for her own reputation.

She felt her cheeks flush when she thought of the scene in the bedroom that evening and how very nearly she had been taken in. Undoubtedly that was a part of his scheme. How very fortunate that she had not succumbed to his charm as so many others undoubtedly had. She thought of Nora's new interest in him and felt a quick surge of guilt. It would be too dreadful if she interfered in Nora's one chance for happiness. The child's time away from Cecilia was coming to a close and she would soon be officially engaged to Andrew Norville.

And a good thing it will be, Elizabeth told herself firmly, refusing to remember her brief joy in Norville's arms. If Nora were satisfied with him, that was all that mattered. She herself already had a perfectly satisfactory life. It was Nora who must be provided for. Dawn was breaking, however, before Elizabeth could seek comfort in sleep.

Chapter Seventeen

Early the next day Elizabeth and Nora received a note asking them to come to Lady Gregory's to meet with Mr. Norville and Lord Mallory. Mallory arrived soon afterwards, offering to take them in his carriage. Accordingly, they were all seated in Lady Gregory's drawing room by the time Norville made his entrance. His face was slightly drawn, but apart from that, he looked and moved as he usually did. No one would have been able to tell by glancing at him that he had suffered a shoulder wound.

The others had informed Lady Gregory of the happenings at the masked ball, for it was obvious that Mr. Norville intended to proffer his explanation of the Duke of Diamonds to her as well. And so it was with considerable curiosity that she studied him as he was shown into the drawing room.

"You told us as a young man that you intended to do something exciting with your life, Mr. Norville," she commented as he was seated. "I cannot think that becoming a highwayman was a part of your plan."

He smiled at her. "No, Lady Gregory, I assure you that the Duke of Diamonds is quite an incidental part of the plan."

"And is your wound mending?" she inquired politely.

"Indeed it is. Thanks to Miss Harrington's quick action, I lost far less blood than I would have, and my man says that it will heal quickly." He turned to Elizabeth. "It appears that I owe you a debt of gratitude, Miss Harrington."

Elizabeth, although surprised by his thanks, was determined

227

not to allow him to believe that she had made any special effort on his behalf. "Not at all, Mr. Norville," she replied coolly. "I would have done the same for any injured person."

He smiled at her retort. "I do believe you, Miss Harrington. I believe, in fact, that it probably took a special effort to force yourself to come to my aid. Helping a stranger would doubtless have cost you less effort than helping someone whom you have taken in dislike."

Elizabeth was confused by his directness, but she did not have to think of a reply, for he turned quickly to the business that had drawn them all together.

"There are some things that I feel you must know about the situation in which we find ourselves, but it is vital that you keep the information entirely to yourselves," he began.

The others looked startled by his seriousness and the allusion to secrecy, but they nodded, and, satisfied, he continued.

"During my time in the army, I was frequently called upon to perform special tasks. These assignments varied greatly: some took me among enemy soldiers as one of them, some took me among the civilian populace to learn what I could for our intelligence operations, some took me into the official circles of foreign governments. Occasionally, I was a government courier."

His audience was listening eagerly, Nora wide-eyed with excitement. "And so you truly were a spy!" she exclaimed.

"Well, of course he was!" responded Mallory indignantly. "I told you all that Michael said about him in his letters! And didn't you listen to Norville's stories at the inn when we first met?"

Nora turned pink and hung her head, for of course she had not listened at all to boring stories about the war. Things seemed a little different to her now that Norville had done something as romantic as masquerading as a highwayman. His action seemed to have cast a romantic glow over all of his activities.

Elizabeth, watching her, was aware of the change that her attitude toward Norville had undergone. It was as though someone had waved a magic wand over him and transformed him from a frog into a fairy-tale prince. She wondered for a fleeting moment if this whole masquerade had been a ruse on Norville's part to cast himself in a more romantic role for the maiden who found him so old and so boring. She discounted the thought as unworthy, however, for a man like Norville would certainly not stoop to such measures to attract the attention of a lady. And she forced her wandering thoughts back to the conversation.

"It was while I was with a group of French officers a number of years ago," he was saying, "that I first heard of the diamond." Caught by the word *diamond,* she gave him all of her attention.

"Everyone knew of the famous theft of the French crown jewels during the Revolution. We had heard, too, that one of them, which they call the Regent, was found in an attic in Paris and that Napoleon had pawned it several times to raise money for his campaigns. One of the jewels that was not found was the Blue Tavernier, a superb blue diamond. According to the French officers, the rumor was that it had been smuggled to England and that an important personage here had paid a very great sum of money for it."

"Do you know who bought it?" asked Nora.

"I am not certain who the original purchaser was, but I did learn that a few years after the robbery it had been presented secretly as a gift to the Prince of Wales."

"To Prinny!" exclaimed Lady Gregory, using the Prince Regent's old nickname from his youthful days. "Do you mean that he has held something of such value for all of these years?"

"He has indeed, Lady Gregory. He received it as a gift from a well-wisher, who undoubtedly expected political favors when the Prince of Wales came to power. The gentleman in question considered it in the light of an investment in the future. It soon came to the Prince's ears, however, that such a stone had been part of the French crown jewels."

"And didn't that present a problem for the Prince?" asked Elizabeth. "What would people think if he had property in his possession that had been stolen from another monarch, even if it were taken during a revolution?"

Norville smiled at her comment appreciatively. "You are right, of course, Miss Harrington. He was in something of a quandary. The gentleman who had presented him with the diamond had died, so he could not return it. The Prince was heavily in debt and needed the money that such a stone could bring, but he did not want to sell a diamond that had been stolen, nor did he wish to make public the fact that he even had it. Even though he at first had sympathized with the French Revolution, his admiration had soon dissipated and his sympathies lay with the Bourbon family living in exile. They would doubtless feel that he should return the diamond to them if it were known that he had it, although he could not decide whether the diamond belonged to the royal family or to France. Also, he was afraid that people would question how he came to possess the diamond, and that it would bring trouble to him just as the Pitt diamond brought trouble upon that family. He was uncertain of how to proceed."

"So what did he do?" asked Mallory.

"He did nothing. Every avenue appeared dangerous. He put the diamond away in a safe place, and only a very few people knew of it. It wasn't until Metternich sent his ambassador to us a year ago and it became obvious that Austria would try to cut England out of a Continental peace that the Prince Regent thought of the diamond and determined that he would use it for the good of his country. He would send it to be sold and used in the battle against Napoleon."

"Sir Howard's mission!" breathed Lady Gregory softly.

"Exactly! The Prince Regent thought that it would be a dramatic way of reminding the allies that England has wealth to offer their efforts against Napoleon and that they need us. Few things speak more loudly than money."

"And what of the Bourbons?" asked Elizabeth. "By sending the diamond to St. Petersburg, the Prince Regent was obviously making his ownership public."

"Ah, but what he was doing was in the best interests of the Bourbons as well. They have no prospect of returning to power unless Napoleon is defeated, and he was contributing to that effort. If Napoleon were defeated completely and removed from power, it would be very possible that they might be invited to return. And everyone knows how outspoken the Prince Regent has been in his position against Napoleon. Once France is defeated, he does not wish Napoleon to be allowed to rule. He wants his removal. What more could the Bourbons ask?"

"And so he sent the diamond in the package that my brother carried?" asked Lord Mallory.

"That had been my speculation," Norville replied. "This is information that I have pieced together over the years and Sir Howard's mission was one that I heard about only after it had gone awry. As you know, the whole mission was kept quite secret, and only the Prince Regent and two others knew exactly what was taking place. They wanted to keep everything as private as possible so that the mission might be accomplished and the diamond arrive safely."

"But it didn't," stated Lady Gregory flatly.

Norville shook his head. "No, it did not. Sir Howard disappeared and the diamond disappeared. There was no meeting in St. Petersburg." He turned back to Lord Mallory. "I had believed, as you do, that Michael carried the diamond, but I no longer think that was the case."

"Did you ask Michael?" inquired Mallory anxiously.

"No. At the time of his death, I was involved in other matters, and I did not know any of the details about his mission until after his death. Even had I known of it, I would not have asked him, nor would he have told me if I had."

"Even after my husband's disappearance?" asked Lady Gregory.

"He did not know of Sir Howard's disappearance, Lady Gregory. Of that I am certain. He returned straight from St. Petersburg to his regiment in Spain, and his death occurred almost immediately."

"And so it is the diamond you have been looking for as a highwayman," mused Elizabeth. "But why look here in England—and why choose the people that you have?"

"When I returned to England this winter, I was told by one of the two gentlemen who advised the Prince Regent in the matter of the diamond that Lord Mallory's brother carried the case for the diamond and a paste replica. The real diamond was sent in a small black velvet pouch with a third traveler."

"A third traveler!" exclaimed Lord Mallory. "Who was the third one?"

Norville smiled. "We will get to that soon enough. First, let me tell you that Sir Howard was to place the real diamond in the case that Michael was carrying and to present that to Tsar Alexander in St. Petersburg. And the case itself was a thing of beauty."

"What did it look like?" asked Elizabeth.

"Like a jeweled Easter egg," replied Norville calmly.

"A jeweled Easter egg!" they chorused.

"Do you mean like Sir Howard's egg?" inquired Mallory.

"Exactly like Sir Howard's egg," was the reply. "In fact, Sir Howard's egg was the case for the diamond."

They all stared at him blankly.

"Do you mean that the egg that we found is not my husband's?" asked Lady Gregory.

"I'm afraid not. It had been described to me, but when I took your egg the other evening, I took it so that it could be identified. It belongs to the Prince Regent."

"Then he must have it back," Lady Gregory insisted.

"He does not wish that, Lady Gregory. He would prefer that you keep it. Your husband was chosen for the mission because the Prince Regent has such confidence in his integrity. The jeweled egg is the least that he can allow you for your loss."

"But if that was not my husband's egg, what has happened to it?"

Norville shook his head. "I wish that I could tell you," he said.

"But what about our riddle?" cried Nora. "And Sir Howard sent the egg to Elsa! What can that mean?"

He shook his head again. "I am not sure," he admitted. "But we do have the key, and we do know that Sir Howard intended for someone to possess it because he did send the egg to Elsa and he did leave the riddle. Indeed, it was hearing Chawton's riddle that night that made me doubly determined to look into Sir Howard's disappearance."

Elizabeth looked at him directly. "Mr. Norville, who was the third traveler to St. Petersburg?"

He paused a moment before replying. "Lady Brill," he responded.

Everyone stared at him again. "Lady Brill has been quite

useful during our years of war with France," he explained. "Her marriage took her to Paris at the time of the Treaty of Amiens, and she has been considered more a Parisienne than an Englishwoman. In fact, many of the people with whom she spends her time belong to the highest circles of power in France. Since her sympathies are with us, that has made her very helpful indeed."

"Indeed," responded Elizabeth dryly, thinking of what she knew of the lady. "I'm certain that she had means of supplying you with information that would not be readily available otherwise. But I see that she is back in England once again."

Mallory was frowning. "But, Norville, isn't she one of those you robbed? Why were you checking on her if she is a spy for England?"

"Or perhaps she is a spy for both sides," commented Lady Gregory. "My husband said that there are those who think that is the best way to handle the situation. Then, regardless of which side wins, they are safe."

"Such things have been known to happen," agreed Norville, avoiding a direct response to Mallory's question.

Nora, as usual, had been planning ahead. "I think we need to go directly on to Chanderley and see if we can find Sir Howard's desk among Michael's things."

"I agree with Miss Lane," said Norville. "I think that it is important to check every possibility as quickly as we can."

Elizabeth, seeing that everyone else seemed to be in agreement with him, felt called upon to interfere. "Just a moment, Mr. Norville. There are still a number of questions I have for you. For instance, you haven't told us whether or not Lady Brill saw Sir Howard and delivered the diamond."

"Lady Brill said that she delivered the diamond and left St. Petersburg that same afternoon, eager to avoid being associated in any way with Sir Howard's mission."

"Do you believe her?" Elizabeth asked.

Norville shrugged. "What can I say? There is no way to prove that she did or that she did not."

"Unless you found the diamond in her possession," countered Elizabeth.

"Which I did not," he replied firmly. "I grant that she might

233

not have kept it with her in her other jewels, but I found nothing, and she assured me that she does not have it."

"And naturally you believe her," said Elizabeth tartly.

"As a matter of fact, Miss Harrington, I am inclined to believe her."

I'll wager that you do, thought Elizabeth to herself resentfully. The power of a pretty face on a man could be most annoying. Lady Brill could wear the diamond in her hair, and he would probably believe her when she said that she didn't have it.

"Will you be able to travel by tomorrow, Mr. Norville?" asked Lady Gregory. "Won't your wound prevent your being on the road so soon?"

"Not at all, ma'am. I traveled with worse than this during the war. But I will beg the privilege of riding in the carriage with the ladies on the way down. I believe that would be wiser than on horseback."

"Oh, yes, do ride with us!" exclaimed Nora. "You can tell us some of your stories of the war!"

Elizabeth stared at her in amazement, and Nora had the grace to blush. "Well, it would be interesting," she defended herself.

"We will be a very snug group," commented Elizabeth. "That will make five of us in the carriage."

"Not at all," said Lord Mallory gallantly. "I will not be riding in the carriage, so although four passengers will indeed make it snug, it will not be unmanageable."

"And is your poor mother prepared to receive all of us?" Lady Gregory inquired.

Mallory grinned. "Indeed she is. She hasn't had company at all for a year now. She is looking forward to it, and the girls, naturally, are especially pleased that Miss Lane will be joining them."

His smile disappeared as he turned to Norville. "Allow me to ask you one more thing, Norville. What connection does Chawton have to any of this?"

"I am not quite sure at this point. He has been a guest in the home of Lord and Lady Brill, and he was in St. Petersburg close to the time of Sir Howard's disappearance, but the only thing that truly connects him to all of this is the fact that he knew the riddle."

"And you discovered that when we all stayed at the inn during the snowstorm," said Elizabeth. "I noticed that he looked quite upset when he saw you. That was because he realized that you had heard what he said."

Norville nodded. "I imagine that he would have given much never to have told that story. I daresay he wouldn't have, had he not wished to antagonize Mallory."

"Well, he certainly accomplished that," said Mallory ruefully. "And he is still doing so. I received another note from him this morning, reminding me that my time is running out to supply him with Michael's package."

"Judging by his request of Mallory, he does not realize that it was Lady Brill and not Michael who carried the diamond."

Their journey to Chanderley was an uneventful one. The only surprise was supplied by Sir Edmund who, when he heard of his sister's plans, announced that he would accompany her to Chanderley. When Elizabeth expressed her surprise at his decision to join them, he assured her that it would be no great trouble to him, and he would be able to look over Lord Mallory's stable and help him decide which horses to dispose of and which to keep. Unfortunately, it developed that Sir Edmund was no longer permitted to travel alone, and Burton himself escorted Rufus and Sampson to the carriage. The animals were forced to be content with that, for Sir Edmund was riding alongside with Lord Mallory, and they were obliged to make do with the company of the other passengers in the carriage.

They arrived quite late that night, but Lady Mallory and her daughters were waiting for them with refreshments and then they were lighted up to their chambers for a well-deserved night's rest. The next morning they assembled for breakfast at a respectable hour and made their plans for the day. Sir Edmund, who was still completely unaware of the true reason for their journey, was shocked to discover that no one else was planning to ride that day. Thinking that they merely needed a bit of encouragement, he did his best in that direction.

"It would be just the thing for you, my dear," he told Elizabeth. "A little ride will brush away all of those city cobwebs.

I'm sure Mallory has a mare that is gentle enough for you."

"I suppose that next you'll offer to walk alongside and hold me on!" retorted his sister tartly. "Thank you, Edmund, but I believe I will spend my time more profitably."

"What could be more profitable than spending it riding?" inquired her brother, shocked by such heresy.

Nora, who was about to respond with glowing honesty, received a sharp kick under the table from Elizabeth and looked up to receive a warning glance. Neither Sir Edmund nor Lady Mallory had been admitted to the secret as yet. Lady Mallory knew that her son would be going through Michael's things, but he had told her that Mr. Norville was hoping that a book of his had gotten mixed in with Michael's things.

Later, in Michael's room, Nora had asked Mallory how he had explained the presence of the three ladies at Chanderley to his mother.

"Well, of course she would be pleased to have you as guests at any time, but I had indicated to her that I was quite drawn to Miss Harrington and wished the two of them to become better acquainted."

"I see," replied Nora in a curiously flat voice. "And what of Lady Gregory and myself?"

"Naturally my mother knows that you are in Miss Harrington's care while you are in London, and Lady Gregory was invited to play propriety on our journey down. Quite a knacky notion of mine, was it not?"

"Oh, yes," agreed Nora. "Very clever of you. And she would believe your *tendre* for Elizabeth, for I have noticed myself how much you enjoy her company."

"She is a rare one," said Mallory with what Nora could only consider to be a smug, self-satisfied smile.

After Sir Edmund adjourned to the stables that morning, the other two gentlemen retired to Michael's chamber to begin their inspection. The ladies made a party in the morning room, for it would have been rude to abandon their hostess on their first morning, and it would have been rather difficult to explain as well. Lady Gregory and Elizabeth conversed with Lady Mallory and her daughters with ease, but Nora suffered from her normal lack of patience, and Elizabeth was obliged to take her to one side and caution her.

"But I want to be helping, Elizabeth, not sitting down here talking!" she complained.

"I would also like to help, Nora, but what do you think we would tell Lady Mallory? That we also would like to go through her son's possessions because he might possibly have something of ours?"

Nora persisted in looking mulish, and Elizabeth continued. "And she is our hostess, Nora. It is only natural that she expects to spend time with us, and the girls will want you to spend time with them as well."

"Splendid! It is back to the schoolroom with me!" said Nora petulantly.

"That could be arranged," replied her cousin with irritation. "But I expect I would have to place you with George. I am afraid that Anne and Maria are too pretty behaved for you."

Seriously affronted by Elizabeth's comment about George, Nora sat down stiffly on the very edge of one of the Hepplewhite chairs, a mahogany piece with tapering square legs and a back designed like a shield.

"I had thought that since the weather is fine, the girls might take you out in the pony cart," said Lady Mallory kindly to Nora, thinking that her stiffness came of being ill at ease. "There is quite a pretty drive, and Maria handles the ribbons very well."

Nora brightened a little at this. "Do you think she would let me try?" she asked. "I did a little driving at Braxton Hall, and I did so enjoy it."

"I'm sure that she would," responded Lady Mallory. "They are with Miss Stevenson now, but I think they could take a holiday from their lessons if you would like to go up to them now and tell them."

After Nora left the room to break the happy news to Miss Stevenson, the girls, and George, Elizabeth looked at her gratefully. "That was very good of you, Lady Mallory. I'm afraid she can be quite difficult when she is unhappy."

"That is usually true of young people," replied Lady Mallory placidly.

Lady Gregory agreed with her, adding, "And I'm afraid that

it is a characteristic that does not necessarily leave us when we are no longer young. The same may be said of many adults." Thinking particularly of Mr. Norville and Cecilia, Elizabeth could appreciate the truth of the statement.

The young ladies departed shortly in the pony cart, accompanied by George on his pony and a smiling young groom on horseback. Rufus and Sampson, being denied the pleasure of accompanying Sir Edmund to the stables, joined the young ladies in the cart. The day being fine, the ladies remaining in the house elected to take a walk in the gardens.

It had been dark when they arrived the night before, and Elizabeth had been unable to appreciate the loveliness of Chanderley and its park of four hundred acres. The house itself was a pleasing red-brick structure in the Palladian style with a white pilastered front. The ladies strolled through the shrubberies and the flower gardens, admiring the daffodils and snowdrops that were already in bloom.

"Given another day or two of warmth and sun and the daffodils will be everywhere," commented Lady Mallory, regarding those flowers with pleasure. "If Trevor had his way, they would literally be everywhere. He loves them."

Elizabeth smiled. "Yes, I understand that they are his favorite. I can understand why. They are like him—cheerful and comforting."

Lady Mallory returned her smile warmly. There is nothing that pleases a mother more than knowing that her child is properly appreciated. "Yes, he has always been that way. Michael was quite mercurial in temperament so that one never knew quite what to expect, but Trevor was always smiling. Even when he had been into deviltry, he was still smiling, and his escapades were never ones that hurt others. He just has a joy in living that escapes most of us."

Mallory and Norville walked into the garden to join them just then, and Elizabeth compared the two gentlemen as they walked toward her: one tall, golden-haired, elegant, and smiling; the other a little shorter, squarer across the shoulders, well-dressed but not elegant, grim and unsmiling. Mr. Norville could not have been placed beside anyone who would show him to less advantage, reflected Elizabeth ruefully. And it was obvious from Norville's expression that they had found nothing as yet among Michael's things.

"Have you not found your book, Andrew?" asked Lady Mallory, echoing Elizabeth's thoughts.

He shook his head. "There are apparently still some other places to check, but we will do that later. We felt that a little fresh air might be in order, and we decided to join you."

"What a fraud you are, Norville!" laughed Lord Mallory. "I was forced to tear you away from those trunks. You came only because I said that I would refuse to show you anything else if you did not."

Norville smiled reluctantly. "I'm afraid that I do become very absorbed by whatever I am doing."

"Absorbed! I should say that is a mild word for it! The only thing that would have slowed you down would have been the onset of darkness."

"You are quite correct, I am sure," admitted Norville. Glancing about the garden, he asked, "Where is Miss Lane?"

"She went out with Lord Mallory's sisters in the pony cart," responded Elizabeth. "She was quite eager to try her hand at driving it."

"Did they go alone?" he asked, his brow creasing.

"No, Andrew," intervened Lady Mallory. "They were accompanied by George and a groom. It is quite all right. They do so regularly when we are at Chanderley."

His expression lightened. "If you assure me that it is safe, then I know that it is so, Lady Mallory," he said pleasantly.

Elizabeth frowned. Mr. Norville was doubtful of the propriety of Nora going out in the pony cart when she told him of it, but he could accept it perfectly from Lady Mallory. It was annoying that he set so little store by her judgment. Elizabeth had long been accustomed to having others accept her actions without question, and Mr. Norville was a decided thorn. He is entirely too fond of himself and his own opinions, she thought in annoyance.

As they walked along the gravel pathway, she fell behind the others with Lord Mallory. Staring after Norville, Mallory said thoughtfully, "I know that Michael thought he was a great gun, but he certainly is not an easy man."

Elizabeth could agree fully with that.

"If I am not intruding, Miss Harrington," he continued hesitantly, "it seemed to me that Norville took a tone about Miss Lane and the pony cart that might more properly belong to one who was her guardian . . . or who perhaps had some other close relationship to the young lady."

Elizabeth could not decide how much she should tell him, so she temporized with, "He knows Miss Lane's mother, you see, and so of course he feels a particular interest in her and her welfare."

Lord Mallory smiled in relief. "Yes, I can certainly understand that. Old General Grover was a friend of my father's, and he was forever turning up in odd places and inquiring after Michael and me. It always annoyed us so, but our father told us that he simply had our best interests at heart and we could show ourselves grateful for that."

He paused, remembering. "We did our best, but I fear that we were not always successful. I remember one time Michael was fishing when he was supposed to be studying with his tutor—Michael was never very fond of his books—and old Grover found him out. He flew up into the boughs and told Michael that he might be able to bamboozle our father, but he couldn't pull the wool over *his* eyes. He went straight off and told our father, and Michael, of course, ended up in his chamber for the rest of the day. Before Grover left, Michael tucked a fish into his portmanteau. I imagine that by the time he reached his destination, his clothing smelled abominably. He didn't come to visit for some time, and my father had a great deal to say to Michael. My brother had to give up fishing for a whole summer and there could have been no more terrible punishment for him."

Elizabeth laughed. "I can see that you were not the only one in your family inclined to play pranks, Lord Mallory."

"Oh, no, Michael was far ahead of me in that respect. He—" Mallory broke off suddenly, and his gaze became abstracted.

"Is there something wrong? Do you feel quite well, sir?" Elizabeth inquired anxiously.

He caught her hand and exclaimed, "That is it, Elizabeth! How could I have forgotten! Come with me immediately and we will see if I am right!" And he hurried her back along the path toward the house, forgetting the rest of the strollers.

"What have you forgotten, Lord Mallory? Right about what?" cried Elizabeth, moving as quickly as she could to try to keep pace with his long strides.

"Michael's fishing equipment! He took all of that to Spain with him. He said that if Wellington and some of the others could keep their hounds and hunt, that he could fish. When his trunks were sent home, we put all of his fishing gear in a storage chamber we use for all that type of rig. I think my man even took down Michael's old wading boots and put them away!"

"Do you really think there could be something hidden there?" So infectious was his excitement that Elizabeth felt her own hopes begin to soar.

"Of course I do," he said confidently, opening a side door for them and hurrying down a narrow corridor. "And it isn't just that there is nowhere else to look. If Michael had anything of value to hide, he would hide it with what he valued most—and that would have been his fishing equipment!"

Chapter Eighteen

Before they could reach the end of the corridor, however, they heard Lady Mallory's voice. "She's calling me," sighed her son. "I might have known she would not let me go loping away with you and leave the rest of them."

He stared ruefully down the corridor in the direction of the storage room he sought. "We'll have to go back. My mother doesn't know anything about all of this, and it would upset her no end if she knew that Michael had been suspected of possessing something he shouldn't have had."

Elizabeth patted his hand comfortingly. "But you know very well, Lord Mallory, that even if we find anything, it does not mean that Michael stole it. We don't know the circumstances. Mr. Norville may be quite correct and Sir Howard may have wished to send back something, the diamond or something else of value, with your brother."

He smiled at her. "Thank you, Elizabeth—you will allow me to call you so, won't you? And you'll call me Trevor?"

"Of course. We have all spent so much time together that I am beginning to feel that we are family." Nor was she making idle conversation. It struck her as most odd that she was coming to know these people very well indeed. The intimacy of their circumstances at the Bull and Barleycorn, coupled with the riddle they had been trying to unravel during the past three weeks, had brought them into a closeness that she shared with few others.

Lady Mallory smiled at Elizabeth as they emerged into the sunshine of the garden, but directed a frown at her son. "I realize that you are eager to talk with Miss Harrington, Trevor, but you must remember your other guests."

Elizabeth directed a startled glance at Lord Mallory, who grinned back at her mischievously. As they walked along behind his mother to join the others, she whispered, "What did your mother mean by that?"

"I hope you don't mind, Elizabeth, but I told her that I felt a deep interest in you and that I wished for the two of you to become better acquainted."

Elizabeth gasped. "You wicked man! Why on earth did you do that?"

"To explain to her the sudden urgency of having all of you down to Chanderley. I knew that you wouldn't mind."

Elizabeth sighed. "Very well, Trevor, but she will be very put out with us when she learns the truth."

"Perhaps not," was the cryptic reply. She had no opportunity to question him further, however, for they came upon Lady Gregory and Mr. Norville at that point, and in the distance they could hear George hallooing and the crunch of gravel as the pony cart came up the drive. Together they left the garden and walked out to greet the children.

"Just see what we have, Trevor!" called Anne, leaping lightly down from the cart. Over her arm was a basket filled with vetch, wild carrot, lady's mantle, fern, and anything else in the way of plant life that had struck their fancy. "We're going to decorate eggs this afternoon! Will you help? John Hatching is going to come."

"Yes, of course I'll help," he laughed. "Don't let John take all of the good leaves," he called after her as she ran inside, followed closely by Rufus and in a more leisurely manner by Sampson.

Anne paused in her headlong run to call back to him. "Don't be silly, Trevor. There's more than enough! You had best look after yourself for the colors though." And she disappeared through the doorway.

"Who is John Hatching?" inquired Elizabeth. "And what a very suitable name for someone who will be decorating eggs."

"He is our gardener, Miss Harrington," replied Maria, who had joined them. "He makes the most beautiful designs on the pace eggs that you ever saw. Will you help us with the eggs, too? Nora is going to."

"I would love to, Maria," Elizabeth responded. She watched with appreciation as the graceful girl, basket over her arm, walked sedately up the walk to the house, stopping to pick up flowers that Anne had scattered in her frantic flight to the kitchen.

"I wonder where Nora could have gotten to," she began, just as the young lady in question came tripping down a side path from the direction of the stables, her cheeks pink with pleasure.

"Elizabeth! The most splendid thing! I drove the pony cart for a whole mile around two very sharp curves, and when we came down the drive, Anne and Maria got out and let me drive it round to the stables by myself!"

"And she didn't smash into anything or overset the cart either!" added George, who had followed in her wake. "Anne tossed us all into a hedge the first time she tried it. I've still got the scar," he added, rolling up his sleeve to display the evidence.

The pace eggs were a grand success. The kitchen was a beehive of activity, for the Grahams, their guests, the cook, Rufus and Sampson, and John Hatching were all bustling about, preparing their works of art. Elizabeth had not decorated eggs since her childhood, and even Sir Edmund felt called upon to make one. A large deal table was covered with a profusion of flowers and leaves and scraps of fabric and ribbon, and the designers labored long over their creations.

"The plants with the finely jointed leaves make the best patterns," Anne advised Sir Edmund in a professional tone, overlooking his progress with interest.

The petals or leaves were arranged on the egg with painstaking care, then a piece of fabric of the colors of choice was wrapped around the egg, then a piece of linen was bound around the whole to keep everything in place. Each little bundle was dropped into boiling water, where it tossed for half an hour, allowing the colors from the material to stain the eggs, leaving an outline of the leaf and petal design, occasionally leaving even the natural green of the leaves.

Nor was it necessary to use scraps of material to achieve their colors, for there were several pots of dye bubbling on the stove as well: cochineal for scarlet, logwood for a deep purple, spinach leaves for green, gorse blossoms and onion peelings for yellow. John Hatching, using an exquisitely sharpened penknife, etched designs of his own onto some of the freshly colored eggs. Elizabeth watched in fascination as he created a delicate garland of flowers on an egg of vibrant purple; then on a scarlet one he drew a dragon for George. The rest of the party contented themselves with using a penknife to scratch simple messages on theirs.

"Even though it's early," announced Anne as they worked, "we can exchange eggs at dinner so everyone gets one made by someone else, and we should pick some of the prettiest to make a garland for the mantelpiece. We can put it up here to admire it, and then take it back to London with us for Easter. The eggs that don't turn out wonderfully well we can use for shackling."

"Anne is the planner in the family," said Mallory to Elizabeth in a low voice as he tried to work his way closer to the pot of cochineal.

Elizabeth edged her way out of the crowd of workers and stood at the side of the kitchen, enjoying the scene before her. Rufus was chewing thoughtfully on some spinach leaves that had floated to the floor, and Sampson was entertaining himself by batting at a fern that was hanging over the edge of the table. Everyone and everything was in motion, making the kitchen a cheerful blur of activity, but it seemed to Elizabeth quite a peaceful, pleasant scene.

"You must be rather bored by all of this, Miss Harrington," said Mr. Norville.

Elizabeth looked up, startled. She had been so absorbed in the scene before her that she had not seen him walk up behind her. She frowned at him as she focused on what he had just said. "Why should I be bored, Mr. Norville?"

"This is certainly not the way you ordinarily spend your time, is it?" he inquired.

"No, but that is no reason for finding it boring. Quite the opposite, in fact. I enjoy change."

"Life in the country does not offer the same type of change that London life does, however. You would grow quite weary without your daily round of parties and balls."

Elizabeth found herself becoming extremely annoyed. "As a matter of fact, I do enjoy London life, Mr. Norville," she retorted, "but does that automatically mean that I must enjoy nothing else? What a very poor creature you must think me if you believe I am able to derive amusement from nothing else!"

He smiled at her tone and bowed slightly. "Forgive me. I seem to have a talent for saying things that irritate you."

"I must agree with you, Mr. Norville. Only I would not call it a talent; I would term it rather a genius. You underestimate yourself!" Turning her back on him, she walked over to join Nora, who was laboring diligently with a penknife.

"What are you writing, Nora?" she inquired, attempting to divert her thoughts into a more pleasant pathway. "Or are you drawing something?"

"Oh, don't look please, Elizabeth. This is . . . sort of a secret."

Elizabeth smiled, amused by her intensity. "Well, of course I won't if you don't want me to." And as she strolled away, she noticed that some of the others had grown quite secretive with their eggs and penknives, stealing away to corners and turning their backs on the others. Anne noticed her look of puzzlement and giggled.

"People are writing their secret messages, Miss Harrington. Didn't you ever write notes on yours?"

Elizabeth shook her head. "We colored eggs, but writing our names was about as far as we went beyond that."

"Then you must try it!" she commanded. "Pick one of the eggs from that bowl and make up a question or a saying for someone."

Elizabeth looked doubtful, and Anne took out the scarlet egg she had been working on. "Look, it's easy." In neat little letters she had printed *Brothers should be banished.*

"And you know who that's for," she giggled. "George always takes on so that it's great fun to give one like this to him. I'll leave it in the basket beside his plate at dinner if Mother will let us get them out. Otherwise, I'll hide it in his room for him to find."

"The baskets at dinner?" Elizabeth inquired.

"Oh, yes," Anne replied. "Usually we have the baskets at the dining table only on Easter Day after our hunt in the morning. They are just pretty little wicker baskets Mother has had for forever, but they're perfect for putting on the table and holding two or three eggs. Then, if we've made any special ones for anyone,

246

we put them in the basket."

"Which one will be the prize egg?" called George, who had been inspecting the eggs that were laid out on an extra table that had been pulled into the center of the room. "I think mine should be," he said proudly, exhibiting a dark brown egg on whose side was printed in uneven letters: *Auk Egg.*

"Why *Auk Egg,* George?" inquired Anne, examining it critically.

"I like auks!" he exclaimed defensively.

His disrespectful sister giggled. "When have you ever seen an auk, George? How could you possibly like them?"

"I *do!*" he exclaimed hotly, snatching his egg away. "Hopper showed me a picture of them during lessons the other day, and I *liked* them!"

"I am sure they are very fine birds," said his mother calmly, directing a quelling glance at Anne. "And I think that an auk egg would make a very good prize egg."

"Yes, but how do we know that it looks like an auk egg?" demanded Anne, who was obviously a stickler for accuracy.

"We will have to trust to George's superior knowledge of auks," said Mallory tactfully. "After all, he is the only one amongst us who has looked into the subject."

Anne looked as though she would like to argue the matter further, but the combined force of warning glances from her mother and older brother restrained her.

"Have a look at this one," called Norville, intervening to divert their attention. "Can you guess who it is for?"

They gathered around the deep blue egg that he held in his hand, and he handed it to Maria to read the motto aloud.

Loveliest of Ladies

"Well, I know who it *isn't* for!" said George militantly. "It isn't for Anne!"

Anne ignored her little brother majestically. "*I* think it must be for Mother," she announced.

Lady Mallory looked touched. "Why, thank you, Anne. What a lovely thing to say."

Lord Mallory looked at Norville with amusement. "Trying to set the cat among the pigeons, old boy?" he inquired. "Writing something like that when there's a roomful of lovely ladies is a great deal like Eros throwing the golden apple marked 'For the Fairest' into the midst of Hera, Aphrodite, and Minerva. Are you trying to start another Trojan War, Norville?"

Sir Edmund glanced up from his own work, frowning. "Don't need another war. The one with Boney will do nicely."

Elizabeth laughed. "Trevor was talking about the ancient Greeks, Edmund."

"Oh, them," he responded in relief, dismissing them with a wave of his hand. "That's all right then. Foolish lot, those Greeks."

The conversation took a more general turn then, and Mallory had an opportunity to whisper to Elizabeth. "We'll go and have a look in the storage room as soon as we can slip away."

Accordingly, they soon found themselves in a small room lined with cupboards, and Mallory began opening doors and checking their contents.

"No, these are my things . . . those were my father's . . . that belongs to George," he murmured, rifling through the gear.

"Here now!" he exclaimed as he opened another door. "These are Michael's boots!" And he hauled forth a pair of high rubber waders and peered beyond them.

"And here is more of his gear!" Mallory hauled out the first case he came to, and they opened it and peered eagerly into its contents. Carefully they lifted reels and lures and lengths of fishing line but could see nothing out of the ordinary. Lifting the boots aside to look into the cupboard again, Mallory overset one of them.

Elizabeth stood staring at it. "Trevor, you don't suppose that Michael would have put anything in his boots, do you?"

Mallory chuckled. "Probably nothing but his stockings, and—when he was younger of course—an occasional frog. But we can look."

Rolling down the top of the boot a bit, Mallory stretched his long arm down inside, probing about with his fingers as he reached the foot. "I don't think it's any good, Elizabeth, but—" His eyes widened and he broke off as his fingers touched something that had been shoved into the toe of the boot.

"What is it?" asked Elizabeth, her voice rising. "Is there something there, Trevor?"

"Yes, I believe so." His face fell suddenly. "But it feels like a woolen sock." He pulled on it, and Elizabeth, ignoring the possibility of dust and cobwebs, sat down on an old wooden bench to watch.

"No, there's a sock, all right, but there's something in it. It's too heavy, and I can feel something solid inside it."

Elizabeth watched with rising excitement as Lord Mallory slowly worked the sock out of the boot and stood with it in his hand.

"Look inside, Trevor! Don't just stand there!" exclaimed Elizabeth impatiently.

"By all means, Mallory. Look inside," said Mr. Norville.

So engrossed had they been that they had not heard the door open, and both of them jumped as he spoke.

"Norville! There *is* something here!" Mallory hefted it judiciously in the palm of his hand as though weighing it. "It could be nothing but more gear, however," he said. "A precious reel that he wanted to protect—or to hide from brother officers who might want to borrow it."

Slowly he slipped his hand into the sock as the other two watched. When he withdrew his hand, he held in his palm . . . another egg.

"I can't believe it!" exclaimed Elizabeth. "Not another one."

Mallory held it up, and they all examined it. "It's not just an egg!" he responded. "Look at this! It's a clock."

And so it was, an egg-shaped clock of cream-colored porcelain with dainty scenes painted on its sides. Elizabeth removed it gently from his hands and carried it over to the window where the afternoon sun allowed them to examine it more closely.

"And see what these are!" she exclaimed. "The clock shows the seasons. Here are daffodils and trees in blossom for springtime, green trees and a sun for summer, trees in gold and crimson for autumn, a snow scene for winter."

"This is it!" said Mallory. "It is just like Chawton's riddle:

> *I am the beginning*
> *I hold the key*
> *I am winter's end*
> *From summer I flee*

We've found it!"

"I do think that this is most unfair!" said a petulant voice from the door. "I am the one who worked out the riddle, and you're all trying to keep me out of things now!"

In the door stood Nora, her lower lip trembling, her eyes angry as she surveyed the group of them. "I saw you all sneak away, and I thought that I would just come along and see from what you were trying to exclude me."

"Nonsense, Nora," said Mallory sharply. "We 'sneaked away,' as you put it, so that my mother would not notice us. I don't want her to know what is going on until we have it all figured out and know that Michael isn't guilty of anything of which she need be ashamed."

"Oh," replied Nora, somewhat abashed. "Well, you could have told me anyway."

"Well, you're here now, and that's good enough," said Mallory with some asperity. It was evident that he had dealt extensively with younger sisters and Norville watched with amusement.

"Does it open?" asked Nora, her curiosity getting the better of her pique.

"We don't know yet," responded Elizabeth. "Do you see anything, Trevor?"

The base of the clock was flat, and Mallory upended it to examine the bottom. And there was a tiny opening for a key.

"We will have to get Lady Gregory and the key," said Mallory. "But we can't do it now because my mother would notice. Perhaps after dinner. It is almost time now. In fact, we'd better go and dress or we'll be late," he said, taking note of the hour.

"Where will we keep the clock?" asked Elizabeth.

Mallory and Norville looked at one another for a moment. "We don't want to take a chance on losing it, but it's too large to carry with you," said Norville. "What is the safest place you can think of, Mallory?"

He grinned. "In the drawer where George keeps his clean shirts."

Dinner that evening was an anxious affair, for they had had no opportunity to tell Lady Gregory what they had found. Nonetheless, Anne had provided a distraction, for she had persuaded her mother to get out the baskets for the table, and she was busily supervising the distribution of the eggs.

"I want to put my own in," demanded George. "We all have some secret eggs to give out, Anne, so don't be trying to take everything over. We can come in one at a time and put our eggs in secretly."

Finally, having followed George's advice, they were able to be seated for dinner and examine the contents of their baskets.

George looked at the *Brothers should be banished* motto and laughed. "Just take a look at yours, Annie."

His sister delved into her basket and brought out a bright yellow egg with the very unsteady saying: *Sisters are sour.*

"Except I didn't mean you of course, Maria," George explained. "Just Annie. She tries to tell everybody what to do."

Before the squabble could escalate, Mallory dipped into his basket and chuckled.

"What is it, Trevor?" demanded Anne. "What does yours say?"

He lifted up an egg that was as bright a yellow as Anne's *Sisters are Sour* one and read, *"To the Daffodil Man.* Now that has to be from you, Mother," he accused her.

"Not at all," she protested. "Although I wish that I had thought of it."

Mallory looked round the table. "Who then?"

Elizabeth raised her hand. "I am the guilty party, Lord Mallory," she confessed.

He bowed to her briefly. "An excellent choice, Elizabeth. And pray remember that we agreed—I am Trevor."

The others looked at her, causing her to flush in dismay, imagining what his mother must be thinking. To hide her confusion, she bent over her basket and drew out a blue egg. Turning it over, she read: *Loveliest of Ladies.* She glanced up swiftly and saw Mr. Norville watching her. He smiled and lifted his glass in a silent toast.

Elizabeth wondered uneasily what he could be up to. Undoubtedly he was about to ensnare her in some way that would make her look most frivolous and vain. She wondered if he had given it to her because he believed that was what she thought of herself. At any rate, she was sure that it was not a compliment.

It seemed to Elizabeth that it took forever for dinner to be over and for the gentlemen finally to join them in the drawing room

251

for coffee. Maria had been allowed to stay with the ladies while George and Anne went upstairs to bed, squabbling all the way. Had it not been for her presence, Elizabeth and Nora could have told Lady Gregory of their discovery, for Lady Mallory had been obliged to go upstairs to help calm the younger children. Instead they made light conversation about Easter egg parties of other years and about their plans for tomorrow. Maria, who was artistic, had suggested an outing if it were fine, telling them that there was a very romantic ruined castle only a few miles away. Nora, always ready for activity, was immediately enthusiastic.

"That sounds delightful, Maria," responded Elizabeth, and was struck by a sudden inspiration. "Have you any sketches of the ruin that you could show us?"

"Yes, I do," said Maria, pleased to be asked. "They are upstairs in my room. If you will excuse me for a moment, I will get them."

"That would be lovely. Nora, why don't you go up with Maria?" suggested Elizabeth.

Nora looked at her in surprise, but Elizabeth nodded quickly in Lady Gregory's direction, and Nora understood. "Yes, I'll come with you," said Nora. "It would be pleasant to walk just a little rather than sitting here."

And so they departed together, leaving Elizabeth to impart the news to Lady Gregory. When the gentlemen entered the room, it was immediately obvious to Norville and Mallory that she knew about the new egg, for she looked brighter and more hopeful than they had yet seen her.

It was not until later in the evening that the interested parties were able to assemble quietly in Lady Gregory's room. With trembling fingers, she raised the dainty key to the lock, slipped it in, and turned it, thereby lifting out the base of the egg and revealing a velvet-lined hollow below the mechanism of the clock. In it rested a sparkling blue diamond.

"It's beautiful!" said Nora softly.

Mallory shook his head. "What was Michael doing with it?" he asked. "Why did he have this and what must be Sir Howard's egg in his fishing boot?"

"This *is* my husband's egg. I am certain of it," said Lady Gregory, scrutinizing its surface. "He had always wanted a clock for his collection. And this perhaps is the paradox he was trying to tell me about," and she pointed to the scenes of the seasons. "He was always fascinated by the changing of the seasons, particularly the magic of spring coming after the ice and snow of winter. He liked to say that it showed us that life sprang from death, that death was not the end of everything, but the beginning."

The rest were silent for a moment, for it was obvious that she was deeply moved by what she had said. Then, cupping the clock carefully in her hands, she looked at Norville.

"What do we do now?" she asked him.

His answer was unexpected. "I believe that we take the diamond to town and determine whether this is the real one or the imitation."

"Of course!" said Elizabeth. "It could be an imitation. I had forgotten about the diamond that was used as a decoy."

"I think it would be better for Michael if this is the real one," observed Mallory heavily. "If it is the paste one, it could mean that he kept the one he was carrying, thinking that it was real."

"Not necessarily," replied Norville, "but it may be that we will still uncover exactly what happened. In the meantime, we need to find out about this stone."

It was decided that both gentlemen would leave early the next morning and ride to London together, and would return with all speed to inform the others of their findings.

to say they heard

"I have seen to that your saline worked handsomely, for Mrs.
Harrington . . . she seems to be in the best of spirits," Anthony continued.

Chapter Nineteen

Lord Mallory and Mr. Norville left for London early the next morning, and Sir Edmund, who was already down at the stables, instructed them to bring back the latest edition of the *Morning Chronicle* and assured Mallory that he himself would continue studying Michael's horses.

Mallory, accustomed as he was to maintaining an easygoing, unruffled approach to life, was finding it difficult going at the moment. He could not decide what he should even hope for when they took the diamond to the jeweler. Michael had carried the paste replica to St. Petersburg, so if this stone were the replica, it was possible, as he had pointed out to Norville, that Michael had kept the stone rather than delivering it to Sir Howard. Since neither he nor Chawton would have known that it was not the real diamond, that would also explain Chawton's eagerness to have that package.

On the other hand, if this diamond were the real one, how did Michael come to have it? Could Lady Brill have given it to him? If so, why? Could he have taken it by force from Sir Howard? Wild as Michael sometimes had been, Mallory could not imagine his brother stooping to such a dishonorable deed. Could it be, as Elizabeth had suggested, that Sir Howard gave it to him to deliver elsewhere? And if so, where and why? The diamond was supposed to have been delivered in St. Petersburg, not sent back to England. All in all, Mallory was finding it very difficult to maintain his usual cheerful attitude.

"Come now, Mallory," said Norville, noticing his glumness. "This won't do. I heard you giving Miss Harrington a speech about allowing herself to be blue-deviled. Follow your own advice."

Mallory smiled reluctantly. "I am realizing that it is much easier to say than to do."

"It appears to me that your advice worked handsomely for Miss Harrington. She seems to be in the best of spirits," Norville commented.

"Elizabeth is a right one," said Mallory absently, still wrestling with his own problems. "She doesn't fly into a pelter when something goes amiss, and she almost never falls into a fit of the dismals."

Norville reflected that this scarcely sounded like a lover's tribute to his lady. "I believe that you have had the advantage of seeing her at her best, Mallory. I have not had that privilege."

"No, you do bring out the worst in her, don't you?" returned Mallory, grinning. "I haven't seen her get on her high ropes with anyone but you. How do you manage it, Norville?"

"It is a rare talent, Mallory, and one that I don't wish to give away."

"You'll have no argument from me. I wouldn't *want* your talent. I much prefer getting along with Elizabeth to having her set her mind against me. She is no milk-and-water miss, you know."

"So I have been told," Norville remarked dryly. "And I have found no reason thus far to dispute the statement."

Mallory chuckled. "Her Miss Lane doesn't fall into that category either. She knows her own mind and don't let you forget it." He stopped a moment, thinking about Nora. "Still, she's a very taking little thing," he added, almost in surprise.

Switching subjects abruptly, he turned to face Norville. "What exactly did you expect to find when you started your robberies, Norville?"

"I was looking for the diamond, either the real one or the replica, and for the jeweled egg. I held up Lady Campion first because I knew exactly when to encounter her coach along the highway and because I knew that she would enjoy it hugely and publicize it. I didn't want people to be frightened; I wanted them to be interested and to talk about the robberies. The only people who might grow nervous, I thought, were those who had something to hide."

"Why the Easter eggs and the riddles?"

It was Norville's turn to chuckle. "It seemed to me that those involved with the disappearance of Sir Howard and the diamond would know both of the jeweled egg and the riddle he left. I hoped that using that twist would make them so uneasy that they might give themselves away. Also, when I returned the jewels that I had taken, I had the opportunity to look about me for anything helpful that I could find."

"And did you suspect everyone you robbed other than Lady Campion?"

Norville nodded. "The ladies all had husbands who had some connection with the mission. I thought perhaps the egg might have made its way to someone's dressing room since it was originally intended to be a jewelry case."

"And Lady Brill?" Mallory inquired.

Norville shrugged. "She was involved herself, of course, and her husband is a gentleman who wears the colors of those he happens to be traveling with at the time. I believe that at one time or another he has probably been in the pay of every government in Europe."

"But you turned up nothing?" Mallory probed.

"Not really anything of value," he replied evasively.

They had the diamond examined at Rundell & Bridge. The jeweler retired to his worktable to inspect the stone and returned to them a few minutes later, his eyes wide.

"It is *real!*" he whispered. "I cannot believe it! I have never seen a diamond its equal! Where did you find it?"

"It has been in the family for a long while," replied Norville, casually pocketing the stone.

The jeweler watched him in horror. "Do be careful of it, sir. You surely will not go strolling about the streets with that in your pocket!"

"I assure you that I will take very good care of it," he said politely as they departed.

Once on the pavement outside, Mallory turned to him. "What do we do now?" he asked, scarcely knowing whether or not to be relieved by the news.

"We will retire to a bank vault to have this safely put away," said Norville, patting his pocket.

"Where do you suppose the imitation is?"

"That is a very good question," replied Norville, "and we will do our best to answer it as soon as possible. In fact, we must," he added grimly, "for you are not the only one being blackmailed and working against time."

Mallory was shocked. "Are you also a victim, Norville? Is Chawton after you, too?"

"I am not the victim," he returned. "Nor am I at liberty at the moment to say who is. I am not even certain that Chawton is the one doing the blackmailing."

Mallory was eager to know more, but judged it best to leave Norville in peace until he felt that he could make himself more clear.

"At least we know that no one has brought in a stone like that made of paste to Rundell & Bridge, or he would have commented upon it," remarked Norville.

"Should we check other shops to see if someone has?" asked Mallory, anxious to be doing something constructive.

Norville nodded. "That is our next undertaking."

While the gentlemen were about their business in London, the ladies and Sir Edmund were left to occupy themselves as best they could, which proved to be something of a task. Three of the ladies were wondering about the diamond and worrying about what they could do next, and their frame of mind was not improved by the onset of two days of damp, dreary weather. Maria's outing to the castle ruin was postponed, and the two younger children, forced inside by the weather, were as cross as crabs and pinched at each other in much the manner of those unsociable crustaceans.

Finally, the others were driven to conjuring up amusements for them simply to ensure the survival of all within the confines of the house. Nora taught them her version of the egg-dance, to the imminent danger of Lady Mallory's carpet; Sir Edmund played whist with them and allowed them to win; Lady Gregory told them stories; and Elizabeth and Maria helped them to get up a play. It was with profound gratitude that everyone at Chanderley greeted the return of sunshine on the third day of their confinement, and immediate plans were laid for the trip to the ruin.

"We can take our luncheon with us," announced Anne happily at breakfast, preparing to retire to the kitchen and worry the cook.

Sir Edmund, who liked having his meals in the comfort of the dining room, looked dubious. "Eat out there just because there's a pile of rubble there that nobody's bothered to pick up for years?"

"It is called dining *al fresco,* Edmund, and it would be a charming thing to do. Have you no sensibility?" rallied his sister.

"If it means jauntering about the country to look at rocks, then no, I have none!" retorted Sir Edmund, but he looked suddenly thoughtful. "Of course, this would be a good time to try that big gray mare of Mallory's . . ."

Elizabeth encouraged this line of thought, and soon he had become quite reconciled to the outing. Accordingly, just before noon the little party set forth: Sir Edmund on the gray and George on his fat little pony; Nora and the children, accompanied of course by Rufus and Sampson, in the pony cart; the three ladies in Lady Mallory's gig. As though trying to atone for the last two dismal days, nature decked herself in her finest springtime array.

When they finally reached their ruin and had duly admired it and enjoyed their luncheon in a sunny spot, they spent their time picking primroses and violets. Maria took out her sketchpad and perched upon a rock to work; George and Anne happily chased brimstone butterflies, which looked themselves like primroses that had taken flight; Nora was playing with Rufus and Sampson; Sir Edmund had tethered the mare beneath a tree and had stretched out on a sunny patch of meadow, his hat over his eyes. Seeing that everyone looked occupied, Elizabeth and the two older ladies decided that they could take a walk down an inviting little path starred with wood anemones.

When they returned almost an hour later, things were much the same as they had been, except that Nora was gone. Elizabeth's anxious inquiry elicited the information that she had put Rufus and Sampson in the pony cart and announced that she was taking a short drive.

"Oh, the foolish girl!" exclaimed Elizabeth. "She doesn't know the country here. She'll get lost or turn the cart over."

"I told her that, of course," remarked Anne, "but she said that she had an excellent sense of direction."

"Just what she would say!" remarked Elizabeth in annoyance. "How long has she been gone?"

"Oh, she left just after you did," said George cheerfully. "I'd say she's much more likely to get lost than to tumble into a hedge like Anne. Nora is much better with the ribbons than—" He was unable to complete his comparison because Anne was closing in upon him, and he took to his heels, laughing.

"If she has been gone an hour, she should surely be back soon. We'll wait just a few more minutes and then I'll wake up Edmund and send him out to find her."

"Yes, we shouldn't wait long," said Lady Mallory anxiously. "We want to get home before dark, and it looks as though it may begin to rain."

The prospect of rain determined their course of action, and the ladies awakened Sir Edmund immediately. It took him a few moments to take in what they were telling him.

"Gone in the pony cart? Where?" he asked.

"We don't know, Edmund," replied Elizabeth patiently, waiting for him to awaken fully.

"Well, then how am I to go and look for her?" he inquired reasonably.

Maria had been absorbed in her sketching, but, to Elizabeth's relief, Anne and George could tell them the direction Nora had taken.

"I'll go with you, Sir Edmund," announced George, preparing to mount his pony. Together they set off, George bouncing valiantly on his fat little pony in an attempt to keep pace with Sir Edmund. The ladies were left to wait anxiously, devoting part of their time to watching the road and part to watching the dark clouds gather overhead, blotting out the sunshine. Elizabeth envisioned herself writing to Cecilia to tell her that Nora had met with an injury while jouncing unchaperoned about unfamiliar country in a pony cart, and shuddered. The only vision that equalled it in horror was the prospect of informing Mr. Norville.

"I wonder when we might expect Lord Mallory and Mr. Norville back from London," she remarked casually.

"Tonight would be the earliest I should imagine," replied Lady Mallory, "allowing them a day in town for their business. It seemed very odd, their rushing off in such a manner."

"Trevor will be back at least by tomorrow," said Anne confidently.

The others looked at her in surprise. "What makes you so sure of that, Anne?" asked Lady Gregory.

"Why, tomorrow is Mothering Sunday, and Trevor would never miss that, you know."

"That's so," agreed Maria. "And we have your gifts ready, Mother. He'll be back. He promised to bring the simnel cake with him. I'm sure it will be an elegant one."

Simnel cakes had become a traditional part of Mothering Sunday, which occurred on the fourth Sunday of Lent. They were rich, dark cakes, glazed with almond paste and garnished with candied fruits and marzipan flowers. The existence of simnels was taken note of as long ago as 1042 in the *Annals of the Church of Winchester*, although not, of course, in connection with Mothering Sunday, but as a royal gift to a convent. Indeed, some believe that Mothering Sunday first referred to the Mother Church.

They were just beginning to wonder if they should all try to crowd into the gig and go searching for the others when George came galloping toward them as quickly as his pony's plump little legs would allow.

"What is it, George? What's happened?" called his mother in alarm. "Has Miss Lane been hurt?"

It took a moment before George had enough breath to answer her, but he shook his head violently in reply to what she had said.

"Gone!" he gasped finally.

Elizabeth, who was standing anxiously beside him, clutched his knee. "Gone? What do you mean, George?"

He made a great effort and managed to reply, his round little face red with his exertion. "We found the cart and the pony, but Nora and Rufus were gone!"

"Were you close to a spinney that she could have walked to, George? Did you check behind the hedgerow and everywhere she could have wandered away to in the area?" asked Lady Mallory.

George nodded. "The cart was just standing in the middle of the lane, and the pony's ribbons were dragging on the ground. She didn't tie him up or anything . . . and we found her bonnet a little farther along the lane and there were carriage tracks over it!"

Elizabeth pressed her hand to her mouth to keep her lips from shaking, for suddenly she feared the worst. "Where is Sir Edmund, George?"

"He said that he was going to follow the tracks as far as he could before the rain came, and then he was going to the nearest village for help because Chanderley was too far away."

"What village will that be, ma'am?" she asked, turning to Lady Mallory.

"Brambleton," she replied. "It's quite a tiny place, however."

"Brambleton!" Elizabeth exclaimed. "That is where the Bull and Barleycorn is!" And she quickly explained to the rest about their stay there during the snowstorm.

"That's right," Lady Mallory nodded. "Trevor told me that he had not gotten far from Chanderley when the storm struck. Do you think that is where Sir Edmund would go?"

"Yes, I do. The landlord and his wife are good people and perhaps they can help us."

All of them except George squeezed into the gig, and Lady Mallory, who knew the way, took the ribbons, although Anne was inclined to think that she could make better time than her parent. Together they hurried down the narrow lanes as the rain began to fall, a cold, heavy rain blown by a rising March wind.

When they arrived at the inn, they were a dreary sight, all of them sodden and shivering. Mrs. Netherspoon threw up her hands at the sight of them, and when she recognized Elizabeth, she hurried over to her and bobbed a curtsey.

"Please come right in, miss. Leave your gig right there and someone will come round to get it. Your brother has gone with my husband and some of the other men to search for the young lady. What a dreadful thing to have happen!"

And as she spoke, she hurried the ladies into the warm kitchen and fixed them mugs of steaming tea while she went to look for enough dry clothes for all of them. George, who had stayed on his pony round to the stable, joined them in short order.

"I took care of Rambler first," he explained. "Sir Edmund says you must always take care of your mount before yourself." Further enlightenment on the subject of Sir Edmund's sayings was denied them, for George was occupied with a huge slice of gingerbread.

Mrs. Netherspoon came bustling in with a stack of dry clothes so that the ladies could go upstairs and change. A stableboy had been dispatched to Chanderley with a note from Lady Mallory to her housekeeper explaining the situation and asking for fresh clothes for all of them and one for her son and Mr. Norville, in case they had returned. While they went upstairs to repair the damage done to them by the storm, Mrs. Netherspoon eyed George speculatively. She had had no children, so there were no spare clothes put by, but she informed George that Tom Macklin's sister had a boy about his size. This was not information that moved George in one way or the other as long as it did not interfere with his continued pursuit of the gingerbread.

The kitchen door swung open suddenly, and rain pelted into the room behind the newcomer. "Good evening, Nell Netherspoon," said Jem Featherstone formally. "And what will we be having for dinner this evening?"

"Jem Featherstone! The very person I was hoping to see!" she exclaimed, displaying an unusual warmth in her greeting that surprised the gentleman greatly.

"I am gratified to see that you prize my company, good lady," he responded, bowing. "It had sometimes seemed to me that you did not hold me in—"

He was allowed to indulge himself no longer, for she swept down upon him with the force of a tropical hurricane. "I need for you to go to Connie Dunlap's cottage and ask to borrow a suit of clothes for this boy," she informed him briskly.

Mr. Featherstone regarded George with some disfavor. He had just brought himself in from a cold March wind and a nasty rain that could send a man to bed with the ague, and now he was to take himself out again for the sake of some unknown bantling. He had been looking forward to a warm fire, good food, and cheerful company, and now he was to exchange it for a soggy trot through the dark, damp night. George stared back at him, chewing his gingerbread methodically. Mr. Featherstone was fond of gingerbread himself and took this ill.

"Where is John?" he inquired, looking about for Mr. Netherspoon.

"John and Tom Macklin have gone with Sir Edmund Harrington—you remember the gentleman that was with us on Shrove Tuesday, the gentleman with the big black horse?"

Mr. Featherstone nodded. "Is he back here to stay then?" he asked, his hopes of a remarkably fine dinner growing quickly.

"He is here because Miss Lane, the young lady with the Scottie pup and the kitten from our Tiger—he is here because she has been

262

kidnapped!" As she reached the end of her tale, she lowered her voice confidentially, so that Mr. Featherstone had to lean closer to hear it.

"Kidnapped!" he exclaimed, his eyes growing round. "When did it happen?"

"Not more than three hours ago, over by that old castle ruin to the south of Farmer Conway's. They found the empty pony cart and her ruined bonnet. The kitten was still in the cart, but the young lady and the pup were both gone!"

Mr. Featherstone's eyes grew wider. "The pup is gone, too?" he asked.

Mrs. Netherspoon nodded and Mr. Featherstone grew grave. "He has gone after her then," he said solemnly.

"Oh, he's just a pup, Jem. He wouldn't be able to keep up with a carriage," she protested.

He rubbed a finger thoughtfully alongside his nose. "Perhaps not, but perhaps he might. And perhaps, Mrs. Netherspoon," he added, "perhaps he is *in* the carriage."

There was a pause as they considered the matter. George was apparently considering it, too, for he stopped chewing long enough to say, somewhat thickly, "Rufus could do it, too. He wouldn't run away from Nora if she were in trouble. He'd stand buff."

Mr. Featherstone regarded him with a more favorable eye. "Is your good husband out looking for the young lady then?" he asked Mrs. Netherspoon.

She nodded. "He and Tom Macklin and the blacksmith rode out with Sir Edmund to see if they could find any trace of her." She walked to the window and pulled aside a curtain to glance outside. "But with the dark and the wet and the cold, I doubt they'll find the poor young thing tonight."

As it happened, "the poor young thing" deserved every morsel of Mrs. Netherspoon's sympathy. When the closed carriage had overtaken Nora on the narrow lane, she had waved blithely back to the driver, planning to pull over at the next possible place so that he could pass. Instead, she saw to her horror that he planned to force his way by, and bit by bit she was crowded toward the hedgerow. Finally, she pulled the pony up short, afraid that he would be hurt if they continued along their present course, and turned to give the driver a healthy piece of her mind.

To her dismay, as that gentleman leaped down from the carriage and walked toward her, removing his hat as he came, she saw that the driver was none other than Lord Chawton. She was frightened, but she lifted her chin and stared at him coldly.

"I trust that you do not think that you drive to an inch, sir!" she said frostily. "Nor that your manners are those that would become a gentleman!"

"Ah, but I have never claimed to be a gentleman, you see, Miss Lane," he retorted, "so that is not a remark that is likely to rankle." He smiled thinly, slapping a leather glove in his hand. "Your comment about my driving strikes a little nearer the quick, however. Perhaps we should talk about the proper manners for a lady, who would certainly never be jauntering about alone in country lanes."

All too easily did Elizabeth's strictures about moderation and prudence in her behavior come rushing into Nora's thoughts. She was indeed alone with this somewhat intimidating man, and it was all through her own carelessness. Most sincerely did she repent her rashness, but as she stared down at his smiling face—somewhat like a crocodile's smile, she thought—she put as good a face on things as she could.

"Of course I am not alone," she said briskly. "Sir Edmund and Elizabeth are following along behind me, as well as Lady Gregory and the Grahams."

He shook his head gently. "I admire your creativity, Miss Lane, but I am well aware that you abandoned the rest of your party to come along on your own. I have been watching, you see."

Nora's fear fought with her anger, and anger won. "How dare you, sir!" she flashed. "How dare you *spy* upon us, like—like a common criminal!"

"Ah, but you see, Miss Lane, you do me an injustice. I am quite *un*common." And here he reached out to pull her from the cart.

Nora screamed and reached for her little whip, which she used to strike him across the face, leaving a line of red to trace its path. Her courage almost failed her as anger distorted his features. Catching her by the wrist, he jerked her roughly down from the perch on the pony cart and dragged her behind him as he moved the cart to one side of the road so that his carriage could pass. Nora's little chip bonnet fell from her head and was crushed underfoot.

As they passed the cart on the way back to the carriage, a sharp little bark rang out, and Chawton's head jerked up. A pair of bright black eyes watched him steadily over the rim of the cart, their owner setting up a series of ear-piercing barks.

"No noise, you little cur!" commanded Chawton, lifting the leather glove as though to strike the pup. Rufus, anticipating a blow, fell back to the bottom of the cart, still barking.

"Well, I'll not leave you behind to set up a din that would bring any farmer from his field for a mile around!" And, jerking the pup out of the cart, he tossed Nora and Rufus into the carriage together.

"You'd best keep quiet and you'd best keep *him* quiet," announced Chawton, taking a length of rope from the carriage. Although she did her best to resist, he bound her wrists and ankles together and then tied a scarf so tightly around her mouth that she could scarcely swallow. Rufus he dropped into a burlap bag with a drawstring top, which he knotted securely.

"Don't talk too much, Miss Lane," he said politely. "And do keep your dog quiet. Remember what almost happened to him when first we met."

And to Nora's dismay, he slammed the door and she felt the carriage begin to move away—away from Sampson and the pony cart, away from Elizabeth and Edmund, away from safety.

Chapter Twenty

Once in dry clothes, a plain cotton gown supplied by Mrs. Netherspoon that hung loosely on her, Elizabeth could not be still. She paced the length of the small inn, pausing to peer from behind the curtain each time she passed a window. Sir Edmund and the others had not returned, and she wanted to hope that that meant they had found some trace of Nora. Visions of Nora lying injured or captive swam through her mind, but she resolutely dismissed them. We will find her, she kept telling herself. It was not possible that they would not.

It was over an hour later when the search party arrived, cold, bedraggled, and downcast.

"We followed the carriage tracks as far as we could, Lizzy," Sir Edmund sighed, removing his sodden hat, "but the rain soon blotted them out quite efficiently. And we stopped along the way at every cottage that stood near the road. One woman had seen a dark carriage go by earlier in the evening, but she could tell us nothing more than that. I'm afraid that there's nothing else we can do for Nora tonight."

It was all that Elizabeth could do to keep from wringing her hands in sheer desperation. The thought of leaving Nora overnight with her captor—for such appeared to be the case—was well nigh unbearable, but she realized that Edmund spoke the truth. She sank onto a stool by the fire and rested her head in her hands, thinking. The others maintained a respectful silence, drinking the hot punch that Mrs. Netherspoon was dispensing without conversation.

When Elizabeth finally lifted her head, she looked about the cheerful kitchen. "Nora was so happy when she was here before," she mused aloud, "setting off on her holiday to London."

Jem Featherstone nodded and sighed gravely into his punch. "A very taking young lady she was," he said, referring to Nora as though she no longer numbered among the living. "I remember well her sitting at this very fire with her pets, trying to solve her riddle." He sighed again and subsided into silence after a quelling glance from Mrs. Netherspoon.

A brief smile flitted across Elizabeth's face as she thought of Nora's determined efforts to solve Chawton's riddle. Suddenly, a startling thought caused her to leap to her feet, exactly like a marionette whose master has pulled the string. The others stared at her, and Jem Featherstone, thinking she was about to become a prey to hysteria, began to make the same kind of soothing noises one would make to calm a baby.

Sir Edmund, too familiar with his sister's disposition to believe for a moment that she was bordering on hysterics, looked at her with interest. "There now, Lizzy, what have you thought of?"

"Mowbry Park!" she exclaimed. "Where is Mowbry Park?"

Sir Edmund began to entertain doubts about her stability himself. He put down his glass of punch, a sure sign of distress of mind, and looked at her with concern. "There now, old girl, what's the to-do about Mowbry Park? Come to think of it, what *is* Mowbry Park?"

"That's where Lord Chawton said he lived, Edmund! When we first met him here at the inn, I heard him tell Mr. Netherspoon that he was Lord Chawton of Mowbry Park!"

For Sir Edmund, who had been privy to none of the further revelations about Lord Chawton and so knew him only as a man who made himself generally disagreeable to everyone he encountered, this was not an illuminating remark. Nonetheless, he decided that perhaps his sister had succumbed to a nervous fit and decided to humor her.

"Well, to be sure, Lizzy, if he lived in the neighborhood, we would want to stop by and pay our respects."

"Don't be such a goosecap, Edmund! Of course, we would not want to pay a social call!" She broke off, remembering that her brother knew nothing of Chawton's efforts to blackmail Lord Mallory.

267

"Oh, I'm sorry, Edmund!" she exclaimed repentantly. "I forgot that you did not know about Lord Chawton—"

"Well, of course I know about Chawton, Lizzy!" Sir Edmund was indignant. "Everyone who's up to snuff in town knows that he's a curst rum touch if ever there was one!"

"Just so!" agreed Elizabeth and the others in the room nodded. "But the thing is, Edmund, and I haven't time to explain it now, it is very possible that Lord Chawton wishes us harm and thinks to strike at us through Nora! I can think of no one else who would do such a thing, and if Mowbry Park is in this vicinity, and I think it must be from what Lord Mallory said, Nora might be there!"

Lady Mallory had been looking quite as lost as Sir Edmund, but she said in a somewhat bewildered voice, "Mowbry Park is located several miles from here, Miss Harrington, but I'm afraid I don't quite follow what you were saying. I know that Lord Chawton is not quite the thing, but to kidnap a well-born young woman would put him beyond the pale. I cannot imagine that he would do such a thing!"

"Dash it all, no, Lizzy!" agreed Sir Edmund. "I grant you that Chawton is something of an ugly customer, but I never heard it said that he was a rake-shame!"

"I think that we should listen to Miss Harrington," said Lady Gregory abruptly. All other talking ceased and attention centered on her, for it was evident that she was deadly serious.

"As Miss Harrington told you," she continued, "there is not time to explain in full now. Suffice it to say that I suspect Lord Chawton of complicity in my husband's disappearance, and perhaps in his death, a year ago." The Brambleton folks, to whom this was news, looked at each other in astonishment.

"I think that he is more than capable of having kidnapped Miss Lane, and if there is the slightest possibility that she is at Mowbry Park, then we must rescue her now. She cannot be allowed to stay the night in that man's clutches!"

Her words had an electrifying effect on her audience. Tom Macklin was standing and putting on his coat before she had finished, and as soon as she had spoken her last word, Mr. Featherstone said, "I will step across the way to Samuel Berry's house. He would wish to assist in the rescue mission, and I believe that we should take as many men as possible."

John Netherspoon nodded. "Mowbry Park be a rundown place by all accounts, and there be no certainty how many servants the lord do keep there now."

While the men were putting on their coats and preparing a buggy equipped with blankets and brandy for medicinal purposes, Elizabeth asked Mrs. Netherspoon if she had a cloak that she might borrow.

"You're never thinking of going with them, miss!" she exclaimed in horror.

"No, Lizzy!" protested her brother. "Dash it all, Lizzy, this is no place for a woman!"

"I quite agree, Edmund," she said calmly. "Nora has absolutely no place there. She is my charge, I took responsibility for her from my mother, and I am going with you. I will drive the buggy."

Sir Edmund, having had extensive experience with his sister's stubbornness, made no further attempt to dissuade her, and set about making plans for their errand of mercy. By the time the motley little group set out, they numbered eight horsemen with Elizabeth manning the buggy. All of the other ladies stayed behind at the inn, but it was with difficulty that George was prevented from saddling his fat pony and joining the party. Not until Sir Edmund pointed out to him that they would be leaving all of the women with no man to protect them from a kidnapper during the long, stormy night did George consent to remain behind. He took his charge seriously and, having secured the front door as they left, bolted the kitchen door and set a bench in front of it, where he made his bed that night with Sampson curled on his blanket.

The progress of the rescue party through the narrow, dark lanes was slow, but they moved with steady determination. The thought that such a taking young woman, so young and so innocent, could be in the clutches of a man whom they all disliked and feared, spurred on the good-hearted men of Brambleton. Elizabeth concentrated on strategies they might be able to employ when they arrived, trying to keep herself from imagining what Nora's predicament could presently be.

And indeed her predicament was not a desirable one. When they arrived at Mowbry Park—for Lady Gregory had been quite correct and the rat was returning to his hole—he had driven the carriage round to a rear entrance and had bundled Nora quickly out of the vehicle and down a set of stairs. So much she could tell by the movement, but she could see nothing because he had thrown a dark cloak over her before lifting her from the carriage. She could tell too as he set her down that she was in a cellar, for the smell of damp and mildew assailed her nostrils.

She heard Chawton leave, and for a few minutes there was a deep silence, but then she could hear footsteps coming down the steps again and the sudden thud of something falling close to her head.

"Here is your dear doggy, Miss Lane," he said in a mockingly sweet voice. "Although you don't really need him to keep you company. After all, you will have the rats." And then the door slammed and she heard the bolt outside shoot into place.

Nora listened carefully as the sound of his footsteps died away, but she could hear no sound from Rufus. Fearful that Chawton had finally killed the pup and had left his body there to taunt her, she worked her way around on the stones of the cellar floor until her hands, which were bound behind her, encountered the bag in which Rufus lay. Desperately she worked at the strings which knotted it shut, but could loosen them only a little. She ran one hand over the outside of the bag until she encountered the small lump that was Rufus. She left her hand there against him, and the tears slipped down her cheeks as she attempted to pat him. He was dead now because of her headstrong ways.

Most bitterly now did she regret setting off on her own. She had been fearful before for her own safety and had regretted her actions because she had endangered herself. She had not until this moment considered the possibility that her carelessness could cause someone other than herself to pay a price.

As to how long she lay there, stiff and miserable, she was never certain. Suddenly, however, she heard a soft, scrabbling noise, and her heart leaped. Was it Rufus? Then, realizing that one hand remained against his still form within the bag, she knew that it was not Rufus that had stirred. She listened carefully, and then she knew. It was the rats.

When she felt one run across her foot, her entire body shuddered uncontrollably, and despite the gag that still bound her cruelly, she began to whimper. After a few minutes, she grew calm enough to realize that the sound of whimpering no longer came from her alone. Rufus had joined her lament.

It is difficult to be joyful in the midst of terror, but Nora found that it was possible to be so. With one stiff hand she gently patted the little lump in the sack, which had begun to squirm about now. When another rat ran across her leg, she shuddered again, but this time she was not alone. Rufus had caught the scent of the rat, and his struggling grew more violent and his whining louder. It was not very long before Nora could feel fur beneath her fingers instead of sacking, and a small rough tongue began to lick her hand frantically.

When another rat scampered across her, Nora heard Rufus's deep-throated growl and heard the sounds of struggle. She listened fearfully, for Rufus was no more than a half-grown dog and had no experience in doing battle. When silence fell, Nora began to cry again, for she was sure that Rufus had been injured. In a moment, however, she heard the sound of snuffling about her face, which was still covered by the cloak. When she managed to struggle free of it a few minutes later, Rufus licked her cheeks joyfully, and the dampness there was no longer that of tears. Even with the gag in place, Nora could not restrain a giggle. Once he had calmed down, Rufus, weary from his experience and the blow to his head when Chawton had brought him downstairs, nestled close to Nora and went to sleep. Whenever a rat ventured close, however, he was up again and at his work, not returning to Nora until the job was done. For the moment, Nora was somewhat comforted by his warm and friendly presence, and even managed to drift in and out of sleep herself.

In the meantime, the rescue party was growing closer. When they came within range of the house, their lights were extinguished so as not to give themselves away should anyone be watching. Mowbry Park was an old, rambling building with wings that had been tacked on every which way over the years, according to the prevailing taste of the age and the wishes of the current baron. The present Lord Chawton had had neither the inclination nor the wherewithal to add to the old place and had used it not as a family home but as a hideaway when he was too far in Dun territory or when some of his less savory activities had attracted too much unfavorable attention. The few servants that he kept there were a slatternly lot and seldom stayed for very long. Sometimes, in fact,

Lord Chawton made a clean sweep of them by offering a package deal to a press gang if they would but make a trip to Mowbry Park by night.

So it was that when Tom Macklin and the blacksmith, Joseph Stewart, approached the lighted kitchen, they could see through an uncurtained window three ill-favored wretches sitting at a wooden table playing cards by the light of a tallow candle. They had carefully noted the two other places in the house where they could see signs of life, one in the far end of a second-story wing, the other not far from the kitchen. The rest of the group remained hidden in the shadows, for they had agreed that Macklin and Stewart would tell Chawton's servants that they had gone out to repair a broken axle at a distant country house and had lost their way during the storm.

Had they been Bow Street Runners at the door, the three miserable creatures could scarcely have looked more guilty. When Macklin and Stewart explained their situation and told them that they were wishful of receiving directions, there may have been a slight hope amongst the three that they could overcome the two callers and help themselves to their horses and the contents of their pockets. However, when one of them raised the candle high enough that they could take in the size of the two before them, such a hope faded and died.

Having received their directions, Macklin and Stewart showed themselves disposed to be friendly, willing to stay and have a drink and blow a cloud with the servants. At this amiability, however, the servants became even more surly and taciturn. A bit of gentle questioning on Stewart's part elicited the information that their master was indeed at home, and, yes, he was an old nip-farthing, and, yes, he did have a guest, a lady. Macklin and Stewart were inclined to be elated by this bit of news until one of the servants, a thin, mean-looking fellow with a face like a ferret, allowed that she was a well-enough looking woman were it not for her yellow hair. Downcast by this puncturing of their hopes, the pair departed, pretending that they were riding away from Mowbry Park and on to Brambleton. Instead, they joined the others and imparted their news.

"There wasn't a sign of the little lady," concluded Stewart, and Tom Macklin nodded his agreement.

"But I'm sure she is in there," insisted Elizabeth.

Sir Edmund nodded glumly. "I think you're right, Lizzy, but how will we find her in that great rambling heap? She could be anywhere!"

"Then we'll look everywhere!" Elizabeth declared sharply. "Just think of it! Nora left to the mercy of Chawton and that gang of thieves in the kitchen! We can't just ride away from here!"

Her speech had a galvanizing effect on the men. "The lady is in the right of it!" declared Jem Featherstone fervently. "We cannot ride away from here and hold our heads up again! We must attack!"

Having made that dramatic call to action, he looked about hopefully to see if anyone else could be slightly more specific as to how the attack would be conducted. After a lengthy consultation, it was decided that Sir Edmund would lead a party to investigate the lighted area closer to the kitchen while John Netherspoon would lead a second party to try to ascertain what was taking place in the second-story wing farther away. Tom Macklin was to remain with Elizabeth.

Elizabeth waited impatiently for what seemed like an hour until the first group returned. Through a parted curtain, Sir Edmund had been able to catch a glimpse of Chawton in what was apparently his library. He appeared to be alone. When Netherspoon's group returned, they had nothing to impart. One room was lighted and the curtains tightly drawn.

"That must be where his lady guest is," speculated Elizabeth, and the others nodded.

"Well, what do we do now, Lizzy? Storm the doors?" inquired her brother. "If Nora is in there, she is either in that curtained chamber or in an unlighted room."

Elizabeth thought deeply for a minute before replying. "Why not?" she asked, her light tone belying the seriousness of her words. "Why don't we storm the doors?"

She could feel the rustle of alarm among the men, who were somewhat leery of openly attacking the home of a member of the peerage, no matter how disreputable a one, without more substantial evidence.

"No, I don't mean literally to attack at this point," she explained impatiently. "Sir Edmund and I will go to the door, and Chawton or one of the servants will answer it. Whichever way it goes, we

273

will see Chawton and tell him that Nora has been kidnapped and that we have been searching everywhere. Perhaps we can even press a point and act as though we are asking for his help—and then watch his reaction."

A resounding silence greeted her suggestion. "Well, what can *you* suggest then?" she demanded of them, only to be met with another silence.

"She be in the right of it," said John Netherspoon finally. "That way we be doing nothing agin the law, but at least two of us are inside the house. The rest of us can watch our chance."

There was a low murmur of agreement, and together Sir Edmund and Elizabeth drove the buggy up the drive in front of the house, and Sir Edmund rang the bell sharply three times. When the door opened, Lord Chawton stood there, staring at them.

"I am thunderstruck!" he said finally. "Sir Edmund Harrington and the elegant Miss Elizabeth Harrington come to call in the middle of the night! I must believe that I am dreaming."

"It's no dream, Chawton, as you'll find out quick enough if you'll invite us in!" replied Sir Edmund tartly, brushing the rain from his hat.

"By all means," he replied, sweeping them a deep and mocking bow as they entered the darkened entryway, lighted only by the candle Chawton had set on a table by the door. Picking it up, he motioned for them to follow him into the next room.

"Are you not going to ask what calls us out in the middle of a dark and stormy night, sir?" asked Elizabeth briskly.

He turned to her with a limpid expression. "Am I to understand by that, Miss Harrington, that it was not a desire for the pleasure of my company that brought you to Mowbry Park?"

Sir Edmund snorted. "We are here because Miss Lane has been kidnapped, Chawton!"

"Kidnapped!" he exclaimed. "How could such a thing have happened? Have you reported it?"

"One thing at a time," said Sir Edmund curtly. "First of all, Chawton, have you seen any strangers about your place today?"

Chawton, who had been bracing himself for an accusation, was thrown off guard, and Elizabeth threw her brother an admiring glance.

"No one any stranger than my servants," he returned after a mo-

274

ment. "Although, to be truthful, they are strange enough. It is so difficult to keep good help in the country these days."

Ignoring his pleasantry, Sir Edmund persevered. "Well, then, if you rode out today, Chawton, did you see anything of a strange carriage?"

"What did it look like?" asked Lord Chawton carefully.

"A post-chaise," Sir Edmund replied promptly. "Back wheels were larger than the front. Not a gig or a phaeton. Not loaded with luggage, for the tracks weren't deep enough. Drawn by two horses, one with an odd star-shaped pattern on the horseshoe."

Chawton looked suddenly wary, and Elizabeth regarded her brother with renewed respect.

Continuing to press his advantage, Sir Edmund added, "Need to bring our cattle in out of the cold, Chawton. Might I put them in your stables for the moment?"

A trifle rattled, Chawton said, still pleasantly, "I had no idea that you planned to make a protracted call, Sir Edmund. I am delighted of course, although I feel that if Miss Lane has been kidnapped, she may be in need of your immediate aid."

"Feel the same way myself, Chawton. Would you like to join us in the search? I could walk out myself and help you saddle up."

"Very kind of you, but I don't think I feel up to it just at the moment. Maybe tomorrow morning when the weather is a bit better and I can see more clearly. I took a bit of a tumble today and haven't quite recovered from my knock on the head," he replied, patting his wounded cheek gingerly. "Don't want to be a bother, you know."

"Just as you say," returned Sir Edmund politely, "but then I'm sure you won't mind if m'sister rests for a minute or two. She's quite exhausted."

"I'm sure she must be. By all means rest a moment before you leave. Let me see if I can find something for your refreshment."

"Mighty pleased I'm not going to the stables, ain't he, Lizzy?" remarked Sir Edmund as the door closed behind their suddenly gracious host.

Elizabeth nodded. "And certainly pleased that we'll be leaving soon. I do wonder how he came by that stripe across his cheek."

Their genial host was back in less than a minute to inform them that one of his servants was even then preparing Elizabeth a cup of tea that would undoubtedly restore her. They had no more than seated themselves when the sound of a pistol shot rang through the house.

Chapter Twenty-one

Nora awakened suddenly to the sound of Rufus growling, and for a moment she could not imagine where she was, for darkness enveloped them completely in their cellar. When she finally recalled her situation, she listened carefully, unable to hear much other than the pup's deep growling, but expecting to hear the scrabbling of a rat across the floor. Instead, she could hear very faintly the sound of voices, and it seemed that Rufus could also hear them, for he set up a dreadful, ear-piercing barking. Panic-stricken, expecting Chawton to come any moment to kill the dog, she tried to silence him by flapping her hand at him in the darkness. He continued barking, however, and to Nora's distress, she heard the unbolting of the door at the top of the stairs. The door opened, revealing an oblong of wavering candlelight, and a dark figure descended the stairs, candle in hand.

"Rufus? Is that you?" Lord Mallory called from midway down the stairs, peering into the darkness.

Recognizing a friend, Rufus shot up the stairs toward him, while Nora did her feeble best to wriggle across the floor in his direction. Mallory heard the sound and raised the candle higher.

"Nora?" He took another step toward her, and she tried to say something against the confines of the gag.

Suddenly, however, another figure appeared at the top of the stairs, and a shot rang out, sending Mallory tumbling to the bottom, candle in hand. Fortunately for all concerned, the candle guttered and went out immediately instead of setting fire to the wooden steps.

Rufus had tumbled back down the stairs, caught in Mallory's

fall, and he stood licking the face of the downed man. Nora could scarcely believe her eyes. Lord Mallory shot!

The unknown assailant laughed and turned back to the light above. "There's a toff what won't be doing any more snooping about—" he began, but was abruptly cut off. There came a muffled grunt and the sound of a body thudding to the floor.

"Mallory! Are you all right?" Andrew Norville appeared on the steps with a lantern in one hand and a pistol in the other. He hurried toward the motionless form at the bottom, drawn by the sound of Rufus whining. As he held the lantern over Mallory, its shaft of light fell across Nora.

"Miss Lane!" he exclaimed, turning from the injured man and hurriedly loosening her gag. "Have they hurt you?"

"No! I'll be fine! Never mind my bonds now!" she snapped as he started to loosen the ropes that bound her. "Can't you see that he has been injured? He may be dying!"

Despite her remonstrances, he quickly untied her hands and feet and rubbed them briskly for a moment to help restore circulation. Having satisfied himself that she had been done no grave injury, he turned back to Mallory.

"Help him, Mr. Norville, help him!" Nora pleaded, kneeling beside the unconscious man.

Norville turned him gently over and Nora held the lantern for him to examine the wound. He was bleeding quite profusely, for the bullet had entered the back of his right shoulder and made its exit through the front. Nora willingly sacrificed her petticoat, for Norville's neckcloth was too stiffly starched to absorb the bleeding readily. They were not left long to deal with the problem unaided, however, for the members of the rescue party came swarming down the steps, armed with lanterns, candles, knives, cudgels, and Jem Featherstone's pistol.

Tom Macklin looked Lord Mallory over and retired upstairs to find a board and ticking suitable for moving the young man from the damp stone floor. When he returned, he and Netherspoon gently eased the young lord onto the stretcher and raised it carefully, moving him as little as possible. Elizabeth and Sir Edmund had arrived on the scene by this time and had rejoiced to see Nora alive and well. The young woman had scarcely noticed them, so absorbed had she been by watching jealously to see that Lord Mallory was cared for properly.

Jem Featherstone raised his lantern to stare around the cellar. "A dank, miserable place for a young girl," he remarked, glancing around him. "For anyone," he amended. His attention was suddenly caught by a mound of something in the corner, and he walked closer to inspect it. It was the stack of rats that Rufus had slain as he protected Nora. Mr. Featherstone scrutinized them by lantern light and turned to look at Rufus, who was once again encamped close to Sir Edmund.

"You have proven your right to be called Rufus," Mr. Featherstone informed the pup gravely.

"Eh?" exclaimed Sir Edmund, called to attention by Featherstone's remark. "Are you talking to the dog, Featherstone?" he asked incredulously.

"I am indeed, Sir Edmund. Allow me to show you something that I think will interest you." And so saying, he led Sir Edmund to the rats and explained the situation.

Sir Edmund looked down at the pup, who had stayed at his heel. "Did you kill these, Rufus?" he inquired in astonishment. Accepting silence as assent, he reached down and patted his head. "Remarkable! Quite remarkable!" he said, and Rufus ducked his head with a becoming show of modesty.

The kitchen at Mowbry Park was a good-sized apartment, but it was scarcely large enough to hold the number that were encamped there. Nora had busied herself lighting every candle that she could find so that Lord Mallory's wound could be cleaned and cared for properly, and John Netherspoon had built up the fire, but it was still a rather shadowy and chilly chamber. A good dozen people hovered anxiously while Mr. Norville labored over the young lord. To their relief, he regained consciousness fairly quickly, although he was somewhat dazed, and Mr. Featherstone quickly presented a flask of brandy to administer to the patient.

When that was accomplished, Mr. Norville looked at the crowd in the kitchen and frowned. "Where is Chawton?" he asked abruptly.

"He came with us when the shot was fired," said Sir Edmund. "We were in the drawing room when it happened, and he and

Lizzy and I all hurried along through this rabbit warren until we saw that fellow," and here he indicated the servant who had shot Mallory, who was now trussed like a turkey, "folded up on the floor with a pistol lying on the floor beside him. When we heard Norville's voice coming from downstairs, we hurried on down there."

Jem Featherstone spoke up next. "After the pistol shot, we were obliged to break out the kitchen window because they had bolted the door. Unfortunately, the window was not very large, and we had some trouble fitting one of us through the opening. But there was no one in the kitchen when we got in, nor did we see anyone as we searched for the source of the gunfire."

"Would you like for us to search the house, Mr. Norville?" asked Tom Macklin.

"I think we'd best," he replied grimly. Leaving Mr. Netherspoon to watch over Lord Mallory and the ladies, the others divided into three parties and set forth to examine the premises. Once again the ladies had the dubious privilege of waiting for news. For once, Nora did not chafe at being excluded from the activities of the gentlemen. She sat close by Lord Mallory's side and bathed his forehead so often that Elizabeth finally felt that she should restrain her so that the poor man would not be washed away in his sleep. Mr. Featherstone's brandy had helped to revive him briefly, but he had soon closed his eyes again, although Elizabeth noticed uneasily that his sleep did not seem to be a restful one.

She was grateful when the search parties began to return. The first party had found no one, but Lord Chawton had apparently returned to his library and hurriedly taken some things from his desk. Papers had been strewn about, and a recess behind one of the bookshelves had been left exposed, for the bookshelf had not been pushed back into place properly. An investigation had disclosed nothing of particular interest, however.

The members of the second party to return looked somewhat more disheveled that those of the first group, for their search had led them through parts of Mowbry Park that had not been bothered in some twenty years. Mr. Featherstone's dark hat and cloak were festooned with cobwebs, but he wore them proudly. They were exhilarated and somewhat disbelieving, for their search had been successful. They had not found Chawton, but in a windowless storage room, far from the inhabited portion of the house, they had found a prisoner, an old man with white hair who had turned his head from the blinding light when their lanterns appeared in the door.

"We almost continued past that room because it was locked," confided Mr. Featherstone.

"Would have," affirmed Sir Edmund. "Too much trouble to beat down an oak door two inches thick to look at a room filled with nothing but cobwebs."

"What made you stop then?" asked Elizabeth, fascinated.

Sir Edmund pointed proudly at Rufus, who was seated neatly on his master's boot. "Rufus stopped with his nose to the crack at the bottom of the door, the way he did the night your jewels were stolen, Lizzy, and he wouldn't budge. Whined and scratched until we did something."

Mr. Featherstone was not to be outdone. "Recognizing the importance of such a reaction, I insisted that we stop and take the door down immediately. It is fortunate that Stewart had brought with him a crowbar as his weapon this night, for together we pried the doors from its hinges . . . and there he was."

The gentleman to whom they referred was seated in the corner of a settle by the fire, too weak to sit on anything that could not support his back. Nora was hurriedly searching the barren pantry, trying to find something that she could prepare for him to eat, for he was so thin and wasted that his pale skin seemed almost transparent. It appeared that one good snap would break him like a china doll. Long white hair curled around his shoulders, and his eyes were closed against the flickering light. His clothes were in tatters, and Tom Macklin had found a blanket to wrap around his shoulders.

"Do we know who he is, Edmund?" Elizabeth asked in a low voice, unsure how much the old man was aware of things around him.

Her brother stared at her. "Well, of course we do, Lizzy. This is Gregory—Sir Howard Gregory!"

It was Elizabeth's turn to stare in disbelief. Sir Howard, whom

281

she had seen occasionally at social functions, had been a tall, vigorous man, fully seventy or eighty pounds heavier than the man before her. His dark hair had been streaked with grey, but this man had hair as white as a fresh snowfall.

"Have you talked to him, Edmund?" she asked, still speaking in a low voice.

"Tried," replied her brother, "but it's my belief that he's been penned up like that all these months, and the light and voices have been too much for him." His usually mild expression was grim. "Chawton has a lot to answer for!"

"Indeed he does!" agreed Norville, who had come in behind them with the third group. "But I am afraid that he has gotten completely away from us for the moment, and unless I miss my guess, he will make straight for the coast and France."

"France?" echoed Sir Edmund incredulously.

Norville nodded. "From what I saw in his desk, it looks as though he must have been in the pay of Napoleon. It would have been in Bonaparte's best interests for his enemies to be divided, and keeping Sir Howard from completing his mission was one way of accomplishing that. He also probably hoped to add to his treasury if he could capture the Blue Tavernier as well."

"Yes, but Bonaparte wouldn't have had Gregory locked up like this," objected Sir Edmund. "He would just have had him killed. Much neater that way."

Norville smiled. "Undoubtedly much neater. I'm sure that's what he expected to happen. The fact that Sir Howard is alive is probably due to Chawton's greed. When they didn't find the diamond, he probably hoped Sir Howard might finally be forced to tell him what happened to it, and then Chawton would have been able to keep it for himself—or at least to strike a profitable bargain with Napoleon."

Sir Edmund appeared ready to cavil at that as well, but their attention was suddenly attracted by the subject of their conversation. Nora had prepared a cup of gruel and was trying to spoon some into Sir Howard's mouth.

"Come now," she was saying gently, "take just a little and you'll feel better."

Hearing her voice, Sir Howard's eyes flew open, and he stared at her as though trying to bring her into focus. "Emma?" he asked in a quavering voice.

Nora looked up at Elizabeth, startled. "Who does he think I am?" she asked.

"His daughter, I believe," she replied gently.

Her eyes grew wide. "Sir Howard?" she asked, staring at Elizabeth, who nodded in reply.

Nora smiled at him and said encouragingly, "You must eat then, sir, for you will soon be seeing your family. Your wife you will see this very night."

It was a slow journey back to the Bull and Barleycorn, for not only were they traveling over muddy roads on a dark night, but they were transporting two invalids as well. When they reached the inn, George moved his bench and unbolted the door, his little face growing pale as he watched them carry his brother in. Lady Gregory, who had placed her arm about Mallory's mother as he was brought in, was about to turn from the door when she realized that someone else was being helped in as well.

"Another injury?" she asked, turning back to see if she was needed. John Netherspoon and Tom Macklin were supporting her husband between them. She stood perfectly still for a moment, staring at the emaciated figure before her.

"Howard?" she whispered, scarcely able to believe her eyes. Slowly she walked to him and, cupping his face in her two hands, gently kissed him. His eyes seemed to focus and for a moment a faint smile played across his features.

"Rachel?" His voice was paper-thin and reedy, but he stretched out his hand to touch her. "Am I really home?"

"You are, Howard. You are home at last." And so saying, she and the two men helped him to the settle close to the fire, while Mrs. Netherspoon bustled about to prepare beds and possets for the invalids and Mr. Featherstone retired to the corner to wipe his eyes and blow his nose.

In an amazingly short time, the inn was relatively quiet again. Both invalids were tucked into their beds, Lady Mallory watching over her son and Lady Gregory tending her husband. The members of the rescue party had been thanked and thanked again and invited to partake of a Sunday dinner the next day. The children were sleeping on their pallets on the floor, and the weary Netherspoons had gone gratefully to bed. Only Nora, Elizabeth, and Sir Edmund, accompanied of course by Rufus and Sampson, were still awake by the fire.

Nora had been staring silently into the fire for a very long time, and Sir Edmund was becoming restive. He had become so accustomed to Nora's chatter that its absence seemed unnatural.

"Are you feeling quite the thing, Nora?" he asked kindly. "A very bad experience you've had today. Could I get you some tea?"

"No, thank you, Edmund." She paused a moment and then blurted out her thoughts. "I deserved the bad experience I had today, but Lord Mallory didn't. If he dies, it will be through my carelessness."

Elizabeth was shocked. "Nora! What a thing to say! You most certainly did not deserve the experience you had today. You were careless, but that does not mean you deserved to be kidnapped."

But Nora would not be comforted. "If I had listened to you, Elizabeth, I wouldn't have been out there alone to be kidnapped, and Lord Mallory would not have come to Mowbry Park and been shot. So, you see, it is my fault."

"But he is not dying, Nora. He has a slight fever, but he will soon be well."

"Just as right as a trivet," affirmed Sir Edmund. "And besides, my girl, if you hadn't gotten yourself kidnapped, we never would have found Sir Howard. Only a room-by-room search would have found him."

Nora had not thought of this, and she brightened considerably. "That's so!" she agreed happily. "And now no one will be able to make odious remarks to her about her husband. I shall *love* telling Lord Dabney about this."

She was soon calm enough to be able to retire with Elizabeth to their pallet and, having reassured herself by a peep into Lord Mallory's room that he was resting, to go to sleep, despite the fact that the dawn was about to break.

Sir Edmund, left sitting by the fire, patted Sampson, who was curled in his lap, and looked down at Rufus, who was again draped across his boots. "I told Jem Featherstone that he was all

284

about in his head because he said a dog could be a gentleman. Appears I was wrong, don't it?"

Rufus wagged his tail once in response, and all three of them drifted off to sleep.

Chapter Twenty-two

The following day was a memorable one for all concerned. Sir Howard awoke to see his wife seated next to him, not in his dreams, but in reality. Nora was free of her dreadful experience and Elizabeth from the dread of losing her. The Netherspoons had more business than they could easily accommodate, and the members of the rescue party had a marvelous time reliving each exciting moment of the night before. Indeed, "the storming of Mowbry Park," as it came to be known among the locals, was a watershed experience for Brambleton. Events were dated from that time for years to come, and people of the village would say things like, "Oh, yes, that happened some five years after the storming of Mowbry Park," or "Edward was born just a year before the storming of Mowbry Park."

Not everyone was perfectly contented, however. Elizabeth had noticed that Mr. Norville did not come in with everyone else when they returned from Mowbry Park, and he had left the inn before she had awakened that morning. She did not particularly wish to see him, of course, but she did wonder what he was finding to do. Also, Nora was naturally pleased to hear that Lord Mallory was resting more easily, but her presence was not apparently required in his sickroom, for he did not send for her. George and Anne were inclined to be upset, for today was Mothering Sunday and their special present for Lady Mallory was still at Chanderley.

"It is all right," she comforted them. "It will still be there when we get home, and I will still love whatever it is."

"But the cake is there, too," George pointed out with the practicality born of a healthy appetite.

286

"Well, perhaps that will still be there, too," she laughed. "Surely the servants won't eat their way through it before we arrive home."

Both invalids remained in bed all day, but to George's joy, a groom from Chanderley arrived bearing not only the required fresh clothing for everyone, but the Mothering Day present and the simnel cake Lord Mallory had purchased in London as well. Sir Edmund was almost as pleased to see his copies of the *Morning Chronicle* arrive as George was to see the cake. Mr. Norville, the groom informed them, had been back to Chanderley to pack his things and had asked him to inform the family that he would be in London for the next few days but would return as soon as possible.

"I wonder what the devil he's up to," mused Sir Edmund as he drowsed over his paper.

"I'm sure I don't know," his sister replied crossly, jabbing her needle into the shirt she was mending for George. It was not to be expected that a healthy ten-year-old with the use of his limbs could keep his clothes intact for more than twenty-four hours. Sir Edmund had been heard to observe of him: "Don't expect he can stay still for more than five minutes at a time. Probably will be kicking his heels from the rooftop next."

"I should imagine," Elizabeth continued, jabbing the needle again remorselessly into the shirt, "that if Mr. Norville wanted us to know what he is about, he would have told us. I expect that he just thinks that he can do as he wishes."

Sir Edmund stared at her. "Shouldn't he?" he demanded reasonably. "Dash it all, Lizzy, what's wrong with that? You think you can do just as you wish! Why shouldn't he?"

Elizabeth, realizing the truth of his statement but not wishing to acknowledge it, gathered up her sewing and marched from the room, leaving her brother to stare after her in astonishment.

"Getting maggoty, that's what," he confided in Rufus and Sampson before returning to his papers.

The surgeon from neighboring Wilton arrived that morning to treat the invalids, and he departed shaking his head over the extraordinary events taking place in quiet little Brambleton. Both Lord Mallory and Sir Howard were in need of rest, he had told them, stating what was all too obvious to them, and advised that they not be moved to Chanderley until mid-week at the earliest.

Accordingly, everyone settled down to a quiet routine, except for

George and Anne, whose course was erratic and somewhat rackety. The Graham children had refused to leave their mother and brother and had opined that they were very content to sleep on the stone floor of the kitchen each night. Lady Mallory had given up the struggle, deciding that they were probably better off there at the Bull and Barleycorn where she would at least hear about their caperings from Maria, than at Chanderley running amuck with no one but the servants to care for them. Little Miss Stevenson had been given a rare holiday to go home to her mother and could not be gotten to Chanderley in time to be helpful even if Lady Mallory had wished to rob her of her long-anticipated treat.

Lady Mallory came down to the kitchen late on the day following the surgeon's visit to announce happily that her son was feeling up to having a visitor. George and Anne demanded a turn and Nora started to her feet, smiling, but Lady Mallory had turned to Elizabeth.

"He would like very much to see you, my dear, but you mustn't stay long, for he is still quite exhausted."

Nora sank back onto her stool, and Elizabeth, troubled by the fact that she didn't even bother to protest, made her way up the steps to Mallory's room. He was propped up on a pillow, still not looking too fit but definitely more like himself than he had earlier. She had been quite frightened by his feverish pallor and glazed eyes.

"Elizabeth!" he greeted her eagerly, raising himself on one elbow. "Mother told me that Norville has gone. Where is he?"

Elizabeth looked at him blankly. "I have no idea, Trevor. He simply told your groom that he would be back in a few days."

He fell back onto his pillow and put his hand to his eyes. "Are you all right?" asked Elizabeth, alarmed. "Should I call Lady Mallory?"

He shook his head. "No, don't do that. It's just that I can't think of what to do. I can't seem to think quite clearly."

"But that is only to be expected," she said soothingly. "Your head will clear soon enough." She sat watching him, her eyebrows drawn close together in thought. "Why do you think you must do something, Trevor?"

"Because of what we discovered in London," he explained eagerly, removing his hand from his eyes. "I had forgotten that you don't know of that yet. The diamond is real, Elizabeth!"

Her eyes grew wide. "Then it must be worth a fortune, Trevor. Where did you put it?"

"Norville was still carrying it in his pocket on Saturday night."

"You didn't put it in a bank vault?" she asked in disbelief.

Mallory shook his head. "We were going to, but Norville wants to keep it a secret, and he thought it would be safest with him."

"But what is he going to do with it?" she demanded. "It belongs to the Prince Regent—or, I suppose, to the war effort against Napoleon."

"He said that he was going to use it to bait a trap. Norville told me that when the trap snapped shut, we would have the diamond, clear Michael and Sir Howard of any charge of wrongdoing, and free England of the threat now hanging over her."

"Which threat? Is he talking about the war? Edmund told me that it was all but over, that Paris will capitulate to the Allies and that Bonaparte is all but captured. What can the diamond have to say to anything now?"

To her alarm, Mallory sat bolt upright. "Norville says that Bonaparte wouldn't be finished even if he were in a prison cell! Even if they capture him, he may still be able to stay in power in France if he will but agree to stay within the boundaries of his own country—only you know he wouldn't, even if he agreed to it."

Exhausted, he fell back onto the pillow once more. Elizabeth was fearful of exciting him again, but she wanted to know more about the diamond. She let him rest in silence a few minutes, then said tentatively, "I don't think I quite understand how the diamond fits into all of this, Trevor."

To her relief, he did not bounce up again, but he spoke in a measured, intense tone so that she wouldn't miss a word he was saying. "If Bonaparte had that diamond in his hands, he would have additional bargaining power. He could use the money from selling it to help keep his officers loyal to him. He might be able to convince a member of the Allies that he should be left in power in France or at the very least that his son should be appointed ruler with his mother as Regent."

"Do you mean offer a bribe?" exclaimed Elizabeth.

Mallory nodded. "Not necessarily one of the top-ranking members of the coalition, but to someone who has influence with them."

"Well, it is a relief to know that he does *not* have the diamond at his disposal," she replied.

"Not at this moment, at any rate," commented Mallory grimly. "But if there is a slip, he may well get his hands on it. Only Norville could tell us that it is safe. Where *is* he?"

Elizabeth thought for a moment, then replied. "I should imagine that he is baiting the trap."

They stared at each other. "Do you know what he planned to do?" asked Elizabeth finally.

Mallory shook his head silently. After a few minutes' thought he added, "After we found that the diamond was real, we went to several jewelers to see if anyone had brought in a paste replica."

"And had anyone?" asked Elizabeth.

"Yes, a tall, blond woman had come in with a diamond precisely like ours. The jeweler said that he had never seen anyone as angry as she was when she discovered that it wasn't real."

"But he didn't know who she was?"

"No. He had never seen her before, but he said that she dressed well, like a lady of some standing, and that she wore a large black pearl ring, a most unusual one, set round with smaller bluish gray pearls."

Elizabeth gasped. She had seen just such a ring. "Lady Brill!" she exclaimed. "It is Lady Brill who has the paste diamond. How that must have distressed Norville!"

Mallory was watching her closely. "Yes, he was upset. It was extremely obvious. But why?"

"Your mother told me that years ago they had been engaged and that she had run away with Lord Brill. It caused him so much pain that he never considered marriage again until —" She broke off, realizing that in her excitement she had said too much.

"Until what?" asked Mallory. "Until he met you, Elizabeth?"

She flushed. "No . . . he has no interest in me, Trevor. It is Nora that he has offered for."

It was his turn to flush. "I hadn't realized . . ." he said awkwardly. "She did not seem to be drawn to him — quite otherwise, I sometimes thought."

Elizabeth, having said this much, decided to clarify the situation. "She did not wish to accept the offer because it had been somewhat awkwardly presented to her and she is young. So I took her with me to visit until Easter, postponing her answer to Mr. Norville, but after that she must make her decision."

Mallory plucked absently at the covers. "I see. And what do you think her decision will be?"

"For the sake of her mother and sisters, I imagine that she will accept," Elizabeth replied reluctantly. "Also, she no longer truly dislikes him. From time to time, in fact, I sometimes believe that she is building a regard for him, which will, of course, be important to their happiness."

"Of course," agreed Mallory, still speaking in a faraway voice. "If you will excuse me, Elizabeth, I think that I need to rest for a while. Then may we talk again?"

She smiled at him. "Certainly we may. Though I'm not sure that George and Anne will let me in again until they have seen you." Closing the door softly behind her, she sought a quiet corner to think over these latest developments.

So Lady Brill had been in league with those that kidnapped Sir Howard! As she sat musing this over, shutting out the newest argument between George and Anne as to which one of them should be allowed to take a bit of sugar out to Devon Boy, she suddenly remembered what the ferret-faced servant at Mowbry Park had said. Lord Chawton had been entertaining a lady with yellow hair, but no such guest had been found during the search. Had she fled to France with Chawton? Would they leave without the real diamond?

How she wished that Sir Howard had recovered enough to tell them what had happened! He had done no more than murmur a few words, however, and Lady Gregory had not yet been able to convince herself that his mind had not been impaired by his long incarceration. Nor had she yet notified her children that he had been found, hoping that rest and care and food would begin to restore him to health and sanity.

What could the trap be that Norville planned to spring? Where had he gone? Elizabeth tried to put together the pieces of the puzzle as best she could. Sir Howard had gone as a private ambassador to St. Petersburg. Michael had carried the paste diamond in the jeweled egg. Lady Brill had carried the real diamond in a small velvet pouch. Michael must have arrived there, for Sir Howard had left the riddle and sent the jeweled egg to Elsa Briggs, apparently in order to lay a false trail for thieves. He had given his own egg-shaped clock and the real diamond to Michael—Elizabeth couldn't bear to think that Michael might have taken them from him—and Michael had taken them with him to Spain, where he was killed before he could return them to England.

Michael had probably thought that he was carrying the real diamond on his journey to St. Petersburg. She wondered suddenly if Lady Brill had been told that she was carrying an imitation rather than the real diamond. If she was truly a double agent in the pay of both France and England and had known that she had the Blue Tavernier in her grasp, why would she not have taken it straight to France where she would have been handsomely rewarded? So, she must have thought that she had the imitation and would take the real one from Sir Howard—or from Michael. If that had been her plan, she had failed.

Elizabeth sipped slowly from a mug of steaming tea, hoping that its strong flavor and steam would clear away the mental cobwebs and help her through this maze. It did not seem to Elizabeth that Lady Brill was an individual who would readily put her trust in another. Why had she not checked with a jeweler before she journeyed to St. Petersburg to see whether the diamond was real or not? Perhaps she hadn't had time. Or perhaps she put absolute faith in the person who gave her the diamond. Another spy? One of the two men who advised the Prince Regent in this matter? That would mean Seaton or Radmore, both of whom the Duke had visited on his nightly rounds.

Why would one of them tell her that hers was paste and that she would switch it with Sir Howard so that he would present the Tsar of Russia with a paste diamond? To undermine England's efforts and embarrass the Prince Regent and the government when the Tsar discovered it was a fake? Bonaparte would have loved it, particularly if he had the real diamond in his pocket.

She frowned. Even if one of the gentlemen in question had done this, and even if he would still like to have the diamond, he didn't have it. Norville had it. Why would he endanger such a prize? Why use it as bait for a trap? If the spy didn't have the diamond for the French effort, he didn't have it. Why look for trouble? But Norville had talked of danger and had mentioned earlier that someone other than Lord Mallory was being blackmailed. The paste diamond couldn't make any difference that she could see. Why try to discover who had it?

"Well, now, Lizzy, why are you so deep in meditation?" asked Sir Edmund, seating himself comfortably beside her.

Elizabeth clapped her hands. "Edmund, how clever you are!" Of course—she had forgotten completely the matter of Sir Howard's desk, his papers, and his volume of *Meditations*. They must contain information that could be used in a damaging manner. Norville had looked for them, and he must have thought that whoever had the paste diamond might well have those as well. He had been to the homes of both Seaton and Radmore, but it had been Radmore and Lord Brill who had been so distressed by the Duke's call that they could not hide their anger.

"Well, I don't say that it ain't true," replied Sir Edmund modestly. "Not that I'm a bookish fellow of course, but—"

"You are clever and kind and brave—" interrupted his sister.

"No—now dash it all, Lizzy, you're coming it rather too strong!" he protested.

"—and you are going to London with me, Edmund dear. We will leave tomorrow morning at first light."

"To London? But your carriage is at Chanderley, Lizzy. There's nothing here but the buggy and the gig and the pony cart."

"Then I shall have to ride. There must be a suitable mount, Edmund. I know that you can find me one."

His chin had dropped. "Ride to London? You don't even have your habit, my girl. It ain't the thing for a lady to do, you know."

She grinned. "Oh, yes, Edmund, I know. And I'm sure that you won't be the only one to point that out to me."

Chapter Twenty-three

Nor was Elizabeth wrong when she said that Sir Edmund would not be the only one to tell her that riding to London, particularly in a makeshift habit put together at the Bull and Barleycorn, was not ladylike. Silvers could scarcely believe her eyes when she looked from the drawing-room window and saw her mistress dismounting. She tottered downstairs to wait on Elizabeth, feeling that no one, except perhaps the long-suffering Fish, could appreciate the exquisite agony of seeing her young lady behaving in such a care-for-nobody fashion while dressed in a manner that would bring tears to the eyes of any respectable abigail.

Silvers was not alone in greeting the arrivals. Burton opened the door to them in his usual majestic manner, but behind him had gathered a small interested gaggle of servants who were sure that there must have been an earthquake at least to cause such a departure from propriety for their mistress. Their curiosity was not to be satisfied, however, for with the exception of Silvers and Fish, they were hurried away into their proper spheres by Burton. The two remaining were horrified and not a little offended to learn that their services would not be demanded just yet because Sir Edmund and his sister needed some refreshment and a chance to confer.

"Am I to infer, Sir Edmund," inquired Burton formally as he brought in the tea tray, "that Miss Lane is not with you?"

"That's right, Burton," replied Sir Edmund absently, attempting to pull off his boot. "She'll be along later."

"But not for several days," explained Elizabeth, seeing that Burton felt that "later" might mean a matter of hours, days, or years.

Burton glanced around the room. "And are the . . . the animals not with you, sir?"

"The animals? Oh, Rufus and Sampson. . . . No, Burton, couldn't bring 'em on horseback, though I thought Rufus was going to follow us until Nora took him up," he chuckled.

After Burton retired, Sir Edmund turned to his sister. "Now, by Jove, Lizzy, explain it all to me again. First of all, Norville is the Duke of Diamonds. Norville! Never would have suspected him of tiptoeing about in his stocking feet! And you've found a diamond at Chanderley that was taken from Sir Howard by Mallory's brother."

"No, Edmund, we don't think Michael Graham took it from him. We think Sir Howard sent it back with him."

"Humph! But you found it in his boot."

"Yes, but that's because he was killed before he could deliver it."

"And who was he going to deliver it to?"

Elizabeth paused. "We're not sure."

"If you ask me," her brother responded, "you're not sure about almost everything you've told me. Never heard so much stuff that sounded like a Banbury tale. I'd think you were roasting me if you hadn't run me all the way back to London."

He thought about it a moment. "And dash it all, Lizzy, why *did* you run me all the way back here?" he demanded.

"To help Andrew Norville."

"To help him do what?"

"To rob Sir John Radmore's government office," Elizabeth replied calmly.

Sir Edmund's eyes grew noticeably larger, and his color began to rise. Spluttering, he declared, "I think that you have rats in your upper works, my girl! Indeed, I'm sure you do. *Rob* Sir John? What do you take me for, a curst sneaksby?"

"No, Edmund, I take you for what you are: a brave man, an excellent rider, and a good friend."

He looked somewhat mollified, but suspicious. "What does being an excellent rider have to say to anything?" he inquired.

"The Duke of Diamonds is known to be an excellent horseman," she replied.

"The Duke of Diamonds!" he exclaimed. "Do you think, Lizzy, that I am going to be the Duke of Diamonds?"

"All you have to do is dress up in black, ride by Sir John as he is

295

coming out to the street from his office, and salute him. Tell him that you will call upon him later."

"And what will I do about all the people in the street just then? Salute them and tell them that I will call upon them later?"

Elizabeth laughed. "I suppose you could do just that. They'd love it. But I doubt there'll be that many about. It's not on a busy street. Before that, though, I'll go in and make an excuse to find out when he'll be leaving, and I'll wait outside and give you a signal."

"And why am I doing this, may I ask?"

"So that he'll think you are going to look in his office that night and he'll bring out the desk and papers and book. Then we can get them."

"And why don't Norville do his own dirty work?" asked Sir Edmund militantly.

"Because he has an injured shoulder and shouldn't be riding like that. Also because he'll be waiting to watch Sir John to see if he removes anything from his office and to follow him without risking the diamond as bait."

"How'd he injure himself?" asked Sir Edmund, interested.

"Oh, someone stabbed him at Lady Seaton's masquerade."

"Someone *stabbed* him? Dash it all, Lizzy, you don't say something like that so calmly. You can say casually that somebody *saw* him or *heard* him, but *not* somebody *stabbed* him! Who did it?" he added as an afterthought.

"We're not exactly sure who it was," she replied.

"Now that's a great comfort," said Sir Edmund tartly. "Somebody wandering about with a nice little knife that they like to use, but we're not sure who it is."

"Edmund, you are refining upon this a great deal too much. Now we will have some dinner after we freshen up, and you must send a note round to Mr. Norville asking him to call upon us tonight to make plans."

Sir Edmund went to his room muttering that he was accustomed to refine upon such things as gratuitous stabbings, but he sent the note to Norville, who turned up promptly at nine.

Elizabeth lost no time in explaining her idea and the manner in which she had arrived at her conclusions. Mr. Norville listened in complete silence, his dark eyebrows rising now and then. Sir Edmund listened, but not in complete silence, and Elizabeth frequently had to pause to clarify something for him.

"Radmore a spy for Boney!" he had gasped finally. "I can't believe that could be so! I've known Sir John for years. Why'd he do such a thing?"

"We don't know that it is indeed so," Norville reminded him. "It is a speculation on our part."

Turning to Elizabeth, he asked, "Has there been no change in Sir Howard's condition?"

She shook her head. "Lady Gregory is afraid that his mind may be permanently damaged."

Norville sighed. "Perhaps not—probably not, in fact. I should imagine that rest and care will eventually bring him back, but not, I'm afraid, in time to help us."

"But you have the diamond, Mr. Norville. The French cannot use it. Do you really think that there is something in the desk or papers that could be used to damage our country?"

He nodded. "I know that is so. I had thought it was the Blue Tavernier, but once we found that and I realized that it had been hidden away all this time, I knew that they must have been hiding something else."

"Is it a letter, do you think?" she asked, afraid that she was treading on private ground and that he would not answer.

"It is possible, I suppose. When I talked with Radmore about Sir Howard's disappearance, he said nothing to me about the government having kept the travel-desk, but we know that it disappeared—and the fact that they were interested in that made me wonder if it could be a letter or a document that they were after." He paused a moment. "I believe though, Miss Harrington, that we are looking for other jewels."

"Other jewels?" she asked, startled.

He nodded. "That is why I asked to borrow your mother's journal. I wanted to read about other notable jewels. There is one, a famed ruby, that your mother noted belonging to a noble family in Andalusia. I recognized their name, and I knew that while Joseph Bonaparte ruled Spain, they were stripped of everything they had, undoubtedly of the ruby, too.

"Do you remember my describing to you what it was like when the French were leaving Spain—that they abandoned wagon after wagon filled with art treasures and money and jewels?"

Elizabeth nodded.

"It seemed to me a possibility that the person or persons who kidnapped Sir Howard and attempted to steal the diamond might also have later been in Spain and taken that ruby."

Elizabeth frowned at him. "Forgive me, Mr. Norville, but that does seem to me a little unlikely. I can see that it *could* be true, but what would make you believe that it is?"

"Because, Miss Harrington, I have seen that ruby. There is a sketch of it in your mother's journal. It was set in a ring in a most unusual and ornate setting, and the stone itself is very large, so it does not escape one's attention. I have seen it very recently on a lady's finger."

"Lady Brill?" Elizabeth asked before she could stop herself.

He nodded. "She has always had an extraordinary fondness for jewels, particularly rings. She still has the black pearl ring that I presented her as an engagement ring."

"But why would she wear a stolen ring?" Elizabeth asked. "Wouldn't she be afraid that it would be recognized?"

"I should doubt it. I would not have known it had I not read your mother's journal. And even if it were dangerous," he added, "she wouldn't care. It would simply make the whole affair more exciting to her—and she is very fond of excitement."

"I understand now why you want a quiet life and a wife to suit it," Elizabeth said, thinking aloud again before she could stop herself.

"Yes," he said abruptly. "I want no one like Caroline."

Elizabeth found that she was quite pleased that he seemed unimpressed with Lady Brill. She had thought that he still found her fascinating. Thinking over what he had told her about the jewels, however, she could see no connection between them and Sir Howard's disappearance, except, of course, for the Blue Tavernier.

Sir Edmund was properly coached for his role as the Duke of Diamonds that evening, and waited around the corner from Sir John's office with his black hat and cloak ready to be popped on at a moment's notice. Mr. Norville and Elizabeth had checked to be certain that he planned to attend the House of Lords that afternoon, so they knew his approximate time of departure.

When the signal was given, Sir Edmund quickly swathed himself in black, complete with mask, and raced around the corner on

Devon Boy in quite a breathtaking style. It was a quiet street and the few passersby looked startled, but no one turned in pursuit. Sir John looked up in alarm as Sir Edmund clattered down the street and pulled up beside him.

In a suitably deep voice, Sir Edmund said, "Good evening, Sir John. I shall be looking forward to calling upon you here later this evening." And then he raced on down the street, discarding his costume around the corner.

Elizabeth and Mr. Norville were watching from the safety of a shop window, and they could see that Sir Edmund's victim stood there for a moment looking after him, then walked slowly on down the street.

"Strange," said Norville. "He had the opportunity to go back inside right then. Could it be there is nothing in his office to check?"

Sir John did not return to his office that night, and a quiet check on his own revealed to Mr. Norville that there was nothing there of interest. The plotters were disheartened, although Sir Edmund had been rather pleased with the manner in which he executed his role.

"I believe that I must return to Chanderley and get Nora," said Elizabeth the next day as they talked over their unsuccessful ploy. "I left her in Lady Mallory's charge, and the poor woman has quite enough on her plate already with Trevor injured and George and Anne squabbling constantly."

Sir Edmund looked startled. "Going to get Rufus and Sampson, too, aren't you, Lizzy?"

She laughed. "Of course, I will, Edmund. Do you miss them?"

Sir Edmund looked down at his shiny boots and spotless trousers and sighed. "Yes," he said simply. "But don't tell Fish."

Elizabeth and Silvers prepared that night for the journey to Chanderley the next day. They would not be staying long, so the packing was not extensive, but Elizabeth found that she was exhausted by bedtime. *I believe that it is because of depression,* she thought. *I am always tired when I am unhappy.*

She did not wish to examine her thoughts too closely, but she admitted to herself that everything seemed oddly anticlimactic. There was nothing to look forward to. The riddle was solved, Sir Howard had been found, Chawton and Lady Brill had been routed, the diamond found, Lord Mallory was mending from his wound, Nora would be going home soon to marry Mr. Norville and move to Devon. She sighed as pulled the covers up over her head. Life was very flat.

When they arrived at Chanderley, for the others had removed from the Bull and Barleycorn by this time, Lord Mallory was sitting in a chair in the garden surrounded by daffodils, animals, and children.

"I see that you must be feeling much more the thing," laughed Elizabeth, "or you wouldn't be able to bear the noise."

"Just so," he agreed, watching the egg-shackling in which George and Anne were engaged, holding their eggs in their hands and pounding them against one another to see whose would last longest. "I shudder to think how many eggs have come to a bad end in this garden during the past day or two."

He studied her face for a moment, noting that she looked less lively than her wont. "Blue-deviled, Miss Harrington?" he inquired.

"Oh, not again, Trevor! I truly do not spend my time being moped. You must believe me."

"I believe you, Elizabeth. But the circumstances we find ourselves in are, I believe, a little unusual."

"What do you mean?" she asked, startled.

"Forgive me for being blunt, Elizabeth. Like everyone else, I know of your reputation—you flirt, but never seriously, and you have shown no desire to marry any of the many gentlemen who have offered for you. And so it seemed to me quite a harmless matter that I should flirt with you and—perhaps—make Miss Lane a little jealous."

"I see," smiled Elizabeth.

"I meant no harm to either of you," he said, looking at her with the same open and engaging manner that had won so many hearts. "I hope that I haven't offended you."

Elizabeth considered this gravely. "Well, to be truthful, Trevor, I did have my cap set for you, but I suppose that I have too many years in my dish for you."

Mallory chuckled. "I was afraid that you would be quite overset when I told you." He stared across the garden and watched Nora playing with Rufus. "Nora—Miss Lane—has said very little to me since her kidnapping. Is she quite all right, do you think?"

"I believe so. Her kidnapping did cause her great distress, however. Not simply because of her fear for herself, but she was distraught because she thought she had been responsible for harming you."

"She thinks she was responsible for my being shot?"

Elizabeth nodded. "She had great difficulty sleeping at first, because she was afraid that you might die."

"Did she indeed?" asked Mallory in a meditative tone. "Why has she not said any of this to me?"

"I think that she feels the awkwardness of her position with Mr. Norville quite keenly."

Mallory straightened up and looked directly into Elizabeth's eyes. "I know that you are not Nora's guardian and I know that Mr. Norville has offered for her, but, Elizabeth, as her temporary guardian, would you give me permission to speak to her privately and ask for her hand in marriage?"

Elizabeth briefly envisioned Cecilia and the girls setting up housekeeping in a two-room cottage, but dismissed it as an unworthy thought and told Lord Mallory that although she had no right to give him permission to speak to Nora about marriage, she thought it was an excellent idea.

Lady Mallory was startled to find her invalid son strolling hand in hand with Miss Lane through the daffodils while Miss Harrington watched them benevolently. She soon discovered that her sympathy for Elizabeth was misplaced and that she was soon to welcome another daughter into her family. A little dazed, she went back into the house to share the news with the rest of her family and Lady Gregory.

Elizabeth, enjoying the happiness on the faces of Mallory and Nora, which was at one with the bright golden beauty of the daffodils, pushed all thought of Cecilia and Norville from her mind. They would have to be dealt with soon enough—but not just yet. Lord Mallory planned to call upon Cecilia as soon as he was able to travel.

Elizabeth allowed herself to relax in the peaceful beauty of Chanderley until Monday, having promised Nora that she would stay until then. She attended Palm Sunday services with the family, having gone "apalming" with the children and John Hatching the day before, gathering the fluffy, golden catkins of the sallow willow for Chanderley and for the church. George and John had tucked sprigs of it in their hats. They gathered daffodils, too—Lent lillies as John Hatching called them. Watching Mallory and Nora, she thought again how like the daffodils they were, bright, joyful, and young. She had the sudden, unpleasant sensation that life was passing her by.

Chapter Twenty-four

Her journey back to London was not a happy one. The country-side through which they passed was bright with spring, but Elizabeth could just as well have been blind. Her thoughts were all turned inward. She must write to Cecilia now and explain what had happened and what an admirable young man Lord Mallory was. And she must, of course, tell Mr. Norville the news. He would be angry, of that she was certain, and he would blame her, of that she was also certain, but that she could bear. He would not, she hoped, be hurt by Nora's defection. But he might be. Lady Brill had left him, and now Nora had left him. Not even having Sampson curled in her lap and Rufus across her slippers could bring a smile.

Sir Edmund greeted her jubilantly, waving the *Morning Chronicle* which detailed the surrender of Paris. "This is it, Lizzy! Boney is cornered now! He'll be negotiating now to save what he can!"

Elizabeth smiled as enthusiastically as she could, but her lack of liveliness was made up for by that of Rufus and Sampson. To the astonishment of the household staff, they spent the first twenty minutes of their homecoming sprinting from floor to floor and running in vast figure eights wherever there was room. They continued until they collapsed in a heap of orange and black fur.

"Have you ever seen the like?" asked Martha the maid of Mrs. Washburn, watching the pair of them race by.

Mrs. Washburn watched them benignly. "They're glad to be home, I should imagine. And I for one will sleep better tonight because Rufus is here."

Martha nodded in agreement. "There's nothing like a dog in the house to make you feel safe."

The only person feeling no satisfaction at all in the homecoming was Elizabeth. She had explained to Sir Edmund why she had not returned with Nora, leaving her instead with Lady Mallory to get to know her better. Sir Edmund had been astounded, but pleased.

"Young Mallory is one of the good ones," he said. "Glad to see the girl has taste."

"Yes, Edmund, but it is possible that Mr. Norville won't think very highly of either her taste or her fickleness."

"Eh?" asked her brother. "What are you talking about, Lizzy?"

"I am talking about the fact that Mr. Norville had asked Cecilia for Nora's hand in marriage and that Nora is supposed to give him her answer just after Easter."

Sir Edmund thought that over a moment. "Has his answer now. Won't have to wait until Easter." He patted Rufus's head absently. "Seems to me that wouldn't answer anyway."

"What wouldn't answer, Edmund?"

"Norville marrying Nora. It's as plain as a pikestaff that he don't love her and she don't love him. Ain't sure they even like each other very much."

"Perhaps not, Edmund, but telling Mr. Norville about this is still going to be unpleasant. I dread having to do it."

"Don't have to dread it long," Edmund informed her chirpily.

She looked at him with sudden apprehension. "Why not, Edmund?" she asked. "Why won't I have to dread it for very long?"

"Because he'll be here for dinner. Thought it would be just the two of us and we'd step out to White's, but Cook can put the covers down here. Just a cozy dinner."

"Oh, yes, Edmund," his sister responded weakly. "A very cozy dinner."

As they sat together in the drawing room before dinner, Elizabeth discovered that she could not bring it up just then and in the most cowardly way possible diverted attention to a discussion of the travel-desk dilemma.

"I'm afraid that there is nothing new to report, Miss Harrington," he told her. "Our deadline approaches, and we still have no answer."

"Deadline?" she asked uneasily, her mind leaping to the Easter-tide deadline set by Cecilia.

He nodded. "Easter week is the deadline. If the Prince Regent

304

doesn't give the blackmailers what they want during this week, they have promised that they will make a public spectacle of him."

"They can't read the newspaper then," commented Sir Edmund. "Don't need anybody to make a public spectacle of him—he can do it himself."

Norville laughed. "I don't say that you're wrong, Sir Edmund, but I think the blackmailers have something a little more international in mind. The Tsar's sister, for instance, is here in London."

"It is the Prince Regent that is being blackmailed then," Elizabeth said slowly. "What do they want of him?" she asked.

"They want him to announce that he favors leaving Napoleon in power when the treaty is made with France."

Elizabeth gasped. "How could he do that? He has been demanding that the Bonapartist system be rooted out completely and that the Bourbons rule France."

"Well, that is neither here nor there. They don't worry about how he could do it, they just want it done. And if they wanted to pick a very public moment for whatever they plan to do, this Thursday would be an excellent time."

"Why?" Elizabeth asked.

"The Prince Regent has decided to attend the Maundy Thursday service at Whitehall this week," he replied, "and that will be his only public appearance for some time. So when the Lord High Almoner is presenting the gifts to the poor, our blackmailer could easily decide to use that time and place for his forum."

The Royal Maundy ceremony was said to date back to the twelfth century. In accordance with Christ's command to be humble and to serve others, the ruler presented the Royal Maundy in a special service. On this Easter, George III would be seventy-six and accordingly the gift of money would be given to seventy-six men and seventy-six women. There was a time when the king or queen washed the feet of these people, just as Christ bathed the feet of his disciples, but William III was the last monarch to do so. Those chosen also received gifts of food and clothing.

Elizabeth had toyed with the possibility of keeping the conversation away from Nora for the entire dinner, but it was not to be.

"Did Miss Lane not return with you from Chanderley?" he inquired.

Elizabeth and Edmund looked at each other in mild apprehension. "No, she did not, Mr. Norville. And I have news for you about Nora."

"Indeed?" he said politely. "I hope that she is well."

"Oh, yes, never better." And I do mean that, she thought to herself. "But the news is, Mr. Norville, that she is engaged to Lord Mallory. Or she will be as soon as her mother gives her permission."

He looked at her mildly. "Is she indeed? Then I must wish her happy. Is Mallory recovering from his wound?"

Elizabeth stared at him. "Yes, he is," she replied weakly. Then, unable to stand it any longer, she asked, "Are you angry with Nora, Mr. Norville?"

"No, of course not," he responded. "I think that they will deal together very well."

"And do you hold me responsible for their engagement?"

He smiled at her. "Oh, yes indeed, Miss Harrington. I do believe that this is something that we can place at your door."

"I expect that's true, Lizzy," chimed in Sir Edmund. "If you hadn't brought Nora along to London, she never would have met Mallory during the storm and gotten to know him."

Elizabeth looked at him in exasperation. "I suppose that is true," she conceded. "But I thought it all for the best."

"And indeed it was," said Norville briskly.

"But . . . what will you do now?" she asked.

"Do? I shall try to solve this one last problem for my country, and then—then I am going home to Stoneybrook."

"And is it so important to you to solve this problem, Mr. Norville?"

He looked at her gravely. "It is."

Their conversation weighed heavily on Elizabeth's mind after he left that evening. He would be going home, once again abandoned by a young woman. He should at least be able to go home satisfied that he had resolved the problem. She wrote a letter to Lord Mallory and called Robert to take it for her, urging him to make all possible speed.

She did not go out the next day, but instead waited anxiously at home, going to the window each time she heard the sound of an approaching rider. She did not truly expect Robert back that day, but she could not help hoping. All through

306

the day and into the night she kept her vigil.

It was late in the afternoon of the second day when Robert arrived. He was exhausted and travel-stained, but exuberant, for he carried a package strapped to his saddle.

"I believe I have what you wished, Miss Harrington," he told her, handing her the package. She took it into the library and shut the door. Opening the note from Mallory first, she read it through and stared at the wall for some time before she could open the package.

He had done just as she had asked. Remembering that their search through Michael's fishing gear had ended abruptly when they found the diamond, she had asked him to continue it. She had also asked that someone reliable be dispatched to Mowbry Park to examine the rooms that the young lady had stayed in—not Nora, but Lady Brill. John Netherspoon, Tom Macklin, and Jem Featherstone had conducted the search.

Mallory had been jubilant in his note. He had not found the desk, but he had found Sir Howard's copy of *Meditations*. It was, as Lady Gregory had said, a slender volume, and Michael had stitched it into the lining of a heavy woolen cloak. "Sir Howard will be able to tell us about it himself someday soon," he wrote, "but in the meanwhile, this books tells it all. He merely left his message by underlining letters very lightly throughout the book. They are scattered and might not be noticed at first, but taken in order, they spell out his message."

Sir Howard had realized his life was in danger and that he would not be allowed to arrive at the Tsar's court. He had worked out the riddle and the wild goose chase of the egg to Elsa earlier, but he had underlined his message very quickly after Lady Brill's visit to him in St. Petersburg. When Michael arrived, he had asked him to wait and had then entrusted him with the book and the diamond in the eggshaped clock. He recorded, too, that Lady Brill told him she had been robbed, and Sir Howard had not been inclined to believe her.

The Brambleton gentlemen had searched the chambers where she had stayed at Mowbry Park and had uncovered some very interesting things. It was obvious that the lady had had little time to pack on the night of the storming of Mowbry Park, and most of her belongings had apparently been abandoned. From the fact that she had two wigs and several suits of men's clothing, including one entirely in black, with a black cape and mask, it appeared to them that she masqueraded as a gentleman from time to time. Also, there were several cases of jewelry that had been abandoned. Nora had recognized three of them as Elizabeth's and those Mallory had duly dispatched with the book and his note.

So Lady Brill had played the part of a man upon occasion! And had masqueraded as the Duke of Diamonds as well. Elizabeth opened her jewel boxes and carefully sorted through her things. Everything was there—everything save the *anello della morte*. Troubled, she sat for a long time and thought about that.

The next morning found Elizabeth preparing for the Royal Maundy service. Ignoring the outraged protests of Silvers and Fish, she had appropriated some of Sir Edmund's belongings and was planning to attend the service as a gentleman. She was aware that her brother would be disapproving, but he was safely off at Tattersall's, and she was free to do as she thought best. Sending Silvers from the room for a minute, she dug through one of her drawers until she found the dagger that had been used on Mr. Norville the night of the masquerade. That she slipped into her jacket pocket.

The Royal Maundy was a colorful service, but Elizabeth was not free to appreciate it as she might. She saw the Prince Regent come in and Mr. Norville, and she placed herself where she would have the best view of all the chapel. Although the foot washing was no longer a part of the ceremony, the Lord High Almoner and his attendants were symbolically girded by linen towels. The members of the procession carried nosegays of daffodils, rosemary, thyme, violets, and primroses. Elizabeth did not allow herself to truly listen to the rich voices of the Choir of the Chapel Royal, nor to revel in the beauty of the silver-gilt dishes which bear the purses of Maundy money. Instead, she was watching a slender, fair-skinned gentleman with a leather pocketbook seated close to the back of the chapel.

As the choir was ending a hymn, Elizabeth saw that the gentleman was about to arise. She hurried down the aisle toward him, noticing that Norville, too, was heading toward him. Together, one on each side, they herded him from the chapel before he had an opportunity to make the scene that he wished to.

"I would have told them what a fraud their Prince Regent is!" he yelled, and Elizabeth was grateful he was no longer in the chapel. "He is here because his father is giving away a few pennies to the poor, and I was going to show them what the Prince Regent takes for himself!" And here he dumped the contents of the pocketbook onto the pavement. A mound of shining stones lay winking up at them, the paste Blue Tavernier on top.

"Why were you going to do it, Caroline?" Norville asked. "What was the point in it?"

"I was going to show them the jewels that their Prince Regent had kept from them and from the fight against Napoleon—jewels looted during the fighting abroad—even a stone stolen from the crown jewels of France. He would have had a pretty time explaining himself! The Grand Duchess Catherine would have heard of it and told her brother immediately. She already dislikes the Prince Regent—that would have sealed his fate and helped to break the relationship between England and Russia."

"And Napoleon paid you to do this?" asked Norville. "Just as he paid you and Brill and Chawton to collect jewels and works of art for him as well as to spy for him?"

She nodded, her eyes still bright with anger.

Norville looked at her sorrowfully. "Why did you do it, Caroline?"

"The Prince Regent ruined my husband!" she said, her voice shaking. "He told them at Whitehall last winter that Brill could no longer be trusted as an agent, and they cut him off without a penny. And France wasn't interested in him unless he had connections here."

"And so you were going to avenge him," Norville stated, looking at her with pity.

She nodded. "He deserves to be ruined, just as my husband was. I intended to humiliate him before everyone."

"What about all the jewels?" asked Elizabeth. "Shouldn't we get these up before they're damaged? And weren't they enough for you to live on?"

"No, they won't be damaged because they're not real—just cheap imitations. And they were enough to live on for a time, but Brill would sell a good piece and replace it with paste until eventually we had nothing but the paste jewels. That is why he was so angry when we were robbed," she told Norville.

"You are the one that advised the Prince not to trust us, aren't you, Andrew?" Lady Brill asked, staring at Norville. "He couldn't quite bring himself to distrust me, because I'm an attractive woman, but you had influenced him. I could see it."

Norville nodded. "Brill didn't have the interests of our country at heart, only his own."

She laughed. "What drivel you do talk, Andrew, but then you always did." She put out her hand to him, looking up into his eyes. "But I am still fond of you, and I do need your help."

Norville started to take her hand, but Elizabeth suddenly shoved his arm away, and he looked at her in surprise.

"Look out!" she cried. "Look at her hand! It is the *anello della morte!*"

Norville leaped to one side, and Lady Brill turned toward Elizabeth, her face distorted with anger. "I should have filled this freshly," she said, holding up the finger with the ring on it. "The poison may well be too old to be effective and that could mean a very slow and painful death."

"You're the one that Rufus barked at, aren't you?" Elizabeth asked. "You're the one that came into our home and stole my rings."

"Of course. I was delighted to hear about them, but that little beast was a hindrance. I did wish that he were running loose. My dagger would have made it easy then."

"This dagger?" she asked, drawing it from her pocket. Lady Brill leaped for her, but Norville was able to catch her and hold her for a moment. Then, jerking the *anello della morte* toward his cheek and causing him to leap back again, she laughed and broke free, disappearing around the corner.

"Are you all right?" she asked him. "Did she scratch you?"

"No, I'm quite all right," he replied.

"Should we not go after her?" Elizabeth asked, staring at the corner where Lady Brill had disappeared.

He shook his head. "We couldn't catch her now. At any rate, there's little enough that she could do at this point, and they'll be watching for her at the ports. This will end it all. There is no fight left in Sir John Radmore and Napoleon's days are numbered."

He stared down at her. "I thought it was only Miss Lane who wished to have a breeches role, Miss Harrington."

310

"I could not see letting Nora have all of the fun, Mr. Norville, so I thought that I would try it. Besides, I knew that it would irritate you, and that is what you expect of me. How could I let you down?"

He smiled. "May I see you home, Miss Harrington, or are you quite capable of going alone?"

She bowed. "More than capable, sir."

"Very well. Then I shall bid you a good day." And nodding briefly, he turned back in to the chapel. And that, thought Elizabeth to herself, was that.

She did not sleep well that night, and early the next morning she lay awake listening to the cries of "Dust-O' " and "Sand-O' " as the men came by to empty the dustbins and sell sand for cleaning the saucepans and spreading on freshly scrubbed wooden floors to protect them from footprints. The rattle of the carts was already beginning. The comforting fragrance of hot cross buns floated up from the kitchen, for it was Good Friday and Mrs. Washburn belonged to the "old school" where traditions were concerned and believed that the efficacy of hot cross buns lay in their being baked on Good Friday. Thus, on that day every year, she rose long before the sun to begin the rolls. It was said that they would keep fresh in a tin all year long and never grow mouldy. When crumbled and powdered, you could use them as a cure for indigestion. Elizabeth smiled to herself, for suddenly from outside her window she heard:

> Hot cross buns!
> Hot cross buns!
> One a penny, two a penny,
> Hot cross buns!
> If you have no daughters,
> Give them to your sons.
> One a penny, two a penny,
> Hot cross buns!

Other people might be purchasing them for breakfast, but not their household. They had Mrs. Washburn.

Sir Edmund was in very high spirits that day, for Bonaparte's kingdom was crumbling about him. When he appeared suddenly in the doorway of Elizabeth's chamber late that afternoon, however, he looked anything but chipper. He looked hagridden.

"Elizabeth," he whispered. "They've come! We've got to get out."

"Who has come, Edmund? And why must we get out?"

Sir Edmund shuddered and motioned to her to keep her voice low. From the entryway below, Elizabeth could hear Burton's stately tones, punctuated by the complaints and shrieks of children. "It's Cecilia and that mob of children!" he whispered frantically. "Caroline Haverton's here, too! It's going to be quite awful to have them all underfoot."

Elizabeth couldn't have agreed more. There were children everywhere. As she made her way downstairs, she encountered Burton's reproachful glance as he announced to her the obvious: "Mrs. Lane and her family have arrived, Miss Elizabeth. Which rooms would you like for me to show them to?"

Sir Edmund gave her sleeve a frantic tug, which Elizabeth calmly ignored. "Why, Cecilia and Caroline, how good it is to see you and the children!" she said pleasantly. "And *such* a surprise! I am afraid that you catch us quite unprepared. You must come in and have some refreshments while Robert goes round to Grillon's and makes arrangements for rooms for you there. They will be quite comfortable, I assure you."

Elizabeth could hear her brother heave a sigh of relief. Cecilia, on the other hand, was beginning to bristle. "I should have thought, Elizabeth," said that lady, "that you would be able to keep your relations under your own roof. But, of course, I wouldn't know the ways of grand London ladies."

Caroline made fluttered sounds of protest at such a remark, but her sister ignored her.

"Now that should put me in my place, I'm sure," responded Elizabeth calmly. "I wonder from whom you have taken the idea that I am such a lady."

"I have come to fetch my Nora home to Chanderley," said Cecilia frostily, "for it is Eastertide now and I understand that you have not been looking after her as closely as I had expected."

Elizabeth was shaken by the truth of this for a moment, thinking of Nora's recent kidnapping. Cecilia, happily, knew nothing of that for the moment.

"Nora has quite enjoyed her visit, I believe," remarked Elizabeth, "but I fear that you will not be able to see her until tomorrow evening."

"Indeed?" replied her mother, bristling again. "And, why, may I ask, may I not see my own child?"

"Your own child is visiting at Chanderley with Lady Mallory," said Elizabeth smoothly, "and they don't return to town until tomorrow."

"Lady Mallory!" cried Cecilia. "Is Lord Mallory with them— the young rake about whom I have been hearing?"

Elizabeth's reply was stiff. "Lord Mallory is certainly one of the party, but he is *not*, as you put it, a 'young rake.' "

"If not a rake, then a shocking flirt, and not someone I wish Nora to be in company with. And why, may I ask, are *you* not with them, Elizabeth?"

"I was with them, Cecilia, until just a day or two ago when urgent business recalled me to town. I assure you that Nora is well chaperoned by Lady Mallory and Lady Gregory."

"Lady Gregory!" exclaimed Cecilia, further scandalized. "Sir Howard Gregory's wife? What kind of company are you allowing my daughter to keep, Elizabeth?"

"Only the best, I assure you," her cousin responded crisply. "And now, Cecilia, do come with Caroline and the children into the drawing room for tea while Robert takes your things round to Grillon's."

Without further caviling, they allowed themselves to be shepherded into the drawing room and later round to Grillon's Hotel. Having promised that they would call on them the next morning to take them to see the sights of London, the brother and sister closed the door behind their unannounced guests with a sigh of relief.

"We will have to do something, Edmund, to dispose Cecilia to think more kindly of Mallory."

"No problem there," said her brother frankly. "Mallory is very plump in the pocket and Cecilia's not. Don't see that she'll cut up stiff if Nora marries him."

Elizabeth looked at her brother with admiration. "Of course, you are quite right there, Edmund. Cecilia won't be troubled with any delicate thoughts about Mr. Norville's feelings as long as she and the girls are taken care of."

"Just so, dear girl, just so," said Sir Edmund amiably.

Elizabeth's face fell. "So everything comes right for everyone except poor Mr. Norville."

"Think he's crushed about losing Nora, do you?"

Elizabeth nodded. "I'm afraid so. First Lady Brill and now Nora."

Sir Edmund eyed his sister thoughtfully. "Perhaps . . ."

Saturday passed in a whirl of visits to shops and entertainments and a culminating dinner at Grillon's. Sir Edmund had been exhausted by the attentions of the girls and Caroline as they made their way from place to place, and Elizabeth was worn to a thread from making herself agreeable to Cecilia and regaling her with tales of Chanderley and Lord Mallory's wealth and important position. The return of the group from Chanderley was too late in the day to allow them to be in the party at Grillon's that night, but it was agreed that everyone would gather in Grosvenor Square after church for dinner and an Easter egg hunt for the children. Sir Edmund and Elizabeth tottered to bed that night, depleted by their efforts during the day.

When Elizabeth and Nora and Sir Edmund arrived home from services the next morning, Elizabeth was surprised to be told by Burton that they had a caller waiting. It was Mr. Norville.

"Norville, a pleasure!" exclaimed Sir Edmund, bustling forward. "Glad you could make it!"

"I appreciated your invitation to dinner, Sir Edmund," he replied, looking at Elizabeth. "I would like to offer you my felicitations, Miss Lane, and wish you very happy," he said, turning to Nora, who blushed a fiery red.

"Thank you, Mr. Norville," she replied in confusion. "I hope that—I do appreciate, I mean—"

"You appreciate my offer for your hand, but you have chosen another and hope that I will go on very well," said Norville, smiling at her confusion.

"Yes, well, I do, of course, but not that bluntly," she said. "I do beg your pardon if I have offended you."

He bowed over her hand. "Not at all," he assured her. "You may enjoy your happiness with my good wishes."

Relieved, Nora took off her bonnet and started up the stairs. "If

314

you will excuse me, I will just go and straighten my hair. Trevor will be here soon."

Norville turned to Elizabeth again. "You have managed very well, it seems, Miss Harrington. Your charge looks very happy."

"Yes, she is, I think," replied Elizabeth, "and I do hope that you are not very . . . unhappy, Mr. Norville. I would not like to think that I have done you an injury."

At that moment, the first wave of children made their entrance, the young Lanes flowing past Burton and into the inner precincts of the house, ready for the hunt. They were followed closely by the Graham children, ably led by Anne—and the hunt began. As promised by their elders, the eggs were hidden on two floors of the house, and the hunt took some little time. Sir Edmund tried not to listen to various ominous sounds of thuds and cracks and to continue a pleasant and adult conversation with his guests, touching frequently upon the gratifying subject of the imminent abdication of Napoleon.

It was approximately an hour later, though it seemed much longer to Elizabeth, who was straining to make polite but distant conversation with Mr. Norville, when George entered the drawing room bearing the Auk Egg triumphantly.

"This is the prize egg, ain't it, Trevor?" he crowed. "Just like we agreed?"

"Indeed, it is," replied his brother, fishing for a guinea. "You have found it again."

"Found it!" exclaimed Anne, who had followed him in. "He followed me and snatched it before I could reach it!"

Before the squabble could turn into fisticuffs, Lord Mallory hurriedly awarded a guinea to each of the gratified children, and they all marched happily off to dinner, their elders following at a more sedate pace.

Cecilia had become quite reconciled to the idea of Nora's marriage, for Lord Mallory had dutifully pledged his promise to place his mama-in-law and her daughters in a London home befitting their station in life, so Nora was glowing. Elizabeth did her best to smile at her guests as they entered the dining room. She saw in surprise that Lady Mallory's baskets were placed all round the table.

"We did not think you would mind," Maria said hurriedly. "And the children did want to have the baskets today."

"Of course not," replied Elizabeth. "It was an excellent idea."

Everyone stood around inspecting the eggs in their respective baskets. Nora squealed with undignified delight when she opened her pink enamel egg and found a sparkling diamond ring—from Lord Mallory, of course. When Lord Mallory opened his, his expression changed markedly. In his hand lay a heavy gold signet ring.

"This is Michael's!" he exclaimed as he stared about the table.

Mr. Norville nodded. "Sir Howard's book disclosed that Michael insisted on giving this to him as a pledge that he would return the clock and the diamond. Chawton must have recognized it and taken it when they kidnapped Sir Howard."

"Well," sighed Nora happily, "it is rather like the egg-dance, isn't it? Where everything is pulled together into a neat little stack at the end and you take off the blindfold and there it is!"

Norville looked across the table at Elizabeth. "Aren't you going to look at yours, Miss Harrington?" he inquired.

Startled, she glanced at her basket and saw that she did indeed have an enamel egg the color of daffodils lying there. Opening it, she saw a tiny scroll tied with red ribbon, and her gaze flew to Mr. Norville, who was smiling at her. She unrolled the scroll carefully and read:

> *The Duke of Diamonds no more I'll be,*
> *But the Queen of Hearts must set me free.*
> *If your heart to mine be true,*
> *Offer me the egg of blue.*

Peering inside her enamel egg, Elizabeth saw a tiny blue porcelain egg. Picking it up delicately, she inspected it for a minute and saw that in tiny letters the word *yes* was printed across its side. She stared at it for a moment in disbelief, then, suspecting a trick, she looked up at Norville, who was watching her intently.

"Another test, Mr. Norville?" she inquired sharply.

He put up his hands to disclaim any such intention. "How could I dare to do so?" he asked, and the warmth of his smile reassured her. He held out his hand, and Elizabeth gently took it.

"I do apologize for the extraordinarily poor verse, Miss Harrington," he said tenderly, taking her hand in both of his own, "but would you go home to Devonshire with me even though I am not a poet nor a member of the *ton?*"

She nodded. For a rare moment the power to speak had left her. Life had not passed her by after all, but stood before her now, dark-eyed and demanding and dear. Beyond Andrew's dark head she could see daffodils fluttering in the morning breeze. It was with an effort that she regained control of herself. He had not, after all, proposed marriage. He had merely asked her to come to Devonshire with him.

"But you wrong yourself, Mr. Norville," she parried, assuming a light tone. "You are a member of the *ton,* whether you will it or not. How could the Duke of Diamonds ever be considered anything but all the crack? I fear that you have made yourself a part of that which you have regarded with such disgust."

He chuckled. "Caught me at my own game, have you, my dear? I shall have to be cautious in my dealings with you."

"Indeed you will," she agreed, refusing to let down her guard. "I am no milk-and-water miss, you will recall. You shan't wrap me in cotton wool and choose my thoughts for me."

He shook his head. "As though I would dare to do so, Miss Harrington!" As he looked down at her, his voice lost its teasing tone and grew gentle. "Nor would I wish to do so, Elizabeth. I wish to marry you exactly as you are."

Elizabeth stared at him, quite unable to believe what she was hearing. Seeing her doubt, he smiled encouragingly and opened his arms wide. Without a word, she walked into them and was folded into a firm embrace.

After a moment, oblivious to the others in the room, he tilted her chin toward him. "Does this mean that you accept my offer, Miss Harrington? Shall we go home to Devon?" he inquired.

Smiling, she dropped the small blue egg into his pocket and cupped her hands gently on either side of his face. "Indeed I will, sir. It is more than time that someone took you in hand."

He shook his head in mock dismay. "I see that I shall be living under the cat's paw. Doubtless I shall be bullied unmercifully."

The chuckle awarded this sally was cut off abruptly as he pulled her closer and pressed his lips to hers.

Lord Mallory, who, like the others, had been watching this exchange anxiously, stood with a glowing countenance and lifted his glass to the couple. "And may we wish you very happy!" he exclaimed.

There was a chorus from around the table, and as it died away, Sir Edmund was heard to murmur, "Devonshire . . . Some devilish good horses down that way, I believe . . ."

DISCOVER THE MAGIC OF REGENCY ROMANCES

ROMANTIC MASQUERADE   (3221, $3.95)
by Lois Stewart

Sabrina Latimer had come to London incognito on a fortune hunt. Disguised as a Hungarian countess, the young widow had to secure the ten thousand pounds her brother needed to pay a gambling debt. His debtor was the notorious ladies' man, Lord Jareth Tremayne. Her scheme would work if she did not fall prey to the charms of the devilish aristocrat. For Jareth was an expert at gambling and always played to win everything — and *everyone* — he could.

RETURN TO CHEYNE SPA   (3247, $2.95)
by Daisy Vivian

Very poor but ever-virtuous Elinor Hardy had to become a dealer in a London gambling house to be able to pay her rent. Her future looked dismal until Lady Augusta invited her to be her guest at the exclusive resort, Cheyne Spa. The one condition: Elinor must woo the unsuitable rogue who was in pursuit of the Duchess's pampered niece.

The unsuitable young man was enraptured with Elinor, but *she* had been struck by the devilishly handsome Tyger Dobyn. Elinor knew that Tyger was hardly the respectable, marrying kind, but unfortunately her heart did not agree!

A CRUEL DECEPTION   (3246, $3.95)
by Cathryn Huntington Chadwick

Lady Margaret Willoughby had resisted marriage for years, knowing that no man could replace her departed childhood love. But the time had come to produce an heir to the vast Willoughby holdings. First she would get her business affairs in order with the help of the new steward, the disturbingly attractive and infuriatingly capable Mr. Frank Watson; *then* she would begin the search for a man she could tolerate. If only she could find a mate with a *fraction* of the scandalously handsome Mr. Watson's appeal. . . .

Available wherever paperbacks are sold, or order direct from the Publisher. Send cover price plus 50¢ per copy for mailing and handling to Zebra Books, Dept. 3709, 475 Park Avenue South, New York, N.Y. 10016. Residents of New York and Tennessee must include sales tax. DO NOT SEND CASH. For a free Zebra/ Pinnacle catalog please write to the above address.